the prudent mariner

the prudent mariner

A NOVEL

Leslie Walker Williams

The University of Tennessee Press • Knoxville

TENNESSEE PETER TAYLOR
BOOK AWARD PRIZE FOR THE NOVEL

Co-sponsored by the Knoxville Writers' Guild
and the University of Tennessee Press,
the Peter Taylor Prize for the Novel is named for
one of the South's most celebrated writers—the author of
acclaimed short stories, plays, and the novels *A Summons to Memphis*
and *In the Tennessee Country*. The prize is designed to
bring to light works of high literary quality, thereby honoring
Peter Taylor's own practice of assisting other writers
who care about the craft of fine fiction.

Library of Congress Cataloging-in-Publication Data

Williams, Leslie Walker.
The prudent mariner: a novel / Leslie Walker Williams. — 1st ed.
p.   cm.
ISBN-13: 978-1-57233-641-4 (acid-free paper)
ISBN-10: 1-57233-641-2 (acid-free paper)

1. Georgia—Fiction. I. Title.

PS3623.I55855P78 2008
813'.6—dc22   2008017219

For my mother, Suzanne Hill Williams

And in memory of my father, Nick Williams, 1927–2008

ACKNOWLEDGMENTS

I am grateful to the many people whose lives and experiences have influenced this book. I have taken great liberties with regional and family histories, which I shaped and altered for the purposes of fiction. The resulting story and characters are my own invention.

I am indebted to numerous people who supported me during the writing of this book. Peggy Shinner's persistent encouragement and keen insights were invaluable. Margot Livesey was unfailingly generous with advice and assistance. The Hackney Awards provided the funds for a final revision. The University of Tennessee Press and the Knoxville Writers' Guild allowed *The Prudent Mariner* to come to fruition.

My thanks to Walker, who helped me start and understand this book, and to Logan, who helped me finish it and begin the next one. I am forever indebted to my mother, for her compassion, spirit, and active engagement with the world, and to my father, for his deep love of books and the water.

Finally, I am profoundly grateful to Michael, for in every circumstance finding, relinquishing, renovating, or building me the best possible place in which to work, and above all, for giving me the time, faith, and silence to do so.

Go, go, be gone, to save your ship from wreck,
Which cannot perish having thee aboard,
Being destined to a drier death on shore.

—William Shakespeare, *Two Gentlemen of Verona, I, i.*

[There is] the double absurdity of separating the dead from the living. It is absurd in the first place from the archivist point of view, when one considers that the easiest way of finding the dead would be to look for them among the living, since the latter, because they are alive, are always there before us, but it is equally absurd from the mnemonic point of view, for if the dead are not kept in the midst of the living, sooner or later they will be forgotten and then, if you'll forgive the rather vulgar expression, it's the Devil's own job to find them when we need them, which, again, sooner or later, we always do.

—José Saramago, *All the Names*

the prudent mariner

PART ONE

CHAPTER 1

Liberty County, Georgia (1913)

She's tired of being dressed up, of having to be ever on the lookout against soiling. The world seems entirely composed of things determined to soil her. It's late summer but she's wearing her Easter dress, for Father has told them they must look their very best. He's given his daughters no choice but to come. Otherwise, he says, they'll never be able to hold their heads up in this county again, much less marry. But Adele can't bring herself to hold her head up. She keeps her gaze trained on the ground, and keeps her distance. She only lets herself look out of the corner of her eye.

Father, passing through town this morning on his way home, had already heard the news, or some version of the news, by the time he rode into the yard. He was often gone, to see to fevers, growths, broken bones, and deliveries, leaving everything in the hands of Riddley, the eldest of the six Glynn girls, and Nancy, who has raised them since Mother died. Nancy's sternness is mostly show, unless you get on her bad side, which Adele never has. For all intents and purposes, she's been Nancy's baby since the day she was born. Nancy and her son Elijah live where they've always lived, in the cabin near the marsh. Elijah knows how everything works, how to fix it if it doesn't, how to make do if he can't. He's well past thirty, with fine, long-fingered hands that belie all the work he does with them. People who don't know him think he's slow. Those who do know he's plenty quick, just quiet.

Sometime earlier in the summer, perhaps as long ago as the spring, Riddley began to blush, to turn tongue-tied and snappish, whenever Elijah was around. He could well not have noticed, but in the churchyard and the dry goods store her sisters began to whisper, to intimate that Riddley had, for the first time, some sort of beau. No harm was meant, or if it was, it was a petty, harmless kind of harm,

what one sister does to another out of the callousness of years spent in close company. And certainly no harm was ever meant for Elijah.

Why Adele said what else she said she isn't sure, though it might have something to do with the fact that she has always felt picked on by Riddley, made to wear the most unflattering of hand-me-downs, and to do the most onerous of chores, ones normally set aside for darker hands than hers: pinching the heads off shrimp, scooping the deadman out of crabs, polishing the ever tarnishing silver. Riddley takes great pains to insure that Adele, the baby, will not be spoiled, though Nancy does the best she can. As everyone knows and no one will say, Riddley blames her youngest sister for their mother's death in childbed, and above all for being pretty, two things about which Adele can do nothing.

But it was not only revenge that spurred Adele on. She'd felt as well the thrill of divulging a terrible secret, no matter it was one she'd invented. What pleasure in saying what ought never to be said, not only because it was unseemly and untrue, but because it was dangerous, though only yesterday had she come to understand exactly how, and to whom. Besides, the fact of the matter was, she was curious. She wanted to see what would happen. But she had only imagined Riddley's embarrassment, or perhaps her mortification. Adele had never even come close to imagining this.

Surely anyone could see she was making it up! For who would ever kiss Riddley? Riddley the homely, the dour, the industrious. How could she have gotten so shorted on looks? It was as if she were never intended for anything but looking after others, a task for which looks are superfluous. Such an easy target for her five sisters, each one prettier than the last, culminating, everyone said so, in Adele, the fairest of them all. But no matter how preposterous Adele's words, they had been believed, or in any case repeated. For the girls she whispered to had brothers and fathers, uncles and cousins, and despite the solemn oaths of secrecy, it was too immense a thing to keep quiet about. As Adele well knew, the words felt too good coming out of one's mouth. As soon as she had said them they took on a life of their own and ran off, never looking back. Last night Nancy burst into the parlor, crying how Elijah had been taken from the back pasture by a group of men

who claimed he'd attacked Riddley. *What would ever make anyone think such a thing?* Nancy said. And then, pleading to Riddley, *You have to stop them.*

Riddley, heat spreading from sternum to brow, looked first at Nancy, then at her sisters. One after the other her sisters looked away and would not meet her eyes, and she knew then that whatever had happened had something to do with them. She lifted a hand to her burning cheek. In one fell swoop she grasped how one thing must have led to another. Whatever it was her sisters had done, her skin told her it was still, at heart, her own doing, despite the fact that not until that very moment had she acknowledged, much less bewailed, her recent spate of blushing.

She stood, determined to ride after them and confess it was all her fault, for being so uncomely and unused to men, that Elijah had only been kind to her in the way he always had, with not a word or glance out of keeping. But then, catching sight of her reflection in the window, she knew she would do nothing of the kind. For decades she would ponder that decision, but at that moment she believed that even if she protested, whatever was going to happen would still happen. And hadn't a woman, a white woman, been tarred and feathered a few years earlier outside Jesup, for *consorting with a black man?* Riddley will recall that incident again the next day, as she makes her way through the crowd, her presence and her silence taken as corroboration, though by then, of course, corroboration hardly matters.

Had Father been home, things might have ended differently. But he was gone to Riceboro to see to a riding accident, and Riddley was only a woman, and plain to boot. After her sisters had retired to their rooms and Nancy had at last headed home, Riddley went out onto the porch. All through the night she sat there, while down by the river, not three miles away at the McClure's plantation, under a moon one day shy of full, they had done what they did to Elijah. Perhaps they had only meant to frighten him, but even to his own surprise his sense of justice lasted far longer than most. By the time he relinquished any final remnants of pride, they were no longer interested, or maybe they simply couldn't understand him through the mess they'd made of his mouth. In the morning Mr. Sanderson rode out to tell Riddley she

could breathe easy now, something she was, in fact, never again able to do. What Elijah thought of her when he was alive—not to mention the still greater mystery of what she herself thought of him—she never could fathom, but that he died hating her she was quite sure.

Marriage prospects having no doubt been endangered, Dr. Glynn will send his daughters, one after another, elsewhere—to the houses of distant cousins and maiden aunts, to study at the Normal College, to serve as an instructor of Comportment and Embroidery at the Aiken School for Young Ladies. The sisters will come home rarely, and stay briefly when they do. Beyond the obligatory Christmas and birthday cards, they'll seldom have contact once they are married. And Riddley will never leave, nor marry, nor, it seems, recover, from what has been done in her name, in the name of her virtue. For how could she leave, how could she marry? Nancy fled as soon as she'd buried what was left of Elijah, and someone has to look after Father, someone has to run the house. Besides, any possible suitor—of which there are none—might have been among those who did what they did to Elijah, or the next day celebrated that it had been done. As Riddley moved through that crowd, through the murmurs and muffled gasps, the stares and averted eyes, she felt, even when a hat was tipped or a greeting offered, that she was being slowly flayed. Until, that is, she saw how utterly intact, in comparison, her own body was.

By mid-morning, people were already packing their picnic baskets and heading to the McClure's. Now, hours later, there's a crowd to rival the county fair. It doesn't hurt that it's a Saturday, in the lull between Independence and Labor Days, and clear weather, and the roads are good from ten days with no rain, though the heat is, as people like to say, *infernal.* Word has spread through the county and beyond, as seen by the newspaper reporters and photographers, the carriages and carts, wagons and buggies, and the few model T's that have been arriving all day, from as far off as Brunswick and Waycross, Hazlehurst, Vidalia, and Statesboro. The police keep people orderly, and some colored boys keep the horses fed and watered. Hawkers crisscross the area, selling everything from boiled peanuts to divinity fudge, postcards to fans.

Adele, a nickel clutched in her fist and dust clogging her throat, enters the throng in search of something cool to drink. Her white frock clings in the late afternoon heat and her hair is heavy, the white bow like a weight on the back of her head. She wonders again if Riddley or, worse yet, Nancy, has learned what she said, something she'll continue to wonder for more than half a century. After today, however, what happened will seldom be mentioned, and then only indirectly, and by accident, for this is a family story never told, much less passed down or elaborated on years later. Others, however, will speak and write of it for weeks to come, these events making the papers throughout the South and as far away as New York and Chicago, *The Times* and *The Tribune, The Crisis* and *The Defender,* though the accounts will in some cases vary so widely as to seem to concern different incidents altogether.

It's a trifle cooler under the oaks, nearer the river with its slight breeze. Many boats are tied up at the dock. How fine it would be to go out on the water, or better yet, to swim, like those boys jumping in and whooping. She plucks her camisole away from her ribs. *Lemonade, fresh lemonade,* a hawker cries, and her mouth begins to water, for lemonade is her favorite. She heads in that direction. The next time he calls he's moved behind her, or else she's lost her bearings. She tries to spot him, but the crowd has thickened and she can't see anything but the damp shirts of the men in front of her. They turn and say, *Make way for the little lady,* and jostle her forward, into a small clearing at the edge of the bluff.

She had no idea she'd come so close. A yard away, feet dangle at eye level, mud dried and clotted in the arch, and at the back of the heels. Or is it blood? And how completely limp both feet are. She doesn't understand, then or ever, that his Achilles tendons have been cut. She sees no red, though doesn't blood dry black rather than red? The torn cloth of his trousers ripples in the breeze, as if he's shivering, and there, in that heat, Adele also shivers.

Her gaze rises to his hands, scraped and filthy, but still the same ones that have lifted her in and out of the saddle and the crooks of trees, repaired fencing and bridles and chairs, and handed her the

wagon reins or the eggs from beneath her favorite hen. She lifts her eyes farther along his body and sees how a man's neck is as flimsy as a doll's, or a chicken's, when it's fresh broke and not yet bleeding, though maybe she can't see the blood for the rope. Then she lifts her eyes to his face and in that first glance she thinks she's wrong about the hands, that they can't be Elijah's, this can't be where her words have come to rest. His eyes are blank, like the blind's. There are marks on his face, and in the places where his ears were. And how entirely ears can be removed, leaving no trace of themselves but blood and flies.

They'll be sold later, in nearby towns, along with fingers, toes, genitals, charred bits of bone, pickled in alcohol, in jars otherwise used for putting up quince chutney, pear preserves, gherkins, pole beans, and okra. Adele won't know what she's looking at when she first spots those pieces of him a few weeks from now, in Clarkton's General Store. Beside the register will be the tall jar of hard candies, butterscotch, green apple, cherry, grape, the sun slanting in and turning them into smooth nuggets of colored glass, and beside that, tucked back a ways, will be another jar, smaller, stuffed full of shapes knotted and curled, dull yellow or brown in a murky liquid that the sunlight can't quite penetrate. She'll briefly take them for pig parts, chitlins maybe. They'll keep almost turning into something she can recognize. She'll think of creatures from the deepest parts of the ocean, ones that never surface, and gazing into that sealed sea she'll be for a moment transfixed, much as her granddaughter Riddley will be, many years hence in the vet's office, peering into the formaldehyde jars of dog intestine, dog fetus, cat lungs, rabbit heart. And then Adele will read the name on the lid, the label that says *Souvenirs* and, as if she'd toppled the jar over and Nancy were not gone without a word but there beside her, Adele will hear her scold her familiar scold, *Now look what you've done.*

CHAPTER 2

Given Names (1970)

Nearly six decades later a girl descended stairs to a dock. She was Adele's granddaughter, Riddley Cross. From a bin outside the dockhouse she removed an orange life jacket. She slipped it on and fastened the clasps. She crossed the upper deck and squatted at the top of the steep ramp to the floating dock, gazing out over the water and marsh. Even in winter or bad weather she was often to be found here. She was only nine, but most people had already proven themselves to be, by and large, poor company in comparison to the river.

The tide was near low, the mudflats gleaming in the sun. It was the twenty-second of December, the shortest day of the year and the first day of winter, but the air was warm enough for swimming. The river, however, would not have been. The latest Riddley had ever swum was October, the earliest a March Easter, and that had been an accident, though not one she'd regretted. She had never regretted being in the river.

Riddley thought of all rivers as salt rivers, which flowed in both directions. She did not directly attribute the currents to the ocean, or to the moon for that matter, though she knew, of course, of the connection. But no one ever spoke of the tide as incoming *from* or outgoing *to*. Rather, the water seemed to move for no reason other than habit or momentum, the river a consequence of nothing but itself.

Twice a day the departing tide gnawed into the bluff. An outgoing tide was like someone slighted, who wants to take whatever you have away, whether or not she wants it for herself. Riddley, being quite accomplished at spite, knew it when she saw it. According to her mother Pauline, Riddley ought by now to have no nose to speak of, for all the times she'd cut it off.

Incoming, though, was another story. That was the time to ask for what might otherwise be denied. Her mother was more apt then to forgive transgressions, and likewise her father Sam's temper lengthened almost visibly. For when the tide turned toward the land the people on the bluffs and docks, in the houses, crossing bridges and causeways, turned, unwittingly, with it, their bodies eased as steadily, even a trifle smugly, the water flowed in.

Children who lived along that bluff were put into the river early. A few, like Riddley, could swim before they could walk. She seemed, indeed, to have always been able to swim, or to have always believed that she could. As soon as she could crawl, she made a beeline for the river. She felt both a longing and a calm while near the water. When as an infant she would fuss, and could not be soothed by bottle or sugar teat or song, her nurse Ida Mae would take her down on the dock. The moment Riddley saw the river she would quiet, especially, Pauline claimed, if the water was rough.

Riddley had never had any fear of water, and, because of what she had been told about her birth, she had no fear of drowning. Nor did she know of anyone who had disappeared at sea, gotten thrown overboard, capsized, or sunk. There were mishaps and close calls—boats run aground or out of gas, caught in lightning storms and deluges, masts snapped and motors broken, people falling off bluffs and docks and decks—but though the water surrounded them, it did not take them in. Perhaps its danger was too blatant, or maybe it simply didn't want them settling there, in body or spirit or someone else's memory.

The only drowning Riddley had heard of in those parts had happened a very long time ago. Some said it had never happened at all, that it was just another of the countless local ghost stories. Yet how, Riddley wondered, or why, would anyone have thought to make up that particular one? The story went that a shipload of slaves, upon landing on one of the sea islands, had turned around and walked right back into the water. What had they heard or seen, to make them resolve at once what to do? Or had they planned it on the way over? She wondered as well if they had all agreed to it, or if some had to be pulled under, and held under, by the others. *Why didn't they even*

try to swim away? she had asked their maid Esther, pressing linens in the laundry room, the top button of her uniform undone for the heat. *Now tell me, child, just where was there to go?* Esther asked back, adding, with a grimace and a shake of her head, *Plus being all chained together like that.* Esther, Riddley knew by then, did not know how to swim.

Although Riddley could no longer remember where she'd first heard that story, it had stayed with her over the years. She had told it to others, though she told no one what had sometimes occurred when, while swimming, she opened her eyes underwater. At the time, she did not stop to wonder what led her to see such things in the first place, or whether others could as well, but she knew enough to know what she saw, and she also knew enough to keep silent. The drowned slaves were down there, a line of people stretching far beyond where the murky river allowed her to see. They were joined at the wrists and ankles like paper dolls. She always had to come up for air before she was done looking, and when she dove again, they were gone. She could still envision how the children swung between their parents' hands, as she had once loved to do between Sam and Pauline, until they said, *You're too big for that, time to stand on your own two feet.*

Riddley looked now at the rippling surface. There was no sign of the slaves, but she did not expect one. The muddiness of the water meant that you had to be in the river to see into the river, and even then you could not see very far, or at least not as far as she would have liked. And how long would it be until she could go in again? Her body missed it as it would've missed sleep, or food, or touch. In the spring she was always eager to swim long before Pauline would let her.

Just then she heard a spluttering hiss of exhalation, followed by a rush of air being drawn in. She jumped to her feet, scanning the river, looking for a break in the water, for circles widening around the place where the porpoise had surfaced. They came up the river often to shrimp and fish and pry crabs out of the mud. She heard the blow again and spotted them upriver, between her and Cougar Island. There were three or four, riding the outgoing tide, on the far side by the marsh.

She ran to the dockhouse, grabbed an oar and dashed down the ramp to the edge of the floating dock. She struck the dock planks with the handle once, and again, and then stomped her foot. Over and over she repeated this pattern, for it was said that porpoises would sometimes draw near to investigate a rhythmic sound. She had tried this many times but never had one approached the dock. She'd had better luck on the water, beating the sides of the bateau, which the sea island fishermen did, for the approaching porpoises herded the fish into the waiting nets. A few times porpoises had surfaced near her bateau, though she could never be sure if they had been attracted to her pounding, or if they had been there all along and just happened to come up right then.

Now, on the other side of the river, almost directly across from her, the porpoises surfaced in close succession. She pounded and stomped harder. A supposedly infallible way to summon the porpoises was a method sea island slaves had brought long ago from Africa. At low tide they waded into the water while beating drums. Riddley would have tried this from her own shore had the river bottom not dropped off so sharply, and the mud not been so soft, and had the drumming not also been rumored to draw sharks. But she intended one day to test it.

The porpoises surfaced again, much farther downriver. She rested the end of the oar on the dock. They were going where she would have liked to, under the power lines and alongside the shrimp boat dock, past marsh and bluffs and the last house at Oyster Point, across the mouths of other rivers and on into Moss Island Sound, between the shorelines of islands and keys and then into Indigo Sound, beyond which lay the Atlantic. It had been months since she had been on the water, months still until she would go again, but she could see the route from her dock to the ocean as clearly as if she were at that moment traversing it.

Two of the porpoises blew at almost the same time. "Spiracle," she murmured. It was a term she much preferred to *blowhole*. Pauline said it came from the Latin for breathe, and also from the word for spirit, because people had once believed that the spirit resided in the breath. *Where do they think it is now?* Riddley had wanted to ask, but

refrained. That was just the kind of question Pauline tended to talk about at great length, without ever really answering.

* * *

Riddley was the youngest daughter of Sam and Pauline Cross. Shortly before she was born they had moved to the house beside the Ashburn River, a few miles south of Savannah, where Pauline had lived nearly all her life. Sam Cross had left his own home in Michigan to join the Navy in 1944. When the war ended he attended college in the Northeast, after which he found a job selling industrial tubing. There followed five years of steady advancement and mild debauchery. He met Pauline Wells on a business trip and within the year had moved south to marry her. He joined the family's shipping firm, for Pauline's father, having only a daughter, aimed to treat his son-in-law like a son. The good standing of Pauline's parents did much to overcome people's natural misgivings about someone from so far away, and with so disagreeable an accent. Sam's skill at money-making, and the telling of off-color jokes, soon made him as welcome as any native, though his true origins, of course, were never forgotten. But over the years he made it past the blackballs of the James Club, the Boatmen's Club, and the Founders' Club, where Pauline had been presented in 1951, and Sam expected to present his own daughters one day.

Three years after she came out, Pauline had graduated from the state university and moved to Atlanta, where she worked at a cousin's law office. Her roommate wed and Pauline, having no prospects in that regard, returned home and took a job at an upscale gift shop. Soon afterward she met Sam, who was at once smitten by her deep-seated naiveté, just as she was charmed by his rakishness. Although Pauline's mother remained unconvinced that Sam didn't mind if his new bride worked, Pauline stayed on part-time at the shop until the twins, Charlotte and Emmeline, were born. Three years later Riddley arrived, by which time Pauline could barely recall what she had done with herself before children.

Years went by at a relentless clip until, seemingly all of a sudden, the girls had much less need, or want, of their mother. The twins were now twelve, with a similarity in bearing, opinion, and predilection

that went deeper than ordinary siblings, as it did with Sam and his own twin sister. As much as Charlotte and Emmeline were cut from the same cloth, Riddley seemed to be made of some other material entirely. This was true of temperament as well as looks. At a distance the twins looked very much the same, though up close they were easy to tell apart. They had their mother's paleness, but their hair was silky and blonde rather than dark and heavy. Riddley had the quick-tanning honey-toned skin of her father, and her mother's strong chin, easy blush, and blue eyes. She came closest to Sam's light brown curls with her unruly, sand-colored hair. Braiding was the only means of attaining any semblance of neatness, especially if rain was imminent. The twins were said to have Sam's mother's nose, while Riddley had her maternal grandfather's brow. Whose body any of the girls would get was unclear, as none of them had begun to fill out.

The twins were named for Sam's grandmothers, while both Riddley's given names came from Pauline's side. Many overlooked her middle name, *Frazier,* but Riddley never did, for it was also her grandfather's middle name, and the one he had always gone by. At just under six-and-a-half feet tall, he towered above everyone, a condition made more noticeable by the fact that his huge head was entirely bald. He held it at a slight tilt, as if you'd just said something he hadn't quite caught. Chances were that this was the case. *Pardon?* he frequently bellowed, with remorse rather than impatience. He fiddled a great deal with his hearing aids, like a man trying to clear static on the radio. Often in the midst of a conversation one of them would emit a high-pitched squeal, as if thrilled or shocked by what it heard. Riddley had always rather liked how he had to lean close to hear her, and how she was supposed to shout at him, that shouting in this case meant not anger or danger but affection. In anticipation of his decline, Riddley had learned sign language for the alphabet. Frazier himself had no idea how to sign, but she figured she could teach him when the time came.

He had been born and raised a few miles from the Alabama line, in Gabbettville, Georgia, where his family ran the town icehouse. The prosperity of the twenties had allowed Frazier to attend Georgia Tech and leave behind his icehouse heritage, though he remained a

lover of cold, dim, low-ceilinged places that would've made other tall men shudder. He entered caves and the rare Southern cellar with an ease that bordered on joy. He was a man who instantly took note of ceiling height and bent his body unbegrudgingly, as though being hunchbacked were a natural, preferable condition. He had never been known to bump his head.

According to Frazier, he had taken one look at Adele Glynn and determined to marry her. Adele hardly seemed to her granddaughters the type to inspire in a single glance. As long as they could remember she had worn skirt and jacket ensembles of a puffy fabric resembling sofa upholstery. *Your mother is one cold fish,* Sam had been heard to say to Pauline, who could not disagree. Frazier had, it seemed, found his icehouse. But in 1927 her black hair was bobbed, her skin was cream, and hanging in her closet was a dress whose hem fell in a startling diagonal, and, much like a parlor curtain, sported a rim of fringe.

Riddley's first name came from Adele's eldest sister, who had died the year before Riddley was born. Pauline had been astonished to discover that her mother was neither flattered nor pleased by the resurrection of the name *Riddley.* She understood then that what she had once vaguely suspected was true: between the eldest and young-est sisters stood something dire and irrevocable. Pauline never could bring herself to inquire what that might be.

Riddley had seen a photograph of Great Aunt Riddley and her five sisters, sitting in an open wagon driven by a black man. Aunt Riddley had treated her sisters more like offspring than siblings, since their mother died moments after delivering Adele. According to family accounts, soon after their mother's death Aunt Riddley had donned an air of rancorous martyrdom, which, in much watered-down form, she had bequeathed to Adele, who further diluted it in its passage to her only child, Pauline. Riddley intended to refuse the legacy altogether, not yet realizing that inheritance seldom had anything to do with choice.

She did, however, intend to follow Aunt Riddley in never mar-rying. As a spinster, Aunt Riddley had done all that was expected of her until her she reached her fifties, at which point what had been an

occasional nighttime ranting about spooks and apparitions took hold and would not let go. What began as fear blossomed, after a while, into other, less palatable sentiments, and she eventually had to be put in a sanatorium, her mind swept free of all clutter but rage. Eventually this too had gone by the wayside, replaced by over a decade of unbroken silence. Her family assumed she eschewed speech in order to make them uncomfortable, silence being, to them, simply another form of spite.

Adele, like Aunt Riddley, seemed well on her way to giving up on, or being given up by, speech. Some days she might still exchange a courtesy or two, or appear to partake very briefly in a conversation, but for the most part her speech had, like tallow or maple syrup, been boiled down to its most potent forms. *Whippersnapper,* she'd said to Sam, who took it as a kind of homage. *Yankee,* she called him on another occasion, further confirming her opinion of her son-in-law. Her other decoctions were not so benign. *Hussy,* she hissed to her closest friend of almost half a century. *Swindler,* she snarled at the grocery clerk, *Pervert,* to the plumber. Nor were her incivilities limited to name-calling. *No, no, no, no, no,* she yelled at her neighbor, apropos of nothing discernible. *Mine,* she said to Pauline, seizing a box of chocolates. At times Adele seemed nearly as likely to say anything as to say nothing, leading many who knew her to hope, eventually, for the latter.

* * *

Two days after Riddley tried to summon the porpoises, she and her family made their annual Christmas Eve visit to Frazier and Adele, who still lived in the house where Pauline had grown up. On the drive into town the girls, sweltering in tights and velvet dresses, speculated among themselves about whether Adele would have arranged the traditional winter scene on the dining room table. Charlotte doubted she would still be capable, and Emmeline thought she would simply have forgotten, while Riddley insisted she would set it up exactly as she always had.

Riddley knew the scene by heart. Hunched down in the back seat, she shut her eyes and envisioned it. An oval mirror would be

transformed into a tree-lined lake, on which cheerful villagers would ice skate. The surrounding farms and towns would be lightly dusted with snow. The lake itself would be left bare, the surface reflecting the skaters faithfully, as Riddley suspected a real frozen lake could not.

When they came into the house, they found Frazier alone in the living room. He knelt beside the fireplace, balling up newspaper. Despite the warm weather, he insisted on having a fire on Christmas Eve. Adele sat at the head of the dining room table, on which was spread the winter scene. The girls went in and greeted her. Adele, once a strict proponent of the mandate, *speak when spoken to,* stared silently at the scene, where, in the middle of the lake, the village bakery perched atop a few hapless skaters. The snow had not distinguished between land and lake but had fallen everywhere. On the lake it was piled too thickly for the skaters to be reflected, or even for most of them to stand, as if they had gone ice-skating in a blizzard. Worst of all were the faces, though Adele had not altered them. But their happiness now looked fake, as if someone had ordered them, on pain of punishment, to enjoy themselves.

Charlotte pulled her sisters back toward the doorway. "I told y'all she wouldn't be able to pull it off."

"Do you think he knows?" Emmeline tilted her head toward their grandfather.

"He must," Charlotte said.

"No, he would've said something." Riddley's hands, pulsing and sweating inside her new rabbit fur muff, did not seem like hands, but as if the luckless rabbit had come back to reclaim its skin. *A muff in Georgia?* Sam had said. *Just you wait,* Pauline had replied, suggesting that even more inexplicable hankerings were yet to come. Now Riddley burrowed her fists in deeper.

"You look like you're shackled inside there," Charlotte said.

"If you wear it all the time you'll ruin it," Emmeline claimed. "Your body heat will make all the fur fall out."

"It will not. Rabbits have body heat," Riddley hissed. "They probably have even more than we do."

"Merry Christmas, Mother." Pauline scrutinized her daughters. "What intrigue are y'all up to in here?"

The sisters all looked at their grandmother, and Pauline followed their gaze. Then she saw the table. "Oh, dear. I didn't realize." She smoothed back the curls escaping along Riddley's brow. "Grandfather's fixing your Shirley Temples," she told them, heading toward her mother. Charlotte and Emmeline scampered over to the fireplace.

Riddley leaned against the doorframe between the living and dining rooms. She lifted her clasped hands and blew into the muff, her breath parting a trail in the fur. It smelled faintly rank, much like when a mouse had died inside the attic wall. Closing her eyes she saw the flayed rabbit. How could she have ever wanted, even craved, such a thing? But she had. She still did. She pressed her cheek into the fur.

At the far end of the living room, where the bar was, Frazier arranged glasses on a tray. He had to know what Adele had done. So why then hadn't he warned them?

Frazier approached Riddley. "Here's your cocktail," he said, his voice quieter than usual.

She thanked him and took her drink off the tray. "Look, Grandfather." She lifted the muff toward him. "It's real fur. It's softer than anything."

His hearing aid gave a shrill cry and he darted a glance into the dining room, as if the sound had come from there. "Take this one to your mother." He thrust the tray toward Riddley. She tossed the muff on a chair and grabbed the last glass.

In the dining room, Pauline was attempting to fix the scene with one hand, while Adele grasped the other. Pauline removed the bakery from atop the skaters. "Do you want to be on the rescue squad?"

Riddley shook her head. She set Pauline's drink on a coaster on the table, beside a can of fake snow. Then she retreated to the doorway. Her Shirley Temple reminded her of medicine. It was far sweeter and redder than usual, and not very cold. It appeared to have more maraschino cherries than ice. Frazier must have forgotten that, unlike her sisters, she didn't much care for maraschino cherries. She stabbed one with her straw. She didn't know how she would manage to finish them.

"We could sure use your help. I can't make heads or tails of this." Pauline deposited the bakery on the shore.

"It doesn't go there," Riddley blurted out.

"What doesn't?" Pauline took a sip of her drink.

"The bakery doesn't go by the lake. It goes in the village."

"See?" Pauline relocated the bakery. "You know where things belong much better than I do." With her free hand Pauline brushed snow into a ridge around the lake.

"That snow doesn't look real at all."

"Then next time we don't have to have it."

"But it's got to have snow. It's not right if it doesn't have snow."

"Well, we can use something else."

"Like what?"

"I don't know, hon." Pauline straightened and tried to pull her hand from her mother's. Adele held tight. "Flour maybe, or sugar."

"Then it'll just be covered in ants and roaches. Maybe even maggots."

"I'm afraid it'd be a disappointment to maggots, though you may be right about the others. So why don't you come up with something better?"

"There isn't anything better." The problem wasn't the snow itself, but that Adele had used far too much of it. Another can stood lidless on the sideboard.

At that moment, Josephine pushed open the swinging door between the kitchen and dining room. She'd worked for Adele since Pauline was in college. She had lasted so long because she was able to clean the house to Adele's very exact specifications.

"Why, Josephine, Merry Christmas! I didn't realize you were here," Pauline said. "Riddley, what do you say."

"Hello, Josephine."

"I'm on my way home but wanted to wish y'all Merry Christmas." Josephine wore a blouse and slacks, rather than her usual pale green uniform and apron. On her shirt collar was a Christmas tree pin. "Mr. Wells had me come in for the extra half-day." She lowered her voice a notch. "He wanted the house to look just right."

"Well everything looks perfect, as usual." Their gaze fell on the table. Pauline forced a smile. "Well, most everything. Everything you had a hand in, anyway."

Josephine stiffened. "I tried to fix that but she wouldn't let me or Mr. Wells anywhere near. He was mighty upset, after he'd spent the morning setting it up."

Pauline shook her head. "Poor Daddy."

Adele stared at Josephine in a way that her granddaughters had always been told not to. Then she extended her arm and pointed at Josephine. "Thief," she said.

Pauline gasped. The look that passed over Josephine's face was so fleeting, so instantaneously concealed, that it could well have been imagined, especially as nowhere else on her body did she register what had just been said to her. But Riddley didn't think she had imagined it. How could she have? It was not an expression she had ever seen before.

"Thief," Adele repeated, in case anyone had any doubt she'd said it. Riddley, who had done her share of stealing, felt a rush of queasiness, almost as if she were the one accused.

"Mother, that's enough, don't be ugly." Pauline turned a deep red. "This is Josephine, Josephine who's been with you for almost twenty years!" Pauline glanced at Josephine. "I'm terribly sorry. What a shock. And on Christmas Eve! Of course you know she doesn't mean it."

Josephine seemed to know nothing of the sort. But nor did she look particularly surprised. She touched the pin at her collar. "She doesn't remember giving this to me." She unpinned the Christmas tree. "Mr. Wells knows she did. It was two Christmases ago, after he got her that one with the diamonds."

"Of course, I haven't a doubt in the world." Pauline watched Adele push a skater headfirst into the snow. "Just look at her," Pauline murmured. "You know she doesn't know what she's saying anymore."

"Yes, ma'am," Josephine said.

Adele's face was calm now, intent on the figurines before her. But when she had spoken to Josephine, she'd drawn her lips into a tight line and narrowed her eyes, and even Riddley could tell that her grandmother had known full well what she was saying, that, indeed, she had

enjoyed saying it, that she may well have been wishing to say it for a very long time. And if Josephine's expression right afterward were any indication, she too had seen that Adele was not just crazy, not just old, or that, even if she were, she'd still meant exactly what she said.

"Why, Josephine, I almost forgot your Christmas present." Pauline headed for the living room. "If you'd just wait for me one minute in the kitchen, I still need to wrap it. You know me, always running behind."

"Yes, ma'am." Josephine pressed the pin into her palm, nearly breaking the skin's surface, but her hands were tough and not easily pierced. In her own family she was known for her temper and quick tongue, and for a moment she was of a mind to speak her mind, but she had a bad back and arthritis, eleven grands and three greatgrands and a fourth on the way. And black people did not get to sixty-three years old—not in this time, not in this place—without being called names, and more times than she could count or cared to remember. And nor was this the first time in this house.

Josephine glanced at the clock. She needed to go. The buses were fewer on holidays, and in two hours' time her son was picking her up at her house to bring her home with him. The rest of this day and all of the next, she would eat food prepared and brought to her by others, and she would do no cooking or cleaning or serving of any sort. She had been working for one white lady or another for over five decades now and she deserved what rest she could get. In two strides she was beside the table, polished by her that very morning. She placed the pin on the gleaming wood. "Merry Christmas, Miz Wells," she said, as if the pin were her gift to her employer. Then she turned on her heel and headed back to the kitchen.

"Merry Christmas, Josephine," Riddley called. It seemed the wrong thing to say, but it seemed she ought to say something.

Josephine paused in the open door. She'd nearly forgotten the girl was there. She had a grandchild right around her age, who could already cook a decent meal and wash up afterward and brought home good grades besides. She doubted this girl could even so much as boil herself an egg. "Merry Christmas, Miss. I know Santa be good to you."

"You have a Merry Christmas, Josephine," Frazier called from the living room.

"Thank you, sir," she called back. "Merry Christmas to you."

The door swooshed shut behind Josephine. "Nigger," Adele said, or Riddley thought she said. Adele's voice was so soft, and her tone so mild, that Riddley couldn't be sure. But how could Adele have said such a thing? *Nice people don't use words like that,* Pauline had always told her daughters, though Riddley knew that plenty of nice people did, just not around Pauline. All kinds of people used that word. But not people like her grandmother. What else, though, could she have said? No other word that would've made sense sounded anything like that one. But maybe she hadn't been making sense. Maybe Pauline was right, that Adele didn't know what she was saying.

And what if, on the other side of the still slightly swinging door, Josephine had heard Adele? Riddley realized that, for all the times she'd heard the word, she'd never heard it said in the presence of anyone black—if that was indeed what Adele had said. Now, watching her move the figurines over the table, it was easy to believe that she hadn't said anything at all.

Pauline returned with her purse and a wrapped package of scented soaps. She pried open the sealed Christmas card and slid in a five dollar bill, and, after a moment's consideration, added another. Riddley wondered if she would also include the Christmas tree pin, but Pauline didn't notice it. She taped the envelope shut.

After Pauline had seen Josephine off, she came back into the dining room and stood beside Adele, shaking her head. "For shame, Mother. You won't have a friend left in the world, you keep acting like that." Pauline snatched up the pin and dropped it in her purse. Riddley wondered if she aimed to give it back to Josephine, to whom, technically, it still belonged. Riddley felt almost sure Josephine would refuse it.

Pauline turned to Riddley. "Grandmother has always been a lady, first and foremost, and a lady would never point, much less speak to anyone, *anyone,* like that, it doesn't matter who they are." Pauline cast a quick glance at her mother, piling a handful of skaters inside the village. "Grandmother forgets that, sometimes. She forgets her*self*

sometimes, who she is, where she came from. It's up to us to keep reminding her."

"Yes, Mama," Riddley said. But she wondered how Pauline, or Frazier for that matter, would have responded had they heard Adele say, and in Josephine's vicinity, *nigger.* It was about more than mere manners, more than just what it meant to be polite or nice or a lady. In the face of a word like that, it seemed it would do little good to say, *Remember who you are, Remember where you came from,* much less, *That's enough, Don't be ugly, For shame.* Such things had, in fact, often been said to Riddley, and though those reprimands had silenced her, seldom had they changed her mind.

CHAPTER 3

Georgia Day

After Christmas the weather turned cold, and Riddley set aside, for the time being, all thought of swimming. Still, she frequently went down on the dock and watched for the porpoises. They appeared but once, heading upriver. They rounded the bend before she had a chance to summon them.

During the last week of the holiday, Pauline often visited Frazier and Adele, but she did not bring any of her daughters along, as she always had in the past. Riddley's inclination to tell Pauline what Adele said on Christmas Eve had faded, for day by day, she grew less certain of what she'd heard. Could it simply have been some bad part of herself that had conjured the word? For it was indeed one that Riddley heard sometimes inside her own head. Every once in a while, with no warning, she heard it when she was with Esther. It was as if someone had whispered it, almost inaudibly, in Riddley's ear. She would glance at Esther, worried that she could tell what Riddley was hearing, or even that Esther might be able, in her own head, to hear that same voice. But Esther just kept mopping or dusting and paid Riddley no mind.

Riddley was almost glad when the holiday ended in early January, for her teacher, Miss Byrd, had a way of making school not seem like school. It was Miss Byrd's first, and to be her only, year there, though none of them knew that yet. She was strict and lenient at the same time, and given to great spasms of affection. Her fourth grade was what she called an Open Classroom, which Riddley had at first taken to mean that one could come and go as one pleased, a notion Miss Byrd had put immediately to rest. What it meant was that they performed a puppet show of *Julius Caesar,* danced in free form to the *Waltz of the Flowers,* and, during a thunderstorm, sat mutely in the dark for a full five minutes, after which they turned the lights back on and everyone, including Miss Byrd, composed haikus.

Miss Willa Byrd was older even than the mothers, by as much as a decade, though she seemed that much younger. To Riddley, Miss Byrd seemed not only younger, but like a different species altogether. With her large, slightly bulging green eyes, magnified by her black-rimmed glasses, she made Riddley think of a tree frog. She was one of those people whom Pauline, with a sigh, called *naturally thin*. Miss Byrd was tall, long-limbed and big-boned, with arms and legs of nearly the same thickness at either end. She gave off an unsweet smell, like mulch. Her voice was deep and raspy, as though she were coming down with something. She was spattered with freckles, which she made no attempt to hide, as if she'd been standing beside a puddle when a truck sped by.

She was the only lady Riddley had ever seen who wore no make-up, not even lipstick. *She could make something of herself with a little effort,* Pauline had said, but apparently Miss Byrd preferred, like a bed, to remain unmade. Her hair, to which she also did nothing, was short and frizzy and a red-tinged brown. Even in the hottest weather she dressed in slacks and blouses, in shades Pauline called, somewhat disparagingly, *neutral,* as though these colors had, through cowardice or indifference, refused to take sides. But Riddley liked her teacher's browns and grays and beiges. It was as if Miss Byrd wanted to be able, in a pinch, to run off and disappear in the woods. To that end, she wore flat, cork-soled shoes and thick cotton socks. She was not now, nor had she ever been, married.

Miss Byrd had taught history in a somewhat haphazard fashion, saving the colonial period to coincide with the run-up to Georgia Day, some six weeks away. The first day back from vacation, she read aloud their textbook's section on Georgia's founding. Mid-sentence she came to a stop. "Aren't you sick of Tomochichi and Mary Musgrove and James Edward Oglethorpe?" Miss Byrd said, causing a number of the children to gasp. "And why does no one ever mention the fact that Oglethorpe, regardless of his original ban on slavery in the colony, was once a director of the Royal African Company, a slave-trading corporation?"

The class gazed back at her in silence. Miss Byrd had already told them far more than any other teacher had about slavery, more indeed,

according to some parents, than their children needed to know. *She's near as bad as the blacks,* Wiley Brown's mother had said to Jane Tibbett's, *with how she goes on about something over and done with, for heaven's sake, more than a century ago!*

Miss Byrd declared that their class would put on a play to commemorate Georgia Day. The following week they picked numbers out of a hat to determine roles. There was much commotion over who got to be Indian, who had to be black. Walter Screven Sr. phoned Miss Byrd that evening to say that he did not pay good money for his son to be some Negro convict in the school play. Word had it that Miss Byrd had insinuated that such an impersonation might do him good. Mr. Screven had then called the principal, and consequently Walter Jr. played an overseer and a lunch counter clerk and lost his part on the chain gang, a role to which he had seemed particularly suited, given as he was to foot-dragging and a hangdog expression.

Riddley would be both Indian and black. For the former she needed a costume, dashing Pauline's hopes that Riddley might use the one from last year. For the previous Georgia Day pageant, Pauline had made her daughters ankle-length calico frocks with poofed sleeves and round white collars, and flounces over where their hips would one day be. She had intended to make them matching bonnets as well, but time had caught up with her. *Alas,* she'd said, *bonnets were not meant to be.*

Sewing was the only activity during which Pauline permitted herself to swear. *Dammit,* she would mutter through her clenched jaw, for even when not hemming or tucking she gripped straight pins between her teeth, as if sewing pained her to such a degree that she needed something to bear down on. *Hold still* and *Stand up straight* were hissed with equal intensity, as if these words too were curses. *No pockets, no darts, no frills,* was her motto, but even without these there were few things—cooking, baking, housecleaning—she disliked as much to do.

In the storage room off the attic stood Pauline's left-handed sewing machine. She bemoaned the bias of everything from faucets, doorknobs and gear shifts, to the pull cords of chainsaws and lawnmowers, which would explain, Sam said, why she'd never been

known to crank one. As a child she had been sorely put upon for her left-handedness, which she'd inherited from Frazier and passed on to Riddley. Until third grade Pauline had been forced to write with her right hand. One teacher tied her left hand to her side each day for a month, but her right hand remained incorrigible. By the time the teachers conceded, Pauline's handwriting had skipped clean over print, landing somewhere between that and cursive, the strokes and loops by turns furtive and jubilant. It was barely legible. Some, such as Esther, could not decipher it. If Pauline left an instruction or request propped between the salt and pepper shakers, Esther had one of the girls read it aloud to her. Likewise, as though Pauline might read as poorly as she wrote, Esther never left notes for Pauline but would call later from her own house to deliver phone messages, or to remind about the chicken in the oven, or the linens drying on the line. *I wish I had such a memory,* Pauline would say after one of those calls, shaking her head and marveling, *They never seem to forget a single thing.*

Despite the leftie sewing machine, Pauline's sewing skills were not much better than her handwriting. There were, however, endless outfits and costumes to be made, for school and church events, recitals and holidays and special occasions. Riddley flipped now through the fabric store's pattern books in search of an Indian Maiden outfit. In the Holiday section of *Simplicity* she found a square-necked Squaw Frock, fringed at elbows and knees. Pauline frowned over the torso darts, but thought that, with Riddley's figure, no harm would come from skipping them.

The saleslady advised them to select a cotton blend, to thwart the fringe's penchant for unraveling. Riddley unwedged a brown bolt. The saleslady smoothed the cloth along the length of the table's fixed yardstick, snipped a notch with her scissors, and with one yank tore clean to the other side.

"Are you Mary Musgrove? I always wanted to play Mary Musgrove," Pauline said on the way out of the store. "She was a half-breed, part Creek, wasn't she?"

"Yes, but that's not who I am. She's not in our play."

"One of the Indians at Yamacraw Bluff, then? A daughter of Tomochichi?"

Riddley shook her head. "It's not about that. You'll see." At Pauline's wounded look, Riddley added, "Okay, I'll give you a hint. I'm Cherokee, not Creek."

"Ah," said Pauline, "I see," though it was obvious that she didn't.

*　*　*

Usually Pauline brought her daughters to visit her parents once a week, or else Frazier and Adele came for Sunday dinner after church. And every other Thursday for over a year, Riddley had stayed with Frazier while the twins attended ballet lessons and Pauline took Adele to the hairdresser's. Thus Riddley had spent many hours alongside him in the den, playing dominoes or checkers, or looking through his travel books or postcard collection or well-illustrated dictionary.

But weeks had passed since Frazier and Adele had last come to dinner, and their church attendance had been irregular. Since Christmas Eve, Pauline had taken the girls to visit only once. Then Frazier, normally so patient and attentive, had been distracted and distant and very nearly short-tempered. Adele had disappeared into the bedroom soon after they arrived. Frazier had rapped on the door numerous times and said, in as close as he came to a whisper, *Please come out, the girls have come to see you.* Afterwards Pauline had said to Sam, *I'm afraid Mother will bring Daddy down with her,* for Frazier's heart, which had troubled him many years before, had lately been threatening to do so again.

In early February, Pauline took to visiting her parents at least once a day to assist with housecleaning and meals, for Josephine had, as Pauline put it, *retired,* and Pauline had yet to find anyone to take her place. Riddley couldn't help but think that Adele had something to do with Josephine's abrupt departure. According to Pauline, Adele had recently been speaking a bit more, though mostly she said the same things over and over, and asked questions. Riddley wondered again if Adele had indeed said *nigger* on Christmas Eve, and if so, whether she'd had the nerve, or the spitefulness, to repeat it.

But if not that word, then another. Why else would Josephine have left the way she did? *With not so much as a warning or a by-your-leave,* Pauline had said, *much less a proper farewell.* Josephine

had simply called one morning and told Frazier she would not be coming back again. As if she hadn't worked for them for almost two decades! But Frazier said he could hardly blame her. When he mailed her check he had added an extra twenty. *A dollar a year,* Josephine thought when she received it, though still she was grateful. And he was always a gentleman. She'd have lasted much longer had it been only him. Not that he had that much longer himself, she didn't think, the years piling on top of him even faster than his wife could shed them. What went on in that house would've made any number of grown men cry, as it had him, something Josephine would have gladly told their daughter, had she ever bothered to ask.

* * *

On the evening of Georgia Day, Miss Byrd's class performed their play. It consisted of a medley of scenes from Georgia's past, set to music. Brief explanatory remarks or quotations introduced each scene. The only dialogue was on the auction block and at the lunch counter. Included were vignettes from the Middle Passage, the slave trade and the Trail of Tears; belles waltzing on the plantation with their beaus; the ginning of cotton, the stomping and stirring of indigo, the threshing of rice; Sherman and carpetbaggers; sharecroppers and chain gangs; Jim Crow and the Ku Klux Klan; and the most recent scene, of protesters conducting a sit-in at McCreary's.

Frazier and Adele arrived just in time to hear Riddley read the excerpt from the Scottish settlers' petition against bringing slavery to Georgia: "Introduce slaves and we cannot but believe they will one day return to be a scourge and a curse upon our children or our children's children!" A little while later, Riddley marched and died in her Squaw Frock en route to Oklahoma. In between scenes Frazier waved at Riddley. Adele twisted her hands together, as if she were anxious or cold. Although Adele tended to be on her best behavior when beside Frazier, nonetheless Riddley worried her grandmother would do or say something untoward. But they were gone by the time Riddley sat, in blackface, at the McCreary's lunch counter, where she ordered and was refused a hamburger, fries, and a cocola.

* 3 2 *

At the gathering afterward Nel Bleecham—whose daughter Suzy had first been sold, wailing, down the river away from her children, only later to don a white sheet—was heard by some to say, "In *my* time, Georgia Day was a day of celebration."

Doug Potter said, loud enough to be heard by all, "This Byrd woman's not from around here, is she?" It was true. She was from the western part of the state, near Albany. Something about the way he spoke made Riddley's skin feel prickly, much as when she didn't rinse off after swimming. Had she ever known anyone before who had been called a woman? The way he made it sound, it was certainly not a word she hoped ever to hear applied to herself.

"*That* was harrowing," Pauline said on the drive home. "But you shone. Plus you can wear your splendid Indian costume next Halloween."

"It's already falling apart," Riddley said. Under the streetlights the blacktop shone. There had been a brief downpour during the auction. The sound of it had added to the gloom.

"Only because you picked at it," Pauline said. "If you leave it alone it will last just fine."

"I liked the part with the carpetbaggers, myself," Sam remarked. Pauline said that would no doubt have been his own line of work, had he lived back then.

"Why'd Grandmother and Grandfather leave early?" Riddley pictured Frazier's pained smile, Adele's twisting hands.

"Oh, Grandmother had the fidgets." Pauline rolled down her window a crack. "You know how she gets sometimes."

Charlotte informed Riddley that her face was still black in places. Riddley scrubbed at her forehead with the heel of her hand.

"Maybe it's permanent," Emmeline said.

"We could sure use more help around the house," Sam said. "Can you cook?"

Pauline remarked how Natalie Lyddell had certainly blossomed. "Wherever did she learn to waltz?"

"She and Kitty took lessons at the Boatmen's Club," Charlotte answered.

"I guess the time has come for that. As with most things, it's best to learn early," Pauline said. "You girls can take lessons this summer."

"But you said I could take sailing lessons," Riddley wailed.

"Your father can always teach you that."

Sam pointed out that it'd be a lot cheaper if she taught them to waltz as well.

"Nonsense." Pauline swiveled toward the back seat. "The only reason I'm able to dance a step is because your father leads so well. Once you learn the basics, he'll be marvelous practice."

"Why can't he teach us the basics?" Riddley said.

"Then you'd just learn everything backwards, or else he'd have to teach it backwards," Pauline replied. "Either way it's too confusing. Like being made to write with your right hand when you're left-handed."

"And we know what a fiasco *that* was," Sam said, adding that many people suspected Pauline was illiterate.

"Don't be ridiculous," Pauline said.

"What's illiterate?" Riddley inquired.

"When you can't read," Charlotte said.

"Like the kids who have to meet with Mrs. Trowbridge in the Special Needs room." Emmeline pronounced *Special Needs* with the same exaggerated emphasis as Pauline used for such words as *menstruation, integration, intercourse.*

"Those children are not illiterate," Pauline said. "They just need a little extra help."

"Like Esther then," Charlotte said.

"Esther can read," Riddley said.

"Have you ever seen her?" Emmeline said.

Riddley thought then of Esther's phone calls to deliver messages, and how she had Riddley read Pauline's notes out loud. *I couldn't make out your Mama's hand to save my life,* Esther said every time, after staring at the paper for a moment.

"Well, have you?" Emmeline repeated.

"Not that I can think of right now." Riddley felt as if she'd been forced to admit something not so much about Esther as about herself.

Pauline said Esther could read a bit, having gone to school a few years.

"Why'd she drop out?" Charlotte said.

"Chances are that was as far as the school went," Pauline answered, rummaging in the glove compartment. "She grew up out in Jeff Davis county, I think it was, or maybe Toombs. Back then some of those little country schools used to have only a few grades, if they had a school at all."

"Too busy pickin' cotton," Sam said, then sang, as had been sung in the play, "Jump down turn around pick a bale o' cotton." Charlotte joined in. "Jump down turn around pick a bale a day."

Pauline, humming along, dampened a paper napkin with her tongue. "Lean here, Riddley. I can't stand to look at that smudge any longer." She rubbed at Riddley's forehead.

"How much is a bale?" Emmeline said, and Sam said he thought it was five hundred pounds. Charlotte said there was no way somebody could pick that much in a single day.

Riddley took the tissue from Pauline. She leaned back and began to scrub. Had she ever before known a grownup who couldn't read? If she had, or did, she didn't know it, though it seemed like something you should be able to tell about a person. Now that she knew this about Esther, it seemed obvious. But things always seemed that way, after the fact. Riddley's ignorance was not, as was so often the case, because they had been keeping something from her. It was because she had not been looking where she ought to, or paying enough attention, to see something that was there, right in front of her, what others had seen all along. As they pulled into the driveway Riddley sternly told herself that she mustn't let it happen again.

CHAPTER 4

The Eye of the Beholder (1913)

What he appreciates most about a photograph, he muses as he peers through the lens, is its precision—its focus, if you will—on one exact time and place, and how it transforms a volatile, shifting instant into a still, unchanging, everlasting fact. He straightens and steps back from the tripod. He looks around him, contemplating alternative angles, but according to the light, he's perfectly situated. Over the past hours he has taken numerous pictures of the scene, from various aspects, including this one. He's about to call it a day when a girl stumbles into the clearing, dressed all in white, from the bow in her hair to her patent leathers. He puts his eye back to the lens.

It makes a nice juxtaposition: white dress, black man, amid the light and shadows. The girl is facing the other way, but she looks to be a pretty little thing, from what he can see of her, and pretty never hurt. He fancies himself something of an artist, having long been drawn to the canvas and the brush. He aims to pick it up again when his children are grown and looking after him for a change, but in the meantime you can't feed a family on paintings, landscapes and still lifes and the like. There is, however, money to be made in photography, fame to be had not in art but reality. He knows that folks like to see a picture of what they've only heard about. He bought his first Kodak as a young man back in '99, and that very year he was visiting his cousin in Atlanta when Sam Hose got his what for. He hopped on one of the excursion trains out to Newman and found there his subject: the crowd, the criminal, the rope, the fire. He himself was not, he was quick to point out, a violent man, but he could see how violence did have its attractions, not to mention its value, and its price. He'd sold those photos to newspapers across the South.

But far and away your best money, as much sometimes as a quarter a piece, is to be had in the picture cards. In the early days,

he'd had them developed as soon as he could, and sold them door to door. Once he determined that photography was indeed his calling, he invested in a portable printing plant. Then he could develop the pictures right there and sell by the hundreds. Nowadays, folks who'd heard tell of his specialty would come in and ask at the shop. He was building up a nice little mail order business, as well. After '08 it was forbidden to mail so-called *incendiary material,* but with a little brown paper wrapping and a thick envelope, no one was the wiser. The postal restrictions might've in fact improved business in the long run, for many a man was partial to the forbidden. And there was no law against taking the pictures, making them into cards, or owning them. In this country, at least, folks had the right to that. Thus he felt no hesitation in having printed on the back of those he developed in his shop, *Copyrighted by T. M. Smythe, Photographer.* As he'd said to Jenny, *Credit where credit is due.*

He has built up quite a collection over the years, having traveled all over the state—Wrightsville, Statesboro, Trenton, Bainbridge, Oxford, Decatur City. He can't remember them all, from tiny cotton towns to county seats, from the middle of nowhere to downtown on the central square. On occasion he ventures to Florida and South Carolina. The last one he'll make it to, a couple of years from now, will be outside Atlanta, for a Jew. His cards of Leo Frank will sell well into the next decade, by mail and in shops in Marietta, which will buy them by the gross.

Timing is the key. He has connections in most of the bigger newspapers, and they telegraph him when something is in the offing, in exchange for first dibs on his pictures. With the few that are advertised beforehand, or known in advance, special trains are often provided, and sometimes special fares as well, but usually a little ingenuity on his part is required, which often meant finding some fellow with a sense of adventure and an automobile who would let him hitch a ride in exchange, say, for twenty postcards and a personal photograph at the scene. But sometimes he wasted a whole trip and got there too late, when the best he could get was a shot of the rope or the tree, or some nigger's head on a pole. Jenny said she didn't know how he had the stomach for it. Sometimes by the time he arrived there was just a

charred stake and a heap of ash, in which case he had to get creative, with photographs of the victim's home or the crime scene, which sold well enough, but never as well as those of the criminal, in any and all conditions. Once he traveled six hours with his eldest, seven at the time, and much to his boy's disappointment not a damn thing had happened, or would, the sheriff having taken it upon himself to move the man nobody knew where, saying he'd suffer no vigilante justice in *his* county. No doubt the sheriff had suffered otherwise in the next election.

But nowadays he has too many responsibilities to go gallivanting around the state, even if it is on business. He has nearly more work than he can handle, photographing families, weddings, christenings, graduations, and portraits. He opened the shop a decade ago, and within the year married Jenny, who had, on her father's side, one-thirty-second Negro blood, something neither of them ever knew, though their grandson, an amateur historian, would one autumn day in 1959 abruptly discover this fact, and just as speedily cover it back up, and for good.

But despite how busy he is at the shop, he has ridden out here today with his family because it's just too close to town to pass up, and besides, he long ago promised his children to bring them along if the occasion arose. They've gone with Jenny to sell picture cards near the road while he finishes up here. Now, if he can just get the girl to turn his way so he can catch her full face and get one last shot. He adjusts the focus a final time and calls out, "You there, pretty young lady in the white." After a moment's hesitation she turns, and he can see the picture then exactly as it will look, and it will be a real beaut, he thinks, one of his best yet, if only he can get her to smile.

CHAPTER 5

Lent (1971)

Lent was Riddley's favorite holiday. *It's not a holiday,* Emmeline said, *if you suffer like you're supposed to.* But Riddley relished the giving up, the austerity in the face of plenty, not to mention the plenty before and after, and the looking forward to getting back. So each spring she lent to God some earthly pleasure—candy, cake, bubble gum, chocolate—while to the poor and suffering she lent, for good, her change. Every year she tried to give up more than she had before.

Charlotte and Emmeline relinquished something they didn't much care for, while Sam wouldn't give up anything at all for Lent. *Oh, lots and lots,* he'd answered gravely, when Riddley asked him if he ever had. He said he was too old now to do without his vices just for show, but Pauline said it was good practice. *Practice for what?* he said, and she made the face that meant, *You know what,* a look she was frequently casting on one or another of them, and not without reason, for usually they did.

Pauline gave up sweets, which hardly counted, as she was always trying to do that anyway. She explained that *Lent* was an old word for spring, so named for the lengthening of the days. As the season progressed, time felt to Riddley denser and yet more buoyant than before, the days drawn out in high, slow, slanting light, and the darkness of the nights not sharp as in winter, but smooth and rounded as the heat came on, and renunciation brought her closer to heaven.

In Sunday School the Sunday before Ash Wednesday Mrs. Kensington handed out sheets of thin cardboard shaped like fat crosses. One side was illustrated with dashes and arrows and miniature scissors indicating where to cut, where to fold, where to overlap and tuck in, where to slash for the slot. If made exactly to these specifications the box could, without glue or tape or rubber cement, hold together all by itself. In it Riddley would collect money for the

lame, the deaf, the limbless, the blind and destitute and crippled, the lunatics and lepers and all those unfortunates who there but for the grace of God did she go. The box seemed rather small, considering, but Pauline said, *fill it first, then we'll cope,* by which Riddley understood that Pauline did not think she would.

Ash Wednesday fell in late February, a couple of weeks after Georgia Day. That afternoon Riddley searched everywhere for coins: the crevices of sofas and armchairs and cars, closet floors and coat pockets, under furniture and in the backs of drawers. In the supermarket checkout line she stood at Pauline's elbow and held out her cupped hands, intoning, "Forget not the poor and needy."

"How could I, with you around?" Pauline said, relinquishing two dimes.

After school the next day, Charlotte and Emmeline went to ballet lessons while Pauline and Riddley went to Frazier and Adele's. "Grandmother just has to get her hair done," Pauline said. "It simply cannot go another day."

Frazier opened the door as they came up the walk. "Eighteen times in the last hour your mother's asked me what time it is," he said to Pauline. "That's about once every three minutes. What can a person do in three minutes?"

"Oh, Daddy," Pauline murmured.

"I can barely finish an article in the paper. Yesterday it was the day of the week. All day I had to tell her it was Wednesday." He paused. "It was Wednesday, wasn't it?"

She nodded. "Maybe you should just turn your hearing aids off."

"I could never do that to your mother."

"Daddy," Pauline said, as gently as she could manage, "she'd hardly notice."

He shook his head. "I would."

Pauline glanced at her watch. "It's time for your medicine, and Mother and I need to run to the beauty parlor."

"She doesn't want to go."

"I was afraid of that. Where is she?"

He gestured toward the back of the house. Then he turned to Riddley. "Butterscotch?" he said, leading her into the den.

"No thank you," she replied. "It's Lent."

"Pardon?" he said, leaning down.

"Lent started yesterday," she shouted. "I gave up candy."

For a moment he looked at Riddley the way he used to, with his full attention and affection. "What a good girl you are," he said, cupping her head with his huge hand, and how fine it felt then, to believe that she was. He scooped up some change from a dish on his desk and gave it to her. "For your collection box." Into her pocket he slid a butterscotch. "To save for later." Then he glanced down the hallway, where Pauline was rapping on the door of the master bedroom.

"Mother? It's me, Pauline. Won't you come out and visit a bit?"

There was no reply. Pauline knocked again. "It's been months since your hair's been done. You wouldn't want Sylvia or Marjorie to catch sight of you like this, now would you?" Again there was no answer. Pauline placed her hand on the knob and turned it slowly. The door was locked.

She stepped back and tidied her bun, reinserting some hairpins. Then she approached the door again. "I tell you what. First we'll go to the beauty parlor and then I'll take you and Riddley for an ice at Dominic's." Pauline beckoned Riddley over.

"Just tell her you'd like to see her," Pauline whispered.

Riddley put her mouth close to the door. "Hello." She cleared her throat. "It's Riddley. Won't you come on out? Then we can go get a lemon ice."

Pauline raised her brows in surprise as the door was immediately unlocked and opened a crack. "Where's Nancy?" Adele whispered.

Riddley glanced questioningly at Pauline.

"Do you mean Nancy Cooperton?" Pauline said.

Adele opened the door wider. She did not take her eyes from Riddley. "Where did she go?"

"I hate to be the one to remind you, Mother, but she died a few years ago. Remember? Of emphysema."

"She died?" Adele looked up at the ceiling, but as if it were the sky. "Is it raining?"

"It's a beautiful spring day," Frazier said as he approached. "You'll be glad to be out-of-doors."

Adele looked down at her navy skirt and top. "I'm filthy." Her voice sounded far more stricken than dirty clothes warranted. And in fact her clothes weren't dirty at all.

"You look perfectly fine, Mother."

"Lemonade?" Adele said.

"Lemon ice," Riddley corrected.

"Lemonade?" Adele repeated dolefully.

Frazier took her arm. "You can get whatever you want, dear." He escorted her down the hall, covering her hand with his own. He led her out to his car and drew the seatbelt gently across her lap. She smiled at him. "You're very kind," she said, as if he were a recent acquaintance.

"Not at all." He patted her hand and shut the door.

He gave his keys to Pauline. "Just come right home if there's any trouble."

"We'll be fine. Take your medicine as soon as you go in. Should I bring Riddley along?"

"Heavens no." He pulled Riddley to his side. "She's to keep me company."

"I'll swoop by in a while to pick you up for an ice," Pauline told Riddley. Then she lowered her voice so Frazier couldn't hear. "Entertain yourself now, he needs his rest."

Rest he may well have needed, but he insisted on three rounds of checkers, interrupted only by cups of hot cocoa, which, being liquid, he assured her did not count as chocolate.

*   *   *

In Sunday School the second Sunday of Lent, Reverend Marsden, the assistant minister, explained how the date of Easter was determined. It was, Charlotte said afterward at the dining room table, extremely complicated.

"How *do* you figure that out?" Pauline arranged her napkin in her lap like another article of clothing. "I never have understood."

"It's the first Sunday after the first full moon after the vernal equinox," Emmeline explained.

"*Vernal's* Latin for spring," Riddley added.

"Indeed it is." Pauline had a great fondness for roots and origins, having studied Greek and Latin in college. Her daughters knew the Greek myths as well as any fairy tale. "They certainly never taught such things when *I* went to Sunday School. All I learned was how everybody elsewhere was on the verge of starvation, so I should eat my peas."

"Who's on the verge of starvation?" Riddley said.

"Me," Sam said, carving the roast at the sideboard.

"I," Pauline corrected.

"You don't *look* starved." He handed her and Riddley their plates.

In order to figure out when Easter would fall, Charlotte said, you also had to know the golden number, which indicated where you were in the Metonic cycle. Riddley interjected that the golden number used to be written with ink made out of gold.

"The Metonic cycle," Charlotte continued, glaring at Riddley, "is how, every nineteen years, the full moon and the new moon happen on the same day."

"Now *that* I would like to see," Sam said, handing the twins their plates.

"What she means," Emmeline explained, "is that the full moon happens on the same day of the month as it did nineteen years before, and the same with the new moon."

"Ah," Sam said, joining them at the table. He dropped his napkin into his lap and grasped his knife and fork. Then, feeling the weight of Pauline's gaze, he set them back down. "Grace, girls," he said, as if they were the ones who had forgotten.

After grace, Emmeline explained that you add one to whatever the year is, then divide by nineteen, and the remainder is the golden number.

"This year it's fifteen," Riddley said, scooping a roast potato onto her plate.

"What if there's no remainder?" Sam was always trying to stump them.

Emmeline smirked. She would not be stumped. "Then it's nineteen."

"Once you know the golden number you look in the Prayer Book

to find out when the full moon is, and from there you can figure Easter," Charlotte said.

"Why not just look in the sky?" Sam pressed, taking two rolls from the basket and passing it to Charlotte.

"Because," Riddley said, "God's moon is different than the real moon."

Pauline frowned. "I would think they're one and the same."

"The church has its own calendar," Charlotte said.

Pauline lifted the top of a covered dish. "Who will have broccoli?" She smiled enticingly, as if they had any choice in the matter.

"There's one thing I don't get," said Charlotte, normally loath to admit any lack of comprehension. "Why can't Easter ever be on a real full moon?"

"That would be far too pagan," Sam answered, liberally salting his meat.

"What's pagan?" Riddley said.

"Heathens!" Charlotte responded.

"Witches!" Emmeline said.

"Like Ida Mae?" Riddley said. Ida Mae had looked after her as a baby. According to Pauline, some who worked along the bluff thought that Ida Mae was somewhat of a witch.

"Heavens no," Pauline said. "Ida Mae was perfectly harmless, and kind as could be. As for Christian, why, she went to church more than anybody I've ever seen."

"Wasn't Riddley the only one who could understand her?" Sam extracted a single floret of broccoli. "I could rarely figure out what the devil the old gal was saying."

"It did take some getting used to, I'll admit. I heard Gullah all the time, growing up. Geechee, we used to call it. Now you hardly ever hear it anymore. She was simply from another era, a bygone time." Pauline smiled, but as her memory of Ida Mae came into focus, her smile faltered.

Pauline had last seen Ida Mae many years ago, when she came looking for work. But by then Pauline had Esther three days a week, and she had sent Ida Mae away. Pauline had told herself that she did

not want to risk offending Esther, not to mention that they couldn't afford more help, but in truth Ida Mae had always made her uneasy. Not understanding much of her speech made Pauline feel, after a while, as if she were being made fun of, though she felt sure, or nearly so, that this was not the case. Pauline's lack of understanding made no difference in terms of what got done, for Ida Mae had no trouble understanding Pauline. Many a time she seemed to understand better than Pauline what needed doing, and how best to do it. But her muttering, her singing of familiar yet unintelligible songs, her bright head rag wrapped tight like an old mammy's, and, yes, the rumors of rootworkings and such, made it seem when Ida Mae was around as if there were a stranger in the house. With Esther it was not like that, though there were times when Pauline could not quite make out what Esther said, either. But Pauline was often able to forget that Esther was there at all.

Many of Riddley's first words were ones Ida Mae taught her. After Ida Mae left, there had been a brief spell of tantrums, during which Riddley screamed over and over whatever word it was that Pauline could not understand. For months afterward, Riddley had on random occasions said what seemed to be words, though the grave consternation with which she spoke suggested that she recalled only the sounds.

Later Pauline regretted not finding some task for Ida Mae, who always worked very hard and never seemed to tire, though who knew how old she was. Those old black women seemed to last forever, or at least to look and act as if they just well might. In Pauline's childhood, the woman who did their laundry had been born a slave, though she claimed to recall none of it. She had not a tooth in her head. Pauline and the neighborhood children had taunted her about that, until Frazier shamed them into stopping. To this day, she could still hear him saying, *Do unto others, honey.* Or had that been the time he'd said, *The meek, Pauline, the meek?* And what had the washerwoman's name been? It was one you never heard these days, Delia or Dinah or some such, vaguely biblical but at the same time not quite. Or was it Caroline? No, that was the woman who kept house for them

that summer of scarlet fever. It had been too long ago. She couldn't keep them all straight.

What, for that matter, was Ida Mae's last name? Pauline couldn't recall. Had she ever known it? Last summer she had driven past a rigid-backed old woman who resembled Ida Mae, walking toward Coffee Creek, where Ida Mae had stayed while on the mainland. Some of her husband's people had settled there, *after freedom,* as she always rather tryingly put it. Likewise she said *enduring slavery,* with a tone that suggested that she herself had done so.

Pauline had slowed the car, studying the old woman in the rear view. It was mid-afternoon and very hot. She at least ought to offer her a ride. But what if it wasn't Ida Mae? The woman's face had a wooden look to it, and in that wood had been carved some expression Pauline couldn't name. But she could tell enough to know that it was not one she wished to examine more closely.

"Do you think she still remembers me?" Riddley liked to imagine that Ida Mae had never cared for any other babies. Likewise it was unsettling to think that Esther worked for another family besides theirs, not to mention that she had a family of her own.

"Why would she remember you?" Emmeline said. "She probably looked after loads of babies."

"She was very fond of you," Pauline assured her, taking another spear of broccoli. "She knew you practically since you were born."

"But she knew lots of babies since they were born." Charlotte removed a roll from the basket. "That was her job, wasn't it?"

"Delivering babies is quite different from taking care of them."

"'I don't know nothin' 'bout birthin' babies, Miss Scarlett,'" Sam said in his terrible drawl.

"*That's* certainly the truth." Pauline tore a roll in two and put the smaller piece back in the basket. The twins had been six weeks early, and relatively easy, but after Riddley, who had been in a particular rush to be born, it took Ed Snodgrass over an hour to sew Pauline up. Some weeks later, Pauline, still unable to sit comfortably, stood in the hallway as Ida Mae sorted through a stack of old linens, in search of one too frayed for a bed. Ida Mae put an edge of a tattered

one between her teeth and tugged, making a small rip. She gripped the cloth between her hands and muttered something about how those hospital doctors ought to know that a woman was like a sheet. Pauline's bafflement ended when, in two yanks, Ida Mae ripped the sheet in half. Just the sound of it had made Pauline sting, and, recalling that now, she shifted in her seat.

Ida Mae had torn that sheet into long strips. One she wrapped as a belly-band around Riddley's waist, an old-fashioned practice Pauline would have resisted had not Riddley's navel bulged unbecomingly. With a wide piece Ida Mae tied Riddley to her back, so she could have both hands free while she hung wash or cooked or took the twins out to the sandbox. She twisted and tied off a scrap at the end with twine, then dipped it in a mixture of boiled water and caro syrup. *Sugar tit,* Ida Mae called it, a term that discomfited Pauline. But that sweet knot often soothed Riddley during a spell of colic, when otherwise she might squall for hours. If that didn't work, Ida Mae would take her down on the dock. At night Pauline, to dry herself up and prevent sagging, bound her chest with a wide strip of that same sheet. Sam said it was like sleeping with a mummy.

Pauline could almost feel that sheet against her skin now. It had been thick and supple, worn soft by years of being slept on. A castoff from Adele's trousseau, it was made of what used to be called sea island cotton. These days, in stores and on package labels, such silky cotton was known as Egyptian. When had cotton last been grown on the islands? Pauline wondered, taking the remainder of the torn roll from the basket. And which island was it that Ida Mae was from? Sapelo, or St. Catherine's? But no, Pauline was sure it was South Carolina. St. Helena, then, or maybe Daufuskie.

"Didn't she scold you for not keeping the caul?" Riddley said.

Charlotte, groaning, said that they were trying to eat, and Emmeline pointed out that they'd already heard this twenty times.

Pauline turned to Riddley, who never tired of hearing it. "When I told her I thought you were born in a caul, I thought I'd never hear the end of it. I said I was woozy from the drugs, and might well have imagined it, but she insisted on telling me all these old African wives'

tales about how special that made you, how wise and lucky you'd be. There's a lot of that kind of talk still on the islands, you know." Pauline paused, remembering. "I ought to have dried it on a piece of paper, she said, and tucked it away for future use. Can you imagine? Fortunately the nurses had long since disposed of it."

"This is so disgusting," Charlotte said.

"Wasn't your mother born in a caul, too?" Sam said.

"Goodness, no. She was born feet first, after which her mother died, despite the fact that her father was a doctor. It was one of her sisters. Riddley, I'm almost sure."

"It was?" Riddley had never heard that before. She was not sure how she felt about sharing this particular trait with her Aunt Riddley.

"We should have sold Riddley's caul down at the port, for some sailor to hang in a pouch round his neck," Sam said. "A common practice way back when. David Copperfield sold his, I believe. We could've put the proceeds towards college, or better yet, a dowry."

Riddley felt as if he were speaking of selling her very self, though she had never before thought of the caul as a part of her. She wondered as well what it was made of. Skin, flesh, muscle? She pictured it as similar to the thin white stuff that sometimes clung, like damp tissue paper, to the stalks of mushrooms.

Emmeline asked what anybody would want with it, and Sam replied that cauls were considered a charm against drowning. "That's why Riddley will always be safe at sea. Let me think, what's that line from Shakespeare?" Sam often dredged up bits he'd memorized in school. "Ah yes. 'He hath methinks no drowning mark upon him.' Born to be hanged, as the saying goes."

"I'd rather drown." Riddley glanced through the window to the river. As soon as dinner was done she'd change into shorts and go down on the dock.

"Not your choice, I'm afraid."

"This is all sheer superstition," Pauline said, slicing up the last of her broccoli. Then abruptly she had to put down her silverware, so vividly did she picture her daughters falling off the dock. This was from a dream she'd had many times. In the dream Pauline knew she

couldn't save them, and, because she didn't want to frighten them, she only smiled and waved as they drifted toward the Atlantic, where they would eventually tire and drown. She gave a quick shake of her head now, to rid herself of the sight of her girls being borne away over the water. She picked up her fork and pierced a floret. "As I've told you before, Riddley, just because you may have been born in a caul does not in any way prevent you, heaven forbid, from drowning, no matter what your father says, so don't go thinking you can swim on a full stomach during a lightning storm, or forgo your life jacket."

Riddley asked what the caul was supposed to be used for later, and Sam said crab bait. Charlotte and Emmeline laughed.

"Ida Mae said it could have predicted various things, such as your health," Pauline said.

"How would you be able to tell?" This was another part Riddley had not heard before.

"Its appearance would change if, for example, you were going to fall ill." It would also transform, according to Ida Mae, if Riddley was in danger of death. Ida Mae's words had made Pauline shiver, and she could feel such a shiver coiled now along the length of her spine. She sat up straighter.

"But how?" Riddley said. "What would it do?"

"It would mold or drip or something equally revolting."

Sam said he thought it would, in this ungodly climate, do that regardless. "Didn't she say that people sometimes actually ingested the thing?"

"I'd forgotten that." Pauline grimaced. "The part that had me aghast was when she said I needn't worry if I'd lost Riddley's." She attempted a laugh. "Anybody else's would do just as well."

"But why would I ever need to eat it?" Riddley's mouth puckered at the thought.

"I can't quite recall," Pauline said, though all at once she did, and so clearly that she wondered how she had ever managed to forget it. If Riddley became too frightened by the ghosts she would see, and was already no doubt seeing, then Pauline could secretly feed her a bit of caul, or have her drink a tea made from it, to blind her to those

ghosts. But Ida Mae said it was far better for Riddley to keep what she called her sight. Most ghosts meant no harm, she assured Pauline, though, like the living, there were always those few who did.

Pauline knew better than to tell Riddley that certain people—well-meaning but uneducated, superstitious—believed that the supposed particulars of her birth allowed her to see ghosts. Or, depending on how one understood it, forced her to see them. Pauline herself had dismissed and then forgotten the notion, until around age three Riddley had begun the nightmares and night terrors, the sleeplessness, sleepwalking and dark dread that would plague her, off and on, for the rest of her life.

But all this business about ghosts and foretelling was ridiculous, because Pauline was still not absolutely sure that Riddley had been born in a caul. Once Pauline had mentioned that likelihood, however, everyone had instantly accepted it as fact. Perhaps this was due to the usual auspiciousness of such a birth.

"If Ida Mae was so crazy about Riddley, why didn't she ever come back to see her?" Charlotte said. It was a question Riddley herself had pondered many a time.

"Oh, she probably moved back to the island, or went to live with one of her children, or found work closer to home. Anything could have happened." Pauline saw again that very old woman plodding along the road in the merciless heat. Good Lord, what on earth had she been thinking? She should have stopped and offered the woman a ride, no matter who she was. Her appetite abruptly gone, Pauline placed her knife and fork together, folded her napkin beside her plate, and pushed back from the table. "Anyone for a bowl of fruit salad?"

* * *

Although Riddley had no memories of Ida Mae, she would have liked to see her again. She always pictured a very dark woman standing in a doorframe painted what Pauline called *haint blue*. That practice of decoration had, according to Miss Byrd, purportedly originated on sea island indigo plantations. Slaves had used rinse water from the vats to color the doors and windows blue, a practice still thought to protect a

house from haunting, perhaps in the belief that the dead can be staved off by the sight of what had, in one way or another, killed them.

Indigo work was grueling, Miss Byrd had said, and the dye solution highly toxic. The color had to be forced from the plant. It was picked in full bloom and soaked in huge vats of water. To extract the juice, slaves pressed and stomped, their hands and feet staining blue. Then they beat and stirred with paddles, to mix in air, for only oxygen could bring out the color. The stagnant water of the vats, not to mention of the surrounding marsh, bred mosquitoes, and thus yellow fever and malaria, though it would be nearly another two centuries, Miss Byrd told them, before that connection would be understood. As those diseases were more common in Africa, blacks had more resistance than whites, which was why, Troy Winters had explained at recess, blacks made such good slaves.

*　*　*

Ida Mae Hunter was indeed from the islands, not Sapelo or St. Catherine's, St. Helena or Daufuskie, but Hilton Head, from way back when it was just a sea island and not a resort. She had been born there twenty-odd years after freedom, as she did always put it. In late 1864 her maternal grandmother Rose had, with her family, followed Sherman's army to the coast, seeking, along with thousands of other freed slaves, land of their own—the fabled forty acres. Sherman spared Savannah in order to give it intact to Lincoln for Christmas, a legendary event that would thereafter be drummed into the heads of local schoolchildren. From occupied Savannah he issued, in January of 1865, Field Order Number Fifteen, about which no one in those parts was ever taught in school:

> The islands from Charleston, south, the abandoned rice fields along the rivers for thirty miles back from the sea, and the country bordering the St. John's River, Florida, are reserved and set apart for the settlement of the Negroes.

But by April, Lincoln was dead. By May, President Johnson had pardoned the planters and returned to them all their lands, and rumor had it he'd revoked the Emancipation Proclamation as well. Congress

clarified that the former slaves had been given not the land but merely the right to purchase it, a right which in practice evaporated a few years later, when most whites refused to sell them any land at all. But Rose's future husband, a skilled wheelwright who'd saved money by hiring himself out, had bought land on Hilton Head in 1861, after the North took Port Royal Sound and the masters fled. She settled on the island with him, while the rest of her family went back inland, ending up she never did know where.

It was Rose who taught Ida Mae midwifery, knowledge that served her well for decades. But eventually midwifery was outlawed in South Carolina, and not long after, the bridge went up. More and more people went to the mainland to have babies. Ida Mae lost most of her land to taxes and swindling and the foolishness of her second son and his mainland wife. The first son she'd lost to war in Europe, as a grandson would later be lost in Vietnam.

Ida Mae came to the mainland in 1961 because she needed cash for the taxes on what land was left. She had managed, through perseverance and God's mercy, to never work a day in her life for white folks before that time. Her daughter cleaned house in Bluffton, but Ida Mae did not wish to wind up working for the descendants of those who'd once owned her kin, so she went on to Savannah. She had the address of some of her first husband James' people in Coffee Creek, and appeared at their door one summer morning. Sallie and Ben made her welcome at once, though they warned her she might face trouble in their house. They were in the movement, and as a result had spent many a night in jail, and come up against billy clubs and hoses and dogs. Ida Mae assured them she could handle whatever white folks might put in her way. Why, even at her age and with her poor eyesight, she'd learned to read five years earlier, in order to be eligible to vote. And vote she did, every chance she got, no matter if, on her way to the polls, some redneck walked alongside her and said, *Why you wanna make trouble, Auntie? You want us to make trouble for you?* She kept her head down and kept walking, saying, *No suh,* as she'd been saying all her life.

Sallie had asked around about daywork, and by week's end Ida Mae was looking after the Crosses' new baby, which she did for some

months. Almost a year later she came back to the city, as she wanted to put aside money for future taxes, enough that she could die on the island. Sallie and Ben had recently returned from Albany, where they had again been locked up, along with the Reverend Dr. King. In Sallie's cell had been a pregnant woman who'd been badly beaten and lost the baby. When they mentioned that, Ida Mae remembered something that James had told her long ago. A woman near eight months along had tried to stop her husband's lynching, and they had hung her beside him, upside down, then set her on fire and cut out her baby with a hog knife. *That child cried just the once,* James said, *and then they stomped on it.* James always had to speak of such things. He never did know when to leave well enough alone. No, he knew, he just couldn't, or wouldn't. Still, sometimes when she looked into the water she saw his body, bruised and bloated and sharkbit, lashed to his own anchor by the men who dragged him until he drowned. When she buried him she swore she would never go in that water again, though she had swum in it most all her life. But it would have been like swimming in his blood.

Ida Mae went to the Cross house seeking work again, and Mrs. Cross had been glad to see her, what with the baby walking and always underfoot. Ida Mae had stayed almost six months. Only once more had she returned to the mainland, and that time Mrs. Cross had turned her away. It was no wonder. The night marches had been going on downtown all that summer, and white folks were looking over their shoulders all the time, and about time, too. Ida Mae had worried she wouldn't be able to find work, but Sallie had found her a place with another family. After Ida Mae made what she needed, she returned home for good.

Those last years, she had gone again into the water. She waded in, and then stood or knelt or, if the waves were mild enough, sat in the shallows. When the air was storm heavy, the sea bath soothed her joints. She seldom used fresh water to wash herself anymore. The smells her body made were no longer of work or dirt, but age, and the salt tempered that better than any soap.

Sometimes she let herself float. It was as easy to float as when she was young. She remembered that sensation from childhood, the long

ripple of a swell moving under her back, pivoting her slowly, bringing her toward, then away, from shore. She was surprised she didn't
just sink to the bottom. She was withered and shrunken, her skin
stretched tight over her cheekbones and the knobs of her feet, and
loose everywhere else. Any fat had long since left her frame. Maybe
air blew now through the center of her bones, like chicken bones after
she'd sucked out the marrow. Why she hadn't died yet she couldn't
figure. *God ain't ready for you yet,* Brother Haynes had told her, *He's
got more work for you to do.*

Floating there she thought sometimes of how the ocean, on its
other side, touched where her people had come from, how they still
had that water in common. It seemed they had little else, besides skin.
The few times she'd seen Africans on TV they were starving or fighting, and always they were plagued by flies.

Adrift in the shallows she thought also of her great-great grandfather, said to be the only one to survive the walking into the water,
a sorrow he'd carried with him all his days, for he had believed that
those who'd gone under had made it back to the other side. He had
been but a few weeks old, and never should have been alive at all,
being born on the crossing. Either his mother could not bear at the last
minute to bring him under, or else he'd floated up out of her hands.
In any case, the story went that a sailor had scooped him out with a
fishing net as he bobbed face up and tightly swaddled in the water.
The slaves on shore who witnessed his retrieval had at once dubbed
him Moses, the name he had been buried with, some half a century
later. But the name he'd been born with, the name given him by his
own, had gone under with the rest of them.

As for the woman Pauline saw alongside the road, she was not Ida
Mae, nor any known relation. By then Ida Mae had already passed,
in her own bed, in her own house, the house that Howard, her last
husband, had built. Within a few months of her passing, her children,
as she had warned them against, had sold the land and the house
that stood on it. Some while after that, a bulldozer had removed all
obvious traces of Ida Mae, but for the shards of colored glass from off
her bottle tree, and the tomato and guinea squash and mustard green

volunteers that germinated for years afterward in the soil of what had been her garden.

As she had requested, her children had laid her to rest in the old graveyard, situated near the water so the spirits could more easily find their way home. In that graveyard there lay as well, among many others, Moses and Rose and Phiba, who was what they called a saltwater African, having arrived in 1858 on *The Wanderer,* the last slave ship to reach America. Ida Mae had never forgotten her, though Phiba had died when Ida Mae was still a girl. Phiba had been much admired by children, and more than a little feared, for her tales of haints and hags, and the fact that all her stories were told in a manner and accent different than anyone else's, though she had by then lived among them more than forty years. In the year before she died, she was often heard muttering in her old language to herself, there being no one else who would have understood it.

Near Ida Mae lay her parents, and the partial remains of her first husband James, and Vesey, her war-dead son; the more intelligible remains of Denmark and Howard, her second and third husbands; her daughters, Frieda, Rebecca, and Ruth; and her twins, one a boy, one a girl, stillborn and never named. On top of Ida Mae's grave stood a pitcher, a glass, a small blue jar, and a clock, set to the time of her death. Occasionally a golf ball rolled between graves. Some of those who had passed before the onslaught of that game at first mistook the ball for a loggerhead egg, and they felt then a fierce craving for something with the particular flavor of the sea.

Even Ida Mae, who knew a damned golf ball when she saw one, thought of those eggs and felt that craving. She remembered one hot moonlit night very long ago, when she had seen the turtles lumbering up the beach to nest. Only a few of the eggs and hatchlings would survive the gulls and coons and ghost crabs, every conceivable kind of scavenger, including herself. To mark the place, she thrust driftwood upright into the sand above the high tide line. At dawn she returned with baskets. She gathered every egg she could find, and caught a ride to the mainland on an oyster boat. It was a windfall. By noon she had sold them all in Beaufort, save an egg for each of her children.

CHAPTER 6

Infirmities

aturday of the third week of Lent was cold and rainy, foiling Riddley's plans to coax Sam out in the motorboat for the first time since fall. She wondered what to do instead. Her sisters were still abed when she passed their room on her way downstairs. In the kitchen Sam was making his monthly call to his mother, Isabel. Pauline had Riddley get on the phone, as she did whenever Riddley did not manage to make herself scarce in time. *Just say hello,* Pauline mouthed. What else was there to say? The bulk of Riddley and Isabel's conversation had always been about cards: points, penalties, and rules, luck or its absence. And Isabel had never had much to say, and had even less now, though her kind of quiet, unlike Adele's, did not make people uncomfortable. Isabel spoke little not because words had fled her, but from decades of living with a man who believed that much if not all that women said was foolish.

Riddley answered Isabel's usual questions about school and the weather, and then handed the phone back to Sam. As she poured herself a bowl of cereal she recalled how Sam had once said that his father Ray had stashed money in his wooden leg, which he could extract through a trap door in the sole. *Oh, do,* Pauline had said, which usually meant don't, *You make him sound like a pirate.* Riddley was not so gullible as to believe the bit about the trap door, but she figured it was worth a look, as her collection box, bigger than it seemed, was slow to fill, and she had exhausted her other resources. Besides, it had been a while since she had explored the garage apartment, where Ray and Isabel had lived for years. It would be a good place to spend the morning, sufficiently out of the way of Sam and Pauline, who might otherwise rope her into cleaning her room or the attic. Next door she could well find some change in a drawer, or between the cracks of sofa and chair cushions. There were plenty of places to search if the leg turned up empty, as she expected it would.

Ray would never have agreed to move south in 1965 had they not been running through their savings at an alarming pace, and had he not suspected he was ill. A stubbed toe had long refused to heal, a condition he concealed until the stench and his limp gave him away. By the time he made it to the doctor, gangrene had set in, as in *set in stone.* He lost that leg up to the knee. A few years later, an ingrown toenail caused him to lose his remaining big toe, and around the same time, his eyesight began to fail. Esther said he had the sugar bad. *Diabetes,* Pauline explained to her daughters, *when sweets can kill you.* This had made the girls, for a time, ease up on candy, which they otherwise only did for Lent.

Sam and Pauline, when referring to Ray's missing leg, never said *amputate* or *cut off.* Rather they said, *when he lost his leg,* as if he had misplaced it, or gambled it away on a bad hand of cards, and that he might yet find it or win it back again. Ray could well have thought the same, for he often lifted the stump as though the rest of the leg were tucked underneath him, like the twisted limb of a balloon doll which swells once the kink is taken out. Sometimes the stump jerked and he would look down at it querulously, as though it did not belong to him at all. Before an injection there he would give it a *thwap* with the back of three fingers, as if in warning or preparation for what was to come, as in *you'll get what's coming to you,* though hadn't it already? The other leg sat very still, in fear, it seemed, of retaliation. Rarely did he give the whole leg any attention.

Sam and Isabel had coaxed Ray into wearing his false leg for holiday meals and the like. On the rare occasion when someone touched it, he had looked for an instant as if a ghost leg lived inside the fake one, and he could feel the living fingers through the wood. But most of the time the leg stood upstairs in the corner of his room, in a black sock and shined shoe. *All dressed up and nowhere to go,* Sam said. Likewise, Ray seldom tried to use the walker. It would have provided an excellent structure for a fort or castle, but early on it had been made clear to the granddaughters that if Ray didn't use it, nor would anyone else. As with many things, it was offered to them long after they had any wish for it.

Eventually his deterioration reached a speed neither his wife nor his daughter-in-law could keep up with, so after some three years

he returned to Michigan, to a Veteran's home near Sam's twin sister. Isabel had undergone then a slow blossoming, chiefly in the form of window shopping excursions and lunches at Morrison's, where the waitresses greeted her by name, despite the fact that she was not much of a tipper.

At Ray's insistence, his prosthesis had not accompanied him back to the Midwest. Six months after he left, he lost his other leg. Riddley had worried over the dispersal of his body throughout the country: one leg in the cemetery in Georgia; a solitary toe interred who knew where; and the other leg gone wherever the limbs of veterans went, perhaps to the capital. Emmeline said there were special coffins for all the extra bits that nobody knew what to do with. Charlotte and Riddley had exclaimed over that, but later, in the dark, Riddley did not find the horror of it so pleasurable. She could picture far too clearly that jumble of all the parts that could get cut off a body. Once you started pondering it, there seemed to be little that could not be severed.

Riddley had visited Ray and Isabel more often than her sisters did, and her visits increased after Ray left. Many an afternoon Riddley had gone next door to play cards with Isabel, games of gin, hearts, canasta, and double solitaire. Then about a year-and-a-half ago a place had opened up at a retirement home near Ray, where everyone had assumed Isabel would wish to be. Ray had lasted only a month after she arrived, as if he were just waiting for her to get there so he could die. Riddley had wondered then if his body had at last been reunited, the various parts of him brought back together in heaven. But Pauline had always said heaven was about the soul, not the body.

After breakfast, Riddley ran through the cold rain to the garage apartment. The swollen door wheezed when she pushed it open. As she stepped in, she was at once struck with the particular smell of the place. Pauline sent Esther over every few months to dust and sweep and let in some fresh air, but beneath the odors of ashtrays and rubbing alcohol lingered something sweet and vaguely fetid, which Riddley took to be the odor of gangrene.

She closed the door behind her and leaned back against it, waiting for her eyes to adjust to the dimness. Just as when Ray and Isabel lived there, the thick curtains were tightly drawn. She could practically

see Isabel smoking on the sofa, and Ray parked on the other side of the room, slumped over in his wheelchair. Once he'd been limp for so long she had wondered if he had died, a notion that had been oddly embarrassing. She had not grieved him when he had. It was clear he cared little for his granddaughters, though, to be fair, by then he cared little for anyone. Everybody knew to stay well out of his way, except of course Isabel, who had no choice in the matter.

Riddley moved slowly through the living room, running her fingers over the familiar objects. She had missed coming here. Right after Isabel departed, Riddley had come over frequently to examine the many objects left behind, and to ride the elevator chair, a privilege long forbidden her. But she had not set foot inside since last summer. There was something unsettling here, as if the place itself could not forget what it had been privy to.

She checked for change in the end table's drawers, and in various containers on the knick-knack shelves. In Isabel's embroidered sewing kit she found a dime. Under the kitchen sink she struck gold: a jar with a slot jabbed in the lid, nearly a third full of pennies. She put it in the doorway so she wouldn't forget it.

At the foot of the stairs the elevator chair waited. She knew exactly where to find Ray's leg. For a long while after he departed, it had stood upstairs in its corner, keeping watch. After he died, Pauline complained that it spooked her every time she went over there, and Sam had said, *Throw the damned thing on the burn pile, that would have suited Dad just fine.* Pauline had blanched and said, *Don't be awful,* as if he were referring to his father's flesh-and-blood leg. After that she moved it to Ray's bedroom closet, where it was hidden behind his shirts and slacks and suits, until Pauline donated all these to a good cause, meaning, in this case, the Salvation Army and Henry, the yardman. Pauline loathed waste, and always preferred to give rather than throw a thing away. Thus steak bones went not to the trash but to their black labs Winnie and Coco, vegetable peelings were tossed on the compost pile, and the turkey carcass was saved in a sack and sent home with Esther, for stock.

Riddley sat in the elevator chair and ascended to the second floor. Everything appeared the same as when she'd last been there. But it

was not. The leg was gone from Ray's closet. As she searched his room and then Isabel's, Riddley recalled the smooth, dry feel of the leg, more like bone than flesh, and how it had seemed to give off some sense of what it was to grow, to be alive. She knew that was absurd, that the leg had never been alive, not as a leg, anyway. But even so it seemed wrong that someone else would wear it. For that was what must have happened to it. Pauline had found the leg a home. Sam was right. They should have burned it in the woods out back. Or maybe they should have sent it North to be buried beside Ray. Not that Ray would have wanted it anywhere near him. He had, after all, come to loathe the thing. Once he had stopped wearing it of his own accord, he had protested with increasing venom whenever his wife or son had coerced him into doing so. By the end, regardless of the occasion, they could not convince him to let them put it on him.

Would Frazier become like that, eventually, about his hearing aids? *Just turn them off, Daddy,* Pauline had said. How could she have suggested such a thing? He had refused, but Riddley wondered now if he hadn't been, or wouldn't soon be, tempted, after which she would never be able to capture his attention again. On her Thursday visit two days ago there had been no checkers, much less cocoa, and she suspected that the blissful afternoon two weeks earlier was an aberration that would not be repeated. For this recent visit, Frazier and Riddley had been relegated to the den while the hairdresser, on a rare house call, washed and set Adele as best she could in the kitchen. Frazier had slept motionless in his armchair the whole time, while Riddley flipped through old *National Geographics* and built forts out of dominoes. She had hoped he would wake and propose a game, but he hadn't stirred at all, even when the dominoes fell in a great clatter, or afterward, as she stood beside him very softly repeating, *Grandfather.* Maybe, come to think of it, he had already turned his hearing aids off.

And what, she wondered, would happen to his hearing aids when he died? No doubt they would, like Ray's walker, wheelchair, and leg, be given to someone else to use. Pauline would want it that way. She wouldn't want them to go to waste. But even more than with Ray's artificial leg, to have some stranger use Frazier's hearing aids seemed a terrible invasion of privacy, as if whoever acquired them would also

receive access to all that had passed through them. And just what had Frazier heard, what had been said to him? For the first time it occurred to Riddley that Adele might be more than just irksome to Frazier, that she might be cruel, as she had been to others. And if that were so, how could Riddley blame him for not wanting to hear?

Riddley sat now on the edge of Isabel's bed and rustled half-heartedly through the drawer of the bedside table. Her head was throbbing, a discomfort compounded by the apartment's smell. She thought you were supposed to get used to smells the longer you smelled them, but obviously that was not the case with this particular one. She needed some fresh air. She walked down the stairs rather than take the elevator chair. Although she hadn't recognized it at the time, hadn't she gotten a whiff of something quite similar the other day in Frazier's den? In that case the smell must have to do generally with old age, that being the only thing she could think of that Frazier and Ray had in common, besides, of course, her and Charlotte and Emmeline.

Outside it was still raining, as Sam had reported it was supposed to do all day. She wished she had thought to wear a slicker. She huddled in the doorway for a moment. Then she knew where to find shelter: Isabel's car. And there was a chance, too, that she might find some change there. The jar of pennies under her arm jangled as she sprinted up the driveway.

Isabel's Chevy had been born, as Sam liked to put it, the same year as Riddley. He had purchased it for his parents shortly after they moved to the South. There had been talk of adapting it to hand pedals, but whatever interest Ray might've had in mobility had soon dwindled to nothing. He and Isabel had seldom ventured out. He was too heavy for her to lift in and out by herself, besides which, where was there for them to go? Not to mention the fact that, whenever they had gone anywhere before, Ray, naturally, had done the driving.

After Ray's departure, Isabel had gone out almost every day. A few months before she also departed, her car was hotwired in the mall parking lot and used for a bank robbery, after which it was abandoned across town. She searched the parking lots for hours, theft never occurring to her. As she circled the mall for the third time, a light

rain beginning to fall and a blister to form on her left heel, whatever pleasure she had felt in her independence was extinguished. Why had no one warned her that senility could engulf you in a matter of hours? Her timidity returned tenfold. She knew what people would think. She knew it because she thought it herself: this never would have happened if she had not been on her own. It made no difference that Ray could have done nothing to help. At least then she would not have been entirely to blame, even though everyone, including Isabel, knew she was entirely blameless.

In the year-and-a-half since Isabel's departure, her car had sat in a slot Sam had chainsawed out for it, midway up the driveway. Every once in a while he threatened to give it to one of his daughters as a sixteenth birthday present. It would have been the worst kind of gift: ridiculous, embarrassing, impossible to refuse. But by then it would no doubt be beyond repair. It had ceased to run soon after Isabel left. Riddley knew because she had tried to start it with Isabel's spare keys, which were tucked into the folding armrest in the middle of the back seat.

She scampered now into the front seat and slammed the door shut. She had often accompanied Isabel on drives and errands, and after Isabel was gone, Riddley herself had spent a good bit of time behind the wheel, pretending to be a bank robber. Now, sitting cross-legged in the middle of the seat, she wondered if she'd ever see Isabel again. Especially since most of her belongings had remained behind, Isabel seemed in a way to have died when she left. Or maybe such a process had begun before that. Although the police had returned the Chevy, Isabel had not gone out again. Nor had she shown any interest in card games or company or TV. Sam had taken to calling her Bonnie, and Isabel, ever the good sport, had laughed feebly along. But anyone could see that the robbers had stolen far more than her car, and things that could not be returned.

It reminded Riddley of what Pauline often said about Adele, *She's just not herself.* At first this had seemed to imply that Adele would eventually become herself again, but after a while it was evident that that person had disappeared for good. What Pauline never said was who, instead, Adele had become. With Isabel it was not so much a

transformation as a kind of dwindling. After the car theft she had been steadily emptied out, until, by the time she departed, hardly any of her seemed to be left.

Riddley, watching the rain on the windshield, thought of each of her grandparents, with their various infirmities. Judging by them, old age seemed largely a matter of loss, or, depending on what was to be forfeited, an ongoing process of losing. Ray, of course, had lost his toe and his legs, his sight and his temper, whereas Isabel's losses had more to do with her spirit. Frazier, having lost much of his hearing and vigor, had also, in essence, lost his wife. As for Adele, she had at the very least lost her memory and speech and manners, if not her very self.

Riddley emptied the pennies into her lap. She counted them back into the jar. The windows were fogged when she was done. She wrote her name over and over on the windshield, the rain on the roof drumming loud above her. She reached into the crevice of the front seat and extracted twenty-nine cents and an ancient peppermint. In the glove compartment, along with many packs of matches and a nearly full pack of Salems, she discovered two quarters. She slid the coins into the jar. It had been a lucrative morning.

She crawled into the backseat. Beneath the seats, she found thirty-two cents, a tarnished earring, and the intact skeleton of a bird. She held it on the flat of her hand. It weighed barely anything. Whatever had eaten it had done a good job, for only bones remained. Without plumage, she couldn't tell what kind of bird it was. She wondered how it had died. Probably it couldn't find its way out and had starved, or dashed itself repeatedly against the window in its desperation to escape. How, though, could it have entered to begin with?

She set the skeleton on the ledge beneath the rear window. It must have flown in last summer when she left the window cracked a few inches. Sam had scolded her about that, though his concern had been for upholstery, not birds. She stretched out on the back seat. She'd bury the bird in the woods, she decided, once the rain slowed. That would hardly redeem her for bringing about its death in the first place, but at least then it would be laid to rest.

That night at supper Riddley asked Pauline about the leg. "Oh, I gave it to Esther," Pauline said. "There's someone at her church who could use it. They're not cheap, you know. I was delighted to have found it a new family."

"It's not a pet, Mom," Emmeline said.

"And it's white," Charlotte added.

Pauline claimed that anyone who wore a prosthesis would also wear long pants, but Charlotte pointed out that Ray would not have liked it.

"You're right about that," Sam said. "He's probably done a few rotations in his grave already at the thought of some black wearing his leg." Sam always said not *black person* but *black,* that lone word sharp and blunt at the same time.

Pauline flushed. "You asked me to handle it. If you had been willing to take care of it—"

"Honey, it's fine," Sam interrupted. "You could have used it for a scarecrow for all I care."

At once in Riddley's mind appeared an image of such a scarecrow, standing across the road in Pauline's vegetable garden. Its other leg was a peg leg, which made the wooden leg look real. The scarecrow wore Ray's old clothes, though not the suits or sport coats that he had left behind. It had donned instead what would have been most likely to frighten birds, the red plaid pajamas Ray favored, which he no doubt would have worn, had he had any choice in the matter, all the way to his grave.

* * *

For Frazier it was a bridge game five years earlier, one particular hand in the spring of 1966, that changed, as they say, everything, or rather, revealed beyond any remaining doubt that everything had already changed. He and Adele were at Marjorie and Evan's, with whom they had played bridge every other week for the last twenty-odd years. For months Adele's game had been erratic. He had explained her inconsistencies as due to her coming down with something, or having a headache or a poor night's sleep. At her best, she was an exceptional

bridge player, far better than he. She could seem practically clairvoyant when it came to figuring who had which cards. But it was more a matter of memory than clairvoyance. She remembered nearly every card played, by whom, and in what order.

But on bad nights it almost seemed she had never before played the game. Above all it was strategy, and the precursors to strategy—recall, foresight, motive—that were missing. Later he thought they should have given up their bridge night much earlier. He should not have forced her to undergo that. But they had once so enjoyed those evenings.

For the hand that turned out to be their last, he was the dealer, a role that compounded his sense of guilt. Yet she might well have bid the same way had she been dealt an entirely different hand—that was how little her bid had to do with her cards. He heard a ripple of entreaty in her voice, or so he thought. Then again, what was bidding if not offering, and asking, and replying in the form of another question?

Two . . . ? she had said, and paused for a very long while, during which there was ample time for Frazier to imagine other things she might say. Such a pause, in another player or, at an earlier time, in Adele, might have indicated a hand strong enough to support a variety of bids, but it was clear, at least to Frazier, that at present that was not the case. At last she said, *diamonds.*

Try as he might to make her the dummy, she kept bidding. After a while he could not bring himself to bid any higher, so that, in the end, he was the one who had to lay down his hand. The bid, he clearly recalled, was four diamonds. After spreading his cards on the table, he rose with a strange dread. What could possibly be in her hand that would be worthy of dread? He made his way around the table, not looking at Evan's hand en route, as he was allowed to do as dummy. But he didn't want to disqualify himself from advising Adele, should such advice be needed. As nonchalantly as he could manage, he sauntered to the back of her chair to play the hand with her, just as he had when teaching Pauline.

Adele's cards were arranged not by suit or number but solely by color. She seemed to have bid based more on what she wanted than what she had, for diamonds were her weakest suit. She had opened

her bidding with two, in a suit of which she had only three, and jack high. They went down by three, but at least he got her out of there with some semblance of dignity. He at once claimed he felt a cold coming on, though they were in the middle of a rubber. For the next bridge date, and the ones thereafter, he made similar excuses. It only took a few refusals for the invitations to stop, which made him wonder how much Marjorie and Evan had already surmised, and to contemplate the possibility that his own wife, and her condition, might have been more apparent to someone other than himself.

Driving home that last time from Marjorie and Evan's, he had looked over at Adele in the glancing headlights of passing cars. She stared straight ahead, her focus on the windshield. Her gloved hands were folded in her lap, her back erect, her knees and ankles touching, as when she sat in church or at the symphony. He reached across the wide front seat. He pulled one hand loose from the other and took it in his own. As if she were too shy to acknowledge his grasp, she gave no indication she'd noticed.

And in the car, on the stoop, in the hall, in their bedroom, what, really, could be said? So they said little. It was too late, it seemed, for words to do them any good. Adele had always had a gift for communicating through gesture and expression. Or maybe it was Frazier who had the gift, of understanding the subtext of her movements and gazes, or to believe that he did. He was always on the lookout for the slightest alteration in her mood. At home, she had never been much of a talker. Thus when she began to speak less he had not at first noticed, and later he had thought it a natural result of long companionship, or perhaps some delayed reaction to his hearing loss.

But as they sat together in the den, he would look up to find her staring at him, wearing a face he had never seen before. Sometimes her lips would move, ever so slightly, to coax the caught words out from the trap of her mouth. Once she had silently cried. He had asked her again and again what was the matter, but she had only shaken her head and patted his hand, as if he were the one with something bothering him, some trouble he could not bring himself to express.

He told Pauline nothing of these looks, nor of most of the other things Adele did, or didn't—as in couldn't, as in wouldn't—do. What purpose would that have served? Pauline would learn soon enough.

Such information, he decided, would only have worried her, with the worst kind of worry, the kind you can do nothing about. Also he was concerned her worry might turn toward herself, as his own had. How he had again regretted having only the one child, as if genetics could be diluted or diverted, or worn out over multiple offspring. For in Adele's whole line, for as far back as he had been able to go, at least one in each generation had been cursed with rage and silence.

What he had never forgiven himself for was that he had not realized earlier what was happening. What he could not forgive her for was that not once, *not once,* did she raise the topic of herself, and her condition. Yet her terror was plain. Amid those unraveling habits of courtesy, manners, custom, and hygiene, he saw flashes of raw fear. These did, over time, occur further and further apart. Then, too, he never knew how much she had admitted to herself, or could admit. And why, really, would she have wanted to understand what was happening to her, when it was clear it would not stop happening until it was done? Or maybe she had understood all along. She had, after all, seen what had happened to her sister Riddley.

He had taken his cue from Adele as to how to handle it. That is, he had covered for her, as she had for so long covered for herself. How could he, though, when she walked onto the lawn at nine in the morning in a maroon cocktail dress? But he did what he could. *You're absolutely right, dear,* he said in a voice loud enough to reach any stray neighbors, *that dress goes just fine with those shoes. Go on in and get changed and we'll head to the store.* But she would not go in and she would not get changed. The stubbornness that had previously been tempered by decorum had by then fully revealed itself. She insisted she go to the grocery in that dress. And so he had driven her there. At least by then he had managed to get her to stop driving. In White Brothers he pushed the cart and greeted passersby, pretending everything was perfectly normal.

That seemed to be what she wanted. He declined all but the safest invitations, and took her out at odd hours, and to odd places, so as to lessen their chance of running into anyone they knew. (But they knew so many people!) Strangers, unlike friends and acquaintances, did not pretend. People who didn't know her knew almost at once

that something was wrong with her, and what. They tended to speak in the high-pitched, accentuated voice generally reserved for children and imbeciles. *Don't you just look a princess in that dress!* Or else they might speak about her as if she weren't there. *Taking her out on the town today, are you?* He seldom left her alone, and they went out less and less. She seemed relieved to stay home most of the time, so that she no longer had to pretend to others, or him, or herself.

Long before anyone else noticed anything, Adele herself would, on occasion, catch herself out, as a mother catches a child in a fib— stealing or hiding something, swearing, lying. She hid such aberrations as much from Frazier and Pauline, Marjorie and Josephine, as from the part of herself that recognized these as *just not like Mother,* a phrase she would later overhear Pauline use to Frazier. Eventually, though, Adele won't be able to recall or discern what she is like, or was like, or even what she does and doesn't like. There are too many layers, one atop another. She will lose the power to distinguish herself now from herself long ago, her memory from imagination, the present from the past and future, one moment or place from another, so she asks Frazier the time over and over, and gazes at the den's beige ceiling and says *Buttermilk clouds,* and mounds tuna fish atop an oatmeal cookie, over which she pours a thick glaze of maple syrup, as if to seal the food for preserving.

Before Adele became a person who could not remember, she'd been one who could not forget. Some called her prone to grudges, but it went beyond that. Even were a grudge to be alleviated, she would forget neither its inception nor its apparent resolution, for to her mind an injury once done could not, really, ever be undone. All the sisters were said to be that way. Both Frazier and Pauline were well aware of this trait and strove never to give Adele fuel for that low-burning flame. During the rare quarrel, they spoke with caution, for Adele was capable of bringing up, *verbatim,* comments from ten years previous. She neither forgave nor forgot, until she forgot everything, or nearly so. Not remembering how she had accumulated her various wounds and grievances, however, didn't mean that such were no longer felt.

And too, there were those things she could not forget or that, perhaps, could not forget her. At times certain memories were far

more insistent than they'd ever been, as if the sporadic emptying of memory's receptacle made other, neglected parts enlarge to fill it. Or maybe what remained was simply the grit at the bottom, which stuck to the sides when the rest was poured away. What happened to Elijah was something she'd have liked, naturally, to forget entirely, but her mind or her soul—or whatever part of the self is responsible for what we remember—held to it steadfastly. Even when she was well beyond understanding just what it was she was recalling, she remembered it, if, indeed, you could call it that.

Once Frazier admitted to himself what was happening to Adele— the same thing that had happened to her sister Riddley, her aunt Marianne, her second cousin Bradley, her great uncle Stewart, her grandmother Lydia, and no doubt others before them—he tried to track its causes and effects, both backward, as it had already occurred, and forward, as it was occurring. Everything became evidence. Every recollection of her became tinged with the possibility that she was already ill, even back five, ten, fifteen years ago. For what forgetfulness, irritability, lash of temper, inexplicable and inconsolable sadness, even unreasonable joy, could not be so attributed?

Thus he began to keep his records on her. *Refuses to leave the house, May 3, 1966. Bounces eight checks, August '66. Spreads mayonnaise on ice cream sandwich, 10/15/66. Hangs up on Mildred Swanson, 11/29/66. Slaps me for walking in on her in her slip, 2/20/67.* The point of these was not entirely clear to him, but had to do with tracing the course of the illness, as if he could, or would want to, anticipate its future path. Later these records served as crucial proof that she had not always been this way. Eventually he did need evidence, that what had by then become ordinary—her speechlessness and obscenities, obstinacy and melancholy, ire and cruelties—was once so odd as to be deemed worthy of record. These notes served, too, as some bulwark against his own insanity, in their increasingly sealed and secret life together, a world of silence and repetition, fury, agitation, excuses, pretenses, loneliness, and long-suffering sorrow.

CHAPTER 7

Lagan

s the sandals, pastels, and sleeveless dresses emerged from winter storage, Miss Byrd's wardrobe altered only in that she wore less of the same. She continued to don socks and closed-toed shoes. Her slacks, though of a lighter fabric, were the same plain colors as before. The sleeves of her blouses ended a half-inch above the elbow. Pauline said, *It's a wonder your Miss Byrd never wears a skirt with those long skinny legs of hers.* But Riddley thought she had found out why.

On Wednesday the class tromped into the woods to hunt mushrooms. Later they would make spore prints and try to identify the specimens. In the fall, they had done a similar exercise with leaves.

Riddley found a cluster of yellowish-orange mushrooms with lopsided caps, the edges wavery and upturned. "Miss Byrd, Miss Byrd," she cried, "I found some."

Miss Byrd strode quickly over. She clasped her hands just below the deep hollow at the base of her throat. "Chanterelles!" she said, a lovely word Riddley had never heard before. Miss Byrd clapped her hand over her mouth. She glanced around her, put one bony finger to her lips, then hitched her khakis up slightly and squatted down, revealing on one leg, above her sock cuff, an inch or so of shin. The pale skin there had a covering of hair, which was, like pubic hair, darker than that on her head.

Riddley knew, of course, that women had hair on their legs, and under their arms, or would have it should they fail to get rid of it, by shaving or waxing or applying certain creams. Riddley had had no idea, though, how much hair women were apt to have, were they not to remove it. She had never thought it would be quite so much.

"What a find, Riddley. I trust you'll keep my little slip a secret. You'll still need to record all your observations, to prove these are indeed what I said."

Riddley glanced at the mushrooms, and then, covertly, back at Miss Byrd's leg. Riddley thought of Sam's leg, on which hair seemed both natural and appealing. Indeed, had he had no hair there, his legs would have looked naked and weak.

"Since I've already given it away, I'll tell you these are one of the best edible mushrooms around." Miss Byrd looked up. "Don't look so worried, I won't make you eat them. But after we do the spore print I'll take them home and fry them up." She raised her eyebrows at Riddley. "Unless you'd like to do that yourself."

Riddley shook her head. She squatted beside Miss Byrd and joined her in scooping away dirt from the base of the chanterelles. No one else must see Miss Byrd's legs. This transgression far exceeded Miss Byrd's many others, even those remarks in class—about Vietnam, civil rights and women's lib, slavery and Jim Crow—that had elicited parental calls to the principal. Riddley glanced around them. Children wandered amid the trees. Someone would come over at any minute. She picked up her clipboard and stood, hoping Miss Byrd would follow suit.

"A few pests," Miss Byrd said, flicking a tiny white worm out with a twig, "but certainly worthy of consumption. Are you sure you don't want to cook them up yourself? I promise you they're not poisonous. There is such a thing as a false chanterelle, but I'm certain these aren't."

"No thanks," Riddley said. Behind Miss Byrd, Bea Partridge, Mary Jane Johns and Kelley Teale approached, in frilled ankle socks and pastel headbands, with monogrammed lockets dangling at their throats. Were they to discover the condition of Miss Byrd's legs, that would be the end of Miss Byrd, and they would make sure it was a torturous end. Were boys to find out, they might joke and tease, but, being for the most part bewildered by girls' secret groomings, they would not have taken real offense. Girls, though, particularly these kinds of girls, would not cease until Miss Byrd's full humiliation had been accomplished. Miss Byrd's unwillingness to do what their mothers did every day, and what their own future selves would also do, would be a grave insult to girls, and the mothers of girls, everywhere. It would be the last straw in Miss Byrd's dual refusal to try to be pretty, and to care that she was not. The lack of make-up and

hair-dos, pantyhose and skirts and heels could be tolerated, but this, once known, could never have been borne.

"Well, maybe I could try them." This was the last thing Riddley wanted to do, for fear of also consuming those worms. But she would say anything now, to get Miss Byrd to her feet. "What do they taste like?"

Miss Byrd slowly smiled. "As with most things, they derive much of their taste from what they're cooked with. But underneath that they have a flavor entirely their own, which I am quite at a loss to describe." At last, Miss Byrd stood. Her pants legs dropped into place. "But they're like nothing else you've ever tasted, I'm sure." She handed the chanterelles to Riddley.

Miss Byrd turned toward the approaching girls. "Look what Riddley found."

Bea reluctantly stretched out her hand to take the mushrooms, and Riddley murmured, "There might be a few worms left." Bea pulled her hand back at once.

"I'm pretty sure I got them all." Miss Byrd curbed a grin. "But let me double check." She took the chanterelles back and peered at them closely. Bea made a face at Riddley.

"That's a very interesting mushroom, Miss Byrd, but we came to ask if we could go use the bathroom," Kelley said.

Miss Byrd studied them over the top of her glasses. "Y'all all need to go to the bathroom this very minute."

"We really do," Mary Jane said, shifting her weight from one leg to the other.

"I do hope the plumbing's up to it. You can take the specimen back with you to the classroom. If the field observations are complete."

Riddley scanned her clipboard, with its mimeographed sheet of questions. "Everything but smell."

The other girls looked at the ground and then the sky, their hands plastered to their sides. Miss Byrd gazed at each of them, and then handed the chanterelles to Bea. "Here you go, Bea. You seem like a girl who'd have a particularly keen sense of smell."

Riddley told no one about what she had seen. Whenever Miss Byrd did anything that might expose her, such as crouch, or sit on the rug, Riddley was poised to rush over and somehow get her to assume

another posture, or create a distraction so that everyone would look at her—Riddley—instead. But Miss Byrd took great care not to let her pants legs rise again above her socks, at least not in Riddley's presence. She tucked her legs under her chair rather than cross them, and on the floor, she sat on her haunches rather than Indian style.

Riddley felt sure she would have heard had anyone else seen, unless that person happened to be another of Miss Byrd's devotees. But Riddley thought that even those who adored Miss Byrd would, if they knew, be hard put not to tell. Riddley herself found it difficult. But she was getting better and better at secrets, especially those about others. For secrets about herself, it was still almost impossible for her not to confess, eventually, to Pauline, though that inclination seemed to be lessening.

Observing Miss Byrd's customary caution about her legs, Riddley came to wonder if Miss Byrd had not simply had a momentary lapse, but that she had intended for Riddley to see, that indeed Miss Byrd had quite purposefully let her in on the secret, maybe even the joke of it, though if the latter were the case, on whom would the joke have been? Miss Byrd's expression had implied that it was clearly not on herself, despite her covertness. She did not seem the least bit ashamed. It nearly shamed Riddley, how Miss Byrd was not.

*   *   *

Pauline, unable yet to find any permanent help, and barely able to keep up herself, temporarily hired Esther to clean for Adele two evenings a week, the only time Esther had available. "I'm afraid it won't be an easy job, Esther. Mother can be downright impossible at times. She's, well, she's—" Pauline stopped, and sighed. "She's just not the lady she once was."

"Don't you worry, Miz Cross. I know how old folks get."

But Riddley, reading on the nearby sofa, was worried. How could Esther not take the word *nigger* to heart, should such a situation arise? Pauline went to her bedroom then to make a phone call. It was the perfect chance to warn Esther. Riddley mentally tried out various lines concerning what she thought she'd heard on Christmas Eve, and her hunch about Josephine's reasons for departure. But in the end Riddley

could figure out neither exactly how she ought to put it, nor whether it was something she should say in the first place, especially to someone like Esther, so she let the opportunity go.

The next day she was glad she had, for apparently Adele had taken to Esther immediately, smiling at her whenever she passed by or looked her way. Pauline suggested that her mother had turned over a new leaf, but Esther suspected that she had been mistaken for someone else, for Mrs. Wells' expression seemed far too intense to be merely the result of good intentions. Esther's suspicions were confirmed when, toward the end of the evening, Adele whispered to her, *You've come back.* Esther was about to point out that she'd never been there before, but then thought better of it. *Yes, ma'am,* she replied.

"Well, it's a relief to know your mother's not like the Montgomerys' terrier," Sam joked to Pauline as he poured himself another drink. Their neighbor's dog hated all black people indiscriminately, snarling and barking and nipping at maid and delivery boy alike. For this reason it was hard for the Montgomerys to hold on long to help, but as that kind of terrier was quite rare and valuable, they suffered the inconvenience.

Sunday was the equinox, and Sam roused his daughters before dawn and goaded them outside. Pauline stood looking out over the dark river. Nearby, their dogs Winnie and Coco burrowed in the leaves and branches that Henry had tossed over to shore up the bluff. In the cool air, with the breeze on her face, the fact of spring woke Riddley the rest of the way up. Soon, maybe even today, she would go out on the water, and in a month or two, she would go in it.

Sam handed each daughter a compass. Despite his own excellent sense of direction, he himself was never without one. *Turn not thy back to the compass!* he was fond of shouting at odd moments. He had mounted spherical compasses with revolving, luminous dials on car windshields and boat dashboards, and stashed portable ones, attached to vinyl cords or fishing bobbers, in glove compartments and dock kits. On his person he carried one resembling a pocket watch. The hinged cover prevented contact between glass and cloth, a friction that would have magnetized the glass and distracted the needle. The remedy for that, he had said, was to lick a finger and touch it to

the compass face. On weekdays he carried the compass in the front left pocket of his suit pants, opposite always from his change, so that the needle would not become, as he put it, *bewitched*. That is, attracted to forces other than the pole.

He had told his daughters that he carried a compass because he was so far from home, implying either that he hoped one day to make his way back to Michigan, or that his departure some two decades before had forever cost him his bearings. After a few drinks he was given to proclaiming, *I am a pelican in the wilderness,* to which Pauline felt bound to reply, *You're not any such thing.*

Sam glanced at his watch. "Due east, girls, that's where it'll be." He cradled his compass in his palm, nearly jubilant as he steadied the needle. He was happiest in the very early morning, standing on the bluff while the light changed over the marsh, holding his plastic mug of instant coffee, or in the early evening, anywhere, holding his first drink.

A section of the sky had begun to turn the pink of a boiled shrimp. "Reflected sunlight sends an image of the sun above the horizon minutes ahead of the actual rising," Sam said, "so the sun we'll first see rising isn't even the real sun. Likewise the real sun sets shortly before the image does."

Riddley centered the red arrow on the *N*. Fixing her gaze on the *E*, she slowly raised her eyes, keeping them in as straight a trajectory as possible up from the *E*. The sun was still not visible, but the sky had abruptly brightened.

"Any second now," he said, just as a great blue heron rose, flapping and croaking, from the live oak next door. Riddley turned to watch it glide overhead, though she knew she'd lose her bearings.

Emmeline pointed slightly to the right of Cougar Island. "Between that dead tree leaning against the farthest pine, and the crab trap buoy." Seconds later a sliver of sun appeared there, as if it had only been waiting for some indication as to where it ought to rise. After that it didn't hesitate. A little bloody, a little hazy, it ascended with minimal fanfare, or at least not as much as one might hope for on such an occasion. Riddley could not discern at what point the image of the sun ended and the real sun began.

Sam grinned, as if he had orchestrated the dawn for them alone. "Behold, ladies," he said, gesturing with his empty hand toward the sun, "the orient."

"But don't behold it directly—" Pauline cautioned.

"—or you'll go blind!" Riddley and Charlotte and Emmeline interjected with glee, as if such a condition, like so much they were warned about, were something not to avoid but to strive for.

"I thought the Orient meant Japan and China," Charlotte said.

"It also means east, in general," Pauline said.

"If you set a course by the sun right now, and traveled due east around the world, what would you come across?" Sam said.

"Cuba," Emmeline said.

Charlotte shook her head, geography being one of her best subjects, despite which she would seldom ever leave her hometown. "Cuba's too far south. You'd hit Bermuda."

"Yes, if you kept a very precise course. Though it would be quite easy to miss it altogether." He squinted at the far distance. "What would you come across in terms of water?"

"The Gulf Stream," Riddley said. The previous summer she had accompanied Sam there on a fishing tournament. At that latitude and time of year, the change from longshore current to Gulf Stream was not particularly startling. She wanted to witness what Sam had, patrolling the mid-Atlantic coast during the last winter of the war. He had been on watch on the foggy gunboat deck when the cold green waters of the Labrador Current all at once transformed into a vivid blue. The spray turned warm and the air balmy, the temperature rising almost thirty degrees. For as far as he could see, the ocean was divided, one side green, the other blue. The green meant the water was not very salty, and so contained abundant life, whereas the blue of the Gulf Stream indicated a high salt content. More salt meant less oxygen, he explained, so not as many animals could live there. But judging from their own river, Riddley found it hard to believe that salt could be anything but a nutrient, much less that any animal would prefer to live in cold water.

Sam nodded. "You'd be in the Gulf Stream for about fifty miles. What about after Bermuda?"

"The Bermuda Triangle?" Emmeline said.

"We'd be north of that, but we would pass through another tricky spot. What's our latitude here?"

"Thirty-two point oh five," Charlotte said.

He nodded. "All around the globe, at thirty degrees, give or take, is a region known as the Horse Latitudes It exists on land as well, though it's less noticeable there. But out in the oceans, the winds in the Horse Latitudes are, much of the time, either non-existent or baffling."

"Baffling like confusing?" Emmeline said.

He nodded. "A baffling wind is one that can come from any direction."

"Like in the Doldrums," Riddley interjected.

"It is similar to the Doldrums, though the Horse Latitudes are dry rather than humid, and not nearly as hot."

"Why's it called 'horse'?" Charlotte said.

"Spanish ships bringing horses to the New World often becalmed there, for weeks on end. They would jettison their cargo when water started running out."

"You mean, they threw the horses over?" Emmeline said.

"As a horse weighs probably close to half a ton, they could hardly be thrown, but the sailors did somehow manage to get them overboard."

"How cruel," Pauline cried.

"It's not cruel, Pauline, it's humane." Sam was aggravated, as always, by what he deemed her soft-heartedness. "It's better to die by drowning than by thirst."

"Seems like two sides of the same coin to me," Pauline said.

"Why not eat them?" Emmeline inquired.

"One horse can feed a lot of people," Sam responded. "And meat wouldn't have kept long in that heat."

Charlotte scrunched up her nose and waved her hand in front of her face.

"Horses can swim," Riddley said.

"Not for that long," Emmeline said.

"Or that far," Charlotte added.

"And don't forget the sharks," Emmeline said.

Riddley hadn't forgotten the sharks. She remembered how Miss Byrd, in her lesson on the Middle Passage, had said that slave ships were always followed by sharks. *Eventually netting had to be rigged around the decks, to stop slaves from flinging themselves, or their children, over the side.* Miss Byrd's voice had sounded as if she were telling them a ghost story. *When a ship ran out of food or water, or during danger of mutiny or storm, the sailors nailed the hatches shut over the hold.* That's when Rudy Page had whispered loud enough for those nearby to hear, *It sure must've stunk down there.*

The sun had disappeared behind the overcast. The clouds, ashen and seamless and extending to the horizon's edges, seemed not a veil over the sky but a bleak version of the sky itself. Sam continued to guide them around the globe—to Marrakech, Alexandria, the Dead Sea, Lahore, Shanghai, then across the Pacific to Tijuana, and back into their own country near Tucson, Arizona. Riddley followed along with him, but part of her stayed far out in the ocean, under the clear still sky of the Horse Latitudes. She recalled a word Sam had taught her, *lagan,* though it hardly applied to either the horses or the slaves. The term meant those goods that sink along with a ship, or that are on purpose sunk, with a buoy attached, so that they may be found again. According to maritime law, such goods could be reclaimed by the owner. But for how long was that right reserved, and how, for that matter, could you manage to return to the exact spot?

All through that day and into the next, in the midst of doing other things, Riddley saw in her mind a herd of horses thrashing in the open water, churning it up like surf. Their heads arched back as they began to sink, until their wide nostrils flared, pink like mouths, for the last air, and they disappeared under the waves. While swimming that summer, if she went down very deep, and held her breath longer than it seemed she could, when she opened her eyes she might well see them, because, as with certain sounds, ghosts could travel farther underwater.

* * *

That ghosts or their equivalent could and did travel in all sorts of ways, Adele had first learned nearly a quarter of a century earlier. Some months after her father died, when Riddley's madness was no longer deniable, all the sisters converged a final time on the house in Liberty County. Within the week they had determined what would be saved and distributed among them, what was worthy of the church bazaar, and what would go to the rubbish heap or accompany Riddley to the sanatorium. Thus had Adele discovered, in a drawer of Riddley's vanity, a velvet-lined jewelry box containing a newspaper clipping about Elijah's demise, and letters from the clerks and sheriffs' deputies of the surrounding cities, towns, and counties. The letters, dating from 1913 through 1916, all stated in one way or another that they had no knowledge of the whereabouts of a certain Negress, Nancy Royall. Many of the letters inquired if she were dangerous or responsible for any crime and should thus be apprehended. Adele smuggled the box out beneath a crocheted afghan, assuming that her sisters would wish to destroy such mementos. Adele neither examined nor understood why she did not wish that as well.

Once home, she wrapped the box in butcher paper, bound it with string and stashed it at the bottom of her hope chest, knowing Frazier would not venture there. She all but forgot it until a decade later, when she came across the postcard. It was the first time she'd laid eyes on it. While fetching stamps from Frazier's desk, she had happened upon an open envelope bearing the return address of her sister Sophia and brother-in-law Wyatt, so she had naturally assumed the contents were also intended for her. As perhaps they were.

At first glance she didn't recognize herself, having long ago forgotten the existence of that photograph, as well as the immense relief she'd felt that day to have reason to turn away, to at last stop looking. Who she recognized immediately was Elijah. Then, upon recognizing him, she couldn't help but recognize herself.

She sank into the desk chair, the postcard still in her hand. Adele had never told anyone, least of all Frazier, what had happened almost forty-five years before. Why in heaven's name would you ever tell a person something like that? Much less how. But maybe there had been no need to tell him. Maybe he had long since known. She well knew

how people could talk. Or perhaps, thanks to Wyatt, he knew now, or suspected. But how would Wyatt have found out? All her sisters were surely as close-mouthed as she about that. But Wyatt could have met someone from Liberty County who, upon learning he'd married one of the Glynn girls, couldn't resist telling the story.

A little something for your collection, Wyatt had written in a brief note. Everyone in the family knew Frazier collected postcards. But only Wyatt was so crass, so downright boorish, as to send something like this. The sisters had long ago agreed that Sophia had married beneath her, though they had refrained from suggesting such a thing to Sophia, who'd had a hard enough time finding herself a husband, she being nearly as bereft of charms as Riddley.

Something occurred to Adele as she glanced again at the other cards in the envelope, which documented similar events elsewhere. Beyond Wyatt's vague remark, *from your neck of the woods,* no mention was made of any personal connection. If Frazier didn't know already, there was nothing here to inform him—except, of course, her glaring presence in the photo. But if he had no inkling to begin with, wasn't there a very good chance that he wouldn't recognize her, just as she had also, at least initially, not recognized herself? She had only been a child then, after all, and a blond one at that. By the time she met Frazier, her hair had long since darkened. Frazier could well take these postcards as simply another of Wyatt's so-called contributions, for over the years Wyatt had sent a variety of tasteless postcards of freaks and disasters and scantily clad starlets. And maybe contributing to Frazier's collection was indeed all Wyatt was doing, though such a confluence of innocence and chance seemed highly unlikely, especially in someone like Wyatt.

Perhaps she ought to mention these postcards to Frazier, to discover what he knew. Yet if he knew nothing, such an inquiry would surely pique his curiosity, for normally neither of them would ever bring up this kind of thing. No, it was better to keep quiet. He was far too much of a gentleman to broach such a subject, even if he did have his suspicions. If he didn't know it was her then he would assume, correctly, that she'd never wish to contemplate such atrocities, and if he knew it was her he would assume, also correctly, that she

would much prefer not to be reminded. With that thought, she put the postcards back in the envelope and put them firmly out of her mind, where for a good long while they stayed, at least in the daytime.

Every once in a while the girl she'd been, the girl from the postcard, surfaced in a dream. Usually she was wandering in a crowd, looking for somebody, Nancy or Riddley or her father, her view obscured by backs and midriffs. Elijah seldom appeared, but when he did, he was driving the wagon and she couldn't see his face, which from the outskirts of her dream she'd been glad of, considering what it had looked like the last time she had.

CHAPTER 8

Trespassing

he one bluff or yard or dock all neighborhood children had for decades been forbidden to set foot upon was the Varnells,' for Reed Varnell would brook no interruption in his brooding. The Varnell place was more than a century older than any other house, and long rumored to be haunted. It was three houses downriver from the Crosses, and sporadically visited by great misfortune. Some two years earlier, Carver Varnell, home recuperating from a difficult divorce, had been asleep upstairs when her father Reed, sitting on the bluff watching a storm come in, had been struck by lightning.

She would've seen it plain as day had she been awake, Pauline had said, relieved, apparently, that Carver had been spared such a sight. But also in Pauline's voice was something close to blame, that Carver had not borne witness, as if that might have changed the outcome, instead of merely searing in Carver's mind the image of her father's hand melded to the wrought iron chair. It was the chair that got him, its foot touching the shallow spreading root of the pine, whose height drew the bolt from far away. It had cracked the sandy soil wide, leaving a black scar. Weeds soon shot up thick and vivid, for fire, Sam said as he set the lawn ablaze each spring, was a kind of fertilizer.

Reed's prohibition on trespassing was assumed, by all children along the bluff, to have expired with him. Their explorations began in the vast overgrown gardens, where it was as easy to hide as it was to get lost. Next they ventured into the many dilapidated structures: the hothouse, the stable, the tool shed, the garage. Along the property's northern boundary stood what had for some decades been referred to as a carriage house. Outbuildings were often called that, whether or not they had ever held a carriage, which this one never had. It was an old slave cabin, the last one standing in the area. But whatever remained of its past had been obscured by plumbing, windows, flooring, and electricity. In front of it, where an old cemetery

was rumored to be, a swimming pool had been dug in the 1920s. It had not held water during any of the children's lifetime. But it made an excellent holding pit for prisoners and slaves, when the neighborhood children converged for games of War and Runaway. For hours they ran across the grounds in squads and armies, until dark fell and they disbanded.

Last summer Carver had come back to live at her family home. One afternoon when the driveway was empty, Wallace Kane sprawled in the spot where Reed was said to have expired. The Wheeler boys made sizzling, crackling noises while Wallace flopped about. Since her car was in the shop, Carver had, from an upstairs window, observed the boys' rendition of her father's death. She made a single phone call, to her former classmate, Olivia Wheeler. Since then, the ban on trespassing had been reinstated, though having once been breached, it could not but be breached again.

The place, once more forbidden, became newly alluring. Whenever Carver had been seen to drive away, children dared each other to sit upon the chair where Reed was said still, on occasion, to sit. One day the chair disappeared. The remaining bench came to be thought of as the one in which Reed had died, to which he returned to sit, and from which his charred hand could, on rare occasions, be seen still clinging to the armrest.

The children agreed that, on Halloween, the ban on trespassing did not apply. That Carver appreciated the tenor of the occasion was demonstrated by the reappearance of the wrought iron chair. It listed at the edge of the driveway, in the shadows beneath a live oak. Emmeline claimed that Carver would not be able to identify them in costume because, being childless, she would think all children looked alike. Whether or not Carver could tell them apart, she did not come out to reprimand them for taking multiple handfuls of candy, a laxity that further gained their admiration. Not that it would prevent them from trespassing, or spying, or concocting stories about her, which they passed on to their parents. The children well knew what the adults wanted to hear about Carver.

Long after all the other houses had stopped dispensing candy, some of the boys dared a final return to Carver's, where the porch

light still burned and candy brimmed from the bowl. Just as they were about to climb the stairs, they had seen Reed's hand dangling from the armrest of the wrought iron chair. Their story might well have been true, there being, as everyone knew, no lack of ghosts at the Varnell place. More likely, though, depending on who was trying to scare whom, one of the children, or even Carver herself, had attached a fake hand there. That was, thought the adults as well as many of the children, just the kind of humor Carver tended toward: dark, perverse, and really, once you thought about it, not funny in the least.

Nonetheless, in mid-December, Riddley had gone alone to the Varnells' to collect for the newspaper's Empty Stocking Fund, which distributed money to the poor at Christmas. The house was barely visible from the road, shielded by drooping sheets of moss, and magnolias and azaleas long unpruned. Even previous to Reed's death the place had been poorly maintained, he having years before *gone to drink,* as Pauline put it, which made liquor seem an actual site to which one could relocate.

Riddley climbed the wide, steep steps to the door. The radio was on inside, and someone was singing along. The bell gave a weak chirp, hardly what you would expect at a mansion. After a while, she knocked. The waiting made her nervous. She had only seen Carver from a distance before, and had never spoken with her. What if she got angry about being bothered? Riddley decided she'd leave after she counted to fifty. Shortly before she reached it, the door swung open and there stood Carver, in a paint-stained gray sweat shirt and jeans. Her dirty blond hair was gathered on top of her head. She was barefoot, and the easy way she stood there made Riddley think she was not unused to being so. She smelled of cigarette smoke and turpentine and something pungent, a tangy salty smell, which Riddley realized was the odor, uncommon in those parts, of female sweat.

Riddley launched into what Pauline called her spiel, about how your own life and the lives of the needy would be enriched by a generous donation to the Empty Stocking Fund. There followed a lengthy pause, during which Carver studied Riddley as intensely as if she aimed to paint her, for Carver was, or had once been, something of a painter. Then Carver held up her forefinger and shut the door.

Some minutes later she returned with a wad of crumpled bills. She handed the money to Riddley. "Here you are," she said, in a voice entirely devoid of accent. Where, Riddley wondered, had she lost it? In New York City or Paris or Rome? "But for God's sake don't use my name, lest I be deluged with solicitors."

Once around the bend in the driveway, Riddley stopped to count the money. It was fifty-three dollars, the largest donation she had ever received. On the donation form Riddley wrote, *From a true friend to the poor,* which was what the newspaper suggested for those who wished to remain anonymous. Later, when Pauline tallied up the amounts, checking Riddley's math before making out the check, (*don't send cash,* the newspaper warned,) she said, "Fifty-three dollars? From whom did you extract fifty-three dollars?"

Riddley hesitated, worried that Pauline might scold her for trespassing, and because Carver did not want her generosity to be known. But surely that was only in public. Besides, Pauline always got such secrets out of her eventually.

"Carver Varnell."

"You went to Carver's?" Pauline said, and for a second Riddley thought she would get in trouble. Then Pauline laughed. "Well, good for you. And good for her."

"She didn't want me to use her name."

"It will be our secret," Pauline said, but Riddley was not entirely convinced that Pauline would be able to resist telling the other mothers along the bluff, all of whom thrived off any bit of gossip, especially about Carver Varnell. But Riddley could understand that. She, too, was intrigued by Carver. She often went on Carver's property, occasionally alone, but more often with her friend Hayden. Hayden Gray was distantly related, on his mother's side, to Carver, and hence felt himself entitled to trespass, or at least he trusted that, should he be caught, she would mete out a lesser punishment for kin. Some said Carver bore a vague resemblance to Hayden's mother, before the bearing of children, and the divorces, marriages and gin got the better of her.

Hayden was the youngest of six siblings who had been dispersed and distributed among various family members, reunited, then dispersed again. Off and on for the last six years, singly or with a sibling

or two, he had lived with his widowed grandmother, Mrs. Abbot Gray, from whom he was less likely to run away. Her house was on a thickly wooded lot in the marsh. The long dock jutted into a shallow waterway called Mosquito Creek, which had access to the river only at high tide. At low it was all mud flats, pocked with crab holes and loud with insects.

Poor at both sports and school, Hayden was already remarkably adept on the water and in the woods. He was small-headed and slight, a boy whose appearance gave little hint of what he would look like as a man, unless he turned out to be one of those men who always resembled a boy. At eleven, he was closer in age to Charlotte and Emmeline than to Riddley, but he was usually willing to let Riddley tag along when, during the hot months, he went upriver to Cougar or Oak Island, or crabbing along one of the nameless dead end creeks. During the cooler months, when he was not permitted to go out on the water, he kept himself busy building forts and shelters and fires, and exploring the woods and the Varnell property.

He and Riddley were headed now to the Varnells' garden, one of their favorite haunts. It was the Saturday following the equinox. Hayden led the way through the woods. As he walked, he snapped off dry twigs and branches. Riddley did the same. From pine trees they pulled drips and clumps of sap. They climbed over a crumbling brick wall, continuing on until they reached a small clearing paved with flagstones. Riddley hunkered down beside him. With his pocket knife he stripped the bark from a handful of sticks. Then he peeled back thin curls from the inner wood, which he left attached at one end. From some of these sticks he made a small teepee, on the roof of which he set pine straw and sap.

He hunched over and struck a match, at once sheltering it with his cupped palm, for he liked to act as if he had only the one match. He held a peeled stick upright above the flame. The curls of wood caught and flared. He inserted the burning stick into a gap in the teepee. The flames made a few tentative forays onto the roof. When they found the sap they leapt up, sizzling. Hayden added more sticks. Lowering his torso nearly level with the ground, his elbows poking sharp toward the sky, he turned his head sideways and blew into the underside of

the fire. *Every fire has a door,* he'd told her once. That was where air could most easily enter. As always, he knew exactly where such an opening was.

"So this explains it," said somebody above and behind them. Riddley did not at first recognize the voice, but Hayden's face told her that it belonged to Carver. There was a loud thud, of something hitting the ground. Carver must have been in a tree. Riddley could think of no one much over, say, thirteen, who would climb a tree.

"I was beginning to think some hobo was living back here." Carver strode toward them. "But instead it's just my cousin, the Boy Scout. Or is it the pyromaniac?"

"Don't worry. I'm always careful to put them out."

"And to make them."

Hayden gave a rare grin. He was glad, Riddley saw, to be caught. But Riddley was worried. If Pauline had told anyone about Carver's donation, chances were that Carver would have found out. Yet she wasn't looking at Riddley with any particular animosity. If anything, she seemed not to recognize her.

"You'd better feed it," Carver said, gesturing toward the smoldering fire. She sat on the ground across from them. "Who's your friend? She took my money but never told me her name."

"Riddley Cross," Hayden said. Riddley had told him about the fifty-three dollars. "She lives up the bluff."

Carver turned her head then to contemplate Riddley, with the same intensity as when Riddley had stood at her door. "Your mother was a few years ahead of me in school, before I went away. Always such a good girl. Easy prey for that Yankee and his wiles. I heard her mother never recovered from that."

Something about the way she said these things made Riddley uncomfortable, as if Carver knew something about her family that she, Riddley, did not, or even that Carver might not much care for them, an attitude Riddley had never encountered, or ever, in fact, imagined. She remembered how Pauline once said, *You just never know what will come out of Carver's mouth.* Sam had laughed and said, *But you can bet, thank God, that it won't be nice,* and the way he said *nice* made it seem like something Riddley, for the first time, was not certain she wanted to be.

"How old are you, Riddley Cross?" Carver asked that question adults always did.

"Nine." She bit back the urge to add the half.

"Third grade or fourth?"

"Fourth."

"Mrs. Toole, Miss Delanahey—either of them still around?"

"I had Mrs. Toole," Hayden said. "She was practically dead then, and that was two years ago."

"She was practically dead when I had her, and that was, Christ, twenty-seven years ago."

"I don't have her," Riddley said. "I have Miss Byrd."

"Isn't she that new teacher people say is so strange?"

Riddley stiffened. "She's not strange. She's the best teacher I ever had."

Carver examined her. "And why is that?"

Riddley shrugged. "I don't know, she's just—" she looked down, ashamed she had no better way to describe Miss Byrd, "—different."

Carver nodded thoughtfully. "That can be quite dangerous after a certain point. Not that she'll know what that point is, before she gets there." She extracted a Camel. "But they'll let her know when she's arrived, rest assured. You can mow your lawn in the nude or sing barefoot in the choir if you're a man—"

"You mean like Billy Lee Bradley," Hayden interrupted, referring to someone who went to their church.

"Exactly. But eccentricity in ladies is not always so appreciated." She pulled a stick from the fire. Pressing the coal against the cigarette, she took long drags to light it. Then she leaned back on one palm. "In any event, I'm afraid that her days are numbered." She sighed the smoke out. "But whose aren't, when you get right down to it?"

Riddley looked down, so her face wouldn't give anything, Miss Byrd included, away. She felt a bit sick to her stomach. Could Carver have heard about Miss Byrd's legs, or could there be something else about Miss Byrd, something Riddley didn't know? She resolved to watch her even more carefully in the future.

Hayden added wood to the fire. Carver seemed to have forgotten all about them. She studied the trees and sky. She smoked until there was nothing left to smoke, all the way down to the brown filter. She

ground it out and then tossed it over her left shoulder, just as, to avert bad luck, Pauline always did after spilling salt.

*   *   *

Although Carver had not reprimanded them for trespassing, Riddley thought it best not to mention seeing her in the woods, especially as Riddley had every intention of returning. *Another belle gone bad,* Sam had joked once about Carver, and Pauline had shaken her head and said it was a terrible shame. *She's a grown woman, for heaven's sake,* Pauline had said another time, having caught sight of Carver, in a halter top and cut-offs at the Kwik Stop. The ruin of Carver Varnell was held over many a girl's head as evidence of what would happen to you if you stayed too long out of the South, or left it too early; if you lived in Europe and New York City; if you got divorced; painted; lived alone; wore cut-offs; swore; had too many boyfriends; had too much money; went braless; drank too much; voted (or so it was rumored) Democrat; ran around with all sorts; sunbathed topless on the dock, and worse yet, did so while Luke mowed the Shippingtons' lawn next door; failed to bear, or perhaps to even *want* to bear, children; or to join the Junior League, the Garden Club, the Daughters of the Confederacy or the American Revolution, the Colonial Dames or the Married Women's Card Club.

Carver was hardly what anyone would call pretty. She was too tough, too raw and sharp-edged to be pretty. And her figure was far from the ideal. She had little in the way of hips or waist or bust. Nor was she what anyone would call thin. She had too much muscle on her for that. Her shoulders were as broad and square as a man's, and she had clearly defined biceps, no doubt from all the paddling she did in the creeks, kneeling on an old surfboard. Her thighs were likewise over-developed. Her body was, if seen straight on, almost boyish, but from the side or back, her high, well-rounded rear end made it clear she was no boy, as did the way she could sometimes walk.

But despite her many and obvious flaws, there was something about Carver, and her body, that incurred the ire, which is to say the jealousy, of all the mothers thereabouts. Part of what so grated was that Carver, despite her purportedly dissolute lifestyle, had retained

whatever looks she did possess, along with what could, for lack of a better term, only be called youthfulness, despite the fact that, in her actual youth, people had said she'd grown up too fast. *It's because she never had any children,* Pauline had said, in a tone suggesting that Carver had not done so with the express purpose of slighting those, such as herself, who had. *You can do sit-ups and leg-lifts and starve yourself 'til the cows come home, but it's near impossible to make a comeback after babies, isn't it?* sighed Marcia Olsenson, mother of four, or five, if you counted her husband, as she often did. *You said it,* said Bitsy Doolittle, popping an olive into her mouth from off the tray Riddley held out, *We might as well just give up.* Marcia whispered, *Oh, let's do.* At that, they had all laughed themselves nearly to tears. Riddley had been uncertain if they were laughing because they did indeed intend to give up, or because they never would.

The crux of it was that since her early teens, Carver had been powerfully attractive to men. Some might well claim that such was due to Carver's reputation, to her years spent gallivanting around, the rumors of her many Yankee and foreign beaus, and the fact that, well, she had long been said to be easy. But it was more than just that. Carver had, for one, a kind of physical confidence rarely glimpsed in the Southern female. It was evident, from how she carried and held herself, that she took great pleasure in her body, not merely because men found it attractive, but because of itself, and what it could do, what it could feel. That her form clearly did not merit such self-satisfaction did not discourage Carver in the least.

Men derided her when not in her presence, but on the rare occasion she deigned to show up at a party—to which she was still regularly invited—she never lacked for male attention, someone to fetch her another whiskey and soda or an ashtray, offer her a light, argue with her about politics, watch her behind as she stalked out the door. At a cocktail party at the Stones, when Bucky Flanders told the joke about the pink rabbit and the black man, she had spat out numerous obscenities as she departed. For, despite her good family, Carver Varnell had few or no manners, or else—and this was a far more disturbing possibility—she simply declined to use them. This shortcoming was attributed to the fact that Carver's mother Evelyn had

died when Carver was twelve, after which Carver had been left to run wild. She had been deposited not in one of those nice girls' schools in Virginia, but in a boarding school up North, in one of those states where the people were as cold as the climate.

For years after Evelyn's death, Carver came home only for Christmas and a few weeks in June. Then, the summer she was eighteen, she had come back to come out, alternating her time between luncheons, oyster roasts, dinners, cocktail parties, receptions, dances, and sessions at one of the city's only psychoanalysts, about which she had been neither ashamed nor discreet. Bernadette (Boo) Zahn, nee Lanier, had often repeated how Carver, peeling off her elbow length gloves after the Cotillion, had said, in the exaggerated, mocking drawl that she had, even then, frequently adopted, *that's it, honey, I'm agoin' on back in.* Which, indeed, she had, not making another appearance in her hometown until she was a bridesmaid in a cousin's wedding, some two or three years later.

After boarding school, Carver had attended college in another small, cold state where the light in winter was gone by four-thirty. Then she spent years in Italy, studying the masters, as she aimed to be a painter. Or was it a sculptor? Whichever, after a number of years in New York, she had finally settled down and gotten married.

The upshot of all that time up North and abroad was that, as everyone well knew, she thought she was better than they were, a prejudice no doubt enhanced by her seldom seen and short-lived husband. His name, which she had briefly taken, had since been forgotten, as no one had ever referred to her as anything but Carver Varnell. Not much could be recalled about him except that he was a Jew from New York City, two traits about which nothing more, really, needed to be said. They had never lived in the South together, residing instead in a brownstone on the upper West Side. But they had visited in winter, and once in spring, for the blooming of the azaleas. He was said, by the few who had seen him, to be just as rich as she, and somewhat swarthy, especially beside her fairness, yet nonetheless quite handsome, except, of course, for his nose.

PART TWO

CHAPTER 9

Passiontide

assiontide was the last two weeks of Lent, from Passion Sunday to Palm Sunday to Easter Sunday. At dinner on Passion Sunday Emmeline reported how Mrs. Kensington had said that, when it came to Jesus, *passion* meant suffering.

"Doesn't it just," Pauline said, then blushed from hairline to collarbones.

"Pau*line,*" Sam said, grinning at her.

The Wednesday between Passion and Palm Sundays, Frazier's heart failed him at last. Pauline found him on the floor of the den, a pillow beneath his head and a washcloth on his brow, Adele seated nearby in an armchair. His death gave Riddley new resolve. She would give up more than she ever had.

The well-attended funeral occurred on Saturday, and after church on Palm Sunday, Riddley did extra jobs for cash. She weeded garden beds, then swept out the dockhouse and sponged off all the boat cushions. In late afternoon she went from bluff to road, pulling Spanish moss out of the trees. From Pauline she knew that Spanish moss was neither Spanish nor moss, but was distantly related, despite the lack of any resemblance, to the pineapple. Also, despite belief to the contrary, Pauline said Spanish moss took nothing from its host, but got whatever it needed from the air, a skill Riddley would not have minded having. Spanish moss, like the resurrection fern it often grew alongside, could look and feel quite dead when the weather was dry, but revived by filling itself with rain. The weight of it waterlogged could cause weak limbs to break, onto roofs and windshields, which was why Sam paid her to remove it.

Across the road, at the edge of the woods, Riddley heaped the Spanish moss alongside the burn pile. The previous July, in the midst of a dry spell, Sam had tried to burn the moss out of the live oak in the driveway. He had held his lighter to the furred gray strands.

Flame flared up the tree like lightning in reverse. Bats whirled into the bright sky, then swooped down so close that Riddley could see their scrunched up faces. One long thick clump of the moss caught and hung there in flames, before falling, in pieces to the ground. The embers glowed like live, snarled wires.

Most of the moss did burn itself out, as Sam had predicted, but the oak caught fire as well. They sprayed water as high as they could into the branches. The bats circled the tree, flitting into and out of the smoke. When checking later that all the fires were out, Riddley found the charred, balled-up body of a bat. With its open eyes and large ears, the bat looked both wise and startled. Because of its size, as well as its failure to escape calamity, she took it to be a baby, though it had none of the qualities she had come to expect in young, neither an endearing expression of helplessness, nor a softness that would have compelled her to stroke it. When she pried open the wings with sticks, she discovered four swollen teats in the chestnut fur. She scooped it up with magnolia leaves and buried it. She didn't want the babies to find their mother in that condition, though they might keep searching if they never found her. But Riddley didn't see the babies after that. Pauline said they must have found another place to roost.

Riddley took two more loads of moss to the burn pile before Emmeline called her for supper. The girls made sandwiches of funeral cold cuts while Sam had a drink. Pauline, unwilling to leave Adele alone, and unable yet to find anyone to stay with her, had seldom been at home the past few days. When she was, she was either on the phone, or lying down with the curtains drawn and the door closed.

After supper, Riddley went out again. In the twilight she added a last armload. Spanish moss had once been used as stuffing for sofas and mattresses and the seat of the Model T that Frazier had long ago driven across the state. Remembering that, she lay down on the pile. It had more give than she expected. She closed her eyes. She was sure she was being attacked by hundreds of chiggers, who were said, like red bats, to prefer Spanish moss as a roosting place. Nonetheless she felt, for that moment, so comfortable, enclosed in the scent of the moss flowers, which had just begun to bloom, and did so, she knew, only at night.

When she stood, the moss had compressed to less than half its height. She pushed it together in a tidy pile, then took a stick and flailed the pile into a dense mound. It made her think of a grave in a place where the ground froze and had not yet fully thawed, or where the soil was too hard or rocky to be dug deep. Not, as she now well knew, like any grave around here. Yesterday morning in Bonaventure Cemetery, she had seen just how sandy and penetrable was the soil, how easily and entirely even a very large man could be swallowed whole.

* * *

Dying, this is what he heard: rain falling, the hush and lisp of it coming down through pines, pattering onto pine straw; Adele singing cheerily to herself that sad song, *O Come O Come E-ma-a-a-nu-el;* the rhythm of a ceiling fan and the weighted end of the shades flapping in that same rhythm against the sill; *That mourns in lonely exile here, Until the son of God appear;* soup simmering on the stove, and the hiss as moisture from the lid hit the coils of the range; *Rejoice, Rejoice, E-ma-a-a-nu-el;* and Adele whispering his name, as she had not for how long? All these sounds that had for decades been denied him, or delivered via the muffled, over-amplified crackle of the hearing aids.

The light dimmed and a coolness came over him, as when stepping off a shadeless road to enter a patch of woods beside a stream. He stretched out a hand and felt a surface solid and cold, as a boulder would be beside such a stream, a slab of ice in the icehouse. The ice slickened with his skin's heat, and sliding his palm over it soothed him as had washcloths, wrapped around chunks of that same ice, and placed on his cheeks and forehead when he had the whooping cough. There's a washcloth on his forehead now, a pillow sliding beneath his cradled head.

Beside his bed his mother has been sitting for days, wringing out the cool cloths which his fever dries and heats over and over. She turns the pillow for the cooler side and tells stories of Brer Rabbit and the Bluebird and Jack and the Beanstalk. Amidst these characters there appears a boy named Frazier, familiar happenings made strange in the telling, in her telling of these tales of himself. Ice slivers are slid into his

mouth, *Take, eat, do this in remembrance of me.* He has always loved ice, she tells him, and how he cried as a baby when a piece melted too small and she had to take it away, for fear he'd choke.

His chest hurt now as it had then, caving in and expanding simultaneously. More than anything he wanted to yawn, to get a full breath. His mouth gaped in a choirboy oval, like a hooked trout yanked above the surface, but he was not in air, no, he was in the water, in the Chattahoochee before they dammed it and shot the fishing all to hell, and it was late winter or a very cold spring, for the water was cold, bone cold, joint cold, and he was under.

*   *   *

Pauline claimed Frazier would have wanted them to return as soon as possible to normal, whatever that was, and as if, considering Adele, such a state could exist again. But in any case, they would do all the things they usually did on Easter. Adele had spent the night before in the guest room, so she could be readied in time for church, but she had adamantly refused to go. Probably it was too soon, Pauline thought. Then again, it might be too late.

On the drive into town, Pauline had them meander past squares and churches, to see people out in their finery. It was a warm, clear day, something blooming everywhere you looked. Pauline switched on the radio and spun the dial. "Oh, gospel," she said, turning it up. "Daddy loved gospel, back when he could hear." She gave a little sigh. "Mother never could stand it. He'd turn it off soon as she came home."

Everybody grew quiet for a moment at the thought of Frazier, and then of Adele, who'd been sitting in the front room, staring out over the water when they left. She barely seemed to notice their departure.

On the radio, a woman sang of Jesus on the cross. "Tripp Hammond said that crucifixion kills you because it makes your lungs cave in," Emmeline said.

"And then you suffocate," Charlotte added.

Riddley touched the crucifix at her neck, one of five in her collection.

"I believe Tripp's right," Sam said.

"Dear Lord," Pauline murmured, looking as she did when one of them asked about the workings of their insides.

Sam turned onto one of the main thoroughfares and gave a low whistle. "Look at 'em all," he said, just as he might were he observing a strange species of wildlife.

"Oh I do love the hats," Pauline exclaimed.

"Do black people have Easter egg hunts?" Emmeline inquired.

"Of course they do," Pauline said, then frowned. "Or I would certainly think so."

"Should I speed up?" Sam said as they approached the intersection, busy with pedestrians.

"Stop it," Pauline chided.

"I could beep."

"Don't you dare." Pauline swatted at him, but she couldn't help herself from laughing. "These days something like that would start a riot."

"Mama, isn't that Bernice?" Riddley cried, pointing across the street to a group of girls. "She said she had some cousins here. She must be visiting for Easter."

"Don't· point, Riddley," Pauline admonished. "I'm sure that's not her."

"You're not even looking."

"Who's Bernice?" Sam said.

"That black girl who was in Riddley's hospital room last summer," Charlotte said.

"The one who was all burnt up," Emmeline added.

The previous June, Riddley had gone to Atlanta for plastic surgery, because when she was five she'd fallen on a neighbor's sleeping dog and been bitten on the face. The scars were quite faded, and Riddley, oddly enough, claimed to like them, but for a girl, of course, any scars on the face were a liability. The children's wing had been full, and there were no private rooms available, so Riddley was put into a double room on the burn ward. She and Bernice made friends at once, though Bernice was almost three years older. But she never lorded it over Riddley, as many an older girl might've.

"The one who died," Charlotte said.

"She did not die." Riddley whirled on Charlotte. "I sent her a letter."

"I bet you didn't get an answer."

"Charlotte," Pauline said, sharply.

"I'm only telling the truth."

Riddley looked at Pauline and saw that Charlotte was right. Still she had to hear it from Pauline. "Did she?"

"You'd already been through so much. I was going to tell you eventually, but after a while you seemed to forget about her."

"I never forgot about her." Sometimes, even still, Riddley dreamed about her. Often in these dreams they were swimming, in the river or at the beach, though Bernice had never been to the coast. In the dreams the water did not hurt Bernice at all, not like it had in the hospital. Nor was her skin drawn tight where it ought to have give, bunched and tucked where it ought to lie flat. Instead her skin was smooth and seamless and everywhere the same color. "Was my letter returned?"

"I didn't want that to be how you found out."

"We caught her taking it out of the mailbox," Charlotte explained. "That's when she confessed."

"Your mother never has been very good at being sneaky. Unlike some of us." He looked at his daughters in the rear view mirror and raised his eyebrows.

"When did it happen?" Riddley said.

Pauline looked at her hands. "It must have been the day we left."

"She died while I was there?"

"She went into intensive care in the middle of the night and died before morning. The nurse said burn victims often go fast like that. It was a blessing, really."

"You told me she was having more skin put on."

"The poor thing had one graft after another, and none would take. Her body kept rejecting them, and she didn't have any of her own skin to spare."

"She could have had some of mine," Riddley said.

"Likely she'd have rejected yours," Sam said.

"That's right," Pauline agreed. "Different kinds of skin would be incompatible."

"Like blood types?" Charlotte said.

Sam shook his head. "If the girl's body had already rejected numerous grafts, it probably wouldn't have accepted anyone's skin, regardless of the color."

"Heaven knows she'd suffered enough already."

"You make it sound like she's better off dead," Riddley murmured. Hadn't the nurse said as much about Bernice's brother? The brother Bernice had carried out, the both of them in flames. He hadn't lasted long, though the nurses hadn't told Bernice that. She had asked Riddley to visit him in intensive care. It was Riddley who inadvertently revealed to Bernice that he had already died. Bernice claimed to have suspected as much, but nonetheless she'd cried for a long time.

"I'm just saying that she didn't have much of a life ahead of her," Pauline said. "All her family had died in the fire, so there was no one to take care of her."

"We should have taken care of her."

"Oh Riddley, how could we have done that? But I know your kindness made her last days very happy."

Riddley slumped back into the corner.

"I should have told you, and I'm sorry I didn't. But I was worried you'd take it in just this way."

Riddley, looking back, thought that when she woke alone in the hospital room, she had known what had happened. It was knowledge she had gladly forsaken when told otherwise. By asking, *Where's Bernice?* not, *Is Bernice dead?* she had provided Pauline and the nurse with a way to not tell her. Worse, she had let herself believe them, despite the fact that she could always tell when Pauline was telling less than the truth. Pauline had clearly suffered from having no siblings to instruct her, by word and example, in the art of lying.

Now it made sense how Pauline had been jumpy and flustered and in a great rush to leave the hospital. What should have made Riddley most suspicious was that Pauline, usually one to encourage any altruism, had been far from enthusiastic when Riddley declared she intended to leave behind all books, games, art materials, and stuffed animals for Bernice. Pauline's clipped speech and strained

expression had caused Riddley to wonder if she did not want her to remain friends with Bernice because Bernice was black, whereas now Riddley saw that the problem was that Bernice, by then, was already dead.

* * *

In the church vestibule the Sunday Schoolers stood, eyeballing each other's offerings as they awaited the procession to the altar. A number of girls had flowers, magnolias and lilies and bouquets of the last azaleas. Each child carried a blue box, many of which would have been near empty, Riddley felt sure, had not the parents replenished them that morning.

Mrs. Kensington, singing along with the hymn, tightened their line and moved them closer to the swinging entry doors. With white gloves, Riddley clutched a flowering dogwood branch and her box of coins. *Hold it with both hands, now, from the bottom,* Pauline had instructed, a little worried, before taking her seat. She'd raised her eyebrows at breakfast when Riddley plunked her collection box down beside her plate. The last coin she had stuffed in, a quarter, stuck up from the slot like the sun coming up behind the marsh. *Goody goody,* Charlotte mouthed, when Pauline rose to fill the pitcher of orange juice. Charlotte and Emmeline's boxes were not even half full.

Riddley's new hat made her head itch. She poked the sharp end of the branch under the hatband, scratching back and forth along her forehead and temples, while pressing the box against her abdomen with one palm. Thus she felt it in her innards as the bottom of the box gave way. She bent forward and the branch snapped, scraping slantwise across her forehead. Beneath the singing and the organ and the shock, the crash of coins sounded like an explosion far away. Coins rolled underfoot and into wainscoting, out the open door, down the steps and onto the sidewalk and street.

"Oh. My. God," Emmeline said.

"I could die," Charlotte groaned. "Just die."

"Shhh," Mrs. Kensington whispered. "Never mind."

In the back pews, a number of heads had turned. Boys scrambled for coins, pocketing quarters and dimes and, when Mrs. Kensington

glanced at them, sliding nickels or pennies into box slots. Girls squatted, experiencing anew the injustice of having no pockets. Mrs. Kensington moved among them, pressing her index finger to her lips and imploring them to act like the ladies and gentlemen she knew they were.

Riddley, fingering her crucifix, looked down. The floor's black and white squares seemed to float at different levels. She fixed her eyes on a black one. It deepened and she felt herself about to fall into it. She shifted her gaze to a white one. Blotches of color surfaced there. White itself was not really a color, Riddley remembered, nor was black. *Black is the presence of all colors mixed together,* Miss Byrd had said, *and white is the absence of all color.* Or did Riddley have it backwards? Either way made a kind of sense.

In the silence after the hymn, a last coin vibrated. The bruises on the dogwood were turning a rusty brown, after which no amount of pennies or aspirin in the bottom of a vase would turn them back. She touched her face where it had just now begun to hurt. Her fingers came away bloody, and she put them in her mouth. The saltiness soothed her. She propped the branch in the corner beside the wadded box. She would have to walk to the altar empty-handed. She was glad Frazier was not there to see that.

"Don't you worry, Riddley," Mrs. Kensington whispered, dabbing at Riddley's forehead with a tissue. "God knows what happened. He sees everything."

Riddley knew that Mrs. Kensington meant that God knew how she had sacrificed and labored and saved, and for what, and also how everything had been lost. Yet for the first time it was in no way comforting to think of all that God might know, all that He might have seen.

Soon after their return home, before the potential clothing catastrophes of the Easter egg hunt, the heat, and dinner, Pauline gathered them up for the family photo. She had managed, without too much fuss, to coax Adele into a nice dress and all of the necessary undergarments. Now Adele sat calmly by, in the chair around which the rest of them would arrange themselves. Once Adele could be persuaded to sit, she might do so for hours.

If only Pauline could keep her from mixing mint jelly into everything at dinner, and eating with her hands. How did Daddy do it? Pauline wondered. Probably, every time Adele seemed on the verge of abandoning her utensils, he had made some slight motion with his own. Pauline was almost sure she had seen him signal Adele in such a way before. As for the mint jelly, he would have served Adele one generous dollop, and that would have been enough. She was much more likely to be satisfied with something if it came from his hand.

Pauline had had no idea the extent to which Frazier had buffered Adele from the world, and the world from Adele. Why had he concealed so many of the details of Adele's condition? Her decline had no doubt accelerated in Frazier's absence, though how much that was due to the shock of his death, and how much to the lack of his intervention, Pauline couldn't tell. At times she wasn't sure that Adele even realized Frazier was dead. Certainly Adele had not made any recognizable displays of mourning. She acted much as though he had just stepped out for some groceries.

Between the birth of Pauline's children and the death of her father, Pauline had spent no more than a few hours at a stretch with her mother. Now, after a mere eleven days, Pauline knew more than she had ever wanted to know about anyone, least of all her own mother. No doubt, by the end, she would know far more. Yet Pauline had also had moments in which she felt that her mother was a complete stranger to her, and she to her mother.

Pauline went from one daughter to the next, straightening sleeves and hems, tying bows, refastening barrettes, removing with a moistened pinky the chocolate at the corners of mouths. Pauline had set no limits on Easter basket candy, though she could not but warn of ruined appetites, stomach aches, bad skin, and rotten teeth.

Pauline, arriving at Riddley, frowned. There was nothing Pauline could do for the red slash across Riddley's forehead. At least the cut looked shallow, not bad enough to scar. Heaven knew Riddley had enough scars. Easter four years previous, the family photo had been the first picture to be taken of Riddley since the dog bite. The stitches had come out a couple of weeks earlier. Pauline had worried that

the scars would stand out even more in a photo than they did in real life.

After the photo, they had all gone down on the dock. The girls, because of their new dresses and the adults' proximity, had been allowed to forgo the requisite life jackets. Riddley had promptly fallen in and gone completely under. During those long moments while Pauline searched the water, she had cursed that river, and herself, for treating her own dreams as fears rather than premonitions, and for unwittingly putting faith in the caul, for she realized then that she too had believed that Riddley could not drown. She felt betrayed, by not only her own belief in the caul's power, but also by the failure of the caul itself, that despite its supposed protections, her child was nonetheless drowning.

Then Riddley surfaced, just as Sam was diving in to rescue her. She didn't need rescuing. She was swimming. The incoming tide carried her to the Montgomerys' dock, where the ladder had, fortuitously, been left down. Riddley would have been just fine all by herself. Her hat had not even been lost, attached as it was by its elastic string.

Pauline scolded Riddley for getting her face wet and risking infection. "But you always say salt water's the best thing for cuts," Riddley answered, for Pauline's suggestion for many a wound was to dip it in the river.

"Your mother thinks we live on the Jordan," Sam said.

There was much joking about how lucky it was that they had already taken the photo, and Pauline had laughed along with everyone. But later, bent over the oven rack and basting the lamb, she began to shake. Grease or tears sizzled on the hot metal, and her hand brushed against the broiling pan. *Damn lamb,* she swore, half-laughing at the sound of it, and then she had knelt down beside the open oven and wept.

The following week, when Pauline got the pictures back from Smythe's, the scars were not as bad as she had feared. Riddley seemed in fact to be healing better and faster than expected. Right after she had been bitten, Pauline had looked into her daughter's torn face and known that she would never look right again. Not that she ever would have been beautiful, but up until then Pauline had thought that

Riddley had a good chance, if she put her mind to it and kept at it, of being reasonably pretty. Over time, especially after the plastic surgery, Pauline had come to think that again.

Pauline also thought of that Easter as the beginning of her own acknowledgement of Adele's condition. In retrospect, Adele's behavior seemed mild, but at the time Pauline was still trying to account for it to herself and others. In Adele's first instance of outright public rudeness (or at least, the first witnessed by Pauline), Adele had refused to speak to the Masons when they greeted her in church. Pauline attempted to explain the slight as headache or insomnia, excuses she had made countless times since. Frazier had already ceased by then to make apologies for Adele. He did not want to draw more attention to her offenses, or to make it seem that her behavior was in any way explicable. Instead he became even more courteous, more gracious, to others as well as to her.

Adele had barely spoken the entire Easter Sunday, and when she had, her remarks were quite unconnected to anything that made sense. Tangents and non sequiturs were hardly uncommon, but Adele's comments were far too nonsensical to fall within the realm of the ordinary, especially considering how skilled she had once been at conversation.

But it was the family photo that had forced Pauline to face matters. While they were posing, Pauline noticed that Adele did not look at the camera. When the photograph was developed, Pauline's apprehension blossomed into full-scale alarm. Adele stared at Frazier as if spellbound, while Frazier looked straight ahead, his smile strained. Was he aware of Adele's expression? Since then, that rapt gaze on husband or daughter had become the norm in photos, as well as something of a joke—one of those family jokes which come about because you are, in truth, aghast, but you get used to it, because there's nothing else you can do.

Now Pauline, having tidied up her daughters and her mother and straightened Sam's tie, checked her reflection in a window. The girls crouched on the grass before Adele, while Pauline went to stand behind her mother's chair. Sam readied the camera on the tripod, pressed the button, and sprinted toward his place on Pauline's left. Just before the shutter clicked, Adele's head turned to look to Pauline's

right, which was where Frazier might have stood in such an arrangement, so that Pauline would be flanked by father and husband. It was another of those instances when it was clear to Pauline that her mother, at times, knew more than she let on, or more than others by then expected. Pauline never could tell when clarity would strike Adele. She wondered if Frazier had been able to anticipate such moments, or known at least when one was occurring. Had he said something then to soothe her?

The picture, once developed, would be a travesty of a family photo. Despite her own best attempts at a smile, Pauline's eyes would look very sad. The whole configuration was unbalanced, because she stood more to the center than to the right, her body having, out of habit, left room for Frazier. Sam's tie was off-center, revealing his shirt buttons. Meanwhile, Adele looked, with her usual disturbing gaze, to the space on Pauline's right, as if Frazier had indeed stood there. At Adele's feet, Emmeline, allergic to most everything that time of year, tried to quell a sneeze, while Charlotte stifled a yawn. Riddley's eyes were open very wide, as if, as the saying goes, she had just seen a ghost. Pauline would think then of Ida Mae, and wonder if in fact Riddley had. But if that were the case then Adele and Riddley had seen two entirely different ghosts.

* * *

In the midday heat the girls scoured the bluff for chicken eggs blown and dyed the day before, plastic eggs filled with jelly beans, chocolate eggs wrapped in patterned foil. They searched for bunnies and chicks made of congealed maple sugar or marshmallow or thin hollow chocolate, the faces caving in. Riddley spotted something bright red within a dense clump of azalea bushes beside the bluff. She squatted down and peered into the branches. It had to be an egg. For extra camouflage, it had been draped over with leaves.

She knelt, then turned her torso sideways and groped around until her fingers contacted a slimy surface. She snatched her hand out and peered in. Flies hovered above whatever it was she had just touched. It was, she realized, some kind of mushroom. Her fingers gave off a stench. *Sounds like a stinkhorn,* Miss Byrd would say the next week, when Riddley described it.

Riddley swiped her fingers back and forth on the grass. The reek remained. She rubbed pine straw between her hands, then rinsed them in the birdbath. She sat on the stone bench at the edge of the bluff, gazing out over the river. She was done hunting. She put her basket in her lap and looked down at the creatures and eggs tucked into the glossy snarls of green tinsel. What real animal would ever want to nest in such stuff? But she had watched birds snatch tinfoil and plastic and bits of knotted string for their nests. She thought of those bats last summer, whirling close beside her in the smoke as they fled their roost. At first she had taken their expression for fear and confusion, until she found the body of the burnt one, and she'd known then that what she'd seen on the faces of the living must also have been grief, and rage.

The wind had died and the gnats were coming out. Across the river, parallel to the marsh, Carver skimmed along on her surfboard, dipping her kayak paddle from side to side. The surface was smooth and glassy. How fine it must be out on the water, though it was colder than it looked.

From the other side of the lawn Charlotte gave a cry of triumph. She'd found the prize egg. Made of silver plastic, it had once contained Pauline's pantyhose, since supplanted by a five dollar bill. Now they would go into the house, where Pauline was preparing dinner. In the dining room they would find the place cards newly configured. No longer would Frazier and Riddley, as lefties, be seated on one side.

Long ago, Riddley had considered Easter dinner an extension of church, believing the leg of lamb to be, as in communion, the Lamb of God, that they were eating the leg of the Lamb of God. How very delicious it was, that tender meat made holy, though as she chewed she had to concentrate hard not to picture the lambs' sweet faces, their coats like swirls of cotton as they lay down in green pastures.

CHAPTER 10

Keepsake

"**G**randmother," Pauline announced brightly one May morning, "will be coming to live next door this summer." Pauline's voice sounded as it did whenever she bade her daughters do some activity they must pretend to enjoy, like playing with their retarded cousin Laney, or bestowing biscuits on the soup kitchen's glowering poor. But it was clear that Adele could no longer live on her own. Her behavior had grown increasingly erratic in the month since Frazier's death. So they were selling Frazier and Adele's house, and Adele would move into the garage apartment.

Pauline knew that Adele might well remain with them for years. It was a thought that filled her with dread. Before her decline Adele was a woman who planned meals a week in advance. To church, bridge parties, luncheons, and any event after five she wore gloves. Thursdays at four-thirty she had her hair rinsed and set, in the same style in which it had been done since 1956. By seven-thirty every morning she was fully attired, including girdle and stockings, because pantyhose, as she had many a time told Pauline, were not only unbecoming but unhygienic.

Pauline had recalled that admonition a few days ago, while struggling with Adele over her clothes. Pauline had felt exasperated as well with Frazier, for not preparing her more. Exasperation was something she'd rarely felt for him when he was alive. It gave her a kind of comfort, to be irked at him. It was such a mundane thing to feel, not something you would ordinarily feel toward the dead.

Adele's days of gloves and girdles were long gone, never to return. The loss of the past seemed to mean the loss of the future as well. Whatever had prevented her from, in public, adjusting her undergarments or extracting something from her teeth, and whatever had kept her, as she had always put it, *watching my figure,* so that she only had Jell-O or fruit for desert, and dry vermouth for a cocktail—whatever

these threats or fears or shames had once consisted of, they seemed to have been, like so much else, erased from Adele's mind.

These days she put her hands anywhere she liked, and likewise put anything she liked into her mouth, with no discernible concern for customary order. Hence Adele's meals of pistachio ice cream on a hamburger patty, scrambled eggs mixed with sweet relish and cottage cheese. At least she chewed with her mouth closed, though more out of possessiveness than courtesy, as if someone might try to extract a morsel, as she herself had at times seemed tempted to do, watching every sweet disappear into her granddaughters' mouths.

Before Pauline found and hired the sitters, when most of every day and night was spent with her mother, Pauline's astonishment at her father had grown. He had, presumably, undergone similar struggles, largely without complaint, and for who knew how long? Pauline had always believed that the dead would hold still while you remembered them, that a person, once dead, would cease to change. But instead of Pauline's notion of her father settling into a stable version of him, her knowledge of what he had silently endured caused her idea of him to expand and contort, and to be further confounded by her changing idea of her mother. Had he bathed Adele, assisted her in the toilet, coaxed her into her underclothes, or had Adele been willing to perform such tasks while he was still alive? And had he held his tongue while she railed or swore or spit at him, or had Adele saved these brutalities for her only child?

Since Frazier's death, Riddley had managed to avoid going inside his house at all, though many times she had sat in the idling car while Pauline ran in to fetch or drop off something she'd forgotten during her regular midday visit, which occurred while the girls were in school. Sometimes on weekends Pauline brought Adele to their house, where she sat for hours in the sunroom looking out the plate glass windows at the river, or dozing, or arranging a deck of cards. On this Saturday morning, Pauline took Riddley with her to Adele's, saying she needed help packing up Frazier's things, though she hadn't objected when Riddley brought along a book.

Pauline and Riddley entered without knocking. They found the sitter at the kitchen counter. "I can't say I spend much time sitting,"

said Mrs. McCall, a stout red-haired woman. She collapsed, huffing, into a ladder-back chair. Earlier in the week she had relieved Adele of two bracelets, a pair of earrings, and a brooch, having discovered Adele's costume jewelry stashed within a velvet-lined pouch inside a wooden box in a brown bag shoved far under the bed. She took such concealment as indicative of value, not realizing that Adele had tucked away a vast number of objects, from screwdrivers and toothbrushes to all manner of kitchen utensils. *How am I to flip your egg, Adele, if you've hidden the spatula?* Frazier had asked the morning of the day he died.

Pauline never would learn of those thefts, but somewhere near the end of April, Adele's wedding and engagement rings were stolen from right off her hand, an event that further encouraged Pauline to move her mother close by. Mrs. McCall had muttered, well within Pauline's hearing, *always thinking they can get something for nothing, too lazy to make an honest living, been that way ever since they came over.* Pauline well knew she was referring to the three other sitters, all of whom were black. Pauline had her suspicions, which did not exclude Mrs. McCall, but as she didn't know when exactly the rings had disappeared, and as it was so hard to find sitters who would show up and stay the appointed time and last more than a week, she had hesitated to make any accusations. Not to mention the fact that she was loath to confront anyone but her children, much less, especially in this day and age, if that person happened to be black.

Pauline had been warned beforehand about such dangers, and had removed silver, crystal, real jewelry, small antiques, and good porcelain, as well as those items with sentimental value, though the latter was a far-reaching category into which, at one time or another, most objects could have been put. She would have been willing, under the circumstances, to ignore various forms of dishonesty, but there was something particularly chilling about the theft of the rings. It made her mother seem like a car alongside the road, stripped overnight of all salvageable materials, though Pauline doubted that Adele cared or even remembered that something she had once cherished had been taken from her. In fact, the thief could well have simply asked for the rings, and she'd given them away without objection.

The last weeks, Adele herself had spent little time sitting. She roamed the house. It was, though none of them yet knew it, the beginning of her wandering. "Poor thing," Mrs. McCall said now in a loud whisper as Adele went by, her eyes fixed on the floor. "She's looking for him. She still don't know he's passed."

Pauline stiffened, due, Riddley surmised, to grammar, for which she was known to be a stickler. Also because Pauline could not stand euphemisms for death. *Died,* she'd corrected, when she overheard Riddley telling a classmate that her grandfather had passed away. Esther, too, said *passed,* but she made it seem not death but life was the trial. *Gone to her reward,* Esther had said when Aunt Rachel died. Esther always made heaven sound like the only place you would ever want to end up, whereas Pauline and Reverend Underhill and Mrs. Kensington made heaven seem a place where one would ever after have to behave, and act like a lady.

After Mrs. McCall departed, Pauline, with Adele at her heels, disappeared into the bedroom to deal with Frazier's clothes. Riddley went to the den, her favorite room in the house. Although Frazier had died there, it looked the same. She picked up his special phone, the volume always turned to its maximum. The dial tone jangled in her ear. She hung it up, scanning the walls and furniture and books. Today all of this would be dismantled.

She sat in his chair and placed her hands flat on his desk. Each of its many pigeonholes was precisely labeled. Riddley had been permitted to play with any of the contents. On the far right was a slot she favored for its promise, though she'd never found anything there. It had the label *Whatnot. What's whatnot?* Riddley had long ago asked Frazier. *Things you can't remember the names of at the moment,* he'd said*, or that don't have names at all.*

Only later had Riddley thought to wonder what known things there were in the world that didn't have names. There were many things that she didn't know the names of, but surely they still had them. Pauline had a tendency, when at a loss, to call objects *thingamajig* or *doohickey,* but Sam knew the constellations and the planets and the different kinds of clouds, and could list, in order of atomic

number, all, or almost all, the elements of the periodic table. Pauline, however, remembered the names of people and places—where people had come from and moved to and moved back from, their married names and maiden names, given names and nicknames, the names of people's offspring and ancestors and in-laws, of relatives distant and close, once and twice and thrice removed, the names of family members long dead or long absent. And Pauline remembered as well the stories that went along with the names, stories of scandal and estrangement, ruin and boon, umbrage taken, grudges held.

Riddley scooted the chair in front of the dictionary stand and knelt on the seat. Frazier's massive dictionary specialized in illustrations of obscure animals, and seemed partial to parasites and pests, particularly those deemed *invisible to the naked eye*. It also had a fondness for creatures clearly perceivable but of peculiar habits, such as the obstetrical toad, hopping about with his mate's eggs strapped like a cluster of pearls to his hind legs.

The dictionary was captivating not only for its plates and illustrations, but also for its detail, and for the words it deemed worthy of definition. Since Christmas, she had wanted to look up the word *nigger*. Because it was considered a bad word, she had not found it in their small modern dictionary at home. But Riddley had heard that it hadn't always been a bad word, that long ago it didn't mean what it meant now, that back then anybody, even a lady, might have said it. Didn't Pauline often claim that her mother was stuck in the past? And when Adele had said it, if she had said it, her voice had not sounded mean, the way it had when she'd said *thief*. Riddley herself had intended no cruelty or slight when, years ago, she chanted:

> *Eeny meeny miney mo,*
> *Catch a nigger by the toe,*
> *If he hollers let him go,*
> *Eeny meeny miney mo.*

A few weeks back Esther had even said it when Luke, who gave her a ride Mondays, showed up dressed in Mr. Shippington's castoff tuxedo jacket. *You old fool nigger,* she'd said, laughing.

Riddley flipped now through Frazier's dictionary. There the word was, just one among many. Noun, adjective, verb. The first two definitions were what she'd expected:

> 1) A Negro—often used familiarly, now chiefly contemptuously.
> 2) Improperly or loosely, a member of any very dark-skinned race, as an East Indian, a Filipino, an Egyptian.

The definitions that followed, however, were ones she'd never heard of:

> 3) Any of several dark-colored insect larvae, as of certain ladybirds and of the turnip sawfly *(Athalia spinarum)*.
> 4) A kind of steam capstan for hauling riverboats over snags and shallows.
> 5) Any of several crude African rubbers marketed as dark balls.
> 6) A fault in any apparatus. *Colloq.*
> 7) *Lumbering.* A long-toothed, power-propelled lever arm, used to turn logs on a sawmill carriage.
> 8) *Soap Mfg.* An impure soap (often dark-colored) that settles to the bottom of lye soap after fitting and standing.

As usual when looking something up, many of the words within the definition needed defining. But to look those up would no doubt lead to more unknowns. It was far too easy to lose sight of what you had been trying to define to begin with. So she pressed on through the numerous words she did not understand.

> 1) To exhaust (land) by working it without proper fertilization;—usually with *out. Local, U.S.*
> 2) With *off,* to burn (off), as a log; also, to burn (charred logs left in clearing land). *Local, U.S. & Canada.*
> 3) To subject to the influence of or association with negroes. *Colloq.*

Next came the various terms and derivatives, many of which had to do with plants or animals. *Nigger babies, nigger bug, nigger chub,*

nigger daisy, niggerfish. Nigger chaser was identified as *a small fire-
work that shoots about on the ground. Niggergoose* was a cormorant.
Niggerhead had almost as many definitions as *nigger.* It was the name
for a wide variety of plants, as well as *a boulder; a mussel; chewing
tobacco; a scoter; a spool on which to wind a hauling rope; a particular kind of nail, or the mark made by it; any dark-colored clump or
tussock of vegetation in swamps.*

Last summer, crabbing in the bateau with Hayden, she had spotted, far off in the marsh, a black man. Only his head was visible. What
was he doing, she had wondered, and how did he get way out there?
She knew of no creek that ran that far in. Not until she was looking
from another side did she realize she had mistaken a stray, muddy
crab trap buoy for a man. Its rope, twisted around an old piling, had
suspended the buoy in the marsh. How could she ever have taken it
for anything else? But Riddley was already notorious in her family for
her propensity to mistake one thing for another: a crumpled brown
bag for a fawn, a young man for an old woman, a live oak for a shack,
logs for alligators, sticks for guns, vines for snakes, mushrooms for
Easter eggs. Despite such errors, however, she had not come to mistrust her own eyes. She always believed, until the moment she saw
differently, that what she was seeing was what was there.

Riddley read through the rest of the definitions and terms.
Niggertoe was a Brazil nut, *niggerweed* was joe-pye. But there was
no sign of *nigger rig* or *nigger rigged, nigger lover, nigger lipped* or
nigger heaven, terms which were, along with the phrase, *Do it like
a white man,* popular at school. Nor did these definitions account
for what Esther had said to Luke, or how once when Emmeline was
spinning the AM dial, a black man's voice commanded, *Take charge
of your life, nigger.* And Riddley had come no closer to understanding
how Adele could have sounded so serene when she'd said it about
Josephine, not to mention how someone like Adele could have said
it in the first place.

Riddley stood and stretched. Inside the open closet door hung
Frazier's portrait, painted by Riddley in kindergarten. An orange-
and-yellow-striped tie dangled beneath his overly large head, which
perched, without benefit of a neck, directly on his shoulders. This

hunching, and the fact that each edge of the paper was touched by some part of him, gave a sense of his height. She had drawn him, as her teacher Mrs. Heffernan had put it, from the mind's eye, which Riddley pictured as dark and unblinking and smack dab in the center of her brain, looking backwards, to see what she could not see with her regular eyes, or what she had seen but forgotten, or not, at the time, understood.

The paint had cracked in many places. Riddley pulled at one big flake with her nail. It came away whole, leaving a gap as big as her palm. The lower left corner of the portrait was torn, from where it had repeatedly broken away from its tack. Riddley tugged at the ragged edge until it tore off. As she had often done in kindergarten, she put the bit of paper in her mouth. It quickly formed a wad, as the wafer had the one time she'd been allowed to take communion.

She already knew the congregation's lines and also the minister's, and en route to the altar the words had run jumbled through her mind: *Verily verily I say unto you, Very God of very God, we acknowledge and bewail our manifold sins and wickedness, provoking most justly thy wrath and indignation.* At the railing she'd tilted her head back and stuck out her tongue as far as it would go. *Body of Christ,* Reverend Underhill murmured, placing the wafer there like a coin in the mouth of a dead Greek, without which, she knew from Pauline, you'd be trapped between the living and the dead, unable to cross the river of woe. *Blood of Christ,* Reverend Marsden said, lifting the chalice to her mouth. The sip Riddley got made her mouth drier. She'd held the wafer there until it dissolved on its own.

Now she brought the wad of paper to her lips and spat it into the trashcan. The portrait, with its torn corner and cracked and missing paint, looked wretched. She had done the very thing that Pauline always warned her not to: heedlessly, thoughtlessly, she had picked. Just as she picked at scabs, hangnails, bug bites, dangling threads and loose buttons, she had picked at paint and paper, forever altering her only record of what she had thought of Frazier when he was alive. She knew it changed, how you thought of someone once they were dead and could not think back.

And what if she had begun some irreversible peeling process? Riddley placed the large paint flake on Frazier's desk and searched the

cubbyholes, but found nothing she could use for repair. She closed the desktop to access the drawers below. *Respect people's privacy,* Pauline said, whenever Riddley rushed in without knocking, or got caught eavesdropping. But how could you invade someone's privacy, much less respect it, once that person was dead?

In the bottom drawer, amidst many scribbled-on scraps of paper, was a dispenser of tape. She gently attached the paint flake, and patched the ragged corner. As she returned the tape to the drawer, Riddley's eye skimmed the paper scraps. One, in Frazier's handwriting, said, *calls me Father, 10/3.* Another, also in his hand, said, *sleeps with P's old doll.* Riddley gathered up a bunch and piled them in her lap. A few were stapled together. Most had dates, and some had times. A few had both. She read:

> —*tuna on Graham crackers, supper June 6, 1967*
> —*12/1/67 pours orange juice over cereal*
> —*insults Marjorie, 9:00 service 10/2/70*
> —*leaves stove on, burns through kettle, 7/68*
> —*bridge game, April 28, 1966*
> —*May 9, 1970, 11:30 hides purse from Josephine,*
>   *11:45 accuses J. of stealing purse*
> —*refuses to wear girdle, March 1969*
> —*refuses to bathe, June 12, 13, 14, 15, 1968*
> —*walks to Victory Dr. in slippers, Sept. 1970*
> —*puts phone in toilet, Nov. 6, 1968*
> —*insults Masons, Sept. 2, 1970*
> —*sleeps in dress, February 25, 1968*
> —*J. finds girdle in trash, August 14, 1970*
> —*asks time every 2–4 mins (approx.) for 3+hrs., 2/15*
> —*weeps from 1:30–3:45, for no reason*
> —*takes chocolates from White Bros., April, '69*
> —*slaps Jos., 1/71*

No wonder Josephine had quit so abruptly. Adele was far worse than Riddley had thought. But why had Frazier written such things down? She wondered if Pauline had seen them.

Riddley reached for more of the notes. At the bottom of the drawer, on a large manila envelope, Frazier had written in block letters

DESTROY?? OR DONATE to GHS? UGA? Riddley glanced over her shoulder and then picked the envelope up. UGA would be the university, but she didn't know GHS. What could Frazier have that he might wish to destroy? She untwisted the string from the envelope's circular tab, and emptied the contents out onto the blotter.

Four postcards landed, face down and overlapping. *Place Postage Here—Domestic Is. Possessions Canadian Mexican 1c Foreign 2c* was printed in a small box in a corner of the top one. Below the stamp box it read, *Address Here,* while across from that was written, *Correspondence Here.* None of them had been either stamped or written on. The postcards were on a thin cardboard, thicker than a postcard would be today. Why hadn't he included them with the rest of his postcard collection, stored in a box in the closet?

She flipped one over. It was a black and white photograph, in a clearing in piney woods, like many a woods that could be found around here. At the bottom of the card was a cluster of men, cut off at the waist. Not everyone was facing the camera, and a few were out of focus. A smaller group of men stood off to the left. Something about the picture—the men's clothes, or the quality of the photograph —made her think it had been taken a very long time ago. All the men wore ties and hats, and some had taken their jackets off and draped them over their arms, revealing suspenders. A few were talking, and looking off in the direction of the woods, as if somebody were approaching or expected.

At the top of the postcard was a dark irregularly shaped thing, by turns blunt and jagged. It reminded Riddley of a tree stump that Sam had chained to the trailer hitch, then uprooted and left to dry before burning. The picture had been taken facing the sun, so the looming object, backlit by the bright sky, was blurry and washed out. She couldn't tell how it was suspended there. All of the men were looking elsewhere, apparently unconcerned that it would fall on them.

Riddley looked away for a moment, to give her vision a chance to clear. The eyes, as she well knew, often played tricks. They could make you see things that were not there, or see things differently than they really were. But such tricks could also be used to your advantage, in that you could sometimes fool your own eyes into seeing something

that they had not been able to at first. As with the buoy she mistook for a man, you could alter how you saw a thing if you looked at it from a different angle. Likewise, to look at something very closely could change the way you saw it from a distance, and vice versa, or to stare a long while at a thing, or glance away and then back, could cause it to transform.

Riddley closed her eyes and leaned forward, her nose almost touching the postcard. She opened her eyes and began to raise her head up very slowly, giving her eyes time to focus, to tell her what she was seeing. At about ten inches away, she sat upright. She knew what it was.

It was a person, or what was left of him. He must have been a big man, because even without most of his limbs, he seemed still larger than the men below, though she knew that to look up at something often makes it appear larger. The short stump of one of his legs pointed to the side, while the longer remains of the other slanted down. Both his arms were almost entirely gone. The left one extended to just above the bicep. The arms were what had given it away, for as she had drawn slowly back there had flashed into her mind another postcard, which had for years been wedged into the corner of Pauline's dresser mirror. That postcard, sent to Pauline long ago by Sam, showed a statue of Venus, naked from the waist up and considered a great beauty, Pauline said, despite the fact that she had no arms. But at least she had a head, which this man did not. That was why Riddley had not at first recognized him as a person.

He must have been hung, though in the bleached out top part of the postcard, she saw no sign of a rope. And where was the rest of him? She tasted something acrid in the back of her throat. She thought of Ray's divided body, the pieces of him dispersed nobody knew where. She reached out to turn the postcard over, but her hand was reluctant, much as she could not bear sometimes to touch the pictures of skinks or leeches in the field guides, or certain illustrations in Frazier's dictionary.

Why would Frazier have wanted such a thing? But he had always been interested in history. He had traced the family's genealogy back

to the 1700s, and he was a member of the Georgia Historical Society, which must be what *GHS* stood for.

With the tips of two fingers, she flipped the postcard over. In a faded oval were stamped the words, *Smythe's Kodak Finishing Shop 122 Green St. Savannah GA.* Wasn't that the place Pauline had her film developed?

Pauline's footsteps sounded in the hallway. Riddley scooped the postcards into the envelope and shoved it in the drawer. With her foot she pushed it closed. She was uncapping Frazier's pen when Pauline appeared in the doorway.

"So what did you decide on?" Pauline said.

Riddley shrugged and pulled a notepad from a cubbyhole, stalling while she tried to figure out what Pauline was talking about. She remembered then how she was to choose something of Frazier's, *as a keepsake,* Pauline had said.

"The postcard collection, I guess." Riddley's voice sounded to her ears strained, but Pauline did not seem to notice.

"Daddy would be delighted for you to have those. Maybe you'll carry on the tradition and start collecting them yourself. You certainly have the knack," she said, referring to Riddley's various collections of rocks, shells, leaves, music boxes, crucifixes, and miniature boats. "He also started when he was young. A few are from his parents and grandparents, from before he was born."

"Oh, I'd forgotten that." Maybe he'd inherited the postcards she'd found.

"I'll just finish packing up Daddy's closet. It shouldn't take much more than a half hour. Then we'll all go to Dominic's for lunch."

"Okay." Riddley, anything but hungry, tried to sound pleased.

Pauline gestured at the open closet door. "I forgot about your wonderful portrait. We can hang it up in your room, or the playroom."

"I don't want it."

"But it's marvelous! Daddy just adored it. We'll keep it, in case you change your mind. You never know what you might wish you'd saved, later on." She looked around the cluttered room, muttering, "Or, for that matter, what you wish you'd gotten rid of."

When Pauline left, Riddley removed Frazier's long metal box of postcards from the closet. She set it on the desk. In it were hundreds

of postcards from all over the world, some blank, some written on, bought on Frazier and Adele's many trips, and sent to him by friends and family and acquaintances. Some he had mailed to himself, to have the stamp as well.

She took the envelope from the drawer. She shook the postcards to one end and folded the envelope over, so it would fit in the box. Scrawled on the front, in a large, unfamiliar hand, were Frazier's name and the address of this house, where he and Adele had always lived. The return address was in Atlanta, with no name of sender.

So Frazier had not inherited the postcards, nor acquired them himself. Someone had sent them to him, whether or not he wanted them. Maybe he hadn't wanted them. She tried to make out the date of the cancellation mark, but it was too faded to see clearly.

She put the folded envelope into the back of the box. Then she gathered and stacked Frazier's notes about Adele, and put these in as well. After all that Pauline had been through of late, who knew how such notes might affect her? Riddley could always give them to her later, and read them in the meantime.

She stretched rubber bands around the box, and then rose and turned. In the doorway stood Adele, staring intently at her. Riddley reminded herself that Adele often looked that way at people. Still, under the circumstances, her grandmother's gaze made Riddley very nervous. How long had she been standing there? Riddley had always thought everyone underestimated Adele. Just because she rarely spoke did not mean she only rarely understood.

Did Adele have any idea what was in that drawer? Frazier would never want Adele to see that postcard, or those notes, which was good reason, Riddley thought, to remove them. Good reason, that is, if Adele was capable anymore of reading. Frazier had thought Adele had given it up altogether. But if so, was that because she couldn't, or because she no longer wanted to? Riddley herself couldn't imagine not wanting to read if you were able, but nor could she see how, once you had learned something like that, you could ever forget it. But Pauline had said that people could forget anything.

Riddley cleared her throat. "Hello, Grandmother."

Adele tilted her head to one side. "What time is it," she whispered, her voice a rasp. Only later did it occur to Riddley how astonishing it

was that Adele had spoken at all, something she had not done, as far as Riddley knew, for weeks.

"It's ten to one." She pointed at the wall clock. "See?"

Adele approached. From near a leg of the desk she picked up a small sheet of paper. Riddley's abdomen tensed. It had to be one of Frazier's notes. Without looking at the paper, Adele handed it to her and gave what seemed to Riddley a knowing smile. Could Adele have already read them? Riddley looked down. The paper said:

> F.—*A little something for your collection. From your neck of the woods, so to speak.*
> —*W.S.D.*

The note must have fallen out when Riddley was hiding the envelope. W.S.D. would be the person who had sent the postcards to Frazier. Pauline might know who he was. How could Riddley ask her, without Pauline, in turn, finding out about the postcards?

Adele was still staring at her. "Thanks, Grandmother." Riddley tried to act natural, as Charlotte and Emmeline had told her to do whenever concealing something. "I guess I dropped it." Riddley folded the paper and slid it in her pocket. "It's something to do with Grandfather's postcards. Mama said I could borrow them for a while. Maybe I'll even start a collection myself."

In her room that night, Riddley could not bear to look at the postcard again, or examine the ones in the envelope that she had not yet seen, though maybe they weren't all so horrible. She had a feeling, however, that they were. She worried that they might in fact be worse, though how could they be worse? But there could always be worse. What she didn't know was worse in what ways.

She slid the box far under her bed. All through the night she felt its presence there. Once she could have sworn she heard a low moan, though that could well have been herself, in her sleep. A number of times she almost cried out for Pauline, as she always had before with nightmares. But at the last minute Riddley held back, for she knew that if Pauline came Riddley would have to tell her what she had found, and she couldn't tell her, not yet anyway, and maybe never, though up until that point she had always, in the end, told Pauline everything.

Anyone standing at Riddley's bedside would have thought she was ill, for she was as restless as if she had a very high fever. This was followed by a long stretch where she slept the limb-heavy sleep of a high fever broken. She had then the kind of stillness that causes a mother or father to lean over and check the child's breathing. Riddley, in the midst of her dreaming, prayed for whatever could break her out of that thick sleep, and away from those piney woods and that too bright sky, blank now but she knew that any minute she would see something there, once she stopped looking directly into the sun.

She woke with the raucous calls of the birds at daybreak. She wished then more than anything that she had not pried, that she had left those postcards behind, that she never had to look at the three she had not seen, or look again at the one she had. Not that she needed to look at that picture again. It was, she knew, hers now forever. Nor, having once seen it, could she really wish that she had not. But what was to be done with them now? She would've put them back where she had found them, where they belonged, except that such a place no longer existed, Pauline having spent the afternoon and early evening packing up the den.

The easiest thing would be to turn them over to Pauline. Or, following Frazier's advice, Riddley could mail them, anonymously, to the Georgia Historical Society, or the university. Or she could burn or bury them, or tear them into tiny pieces, or lash them to a stone and sink them in the river. But curiosity and fascination were stronger still than fear, than repulsion, and she could not yet bring herself either to destroy or relinquish them. Sooner or later she would muster her courage, and open the box and the envelope and then, one at a time or all at once, she would brace herself and look at them, for as long as she could bear it. Only after doing that could she decide what else she should do.

CHAPTER 11

The Prudent Mariner

Summer truly began that year, as it did every year, with the first trip to the islands. They went every Memorial, Independence, and Labor Day, and occasional Saturdays in between, as well as the rare Sunday when Pauline could be persuaded to let them forgo church, weather, as always, depending. For as long as Riddley could remember, she had wanted to live on one of the islands, and a true one, singular and unattached, not one of the many to which bridges or causeways stretched.

Pauline, too, had gone to the islands when she was a girl, especially after hurricanes, when what washed ashore was rumored to come from as far off as the Canaries, or at least the Abacos. She and Frazier collected cats' eyes, driftwood, and bits of blunted, cloudy glass. At the base of the dunes, on the rare and right conjunction of moon and tide and season, they found clutches of loggerhead eggs, abandoned in their nests of sand. The eggs were not oval but round, with a shell rubbery rather than brittle. They gathered as many as they could carry. On the boat ride home they dug in with their thumbs, as if prying open oranges. They arched their heads back, draining the shell like a shot glass. The emptied shells bobbed in their wake.

"You ate them raw?" Riddley said.

"Mmm-hmm," Pauline answered, remembering.

"Where were the mothers?"

"Long gone. They don't much like it on shore. Once they lay the eggs, they head back to the water." She arched an eyebrow. "How would you have fared if left like that to your own devices?"

"They should've at least hid them better."

"That's how they'd done it for millions of years. It had always worked before."

"Well it doesn't work any more." The loggerheads, Riddley knew, were running out.

"True, true. But back then there always seemed to be more than enough." Despite herself, Pauline couldn't get the look of pleasure off her face.

"Y'all shouldn't have eaten so many."

"You are absolutely right, and I do wish we hadn't. But back then practically everyone ate them. The settlers learned it from the Indians, and the slaves learned it from the whites, and everybody just handed it right on down."

"Well, you should've known better," Riddley said, with the particular glee of saying what had so often been said to her.

This Memorial Day would probably be the only time they would all go to the islands until Labor Day, for come June, Charlotte and Emmeline would go to North Carolina for two months of camp. Riddley herself saw no need to go inland for mountains and cool air, least of all for fresh water. So she would spend her summer alone. Not that her sisters hadn't always, by virtue of being twins, and older, excluded her, or included her principally as someone to torment.

By dawn of Memorial Day, Sam was down on the dock, a cigarette lodged in his lips, his plastic mug perched beside him on the railing, the smoke and steam rising in twin columns. Long before his family was roused, the boat was made ready: extra life jackets stowed, water canisters filled, the proper charts tucked into the plastic zippered pouch. He did not, of course, do food. He did navigation, transportation, and survival, along with his own personal necessities: sunglasses, rain slicker, two packs of cigarettes sealed in a zip lock baggy, a flask of Scotch in case they got stranded at cocktail hour.

Some twenty minutes past the scheduled departure time, Pauline, having made one last trip to the house, joined them on the dock. "Sweet Jesus, Pauline. At this rate we'll be lucky to leave by Labor Day."

"Name of the Lord, Sam," Pauline said.

"The Lord's named Sam?" he shot back, and even Pauline had to laugh.

After they cast off, Riddley pulled the bumpers in and took her place in the bow. Sam put the boat at full throttle. His tanned neck looked even darker with the thick white strings around it, which

attached to compass, hat, and sunglasses, none of which he would put to sea without. Should he be thrown overboard these would, he claimed, prove essential, especially the sunglasses, which would prevent him from going blind in the glare, and which could, by means of reflection, signal a passing boat or plane for rescue.

When he set out solo in his Sunfish he never went much past the shrimp boat dock, but all the while his eyes were focused on the horizon. In the dockhouse Riddley had found old manuals on boating safety, navigation, and sea survival, along with charts for territory as remote as the Bahamas. This furthered her suspicion that Sam might rather like to be shipwrecked or marooned or blown way off course. Then he would subsist on flying fish, rainwater, and Vienna sausage, and navigate by stars and moon, by swells and ocean color and the habits of sea birds. *Kon Tiki* was, after all, one of his favorite books.

Three pelicans glided alongside them above the flat water, then veered off. A porpoise surfaced, headed in the opposite direction. Sam handed Riddley the rolled chart, sheathed in plastic. "Keep an eye on our course," he yelled into the headwind.

Although she knew that he knew full well where he was going and how to get there, she unfurled the chart and rested it against her legs. It was one she had examined many times. She never tired of looking at any of them. That winter she had taken to climbing down to where the boat hung in the covered hoist. The boat had swayed like a huge cradle as she studied the charts for the area. She had set to memory the names of most islands and rivers, and which waters flowed into and out of one another, and along which shores. But she knew there was more to the charts than that. Some secret knowledge was to be derived from their mysterious instructions and injunctions, those *soundings in feet at mean lower low water.* She wanted to understand, without asking, exactly what was meant by that, and by the water's designations as *hrd, sft, stk,* and by such warnings as, *Mariners are cautioned not to rely solely on the lattices in inshore waters,* and *Improved channels shown by broken lines are subject to shoaling, particularly at the edges.*

With her finger she traced the course they were on, and the one they would take. A buoy would appear shortly, near the mouth of the

Leigh. *The prudent mariner will not rely solely on any single aid to navigation, particularly on floating aids.* That was one instruction she clearly understood.

If they went up the Leigh, rather than heading out to Moss Island Sound, they would eventually come to Runaway Negro Creek, a body of water she'd first seen on the charts in December It was one of the few creeks that actually led somewhere, rather than dead-ending into marsh. From the looks of it, with the right tide, and in a craft with minimal draw, a fugitive could have passed between rivers, and eventually out to the islands, though there was a chance the creek would only be passable on a spring tide. Maybe she could get Sam to take her there this summer. She would like to travel the length of it, to see how far it was possible to go.

She loosened her grip on the chart and it rolled itself up. They entered narrow, shallow Devil's Door, easily passable so close to high tide. They cut through to the other side. Before them lay the northern end of Indigo Island. Heading into Indigo Sound, they skirted the breakers off the point and went south along the coast. Empty boats bobbed offshore, their passengers already on the beach. Sam put some distance between their own and the last boat, and then headed toward shore. Riddley hauled the bow anchor onto the beach. They unloaded, piling everything just beyond the surf. Sam stayed at the helm, popping the motor in and out of reverse, to keep the boat from beaching.

"Can I come?" Riddley called. He would anchor the boat far offshore, so that it would not get stranded once the tide went out.

"Climb on, before she gets swept in."

"Wear shoes for the walk back," Pauline yelled.

In the bow, Riddley fed out the line for the shore anchor. "That oughtta do it," Sam said when the line was nearly taut. He tossed the stern anchor over. "It's a long way in, but better safe than sorry." That was one of his favorite things to say to his offspring, though not, as Pauline was quick to point out, one of his favorite ways to behave.

"Go ahead," he said. "I'm right behind you." Riddley knew this meant he would pee first off the stern, check that everything on board

was in order, and then have a smoke. Riddley put on her sneakers and lowered herself over the side. The water lapped her ribs.

From the shallows, she glanced back at the boat. In a stern seat, facing the ocean, Sam sat the way he always did when between tasks, or when he thought himself alone and unobserved, with his feet planted wide and his elbows on his knees, a way she had been taught never to sit. In his right hand would be a cigarette, and as it shortened he would grip it between thumb and forefinger for the last few long drags, then flick the butt into the waves.

Up the beach, Pauline sat atop the cooler, fanning herself with a *Time*. "It's already hot as the hinges and it's not even June yet. I do wonder what we're in for."

Charlotte and Emmeline greased each other with coconut oil. They aimed to get as dark as possible, without burning, or to only burn the kind of burn that turned to tan and did not peel. Sam strode through the surf, his compass bouncing against his chest, his cigarettes held aloft.

"Y'all can swim here, where I can see you," Pauline said. "Elsewhere only wading. You know the rules."

Riddley went down to the water's edge. In the shallows a couple of yards away, just as she was about to wade in, small fins cut straight up out of the water. It was a young hammerhead shark, only a few feet long. She was surprised that even the young had such monstrous heads, though of course that was something it was born with and would always have, not some trait it would grow into.

She turned to announce her discovery. But mightn't Pauline then put further limitations on swimming here, or prohibit it altogether? Pauline was already inclined to a drastic response to danger. But a shark that size could probably do little damage. Nor did Riddley think that mother sharks were protective of their young. She was not sure enough, however, to swim right then.

She turned back to the water. The hammerhead had disappeared. Despite all the threats and fear of sharks, this was the first live one she had ever seen outside of an aquarium, unless she counted that one last summer. Sam had brought Riddley along shark fishing with

Will Montgomery and Jasper Kane and their boys. At dawn they'd reached the sound, the flat water mirroring the vivid sky. They threw chum overboard. The fathers sat and smoked, stroking their unshaven chins. Jasper opened a can of beer, and the *sspftt* made the air seem stiller. After an hour of nothing Conrad Kane muttered that everyone knew it was bad luck to have a girl on board. *Then you better throw yourself over,* Sam had said.

Returning, they had passed a crowded dock. An enormous shark hung by the tail on a hoist. Something smooth and grayish-pink bulged, faintly pulsing, from its mouth. Riddley took it to be its heart, or perhaps some other organ, though she was uneasy enough not to ask. She waited until evening, until Sam had poured himself a drink. She let him have that first long sip before inquiring. With the whiskey still held in his mouth, he studied her, appraising, she knew, her mettle.

"I'm not Mama," she said, lifting the strong chin that nonetheless marked her as her mother's. "Or Charlotte or Emmeline, either."

He choked a little on his Scotch. "No," he said, using one cigarette to light another, "that you're most certainly not." He took a swallow and glanced at the kitchen door, to see where Pauline was, which fortunately was elsewhere, for had she heard she would've cried out. He looked back at Riddley. "Live birth."

Riddley shuddered. Not from squeamishness, but from the sheer wrongness of it. Nature, it seemed, had momentarily taken leave of her senses. Sharks, as fish, should bear eggs, and should spawn, not mate. The encyclopedia corrected her of this notion. Even when sharks did as they ought and produced eggs, at most only two of many embryos survived, which they did by devouring the others as they lay nestled together inside the mother's body.

After lunch, Charlotte pressed a finger into Emmeline's arm, to see if she'd gotten any color. Riddley put an apple, a soda, her sneakers and a towel in a bag, and took off south along the beach. She was hot, having done no more than splash herself off in the shallows. She hoped to come across a tide pool deep enough to submerge in.

After a while, a smell hit her, and soon she came upon many horseshoe crabs scattered across the beach. They were a creature she found it hard to picture doing much besides dying, as that was mostly

what she had seen them do. *That's just nature's way,* Pauline had said, but Riddley had her doubts. Pauline admitted that some did get dragged and drowned by the shrimp nets, and then washed ashore, but most just got left by an outgoing tide. Sam said Riddley need not worry about their ability to endure, as they had been around already for a few hundred million years. *So have the loggerheads,* she said. *True enough,* he'd replied, *but who likes to eat horseshoe crabs or their eggs?*

A good many had expired in the strip of dried marsh grass near the high tide line. A few had made it to the soft sand farther up. Either they had laid their eggs there, or they'd gotten turned around. But how could they get turned around? A creature from the ocean, she felt certain, would always know in which direction the ocean lay. Likewise she had never quite believed that a person underwater could not know the way to the surface.

She came to a crab that was in what Pauline called *the throes.* As usual in such a state, it was upside down, the complexities of its underside exposed to sun, gulls, flies, and, come dusk, coons. There in the horseshoe crab's belly were the layers and layers of gills, encrusted with sand, and the legs and tail feebly waving. The tail was too weak to do its usual job and turn the creature over. She held a stick at arm's length to flip it over, though she knew neither the tail nor any other part of the horseshoe crab could hurt her. Still, in its armor, and with so many bristling parts, the creature seemed designed to poke or sting.

That horseshoe crabs would not do you harm, even under the direst circumstances, she had witnessed last summer, when her teen-aged cousins visited from Michigan. The beach had been littered with horseshoe crabs. The boys had no interest in the dead ones, but they went from one live one to another, yanking off any append-ages, and jabbing each one in the gills with its own tail. Charlotte and Emmeline, having no qualms about being considered squeamish, returned to their beach towels, while Riddley stayed with the boys. It felt somehow compulsory, to watch.

The horseshoe crabs seemed to take forever to die, or else, like snakes and chickens, it was only muscles or nerves, not agony, which made their bodies keep moving. They did not make a sound,

apparently having no ability to call, unless you counted the snapping, crunching noises, and the bubbling and frothing of what came out of them. Nor did they make any attempt to fight back, which inspired scorn rather than pity in the boys, who grew tired of it after a while. Still they kept on, methodically, as if it were a task some adult had assigned them, which they had to finish carrying out. Riddley retired after a while to the dunes, weary of watching, and agitated, too, by the animals' utter lack of resistance, though what difference would it have made? Still she could not help but think the horseshoe crabs were, in a way, asking for it, with their frail beckoning limbs, and their stubborn unwillingness to go ahead and die. Not as though they deserved it, but she had understood how such mute vulnerability did, for some, make their torment very hard to resist.

She continued walking south in the shallows. Had she come across, say, a pelican with a broken wing, or a beached porpoise, she would have relished its rescue. It would have gazed at her with an expression pained and pleading, with eyes so like a human. Not like the eyes of horseshoe crabs, which not only were there many of, but which Sam had told her did not see details or colors or pictures at all, but only light and dark.

Once Sam had picked a horseshoe crab up by the tail and carried it down to the surf. He wanted to see what it would do upon being returned to the ocean. At the very least it might have shown relief, at being brought into the water, out of the sun. It sat there unmoving as the waves lapped over it. *Oh dear,* Pauline murmured, *maybe it's already too far gone,* and Emmeline said, *You mean fried.* Sam said it just needed time to get its bearings. Soon the water beneath the crab grew murky. Its tail shifted, and then the crab began to move, with more speed and determination than Riddley would have expected from such a creature, as if, because it had existed for millions of years, it would by nature be slow, dimwitted, rather than tough and clever to have survived so long.

As she walked she kept her eye out to sea, hoping for porpoises. Distant clouds indicated a storm was in the offing, though that didn't necessarily mean it would come to shore. After a while she decided to cut inland, on the slim chance she might spot some wild horses,

descendants of those who'd survived the Horse Latitudes. She slipped on her sneakers, crossed low dunes and a slight ridge, and came to a slough. She tried to skirt it but soon lost the dry ground and ended up ankle high in rank water, the mud deeper than it looked. Each step was a struggle, and she did not see the alligator until she was almost upon it. It was partially submerged in the shallows, water pooled in places on its back. Its eyes were closed, which led her to believe it was sleeping. But the moment she was still, it looked straight at her.

It was not a very big alligator, only about her own length, though instead of decreasing in size as she slowly backed away, it seemed to grow larger. Hayden had told her what to do if charged by an alligator: embrace it tightly around the jaws and roll with it, punching the tender tip of its nose. At this proximity, she could not imagine following such advice. She slipped and fell and scrambled to her feet, thinking it would be more likely to attack if she were down.

She could no longer tell if the alligator's eyes were open, but she nonetheless felt its gaze on her, as she would for some time to come. In a single glance it had evaluated her as prey, determining how weak she was, and whether she could be held under the water long enough to drown. She didn't doubt that she could.

She ran down to the beach and headed north, back the way she had come, clouds thickening overhead. She paused in a tide pool to wash the mud off. She was very tempted to tell her family about the alligator, but as with the hammerhead, she worried such a sighting might engender more restrictions. So in answer to Pauline's inquiries, Riddley only said she'd walked far down the beach.

Sam was eager to depart before the outgoing tide and incoming storm made the journey perilous. The sky darkened considerably while they loaded the boat, and as they headed out of Indigo Sound, the gray-green swells were much higher than when they'd arrived. In the bow, the wind was almost cool, and Riddley wrapped a damp, sandy towel around her shoulders.

On the left side of Moss Island Sound a green light flashed, while far away on the other side a red one blinked languorously, like a person fending off sleep. Sam headed for the far one. "Red right returning," he intoned as he passed to the left of the light. When they went

by a signal buoy, he liked to voice whatever rule applied, to teach his daughters how to get home one day without him. Their own mother, Riddley knew, could not have done it. Pauline had no sense of direction, a failing which did not shame her. *I could not find my way out of a paper bag,* she'd boast. *That's fight your way, Pauline,* Sam would reply.

Riddley had believed, when younger, that Sam had invented the rule, *red right returning,* for their instruction. She liked to whisper it to herself, and did so now. It was comforting, like a fragment of nursery rhyme, a secret and repeated wish. When she discovered that the rule did not apply solely to her family, but was useful the entire length of the coast, to as far away as Boston or Key West, she had at first felt cheated, and more than a little foolish, that what wisdom she had thought was theirs alone belonged instead to anyone who traveled the Intracoastal Waterway. But later she liked the fact that she could apply this rule beyond their waters. Nor did *returning* necessarily mean going home. Rather it simply meant coming into port from the sea. The curving of the rivers was such that at times it might be necessary to veer in nearly the opposite direction from where you intended to end up, so that, for example, to achieve the larger southern bearing you might need to go for a spell due north.

Sunburnt and wind-burnt and jarred, she grew very drowsy, as always happened on such returns. She leaned back against the windshield and closed her eyes. Sam's windbreaker snapped in the gusts. Gulls gave their raspy cries and the boat slapped down between swells. Amid these sounds she heard the splutter and hiss of air being expelled, the rush as more was taken in. It had to be a porpoise. She opened her eyes half-way, to see if she could spot it, or them, as porpoises were said never to travel alone. She scanned the water, furled on top with white, but between the waves she glimpsed no fins or flukes. Her lids closed again and she saw the hammerhead zigzagging through the water, already so menacing, despite the fact that it must be too young to do real harm. Not like the alligator, who continued in her mind to watch her, while on the beach the horseshoe crabs struggled to turn themselves over. Her vantage shifted again and she was deep underwater, looking toward the surface, where the Spanish horses

were in the midst of drowning. Their legs slashed back and forth, as though they might yet reach solid ground. *Lagan,* she thought, as if those horses had not all been devoured by now, as if they might still, centuries later, be retrieved.

The breathing sound recurred, and it seemed this time different from a porpoise, more hollow and resonant, as if it came from something much larger, from a body which held more breath. Maybe it was the blow of a whale, a pilot whale or a pygmy sperm whale or a right whale, all of which passed by here on their way elsewhere, none of which she had ever seen. The few right whales that were left, Miss Byrd had told them, calved just down the coast in St. Andrew's Sound, which long ago had been called the Bay of Whales, because it was filled with them, and with whalers.

Again Riddley partially opened her eyes. Ahead of her were dark water and sky and tapering, branching, winding rivers. To her left the wind cut paths through the wide marsh, and to her right was the long beach of Moss Island, strewn with huge drifted trees, washed up there as the bodies of whales might once have been, after they drowned in a storm, or got stranded on a sandbar in an outgoing tide. Those right whales which had survived would, she remembered, all be gone by now. They returned north every spring. The sound she had heard must have been that of the wind, pressing through the marsh grass, or narrowing and dividing as it passed over the rivers, alongside the high bluffs. Before she slid the rest of the way into sleep, Riddley could tell from the faster rhythm of the boat's bouncing that they had left the larger swells of the sound behind, for the sheltered, choppier waters of their own river.

CHAPTER 12

Evidence

Ray and Isabel's belongings had been crowded into Ray's old bedroom, and Frazier and Adele's furnishings had been installed throughout the garage apartment. Its odd odor had been largely covered up by the smells of Adele's talcum powder and cold cream. The uneasiness of the place, however, had not dissipated. That quality had combined with a sense of displacement, of objects being in the wrong surroundings. Nonetheless, the appeal of the garage apartment had been rekindled, and in the ten days since Adele had arrived, Riddley visited often. In Frazier and Adele's house, there had always been the mandate to act like a lady. However, since Frazier's death, and since Adele had taken to eating soap, pocketing anything she took a fancy to, and hiding her own and others' belongings, Riddley had felt much less constrained in her presence. Especially now that Adele had pretty much stopped speaking altogether, Riddley felt as free as she had with Isabel, in that both grandmothers had quite ceased to care how Riddley behaved, much less how she turned out.

Ray's elevator chair had remained, in case Adele's bodily deterioration should catch up with that of her mind, an event that seemed highly unlikely. Her physical vigor was in fact improving, along with her already unseemly appetite. *Your mother's getting quite beefy,* Sam had said one evening, and in that instant Pauline felt almost as though her mother's body, and her mother's hunger, were her own. Adele wolfed down seconds at every meal, intent, it seemed, on making up for decades of restraint.

As a result Adele had, like a child, outgrown most of her clothes. Today, a Saturday, Pauline had taken Adele shopping, while Sam caught up on some paperwork. As soon as Pauline's car was out of the driveway, Riddley had gone to the garage apartment. Upstairs, she opened the door to Ray's room. A dismantled bed frame

partially blocked it. She squeezed through and the door shut by itself behind her.

She made her way through the maze of furniture to where a massive bureau stood against the opposite wall. The day after finding Frazier's postcards, and before she could bring herself to look at the other ones, she had felt compelled to get them out of her immediate vicinity, and so she had stashed them in the otherwise empty bottom drawer of Ray's bureau. Upon closing the drawer, she had promptly put them out of her mind, an expulsion she had thought would be much harder to accomplish than it was.

She never had any doubt, however, that she would eventually have to revisit them. The image of the postcard appeared now with such familiarity that she wondered if, in the meantime, she had dreamed of it again, as she had that first night, though she recalled no further nightmares. But according to Charlotte and Emmeline and Pauline, the past weeks Riddley had been talking a lot of gibberish in her sleep, as well as sleepwalking, something she had otherwise not done much of in the past year. A few times she had woken up in another room. She thought she would remember had she dreamt of the hung man, yet she suspected that, even had he not appeared, her talking and wandering was, however remotely, about him.

She crouched and slid the bottom drawer open. Her breath caught. Stacks of napkins and tablecloths and doilies filled the deep drawer. In the center of one an elaborate *W* stood up like a welt. These had to be Adele's. Pauline must have saved them for her own table, or the tables of her daughters' future dining rooms. But who had put them here? It had to be Pauline, or possibly, before they left for camp two days earlier, Charlotte or Emmeline.

The envelope with the postcards in it had Frazier's name on it, so anyone who spotted it would know it was not Ray's, despite being in his bureau. If, that is, the person who found the envelope could read. The scent of lemon oil swept over Riddley. She sat back on her haunches and glanced at the other furniture, and it, too, had a new sheen. Pauline had sent Esther over here numerous times before Adele moved in, but Riddley had assumed she had cleaned only those parts of the house that Adele would occupy. But Pauline must have had Esther polish this furniture as well, to better preserve it.

At the thought of Esther seeing the postcards, Riddley's face grew hot, as if she'd had more to do with the envelope than opening it, more to do with its contents than merely looking. Just because Esther had been here, however, did not necessarily mean that she had found the envelope. She could have polished this furniture after someone else put the table linens in the drawer. But all of the linens had, Riddley abruptly recalled, been recently washed and pressed by Esther, and then refolded along different lines, despite which Pauline said they'd never be rid of their old creases.

But wasn't Pauline always praising how well Esther respected their privacy, how she behaved much of the time as if she were not even there? Esther might well not have opened the envelope, much less noticed it, for Riddley had wedged it upright against the back of the drawer. But even if someone had noticed, and had looked, and even if that person were not Esther but Pauline, what was Riddley so worried about? She had not done anything wrong, or not exactly. After all, Pauline had given her Frazier's postcard collection, and surely these could be counted as a part of that. Granted, he had kept them separate, and she had acquired them somewhat deviously. But there had been that note from W.S.D., saying that these were for Frazier's collection. Still, Riddley could not rid herself of the feeling that she had done something she should not have, something more than simply prying and taking what was not hers, though that would be what she got in trouble for, should she get in trouble. Nor was it only that she had seen something she should not have. The looking itself was at the heart of her transgression—that, having once seen, she had continued to look, she had not at once looked away—though that was not something, she knew, for which she would be punished.

If the envelope had not yet been discovered, it no doubt would be soon. She lifted out the central stack of cloths and reached back for the envelope. It was exactly where she had left it. Relief surged through her. She took the postcards out, face down. One was missing. Why would anybody remove only one? But she had been flustered at Frazier and Adele's. She could have miscounted.

But she knew she hadn't. Someone else had held these, someone else had looked. She could feel the difference in her hands. The

postcards seemed denser, smoother, the paper compressed and burnished by another person's gaze. She turned the postcards over and spread them across the stacks of linens.

It was the one she had looked at before that was missing. As if to taunt her with its absence, or refresh her memory in case she had forgotten any details, another postcard had a smaller replica of the missing one. This postcard was split into four versions of the same scene, from different angles and distances. The hung man appeared in all but the bottom right square, which showed a tree trunk with a makeshift sign nailed to it, the writing too small to read, except for the first and largest word, *WARNING*. A man with his hat pushed back on his head pointed, grinning, at the sign. In the photograph taken from farthest away, it was clearly a person, or the remains of one, suspended in the air. She wondered, as she always did after the fact, how she could ever have mistaken it for anything but what it was.

There could be no mistaking what the next postcard was about. It did not at first seem, in comparison, as horrible. The man was clearly a man. He knelt in the foreground, his hands tied together before him, the fingers pointing down. A rope around his neck held him upright against the trunk of a palmetto. His open eyes made Riddley think, at first, that he was alive. His mouth, too, was wide open, but on closer inspection she saw that the gaping was more than just mouth. He had been cut or shot there. In the background and off to the far right edge, as if the photographer had not meant to include them, two white men stood beside a car. Their white shirts were bright against the high, rounded hood of the dark car, off which the sun glared.

The last postcard was crowded with people, in clothes that looked like church or party clothes, though that could just be because they were old-fashioned. In the foreground a girl posed, smiling, for the camera. She looked to be maybe a year or two older than Riddley. In her white dress with its big square sailor collar and its bow at the back, she stood out bright in the shade of a live oak. In her glossy blond hair was another large white bow. She was very fair, the kind of fairness that has always been protected from the sun, and against her pale skin and hair her dark eyes and brows were striking. You could tell, too, that she knew she was pretty, and that she was beginning to get some inkling of all that might mean.

A black man hung just a short ways away from her. His head was bent to the side, his chin resting on his collarbone. Mud was stuck to one side of his head, as if he'd lain down in a puddle. To look at the tilt of his head, you could almost think he had fallen asleep in church, or waiting on a bench for a bus. Except that his eyes, like those of the other man, were open. His feet, caked with dried mud, were at about the same height as the girl's face. There was something odd about how they dangled, as if he were pointing his toes, trying still to reach the ground.

The men were talking amongst themselves, smoking pipes and cigarettes. Most of the ladies' backs were turned. A few children dodged in and out, with the frenzied glee that comes when the adults are otherwise occupied. Judging from the wide-brimmed hats, the thin fabric of the clothes, and the occasional rolled-up shirtsleeves, it was summertime, and hot. Most of the crowd was in the shade.

Beyond that shade, at the very edge of the photograph, stood three black men, straw hats in their hands. In their overalls they looked to be yardmen, or maybe sharecroppers, Riddley thought, if this was long enough ago. Their faces were turned in the hung man's direction, but their eyes seemed focused elsewhere, as if they could look and not look at the same time. What were they doing there? Someone must have made them come, or brought them there to teach them a lesson. As with many lessons, it was probably about how you must never do what you shouldn't, and you must always do what you ought, what you know you should and what you're told. Implicit in that lesson, as in all lessons, was what will happen to you if you don't. That, she realized, must be what the WARNING was about.

There was something familiar about this scene that she couldn't quite place. Except for the man hanging in the tree, it could almost be a barbeque, an oyster or pig roast, a party for the Fourth of July. Partly what seemed familiar were the people's expressions. Whenever Pauline told her to be pleasant, to be cheerful, not to be glum, this was what she meant. But something else was recognizable about the scene, something beyond the faces of the people. The tree itself looked almost familiar, like the one next door at the Montgomerys. But that one had much lower limbs than these, too low to hang someone from, unless you did so over the river itself.

That was what was familiar about the picture. It took place, she was almost sure, on a bluff, one very much like their own. She picked the postcard up and tilted it back and forth, thinking of a card Bernice had propped open on the hospital windowsill. When held flat, it showed the face of Jesus. When tilted, it revealed hands pressed together in prayer. If you held it just right you could see both at once, the forefingers of the clasped hands pressing on Jesus' mouth, as if He were saying *shush*.

Riddley squinted, to see beyond the tree and shade and people to what was behind them. Didn't the ground drop off a ways back, or was that just the photo fading out? She was almost sure she saw the glint of water. She looked away, then back, leaned close, then far, but the picture became no clearer.

Had Esther noticed, too, that this one looked as if it took place on a bluff like theirs? For it had to be Esther. Riddley felt a brief relief, that she might yet elude punishment. Pauline would have confronted Riddley by now, if she were going to do so. She would never have left them here for anyone else to discover, Pauline being of a mind that ugliness could serve no purpose, and so ought not to be seen or shown, spoken of or heard. Likewise would Charlotte and Emmeline have wanted nothing to do with the postcards. They would have turned them over to Pauline. In the unlikely event that Sam had found them, he too would have given them to Pauline, not only since they had Frazier's name on them, but also because they were about the South, and thus had nothing to do with him. If Adele had found them, she wouldn't have put them back so carefully, if at all. Esther alone would have left the envelope exactly as she'd found it, and said nothing.

How, though, could Esther say anything? She too had taken what was not hers. But didn't the postcards, by virtue of blood, belong more to Riddley? *Stealing is stealing,* she could hear Pauline say, though on second thought Riddley wasn't sure Pauline would say that. But whatever you called it, why had Esther taken the postcard, and did she aim to keep it or give it back? And why would she choose to have it near her, where she could look at it anytime, and where, in its terrible way, it would look back?

Gravel crunched in the driveway. Surely Pauline and Adele wouldn't be back yet, unless something had happened. Riddley ran to the hall window. Esther was just emerging from the front seat of a car Riddley didn't recognize, the kind boys called a *nigger rig*. Riddley had forgotten it was one of Esther's every-other-Saturdays. She always looked so different in her regular clothes than she did in her uniform. They had driven by her on the street once, downtown, in a hat and high heels, strolling with two teenage boys. By the time they recognized her, they were too far beyond to stop.

Esther waved as the car drove off. Her beige purse slid into the crook of her elbow, and she hugged that arm tightly to her side, as Pauline did when she had just come from the bank. She started toward the side door, then paused and looked up at Riddley in the window. As Esther's eyes met hers, Riddley flushed. Esther gave a slow nod. Riddley lifted her hand to wave, then froze midway. She still held the postcard. Just moments ago, she had been relieved to think it was Esther who had found the postcards, but now she did not want Esther to ever know that she had seen them.

Esther must have taken the missing postcard because, like Riddley herself, she had needed time to recover from the initial blow of it, and time then to consider it. And she would not keep it for long, because she wouldn't want to get caught. But if Esther went to return it and there was no envelope, she would guess, having just seen Riddley here, that Riddley was the one who had hidden the envelope, or at least that Riddley had found it, and put it somewhere else. Riddley imagined them looking at each other later and knowing full well what the other had seen. But Riddley could not imagine what she herself, much less Esther, might ever say.

Only after Esther had disappeared into the house did it occur to Riddley that she should have smiled. She needed to act quickly, in case Esther came over to tidy up, or to see what Riddley was doing, or on the slight chance that she already knew. But how could she know? Unless Riddley had just now, in a single glance, given herself away.

Riddley put the postcards back in the envelope and returned it to its place. She would go into the kitchen and talk to Esther, taking

care to act like nothing was different or wrong. Then she would make herself scarce the rest of the morning, head to the woods or Carver's garden, to Hayden's or down to the dock, to check the crab trap again, and swim. Or maybe Sam would take her skiing. Any of these activities would give Esther a chance to put the missing post-card back before Pauline and Adele returned. And in the meantime, Riddley would consider what she could no longer avoid considering: just what to do about the postcards, now that she was no longer the only living person, or the only one she knew of, who knew of their existence.

*   *   *

Esther was never sure, all the long way until her own death, what had made her take the envelope out from what was plainly a hiding place, and empty the contents on the bureau top. She was not the prying type. She had her pride over that. Likewise she always took great care to put objects exactly back when she dusted, and to leave money untouched, rimmed by dust. That way they could never shame her by suspecting her of taking anything that was theirs.

She knew those who took things that they thought would not be missed, and looked at whatever they could, wherever they ought not to, and made too much of what they had seen. It was easy to be scornful, to judge others and leave yourself out of the judgment. She was not the one to do the judging. There was plenty of time ahead for that. *Judge not lest ye be judged.* Her husband Cole said he might well be damned for it, but damned if he wouldn't judge.

Not that you needed to pry, really. Nothing like cleaning up some-body's mess, taking out their garbage, sweeping under their furniture, wiping the stains off their tables and floors and walls, washing their clothes, not to mention their smalls, their sheets—if that didn't show you who somebody was, then nothing did.

But still she had been shocked when she found these. She shouldn't have been, she thought later, what with those paintings they had on the wall of slave women with baskets on their heads, and the old soap advertisement they'd framed, of the boy washing off his

blackness. And how Cole, steaming oysters at a roast, had heard Mr. Cross telling what amounted to nigger jokes, though he hadn't used the word itself. But nonetheless she had been shocked.

Maybe the shock came from seeing a picture of something she had long heard about, but never seen. She had always thought that seeing suffering in the flesh was the worst. Days and decades later, she wondered if that was so. In ways these photographs were worse. For everything was already over and done. There was no understanding possible, and certainly no forgiveness. The how and why of the wrongs done, and the ways such wrongs had been fought, and repeated, and fought again. Not to mention, who took their poor bodies down, and cleaned and buried them, who mourned and remembered them, and who remembered them still, to this very day, for someone did remember them, didn't they? But all of that was missing from those photos. There was only suffering and hate, and the kind of calm that comes after violence has been done.

At least when she remembered the policeman in Daffin Park, his nightstick raised over the girl on the swings—no older than the girl in the postcard, who was, Lord forgive her, smiling—at least she could think also of those fine brave young people gathered in the square for the voting, and at Tybee to open the beaches, and downtown when the boycott started, and marching in the streets those summer nights, many with candles in their hands, some singing, with voices so steady and strong. And when they fell silent, that silence was full and ringing of that same strength, as during a service, during the pause between song and word, though there, in the street, they were surrounded by dogs, by police, by others standing around watching. You could tell just from the way those white folks stood there, their bodies slanting forward like children eager for sweets, that they were hoping for blood, for screams, for black people crying to them again for mercy, which they would not give.

Nor was she sure why she took the one postcard home, to show Cole. She could have guessed how he would react. Maybe it was just that she couldn't stand to be the only one to have seen it. She could have described it to him, put words to that picture, but that seemed

worse, as if to do so would make it more real. And besides, she didn't think she could. Maybe that was why she had chosen that particular one. It seemed the hardest to describe. She would choke on the words that would describe what she had seen. And she couldn't not tell. So she brought one for him to see for himself. He had barely said a word, except to inquire how she'd gotten it. Then he had looked and looked at that picture until she had gone on to bed. Neither of them had slept well. They lay side by side in the dark hot room, not giving each other any comfort.

The next morning, after the boys had gone out, he told her he wanted to keep the postcard. "We should be able to show our children and grandchildren and great-grandchildren, or send it to some university or museum up North. Black folks need to know these things."

"Everybody knows these things already."

"Some don't, young ones especially, or some've forgotten. And nobody," he said, leaning toward her, "should be allowed to forget this. But even if people know or haven't forgotten they still need to see it."

"Why shouldn't we be allowed to forget?"

He picked the postcard up and looked at it, then back at her. "It's evidence, Es."

She rose from her chair and gathered their plates. "We don't need evidence. We got more evidence than we know what to do with. What good can any more do us?"

"You can't have too much evidence."

"I won't take from them."

"This doesn't belong to them." He dropped the postcard on the table.

She saw that he had already given up. Still they had to finish it. "I can't lose this job, Cole. They're not bad folks. They treat me fine. And Donald has to get eyeglasses, and Marcus has a tooth needs taking out." She stopped, knowing she was only making it worse, going into all they didn't have, all they needed, all that Cole could not provide. "I won't steal. I won't give them reason to mistrust me."

He laughed, a humorless grunt of a laugh. "Don't tell me you think they don't already."

That night she slept badly again, stunned by the risk she had taken. She would return it first thing. But what if she had already been caught? She would be fired, and word would spread to the Wilcoxes' as well. She'd be let go without references, which in these times meant it would be almost impossible to get work in anyone else's house. And where would that leave her? In some laundry or restaurant kitchen, and she was just too old for that. If, at her age, she could get work at all.

This morning she had her blood pressure check, and it was high. It was no wonder, with the postcard boring a hole in her purse. In the driveway, Esther felt someone watching her from the garage apartment. She was certain she'd been found out, until she looked up and saw it was only Riddley. After Riddley had gone down on the dock, and Esther checked that Mr. Cross was still occupied, she went to the laundry room for her purse. She was about to head over to the apartment, but then she thought that, should Mrs. Cross and her mother come back early, or should Mr. Cross spot her, she would look suspicious with her purse over her arm. They would only suspect her of taking something, not of returning it. She slipped the postcard out of her purse and into her uniform pocket, the picture side facing her body, in case it should be visible through the thin cotton. For an instant she saw the picture imprinted on her hip like the negative of a photograph, so that the sky, and the hands and faces of the white men were dark, far darker than her own skin, and the men's suits, the tree trunks, and the hung man's blackened body were all a glaring white, like scars.

Once inside the apartment Esther, just to make sure, called out, "Ma'am? You here? It's just Esther, come to clean." She headed up the stairs, declining to use what Mr. Cross once referred to as *Dad's electric chair.*

In the old man's room, she bent down and opened the bottom drawer. She felt behind the napkins and tablecloths and pulled the envelope out. She slid the postcard into its place, then put the envelope back and closed the drawer. Dizziness flooded her as she stood. She grabbed the edge of the bureau with both hands so as not to fall. Dark crowded in at the edges of her vision.

When she was steady again, she took her hand away. The marks of her fingers stood out on the gleaming surface. She spit lightly on her fingertips and rubbed her prints out. The smear would vanish when it dried. The smell of the furniture polish rose up, too sweet, a little sickening, from her hands.

When Esther had first found the postcards two days earlier, she had felt a powerful urge to pray, and she had done so. That was something she would not be able to do again with true concentration or feeling for the one day and two nights that postcard spent under her roof. The picture seemed to be mocking her for her faith, for her desire to forgive, to hope, to not be afraid for her boys or Cole or herself.

But now, with the postcards put away and the dizziness gone, Esther got on her knees. In the midst of all that furniture, she clasped her hands and closed her eyes. Her mind still seemed infinitely far from prayer. There on her knees all she could think of was that man kneeling, in what at first might, if not for the rope, have resembled prayer. And he was dressed in a suit and tie, in what must have been his church clothes. Had they done that to a man on his way to church, or returning home afterward? The shame of it. The palms of his hands were bound together before him, the fingers pointing not to heaven but to the bare and sandy ground. And Lord how he must have prayed, she thought, though that would not have been how he came to be on his knees. Had he pleaded with them for his life, or had they wanted him to but he wouldn't? Cole would not have. They could have done anything at all to him and he would not have given them that satisfaction. Donald and Marcus, though, would not have been able to hold out for long.

The thought of her sons brought her to her feet. God would forgive her for not kneeling. He'd still hear her. She stood there, her hands open at her sides. She would wait all day if need be. Prayers would come. They had to come. And after a while, they did.

PART THREE

CHAPTER 13

Summertime

s long as Riddley obtained the approval of either Pauline or Sam, she was now allowed to swim solo off their dock, and go a greater distance alone in the bateau, in whichever direction that, should her craft capsize or the motor fail to catch, she would not be swept out to sea. Hence on an incoming tide she could go downriver as far as the power lines, and upriver, on an outgoing, as far as Cougar Island. Both destinations were for the most part visible to Pauline, standing on the edge of the bluff with one hand shading her eyes, though much too far for Riddley to hear her call, and far enough for Riddley not to notice if, a storm approaching or dark descending, Pauline tried to wave her in.

Riddley had earned these privileges because she had endured two weeks of rigorous swimming lessons. Pauline said that only if Riddley passed the Advanced Course, *and with flying colors, mind you,* could she swim off their own dock alone and unsupervised, and extend her boating boundaries. Such liberties did not, however, include the shedding of her life jacket. That she was doomed to wear until at least age ten, except with special permission.

A few times while swimming Riddley had thought she'd seen the horses and the slaves, though she was never as sure as she had been when she'd seen the slaves underwater the previous summer. Such a glimpse could come at any time, but it was most likely to occur in early evening, when she went down on the dock with Sam and Pauline, and usually also Adele. The magnanimity brought on by cocktails meant they often let her swim without a life jacket. Thus she expended less effort and air and could go deeper, and remain down longer.

She would take a running start down the ramp and dive at a diagonal toward the bottom and center of the river. She swam as hard as she could, and as her momentum slowed and the buoyancy began to push her toward the surface, she opened her eyes. Then she

sometimes saw, farther out at the deepest part, what looked to be a horse tossing its head, tapping the ground with its hoof, or the throat of a person looking up, and a row of dark bare legs, chains glinting. But before she could get close enough to be sure, she had to come up for air. She might go down again right after a gulp of breath, but she could never get as deep without the force of a dive. By then the water seemed already dimmer, the light at that time of day fading quickly. When she surfaced again, the tide would have pulled her halfway to the neighbor's dock, and Pauline would call to her to come on in, that dark was coming on. *And the sharks are in search of supper,* Sam would add.

As for the postcards, they came to her occasionally at night, though still she did not remember those dreams. She knew because the postcards would be her first thought upon waking. She would lie there in the dawn light, contemplating what she ought to do. When she visited Miss Byrd, as she had promised to do, perhaps she ought to seek her advice. Or she could ask Hayden what he would do in her situation. Or there were always the options of mailing the postcards anonymously to UGA or the Georgia Historical Society, or surrendering them to Pauline, or destroying them. But after much consideration, Riddley felt no closer to any decision. Contrary to her expectations, seeing all of the postcards had hardly clarified what action she should take. Her options seemed, instead, to be multiplying.

She watched Esther for any change, any veiled references to the postcards, but she detected none. The missing postcard had been returned, though it had been a week before Riddley had been able to check. That lapse in time meant Riddley was less sure it was Esther who had taken it, though she couldn't imagine who else it might have been.

Mostly now the postcards came to Riddley in the daytime. She would be out in the yard or woods or Carver's garden, or puttering in the bateau alongside the bluff or Cougar Island, and out of the corner of her eye she would see something dangling in a tree, a shape that could only be a person, or the remains of one. Sometimes she turned quickly, the way you do to catch someone staring at you, before he or she can look away, and at other times she turned very slowly, as

when you don't want to startle a wild animal. Turning to face whatever it was, she would see that it was not what she had thought, that she was, yet again, mistaken. And oh, for once, how glad she was of that. Never had she been so delighted by the sight of a branch, bent over and partially broken, or a thick tangle of Spanish moss or twisted wisteria, or an empty paper bag, lifted by the wind and snagged in tree limbs.

Yet she also wondered if there really had been something there before she turned, something that had altered in the instant before she faced it. Because sometimes, the tree was empty. There was nothing there that it could have been, nothing that would explain what she'd seen.

* * *

Numerous times a day, Pauline sent Riddley next door to check on Adele. *Just pop your head in to see if Grandmother needs anything,* Pauline would say, which really meant, to see if she was still there. Pauline checked on her about every hour, or she had Riddley or Esther or occasionally Sam do so. Before Charlotte and Emmeline went to camp, they had also taken turns. Such frequent visits, Pauline hoped, meant that if Adele wandered off, she wouldn't get far. Also that she wouldn't, as Pauline put it, *soil herself.* Pauline or Esther took Adele to the bathroom far more often than she could possibly need to go.

In the first days after Adele moved there, she had barely budged. Even her fidgeting had largely abated, though she did from time to time still worry a charm on her charm bracelet, or pick at the fabric of a chair arm or sleeve. But over the last week, she had wandered off regularly. She made no attempt to sneak out. Sometimes she forgot to shut the door behind her. All measures were taken to prevent Sam from finding that out. *Run go get the door before your father sees,* Pauline would whisper to Riddley, who wondered what might happen if he did. Would he say his mother-in-law couldn't have air conditioning, couldn't go out, couldn't live there at all?

There goes Mother, Pauline would say when she spotted Adele heading off. Sometimes Pauline would call for Riddley to follow her. If, as was often the case, Riddley was not around, Pauline put aside

whatever she was doing and took off after her. Pauline felt peculiar, following her own mother, as if she were trying to catch her at something. Pauline would call out, *Wait Mother, wait, it's Pauline.* Such entreaties failed to slow Adele down. Once Pauline had called out, *Miss Glynn, Miss Glynn,* and Adele had come to a full stop. Then she had taken off again, faster than before.

When Pauline caught up, she would walk alongside a little while, until she could coax or bribe her mother into coming back. Pauline would sit her down in the sunroom or breakfast room with a pack of cards or, if that didn't seem to be working, a snack and the television. When Pauline worked in the yard, she sat Adele in a lawn chair in the shade.

But Adele was less and less inclined to sit for hours where Pauline put her. And, despite Pauline's precautions, every once in a while Adele got away from them, though she had not gone far. She tended to go back and forth, back and forth, the way she had paced inside her house. She walked up and down their driveway, or Belleview Avenue or Ashburn Street, again and again. Likewise, she had the same few destinations: the bateau, Isabel's broken-down car, the wooden bench beside the vegetable garden, or the stone one on the bluff.

Pauline worried that one day Adele would not turn back at the end of the driveway or road, or would not be content to sit once she reached the car or boat or bench. What if she got lost, or went too far for them to find her before something happened? But Pauline didn't know what she could do, short of restraining her. *She's too much for just you,* Sam had said, though he'd said as well that they should wait as long as they could to hire someone, for Adele could, as he put it, *last for years,* which made Pauline feel as if they were discussing an appliance.

As yet, Adele had not gone anywhere at night. Pauline had heard stories of caretakers putting sleeping pills in the food of their charges, to keep them from night wandering. She had heard, too, of the same thing done to keep people immobile in the daytime. Stories such as these, as well as Adele's lost rings, not to mention the finances of the situation, made Pauline averse to hiring anyone to help. Why should Pauline need anyone else, now that Adele was right next door, and

Pauline, for the summer anyway, had only one of her children to look after? Frazier had done it alone, all those years. *And look what happened to him,* she thought, before she could stop herself.

Pauline arranged to have Esther come longer hours on Mondays and Thursdays, and every other Wednesday, and every Saturday instead of every other. Esther was not put off by Adele's silence, or by worries over what Adele could and couldn't understand. Esther just did what needed to be done, and with a gentle firmness that Pauline could never quite manage. Adele was, in general, less refractory with Esther, and often seemed quite attached to her, as much as she had been to anyone since Frazier. She put up little or no resistance to Esther's ministrations, and seemed, at times, almost grateful, which she never was with Pauline.

Esther was the only one now who could, in terms of all the necessary undergarments, get Adele properly dressed for a trip to town, or when one of her old friends made a rare visit. But for the most part, comfort had roundly defeated appearances in the battle for precedence. Indeed, appearances, or the concern for them, seemed to have been routed altogether. Pauline was surprised at how rapidly she was willing to let her mother give up such standards as a daily bath, lipstick, slip, girdle, stockings, spotless clothes, even matching clothes, for on those occasions that Adele showed any interest in dressing herself, Pauline did not wish to discourage her, except when, say, Adele selected a floral shirt to accompany a plaid skirt, a combination that might suggest neglect.

Part of the reason she'd wanted to move her mother next door, and part of the case she had made to Sam, had been that Pauline might, through close observation, slow Adele's deterioration. But Pauline now believed that her mother's decline had its own set speed, though Adele did seem less erratic here, less inclined to become enraged or inconsolable. Pauline wondered if that was because there was little now to remind Adele of her former life, and her former self, a kind of blankness that Pauline would never have guessed would be comforting.

* * *

Riddley rapped on the garage apartment's door before entering. As when Ray and Isabel lived there, the living room was thick with smoke. Adele sat in the middle of the sofa, holding the gravy boat from her china set. Within it was a pile of cigarettes, some still smoldering. Both Adele and Frazier used to smoke, but together they had quit after his first heart attack fifteen years earlier. In Adele's lap was a pack of Salems, the brand Sam and Isabel smoked. Maybe Adele had found an old pack in the apartment, or in Isabel's glove compartment.

Adele's head rested against the sofa, her eyes half-closed. She did not resist when Riddley took her makeshift ashtray and emptied it into the toilet. Riddley opened the windows, turned on the fan above the stove, and sprayed air freshener. She stashed the cigarettes and matches in the back of a drawer. She washed the gravy boat, put it in the dish drain, closed the windows and left. To Pauline, Riddley reported that Adele was sleeping. What good would it do to tell? Pauline would find out soon enough.

Most of Riddley's days were spent crabbing, usually with Hayden. They had made signs on white poster board.

CRABS—**Live!! Or Boiled!!**
$1 a Dozen! Caught *Today!*
Call 355-2255 to Place Your Order!!!

Carver had drawn a crab in each corner. Her payment had been one crab boiled and delivered for each crab drawn. It had been Hayden's idea to ask her. Both he and Riddley had been surprised at how willingly Carver had obliged. Most of the crabs were in a fighting posture, claws raised and open, as if they had been backed into the corner of the sign, or, more precisely, had perished there, for their color indicated that they were already dead. They were the orange-red that blue crabs turn after boiling.

Riddley and Hayden had posted the signs along all the nearby roads. They had call-in orders and standing orders, and far more than they could ever fill. They delivered to houses within biking range. Occasionally customers wanted them live, which was easier, as long

as Riddley or Hayden remembered to change the water in which the crabs were held, so that they did not expire prematurely.

They had a trap on each of their docks, but their best luck tended to be with lines and nets rather than traps. Almost daily, weather and grown-ups permitting, they went out either in Hayden's canoe or, most often, Riddley's bateau, carrying thermoses of ice water and sweet tea, and bags of pretzels, cookies, and sandwiches. They frequented the creeks around the bend, and the shallows and eddies around Cougar Island and Oak Island.

Many a morning Riddley pulled on her bathing suit and sneakers not long after sunrise. This morning, eager to see what she'd caught in the trap overnight, she carried her toast down to the dock. She strapped on her damp life jacket and went down the steep ramp to the floating dock. The water drained out in a rush as she pulled up the trap.

Pauline appeared on the bluff. "Have you seen Grandmother?" she called.

Riddley shook her head and Pauline walked back toward the house. In the trap, more than a dozen crabs hissed and blew bubbles, walking backward up and over one another, snapping their claws, sticking the tips through the holes.

Riddley ran up the ramp and banged on the dockhouse door to scare off any water rats. She opened it and there was Adele, perched atop the overturned crab bucket. It reeked of rat droppings and roach poison and bits of sea life dried to hooks and nets. There was also the smell of urine, for nailed to the wall, only a few inches from Adele's left shoulder, was Sam's homemade urinal: an upside down plastic milk jug with the bottom cut off, its mouth attached to an old hose which emptied into the mud below.

Adele smiled at Riddley in a way she never had before. It was a cocktail party smile, a smile never bestowed on children.

"Morning, Grandmother. I'll just let Mama know you're down here. She's looking for you."

Riddley found Pauline by Isabel's old car. "Grandmother's in the dockhouse."

"The dockhouse?" Pauline wrinkled her nose. She looked toward the dock, then at her watch. "Goodness, I have to run. I'm due downtown. I won't be gone long. I'll send Esther down to get her."

"She can stay with me."

Pauline studied her a moment.

"I won't let anything happen to her. I'm good with her. You know I am."

"Yes, you are. And she's good with you. Certainly better than with me. Me she's determined to thwart whenever possible." She gave a grim smile. "Just desserts, no doubt. Remember that later. All right, she can stay with you, but not for more than an hour. Esther's there if you need her. You take good care of her, now, promise?"

Riddley nodded. "Promise."

Adele was sitting exactly as Riddley had left her. "Mama said you can stay on the dock a while. I'll take you back up to the house in a bit."

Adele stared, her smile entirely gone.

"I just pulled up the crab trap. I got a bunch last night." Riddley pointed at Adele's stool. "That's the bucket I usually put them in."

Adele's eyes shifted, watching something over Riddley's shoulder. Riddley fought the impulse to turn and see what was there.

"After I sort through the crabs, I'll put the bateau in."

Adele's gaze returned to Riddley. The bateau was one of Adele's haunts, as Pauline put it, and was thus one of the first places they checked if Adele was missing. She always sat in the bow, facing forward with her hands in her lap. Even if the bateau was on the dock, she would sit in it.

Adele's heavy charm bracelet, coveted by all her granddaughters, jingled as she brushed past Riddley and headed for the ramp. Riddley wondered if she should have her wear a life jacket. But surely her grandmother knew how to swim. Riddley could recall no incident, though, when she had seen her do so. Not that that meant she couldn't. Most ladies gave up swimming at a certain age, because they didn't care to be seen in a swimsuit, or the act itself was unseemly. That Adele had once been able to swim, however, was no guarantee

that she still could. She could have forgotten swimming just as she had, apparently, forgotten reading and speaking, though swimming seemed an even more impossible thing to forget how to do. It seemed in the same general category as sleeping, breathing, and dreaming, actions that Riddley had always believed would be harder not to do than to do. Nonetheless, just in case, she grabbed a yellow ski vest. She could, if need be, toss it to her as a life preserver.

Adele climbed into the bow. Riddley opened the trap's door. "I'm going to dump the crabs in the stern. Don't worry, they can't get up where you are." She hooked her fingers in the chicken wire, turned the trap over and shook it above the bateau. Half a dozen clattered to the bottom. They righted themselves at once and extended their open claws. She shook the trap again and again.

She would, as always, have to throw some back. With metal pincers, she removed the small and the female, and set them free on the dock. She liked to watch them figure out where the water was. It didn't take long. They moved sideways or backwards toward the nearest edge, as if to disguise where they were headed. When they were a few inches away, they made a break for it. Sometimes as they charged over the side their claws and legs flared out, in giddiness or panic at being suddenly aloft.

Riddley put the eight keepers into the bucket. With the bailer she scooped water onto them, so they'd stay alive until it was time to kill them. Then she offered a hand to Adele. "If you'll come out for a minute I'll put the bateau in." Adele stepped onto the dock. Riddley put the plug in, then slid the bateau into the water. She pulled it around to the outside of the dock, and held on while Adele took her place in the bow.

The bluff was empty. "Should we go for a little ride?" Riddley said, feeling a strong wish to please her. The motor caught on the third pull. As Riddley cast off and veered away from the dock, she knew, as she always knew such things without being told, that Pauline would disapprove. If, that is, she found out. But surely someone would see them out there. Neighbors were always talking about who and what they had seen, especially about each other's children. Esther might

see, but Riddley was not as worried about that, for Esther had never once told on Riddley. If Esther thought Riddley had done something wrong, Esther scolded her herself.

At the last dock, Riddley turned the bateau around. Adele continued to stare straight ahead. Riddley passed their dock, and then swung around again. Sam had taught her to always dock against the tide, for that way she, and not the current, would be doing the steering. They glided in, the bow lightly grazing the edge of the dock, bringing the stern close enough for her to grasp the corner 4x4 and stop their forward momentum. It was a perfect landing, the kind she was almost never able to execute when anyone, particularly Sam, was watching.

After that, Adele began to go down on the dock almost as often as Riddley. Along with Isabel's car and the downstairs sofa of the garage apartment, the dock came to be one of the only places where Adele could be counted on to remain for any length of time. Pauline had Sam set up a patio umbrella on the upper dock, so Adele wouldn't get so sunburnt. Adele, who had guarded her skin from darkening all those years, had acquired freckles along her cheekbones, and across the bridge of her peeling nose, for any hat Pauline put on her she hurled at once to the ground.

Riddley quickly got used to having Adele around. She suspected that Adele was hoping to go out again in the bateau, but Riddley figured she couldn't get away with that again for a while. Before Riddley went crabbing, she took Adele back up to the house. Often she could feel Adele's eyes on her as she walked back across the bluff, and Riddley turned and waved before she descended the stairs to the dock. Adele neither waved nor smiled, but Riddley did it just the same.

"Your father and I have been discussing," Pauline said in late June, "about how good you are with Grandmother, how much she likes to be down on the dock with you, how you're both such wanderers. We were thinking maybe you could look after her officially some of the time."

"Officially?" Riddley said, taking a bite of toast.

"You'd spend a bit of time with her each day. I thought start out with an hour or two and see how it goes. Just for those times when Esther or I are too busy. One of us would always be around, if you needed us, for taking her to the Ladies and such, but you'd be the one watching over her, to make sure she didn't go off by herself. And if she did want to walk, you could go with her. I wouldn't want y'all to go far, mind you, but you could go a little ways. And if you didn't like it, then you could quit."

"I wouldn't have as much time for crabbing."

"Not from the bateau, no. I wouldn't want you to take her out in the bateau." Pauline paused long enough for Riddley to wonder if she knew she already had. "But you could crab from the dock." Pauline paused again. "And of course I'd pay you."

"How much?"

"A dollar an hour." Pauline was well aware it was an extravagant sum to Riddley, one that would be very hard to refuse. "It would be a huge responsibility, the biggest you've ever had. You think about it. We can talk about it again in the next day or so."

Riddley accepted the job by supper, after which Pauline told Riddley what to do in the event of every imaginable disaster, from snakebite to rabid raccoon, twisted ankle to heat stroke. She talked as much as either of them could stand about signs that Adele might need to go to the toilet, though that was a task that would normally be taken care of by Pauline or Esther. She laid out all sorts of rules: no walking beyond the Jenkins house, no drinking of sweet tea or other diuretics, no eating of any foods on which Adele might easily choke, no swimming, no boating.

at RiddleyCarver had been in much greater evidence since the weather had turned hot. She was often seen swimming, or paddling by on her surfboard, or reading on her dock in the late afternoon, or cruising by, at all hours, in her speedboat. After dark, if a boat went by without running lights, chances were good it was Carver.

In May, Carver had let it be known that her bluff and backyard were now open for crossing, and her dock for landing, that the trespassing prohibition had been entirely revoked. This was not due to

any newfound love of her neighbors or their children, but because she wanted to be free to trespass herself, for her daily swim. If the tide was going out, she walked upriver along the bluff, then dove off the Glennings' or Waterfords' dock and swam back. If it was coming in, she dove off her own dock and swam upriver, then hauled herself onto the Kanes' dock and strolled home in her modest one-piece. The sight of Carver passing by soon came to be as ordinary as the surfacing of the porpoises, and, to Riddley and Hayden, nearly as pleasing.

They worried though that others might invade what they now considered their territory. There was, however, hardly a flood of intruders. Carver's property was so overgrown it was hard to get through, unless you knew where the paths were. And those who did go there did not linger. The spell of the place had worn off by then, or so most of them thought.

Riddley and Hayden grew bolder, though not as bold as they'd been when the house was unoccupied. They quickly got a sense of Carver's habits, and of Mattie's, the maid who came every Thursday. They took turns standing guard in the high branches of the magnolia along the driveway. The doors were left unlocked, as doors around there always were, but though they longed to, they dared not venture inside. They peered through screens and windows, down halls and through doorways.

Rarely did these investigations satisfy Riddley. Something seemed to be lacking. Only when they were almost caught did Riddley realize that what was missing was Carver. The wind being hard out of the east, Riddley, the lookout, had not heard Carver turn into the driveway. Riddley gave the signal just as Carver's car came into sight around the curve. Hayden jumped into the side hedge while Riddley remained aloft, for the drawback of the lookout tree was that a person descending the trunk could easily be spotted from the kitchen, where Carver soon stood smoking and staring out the window, then preparing and eating and cleaning up her lunch. Everything that Carver did that day Riddley had seen done many times before, but the clandestine watching of such mundane tasks made the tasks themselves seem extraordinary.

Shortly after Carver had moved back last summer, Riddley and Hayden had snuck into the carriage house. This was before Carver took to painting there, and keeping it locked. Propped against the back wall were two huge canvases, populated by larger than life figures, whose hands appeared, even for people of such size, nearly too long and heavy to raise. Their faces also looked elongated, dragged down by the weight of some great burden. *Hard to picture on the living room wall,* Riddley could almost hear Pauline say, as she had once in a museum in Washington, of a painting of ants and melting clocks. And it was true. Carver's pictures were certainly not what anyone would call beautiful. They were in fact quite disturbing to look at, which didn't necessarily mean you didn't want to look at them, or that Riddley didn't, anyway.

Recently, Riddley and Hayden had been spying on Carver at the carriage house, where she spent almost every day painting. They tried to time their observations for her mid-morning or early afternoon break by the pool. They had to be in hiding before she emerged. She would pace back and forth the length of the pool, cigarette in hand, or sit and smoke in one of the many rusted lounge chairs. Occasionally she talked to herself, in a voice too low to understand.

Once they had used binoculars to watch Carver while she painted. She had stood for long periods, looking at the canvas from a few feet away. Every now and then she approached it, and then stepped back again. Riddley had been riveted, though not in a way she cared to repeat. Watching Carver in her kitchen or beside her pool, even that one time Riddley had glimpsed her sunbathing topless, Riddley had not felt particularly ill at ease, or not more than one would expect to feel, spying. But what Riddley had felt while watching Carver inside the carriage house was sharper than the customary twinge of deliberate wrongdoing. It was hard to forgive yourself for something you knew you wouldn't be forgiven for. There was something extremely private about Carver painting, more so even than her nakedness. Riddley knew that Carver would also feel that way. Nor would Riddley have put some kind of revenge past her. Carver would not forgo anger for the sake of politeness or neighborliness or kin, nor because they were children.

Every once in a while, it felt to Riddley that it was Carver who was spying on her, on them. Riddley would be on the dock, in the bateau, on Cougar or Oak Island, crabbing up one of the nameless creeks, alone or with Hayden, and she would turn around and there would be Carver, on her surfboard or dock, watching. Nor did Carver immediately look away, as Riddley did whenever she got caught staring. Carver seemed to want Riddley to know that she had been, and was still, watching. Or sometimes Riddley would turn and see her, and though Carver would not be looking at her at the instant Riddley turned, the feeling Riddley had was that, just before, she had been. How long had she been watching, and why would she want to? Riddley and Hayden could think of no reason, beyond those of parents or teachers, why an adult would be interested in watching a child. Unless she knew they had been watching her.

Now, within the overgrown bushes and weeds, Riddley and Hayden crouched side by side. Carver was some thirty feet away, sprawled in an orange and yellow recliner. A twig snapped behind where they hid, and Carver sat up and looked in their direction. She formed an O with her lips and a thick smoke ring sailed forward. She blew another, and another, and these lined up behind the first. Before they dispersed, Carver blew smoke through all their centers. She picked up a pine cone and hurled it, as hard as she could, into the pool.

Carver apparently preferred, like Riddley, to swim in the river, for she had never had the pool cleaned and patched. Whether it was capable of repair was doubtful. It had not been filled for nearly a quarter century. In it stood an inch or so of tea-colored rainwater, along with leaves, sticks, pine cones, acorns, and the bodies and bones of numerous animals. Those who fell into the deep end usually ran back and forth along the wall below the diving boards until they collapsed, or clawed themselves to exhaustion trying to scale the tiles. Only those who walked in could be relied upon to walk out, the method of departure apparently being determined by the one of arrival.

The steep incline from the deep to the shallow end could, from below the diving boards, seem more like a wall than a slope. Riddley knew this from when, two winters before, she had been held prisoner

there during a game of War. Carver too knew this perspective because, the morning twenty-four years earlier that her mother died, Carver had jumped into the full pool and held herself under by gripping the bottom rung of the ladder. She'd stayed there as long as she could, her ears aching, the raw rims of her eyes stinging. By a couple of weeks after the funeral, much of the water had drained out through the many cracks, as if it no longer wished to remain if Evelyn was gone. Reed had seen no reason to keep having it topped up. He had only done so those last months under the pretense that one day Evelyn would again wish, and be able, to swim.

Before it became too much to do more than rest, Evelyn had spent hours in the pool, just as some years earlier, before she became too weak for the tide, she had swum daily in the river. In the year before she died, she became convinced that the river itself was what had made her sick. She said it was from all the poisons the factories poured into the water. There had been some uncomfortable moments at oyster roasts and cocktail parties, when Evelyn had started ranting about the paper mill or sugar refinery and not ten feet away was somebody on the board of that company, or the wife of somebody who was.

Reed had told her those factories were on entirely different rivers, which dumped out into the ocean miles up the coast. She countered that the pollution came up their river when the tide came in. On the rare day that the wind brought the stench of the paper plant with it, Evelyn would look at him pointedly. As if water, he'd thought, could carry the same things as wind. But by then, Reed wouldn't argue with her anymore, a permanent truce that, he realized years later, must have convinced her she was indeed dying. At a certain point Evelyn had not only refused to swim in the river, she had also forbidden Carver to do so. Carver had just swum off someone else's dock. In one of Evelyn's more lucid moments toward the end, she had sniffed at Carver's neck and hair and begged her to keep out of the river.

Not long after her mother died, Carver had touched the swelling knots of her own breasts and known that her mother had been right about the river, and that she, Carver, would die that same horrible death, because she had failed not only to obey her mother but to believe her. Carver's friend had said she didn't see how you could get

breast cancer before you had any breasts. Even after she had them, they seemed far too small for a tumor to hide in. Nonetheless, she stayed out of the river for some two years. After Reed's death, Carver discovered that for decades her family had been major shareholders in many of those very companies that Evelyn believed had killed her. But money was Reed's business. Evelyn had taken care of other things. Against the advice of her broker, Carver sold that stock. It had seemed, after all those years, the least she could do.

Carver swung her legs now to one side of the lounge chair and stood. She walked along the edge of the pool, toward the river. At the corner she paused, facing the hedge where Riddley and Hayden hid. She flicked her cigarette toward the pool's center. It hissed when it hit the muck. She strode back toward the carriage house, grabbed a baseball cap from a nail outside the door and crammed it on her head. She took the path toward the main house.

Riddley and Hayden shifted their legs, the leaves beneath them loud after the silence. "You think she saw us?" Riddley whispered.

"You never can tell with her. She might not've seen us but could've guessed we're here."

Riddley nodded. Carver seemed a person likely to not only have a good deal of knowledge apart from sight, but also, unlike most people, to trust such knowledge.

The pale yellow floor-length curtains, pushed to one end of the sliding glass doors, rippled at the open screen. Unlike at the main house, Carver never left the carriage house curtains open or the door unlocked when she was not there. "She's probably just fetching something from the house," Riddley surmised.

"Why the hat then?"

Carver's car door slammed. The engine revved. Oyster shells in the driveway ricocheted as she sped out. "Maybe she's out of cigarettes."

"Whatever she's doing, we don't have much time," Hayden said. They made their way out of their hiding place. They paused at the open door.

"Maybe it's a trap," Riddley said.

"Why would she care about us? We're kids."

"But if she knows somebody's been spying on her—"

"If it is a trap, we'll hear her when she comes back."

"Unless she drove out to make us think we're safe, and she'll walk back." Riddley glanced behind her. Carver seemed quite capable of covering large distances, rapidly and stealthily. "Should we have a lookout?"

"There's not enough time. We may never get another chance like this." He slid the screen farther open and stepped in. Riddley was right behind him. They stood in the doorway, getting their bearings, waiting for their eyes to adjust. It looked quite different from the time a year earlier. Nor had looking in from the outside really given them a sense of what it was like. Carver's privacy here must have extended to Mattie, for no one had cleaned in a good while. On the kitchen counters and table were glasses, ashtrays, tubes of paint, brushes of different sizes, a jug of turpentine, jars in which paint had been mixed, jars from which jutted clean brushes. Two rotating fans, left on high, moved the air through the room, but still it was hot and stuffy and smelled strongly of paint and smoke.

Tacked to the opposite wall were some thirty or forty squares, on which were dashes and swirls of paint, in many different colors. As far as Riddley could tell, none of these squares was a picture of anything. Propped against and facing the south wall were two stacks of paintings. The bleak figures Riddley and Hayden had seen before could not have been among them, as these paintings were much smaller.

The canvas on the easel was blank, so they went to the paintings against the wall. They each took a stack. Riddley flipped the first one back. It was of a man, with glasses and curly dark hair. He was handsome and very serious, perhaps to the point of anger.

The next painting was a landscape, though it was hard to tell exactly of what. Certainly it was of no land around here. There were huge boulders, in all varieties of gray. Some of the surfaces were almost shiny, as if it had recently rained. The longer she looked at it, the less the painting seemed to be a landscape. What she had thought were rocks did not look heavy enough to be rocks, and nor did they appear to be touching each other, or what she'd assumed was the ground. The next canvas, bigger than the first two, and very dark, was of a forest, though the trees were not the right colors. There was

not a green or a brown among them. They were blues and maroons and blacks, with mustard and lavender in places. The trees looked to be very old live oaks, the branches knotted and twisting. After looking at them a moment, they began to resemble figures, contorted or possibly dancing.

The next painting was of Carver's house. The picture was from an odd angle, and distorted, the entire house visible but as if seen through some kind of lens, so that it bulged and lengthened in a way a real house would not have. In the forefront, and out of scale from the rest of the picture, was a young lady in a hoop-skirted white dress and a wide-brimmed, beribboned hat. She was looking up, her white-gloved hands framing her cheeks and her mouth wide open, in what looked to be a cry. In the corner was written "Belle, 1853, 1953," and below that, "1965." In the far corner, in a place that should have been marsh and river, was a road, on which drove a yellow convertible.

As Riddley was about to flip to the last one, a car turned into the driveway. Riddley and Hayden slammed the paintings back against the wall, harder than they had intended. They almost knocked the easel over in their bolt for the door, and scratched their arms and legs up as they barreled through the hedge. They were far down the bluff by the time Carver entered the carriage house, carrying a large cup of sweet tea and a carton of Camels.

*　　*　　*

Adele kept her distance, and her quiet. She could be very quiet. She had followed the children through the woods, ducking under branches and through looped vines and crossed trunks. She stood, then crouched, as they did, in the bushes, as she also had as a child, hiding just to hide, for the pleasure of being hidden, or for Hide and Seek. The leaves and branches were thick around her, insects at her ankles, crawling up her calves, buzzing in her ears. She let them have her. Later she would scratch herself until her nails were wedged with blood and hair and skin.

Riddley and Hayden didn't feel her steady gaze upon them. When you are watching someone, it can be difficult to detect that you are

also being watched. Or you can dismiss that sensation as a mere result of the fact that you are watching another.

When they went into the carriage house, Adele stayed where she was, where she would be found by Esther a short while later. You couldn't have said she was waiting for them. She had, for all intents and purposes, forgotten about them. But it was not about *forget* or *remember*. Rather she was guided by the urge to move, or the urge to be still.

A while later, they came out running. They passed within a dozen yards of Adele but didn't notice her, where she sat on the other side of a water oak, her back to the trunk. Nor did she notice them. By then she was already asleep, and dreaming, for she did and would, all the way until the end, still dream.

CHAPTER 14

Carver

ometimes Riddley would be crabbing from the dock or bateau, or exploring the garden or woods with Hayden, climbing a tree or swimming, and she would be struck with a great need to look again at the postcards, to ascertain whether that one with the girl does indeed take place on a bluff, or if she could with a magnifying glass read the warning sign nailed to the trunk. She would get to the garage apartment as soon as she could, and there on the doorstep as she knocked, or inside under Adele's gaze, Riddley would be daunted. She would go ahead on in and sit with Adele, but Adele always looked as if she knew exactly why Riddley had come. How was it possible, Riddley wondered, for Adele to look as if she knew everything and nothing at one and the same time?

Riddley had found it very easy to look after Adele. They usually spent a few hours together in the morning. Adele would sit in the docked or moored bateau while Riddley crabbed and swam. Riddley and Hayden had also taken her to Carver's garden, and through the woods to the marsh. She was willing to go wherever they might lead, a willingness she never demonstrated with Pauline. Sometimes Riddley read in the garage apartment while Pauline ran errands. Adele often held her hand while Riddley sat beside her, or when they took a walk. Every once in a while Adele smiled at her.

Riddley tried to figure out when the postcards might have been taken. At the library she found histories of clothing and cars. Nothing decisive came of it, except that she thought now that the postcards were not nearly as old as she had initially believed. This impression was further confirmed when she looked up Smythe's Photo Shop in the phone book. It had altered from *Shop* to *Shoppe,* and had five branches, including the southside one that Riddley had been to with Pauline. The downtown address was the same as on the postcard. The

advertisement in the yellow pages said, *Serving all your photo needs for over 65 Years.*

One morning it occurred to Riddley she ought to try a different tack. She was surprised she hadn't thought of it before. Later that day, in the garage apartment, she went upstairs to the bureau. She slid open the heavy drawer and took out the envelope, which was just as she had left it. She went downstairs and sat next to Adele on the sofa.

"Grandmother, I have something to show you." Riddley placed the postcards in Adele's hand. "These belonged to Grandfather. To Frazier." It was the first time Riddley had ever referred to him, out loud, by his given name.

Adele looked around the room expectantly. "Here," Riddley said, pointing to Adele's hand. Adele, as if setting up solitaire, laid the postcards one after another on the coffee table. When she came to the one with the girl, she held it up a few inches from her face. For an instant she looked stricken.

"Grandmother," Riddley whispered, not wishing to break whatever spell Adele was under, "have you seen this before?"

Adele, frowning, looked at Riddley and said, in a voice hoarse from disuse, "Riddley." She lowered the postcard to her lap.

Riddley had expected, at most, a nod or a shake of the head. Why would Adele say her name, especially after such a long time without speaking? Perhaps Adele meant to scold or shame her. Adults often supposed that to speak your name would remind you of who you were, and thus, of how you should behave. But though Adele had frowned, she hadn't sounded as if she were reprimanding her. Maybe she was simply letting Riddley know that she knew exactly who she, Riddley, was.

"Yes, Grandmother," Riddley said, picking up the postcards, "it's me, Riddley."

*   *   *

Hayden's mother wanted him back. This happened from time to time. He was, after all, her baby. There was no telling how long until she would tire of looking after him and send him back to his grandmother's. *Just for a couple weeks, three at the most* he'd told Riddley. *Three*

weeks! Riddley had repeated, as if it were a prison term. *Well,* she added, *the crabs'll be glad.* Hayden looked at the ground. He wanted to go, Riddley saw. Who could blame him? But she wished he had a mother like everyone else's.

* * *

Carver walked up to the main house from the studio, where she had been since rising at eight. She had taken her usual breaks out by the pool, when she couldn't stand to be in front of the canvas anymore. According to the heat and sun, it was now mid-afternoon, coming onto three o'clock, she reckoned. She didn't keep a clock in the studio or wear a watch, lest, when it was going badly, she strike bargains with herself about how much longer she had to stay in there, or lest she get discouraged over how quickly she felt tired or distracted or in need of a drink, and how long she had to go before she would allow herself to have one. She'd have made a good alcoholic. It was not the only way she was like Reed.

When her work was going reasonably well time could also be detrimental. She would wonder how much longer she could maintain her concentration, or maybe she could quit early since she'd gotten so much done. But who knew how long it would be until she would work well again? And even when it was going well, she often had to convince herself to continue.

Every morning she carried a roll and a thermos of coffee to the studio, where she also kept fruit and a carton of cigarettes, so she'd have no excuses for leaving. She ate little while working. She liked to work hungry. Up to a point, it made her sharper. After a point, she got distracted by it. That was the point she tried to get to each day before she let herself go up to the house for lunch. That was the point she was at right now.

It had not been a good day of work. It had been many days, weeks, in fact, since she'd had a good day's work. She was in between paintings, a place she invariably hated to be. Nor did she have any destination in mind, beyond color. She had covered pages and pages with different combinations of paints, often of colors it had never occurred to her before to mix. Subsequently she'd made, especially at the outset,

many browns and grays. After her initial frustration at seldom being able to get the exact colors she had imagined, she had concocted different colors, ones that came to her as she went, or ones that were in reaction to a color she had just made. She thought there was a chance she might come upon what she wanted by accident. She tacked the squares to the wall to dry, but then she liked the look of them, so she left them there. At first their placement had been haphazard, but soon she took to arranging them, for the effects of certain colors together.

This wasn't real work. She knew that. It was as absurd as a poet compiling lists of words for possible future use. But it was something to keep her thinking about painting until she was really painting again. If she was lucky, it might help prepare her for whatever she would paint next. At least it kept a paintbrush in her hand. But she was about at the end of it.

In the kitchen, she grabbed a drumstick from the fridge, and headed through the living room to the front porch. She grasped the handle of the porch door and abruptly stopped. A woman's hand and forearm were visible on the armrest of the high-backed rattan chair, where Carver's mother had always sat, until she became too ill to sit up any longer. At that point, Reed had pulled the chaise lounge into the same spot, so Evelyn could still look through the curved frame of live oak limbs to Cougar Island and the river bend. It was that view, she'd told Reed, she wanted to see the day she died. She had not. She had died in the hospital. Before the funeral, Reed had gotten rid of the chaise. No doubt it had been soiled by all the dying done in it.

The chair had been returned to its place. It was arguably the best seat in the house. But since Carver had turned thirty-six, the same age as her mother when she died, Carver had avoided not only sitting in the chair but touching it at all. As if breast cancer were contagious. At one time, no doubt, people had believed it to be so. Carver had recently considered getting rid of the chair altogether, but she was too sentimental, or too superstitious, for that.

The woman in her mother's chair had yet to budge. Perhaps she was an apparition. Carver, never having had any belief in ghosts, did not fear them. She would have liked to believe in them, or so she had always believed. The year after her mother died she had tried to,

much the way she had made great efforts then to believe in God. She had wandered the dark rooms late at night, gathering her mother's objects and surrounding them with lit candles. Had Evelyn returned, she would not have lacked for company. Everybody had always said the Varnell place was haunted. But Carver had never seen or heard a one of these ghosts, though she had bragged about them at boarding school, where being from a haunted house in the South made her, she thought, rather glamorous. But soon enough she learned that it was more peculiar than glamorous, much the way someone is if they have a retarded sibling, or six toes on each foot. By then any apparent advantage of being a Southerner had worn off. It just meant, in the end, that everyone thought she was brutish and backward, a verdict which came as something of a blow, Carver having been reared to view the South as the last vestige of civilization.

Since moving back, she had used the ghost rumors to her advantage. It had given her a certain pleasure at Halloween to scare those boys. It was some revenge for all the times boys had scared her, or she had let them believe they had. Her pleasure, however, had been mitigated by her uneasiness that it was bad luck to even pretend to raise the dead. But how else would Carver have rid herself of all those kids, snooping, treating her place like *she* was the one trespassing? Kids were the quintessential squatters. *Finders keepers* extended to place. She had not forgotten how that was.

And she still hadn't gotten rid of them all. She kept finding marks on windowpanes, small footprints in the soil around the house. More than those clues, though, was her persistent sense of being watched. She knew this was due in part to being almost always alone, and the accompanying feeling she sometimes had of watching herself. But it was not just herself who was doing the watching, of that much she was sure. Maybe she needed a few more ghosts, to scare them off for a while. She did still have that rubber hand, the one she'd attached to Reed's wrought iron chair.

Earlier in the summer, Carver had seen the Cross girl in the big magnolia alongside the driveway. Did she think she was invisible? Carver must once have thought the same, though she could not recall how it was to believe that. It was the kind of notion that, once you

stopped believing it, you could not quite fathom how you ever had. But the desire to disappear, to observe without being observed— those longings she well remembered, and did, in somewhat different form, still have. She'd had a particular fondness for storybooks with invisible characters, or ones so small only children, being attentive to the infinitesimal, would notice. What power, to see without being seen. What power, indeed, to see.

The woman on the porch lifted her arm and scratched her face. Her enormous bracelet jangled toward her elbow, removing any lingering notion that she was a ghost, for no spirit could have hefted that.

Carver slowly opened the door to the porch. The breeze was fine off the water. The woman kept gazing out, at Evelyn's view. Carver recognized her, though at first she couldn't place her. She'd seen her out walking, and sitting on a dock, another time sitting in the passenger seat of a car. Pauline Cross had been leaning across her lap, rolling up her window. She must be Pauline's mother, recently widowed. Mattie kept Carver informed of everything, regardless of whether or not Carver wanted to know. Yes, she looked like Pauline, or rather, Pauline looked like her. Same chin, same mouth.

What was she doing here? Carver sat in the rocker beside her, and took another bite of chicken. Still the woman did not look at her. Her expression had not altered one notch upon Carver's arrival. She looked quite composed, despite the fact that she had a strand of Spanish moss in her hair, and a thin scratch along one cheekbone.

Carver scanned her memory. Mattie had told her that Mrs. Wells had taken to wandering, and sitting for long spells in odd places. She barely said a word anymore, and when she did, it was only to say something nasty. *Like what?* Carver had inquired. *Not the kind of nasty you're thinking,* Mattie had replied. *Curses and name-calling.* Then Mattie shook her head, clearly hoping she'd be spared such behavior herself, when her own time came.

Carver remembered the husband, Frazier Wells, tall and bald and gracious, slow-moving in that well-meaning, exasperating way, the kind of chivalrous Old South gentleman she refused, out of principle or spite, ever to sleep with, though they had a certain appeal. Men in

the generation after them tended to be smug, slick. The few she might have considered had some frat boy edge to them, which made all their charm suspect. Most of them seemed quite capable of rape, though the whole time they would, by their own lights, be treating you like a lady, except, of course, for the act itself. *Don't fret now, Miss, I'll fetch you a glass of cool water soon's I'm done,* and *Darlin' you're the sweetest thing I've come across in a coon's age.* But that was just some Yankee part of her head talkin' Southern. Nobody she knew talked like that. Nor, for that matter, could anybody she'd ever met from up North do a halfway decent imitation of a Southern accent, try as they might. And oh, how they did try.

Reed had some business dealings with Frazier, she remembered. What was his wife's name? It was one of those names you seldom heard anymore, feminine but stern, something along the lines of Maude, Edna, Alice, Edith, Ada—Adele, that was it. Carver glanced at her again. She did not look to be in decline, or anywhere near it. Wandering and silence and the occasional display of venom had, from the looks of it, been a boon to her health.

Carver put the gnawed drumstick on the table, brushed her hands together a few times, then wiped them down her already filthy cut-offs. For the first time, Adele looked directly at her. On her face was an expression of distaste. How dare she judge me on my manners? Carver thought. *She's* the one who's broken in. Then Carver grinned. Here she was, made indignant by some old lady so senile she'd walk uninvited into a stranger's house. But she must have known Evelyn and Reed. She looked about their age, the age they would have been. Could she have been here before? If so, it would have been in the thirties or forties. There had not been any entertaining here since then.

Carver cleared her throat. "Good afternoon, Mrs. Wells. I'm Carver Varnell, Evelyn and Reed's daughter. May I call you Adele? It is Adele, isn't it?" Adele continued to stare at Carver, her face gone blank. "What can I get you, sweet tea, ice water? Bourbon?"

Adele smiled.

"Bourbon it is. You make yourself at home and I'll be right back." In the kitchen she loaded a tray with drinks and potato chips and

cocktail napkins. "I'd sure like to join you, believe me, but it's a bit early for me yet." Carver put the tray down and removed her glass of tea. Adele set to work on the bowl of chips. It had been a long while since Carver had been with anyone old. Except for Mattie, who was seventy-three or four. Old, for Mattie, had nothing to do with frail, nothing to do with feeble, in body or mind. If anything, Mattie had become more formidable with age, certainly more righteous, more fearsome and God-fearing at the same time. Or had she always been like that, and Carver just hadn't been able, or allowed, to see it?

Mattie had worked for Carver's family since before Carver was born. In 1933 Mattie had been hired by Reed's mother, who had, as a wedding gift, paid Mattie's wages for the first year, much as house slaves used to be given to newlyweds. It was Mattie who had nursed Evelyn through her final illness, and the ones that preceded it, and looked after Reed for the twenty-odd years he had survived, if you could call it that, his wife, though Mattie had been left nary a dime in Reed's will. Still she stayed on, either out of loyalty or habit, or some belief that her near forty years of labor and discretion might bring her something more than what it thus far had.

Many a time Carver had tried to convince Mattie to retire, to live off the money Carver had, since moving back, set aside for her, but Mattie did not seem to believe that Carver could get by without her. Not that Carver wanted to get by without her. Mattie was the only person left who had known Carver all her life. Or not exactly—there were plenty of people around here whom she had known since childhood. But they had given up on her somewhere down the line. Certainly none of them had any sense of who she might be now. Probably Mattie didn't either, but nor did it seem to matter. Mattie had never given up on Carver, nor had she ever been shocked by her. Disapproving, concerned, yes, but not appalled, not hopeless. Carver wondered if what she really meant was that Mattie was the only person left who had loved her all her life. If, that is, Carver could call it love. She could just as easily say that Mattie had worked for her all her life.

Carver stared at Adele, as she had since childhood been warned not to do: *Don't stare, Don't point, Don't accept anything unless thrice*

offered. But Adele did not seem to mind. She had devoured the chips and was licking the salt from her fingers. The concerns of the social world, its rules of courtesy and obligation, of euphemism and fabrication and pretense, had been left far behind. What a great relief it must be, Carver thought, to be gone from there. Carver prided herself on her own hard-earned distance from that world, but seeing Adele now made Carver feel she'd never left it at all.

Adele had an almost eerie kind of stillness. She appeared completely occupied by just sitting. She seemed entirely there, and yet also not there at all. Not vacant, but not exactly present, either. There she sat, in her mauve skirt and checked blouse, rubber-soled shoes and ankle-high golf socks, her charm bracelet like a shackle. It was a get-up that, despite itself, did not make her appear absurd. Not with such a face could she be absurd.

Carver crushed out her cigarette. Her legs and arms and hands were jittery, out to the tips of her fingers. She clenched her hands, tensing the muscles in her neck and shoulder blades. Only rarely, when she was very lucky, did the desire to paint something hit her like this: a bit like lust, a bit like fear. Some would call it inspiration, but that was a notion she mistrusted. Her best work always occurred long after that point.

Carver released her hands and exhaled. She leaned forward, narrowing her eyes, to see past Adele's skin, into her muscles and bones and all the rest of her, the parts that could not be seen. She had not done a portrait since last summer. If she could only get Adele's quality of—what? Stolidity, impassiveness, repose? It was throughout her body, not solely in her face. And then when she looked directly at you, there was some vestige of a ladylike expression, belied by her gaze, the wariness in her eyes.

Carver took a pad of paper and a pencil from the end table's drawer. She began with Adele's profile, and her arm along the arm of the chair, her calf and foot. Adele continued to gaze straight ahead. After a few concentrated minutes, Carver stood, the sketch in her hand. It was a fair resemblance. Not that she had accomplished what she wanted. It would take many attempts to paint Adele as she saw

her, if she even could. Most people wanted a portrait to be flattering, which often meant that it not look too much like them. Enough to be recognizable, but not enough to make them wince.

Carver held it in front of Adele, who glanced at it, then back at the river, her expression unchanged. Carver, surprised, placed the sketch on the table. It hadn't occurred to her she'd get no reaction at all.

"I suppose I ought to give Pauline a call. No doubt she's worried about you." Carver looked up the number in the phone book and dialed. "Busy," she said. "I'll try again in a little bit."

Adele did not move, or change in any visible way. But it seemed to Carver that her silence had abruptly grown more forceful, less an inability than an unwillingness to speak. Maybe Adele was upset about Carver phoning Pauline. Or could she be bothered by the sketch? That was the thing about silence. You could fill it in with whatever you were afraid of, or wanted. Carver thought again of how Mattie had said that Adele, when she did speak, only cursed and called names. A half hour earlier, it had been hard to believe Adele capable of swearing and name-calling, but there was something about her face now that made that kind of behavior entirely plausible. What kinds of things did she say? *Damn, goddamn, go to hell,* or nastier terms like *shit* and *fuck, cunt* and *prick?* If, that is, Adele even knew such words, which the local lore would have you believe she did not. But Carver had long wondered just how much the ladies around here really didn't know, and how much they were only pretending, consciously or otherwise, not to. Her mother had cultivated a certain naiveté, though that had soured somewhat during dying.

Carver, having left the South before her own training had been fully completed, had always felt herself to be an imposter, though no one else seemed to take her as that. The longer Carver remained here, the more she realized that it didn't matter how long ago she'd left, how long she had stayed away, where else she had been or what she had done. If you had ever been from the South, you were always from the South. It probably worked that way for anyplace. But maybe with other places, it did not matter so much to begin with where you were from.

Before she moved back, when she told people she was from the South, they tended to look both fascinated and alarmed. In those instances when she had not identified herself as a Southerner, if a person detected it, or was told that fact by someone else, the person would usually say something along the lines of, *Oh, you're a Southerner!* as if that explained everything, or she had been trying to conceal that information, which, in fact, she often did. After so long away, if she avoided sliding into a mocking drawl, or becoming brittle when someone launched into some glib ridicule of the South, so popular among Northerners—if she resisted these avenues of self-exposure, she could easily pass, as it were, as a Yankee, though never as a New Yorker. People were always surprised that someone as *sophisticated and open-minded* as she had come from the Deep South. How could she blame them for their surprise? Often she was surprised herself, where she had come from, who, indeed, she was, and was not. But she did blame them. And at times she assailed them as well, putting herself in the untenable position of defending the South, a place she could not, really, even claim to know anymore, or perhaps ever. Far more often, though, she had assailed the South itself, and Southerners.

Carver tried the phone again. It was still busy. She returned to the rocker. She lit a cigarette and looked out at the river. There was a bateau across the way, with a girl in it, crabbing. It had to be Riddley. She was out there all the time, alone or with Hayden. "Look, isn't that Riddley?"

Adele scowled.

"I'll be right back."

At the edge of the bluff, Carver cupped her hands around her mouth and called to Riddley, beckoning her over. Riddley crossed the river, docked and secured the lines.

"Come on up," Carver called down. "Your grandmother's here." She returned to the porch. Adele was gone. Carver found her in the library, standing in front of the desk, whose abundant contents had been stacked on every available surface, and held in place by ashtrays and paperweights and conch shells. Over the last several months,

Carver had spent most of her evenings going room by room through all the drawers, closets, bookshelves, and cabinets. She read every scrap and sheet of paper she found: lists, records, letters, postcards, bills and bills of sale (cotton, rice, slaves), poems, journals, invitations, condolence and calling cards, and newspaper clippings of obituaries, trials, debutante balls, engagements, cotillions, weddings, scandals, fame, births, bankruptcy.

Carver said Adele's name. Adele did not move. Carver went around to the other side of the desk. Adele's repose was entirely gone. What could have made her so distraught?

"What is it?" Carver asked. Adele looked down at her own hands, but as if they weren't hers. Indeed they did seem to be moving of their own accord. Was she arthritic? Carver thought of Mattie's knotted, swollen joints, to which Adele's hands bore no resemblance. How little use, in comparison, Adele's hands had seen.

"Usually that means she wants to play solitaire," Riddley said from the doorway.

"Solitaire?" Carver repeated, startled. She had not heard Riddley come in.

"You know, cards."

"Oh. I'm sure I've got some somewhere." In the back of a drawer Carver found a box with two decks. She handed it to Riddley. "Let's go on the porch," Carver said.

Riddley took Adele's hand and led her out. Adele went directly to Evelyn's chair.

Carver unfolded a tray table in front of her. "Here you are. I'll bring you some sweet tea. What about you, Riddley?"

"Yes, please." Riddley removed the cards from the box and set them on the table.

In the kitchen Carver handed Riddley two glasses from the cupboard. "You're quite adept at getting her to do what you want."

"Sometimes my mom gets fed up or tries to rush her and then Grandmother digs her heels in. But if you just give her a little time and talk to her, usually she comes around. That's what Esther does. Esther can get her to do almost anything."

"Who's Esther?" Carver removed a pitcher of sweet tea from the refrigerator.

"She's our maid." Riddley was surprised that anyone along the bluff could not know who Esther was. "Oh, I almost forgot. Grandmother isn't supposed to drink tea," she said, blushing fiercely.

"Should you show her where the bathroom is?"

Riddley nodded, her color deepening further. She had never taken Adele to the bathroom before, but if she didn't, she knew she ought to take her home right away. Riddley escorted Adele to the bathroom but couldn't bring herself to go in with her. From what Riddley could hear outside the door, Adele managed fine on her own. Afterward, Riddley returned her to her seat. Back in the kitchen, Riddley said, "I should call my mother."

"I tried, but it was busy." Carver pointed at the phone on the wall. "Help yourself. I'll be back in a minute."

Riddley picked up the phone and slowly dialed. Before it had even rung a full ring, Esther picked up and said, "Cross residence."

"Hi Esther, it's me. I'm at Carver Varnell's. Grandmother wandered over here."

"She all right?"

"She's fine."

"She clean?"

"Umm-hmm. I just took her to the bathroom. And she went."

"You're catching on quick. Your mother's worried sick. She's phoned everybody. She's out looking for her right now. She had me wait by the phone in case somebody called about her."

"Carver tried to call but it was busy."

"We were worried about that. Y'all come right on back."

Riddley lowered her voice. "Carver's just made us something to drink. It would be rude to leave right now."

"She won't like it."

Riddley knew Esther was talking about Pauline. "I'll bring her back in just a little while."

"I suppose you're going to get your eyeful while you're there. Well, I'll let her know where y'all are. Don't be too long."

After hanging up, Riddley crossed to the double sinks. Above them was a large window, looking out to the driveway and the magnolia in which Riddley had sat and watched Carver. Riddley was startled at the tree's nearness, and the distance between branches, how clearly one could see between them to the trunk.

There was a noise behind her. Riddley whirled around. Carver leaned against the doorframe. Riddley had the distinct feeling that Carver had snuck up on her on purpose.

"I always wanted to build a tree house in that tree. The view's so good from up there." Carver gestured toward the magnolia. "Your grandmother fell asleep."

"She's hard to wake once she's out," Riddley said. "She can sleep through anything."

"Where's Hayden? Aren't y'all still in business together?"

"He's at his mother's."

"Cousin Priscilla," Carver said, grimacing. "Did you get ahold of your mother?"

"I talked to Esther. I told her we'd be back in a little while. It's fine now that they know where she is. We can stay as long as we want. I mean, as long as you want."

Carver smiled slightly, then walked into the living room. Riddley followed, taking her tea from the counter. The air moved over her skin, cooling her without making her cold. "It's better in here than air conditioning."

"That's my great-great-great grandfather's doing. He was said to have designed the house with the aim of combating fevers. People back then thought malaria and yellow fever were due not to mosquitoes but to something called miasma, deadly vapors and the like. So he built the house to catch the slightest breeze and move it through the rooms. The shade certainly helps, and the fans, but even without them on it's usually comfortable enough on the ground floor. It can get pretty toasty upstairs. And it's drafty everywhere in winter. Nonetheless, I love this house."

Carver stood in the middle of the room. "Doors and windows are lined up to funnel the wind in and encourage cross breezes." She lit

a match, cupped it, and held it above her head. When she took her cupped hand away, the match made the rushing sound of flame in wind, and then was extinguished. "It's a brilliant idea, except in the event of fire. Then it would in no time become a very bad idea." She tossed the match in an ashtray. "You can look around if you like. I'll sit with Adele."

Riddley would long remember that afternoon when she had, at last, gone throughout Carver's house. Because of her eagerness to do so, and because she was not disappointed once she did, and no doubt also because of what happened later, she would recall it with great clarity. She would remember particularly how the light, after passing through the lattices of vines and trees, had moved across the floors and walls. That light had a liquid quality, like it reflected off water, as if the house were surrounded by a moat, or stood much closer than it did to the river.

The house, though large, was not as big as Riddley had always imagined. She made her way up the broad curved staircase, covered in worn maroon carpet. Above her hung a tremendous chandelier, its prisms caked with dust. She'd expected some rooms to be large and grand, others small and peculiarly shaped. In fact the house had a very orderly, and ordinary, arrangement. Rooms of much the same size led off a wide central hall, which ran north to south. Tall casement windows at each end of the hall were propped fully open, allowing any breeze through, though as Carver had said, it was much hotter upstairs. But Riddley had never much minded the heat.

On the third floor Riddley found what had to be Carver's bedroom. It was the room Riddley would have wanted for herself. It was vast and sparsely furnished, with a starkness not found anywhere else in the house. The bare wood floor increased the sense of light and space, and made the other rooms seem even denser with furniture and knick-knacks. The room was, like Riddley's own, on the southeast corner, with three big windows on the south wall, and three sets of French doors opening onto the eastern porch. The large bed was against the western wall, so that its occupant would face the river and marsh and sunrise. Taking up almost half of the northern wall was

a blackboard, and in the corner beside it stood a large roll-top desk. Riddley walked closer, the floorboards moaning under her feet. The blackboard was built into the wall. Maybe this had once been the schoolroom. On the floor was a chipped bowl full of chalk, beside it an eraser. The blackboard was the only thing on the room's white walls, which looked to have been recently painted.

She went out onto the porch. Magnolia branches and wisteria vines pressed against the torn screens. The closeness of the foliage and the loudness of the insects made the porch seem situated more outside than in. There was a cot, and above it a kind of canopy, which, though white, was not of the usual frilly fabric Riddley had seen draped above girls' beds. Rather this looked like a kind of medical gauze. Rubbing it between her fingers, Riddley guessed it was mosquito netting. This must be where Carver slept in the summertime.

On the porch below, Carver laughed. Adele must have done something funny. She often did, without meaning to. When she wasn't around, Riddley and Sam might make fun of something Adele had done, and Pauline would shake her head and shush them but laugh just the same. Such as when Sam, ice cream cone in hand, said to Riddley, *Squirt some ketchup on this for me, will you?*

Riddley should go down, now that Adele was awake. But behind a hallway door Riddley found what she'd been hoping for, a staircase. It led up, to the attic or the maid's quarters. The steps were steep, and ended at a door in the ceiling, like a ship's hatch. She undid the latch and slowly pushed up. Much to her surprise, it opened to the air.

She was on the widow's walk. She'd forgotten about it, though she'd always longed to go up there. She was facing west when she emerged, looking down into the crowns of trees. Beyond was lawn, road, garden, woods. It made her light-headed, how high up she was, how seemingly precarious. She turned, into the wind, for up here it was not a breeze but a wind. Spread out below her was the river. She had never seen it from such a vantage. She pictured the charts, how this was what was meant by them. Every turn in the river was visible, and how obvious the sandbars and shallows were from this height, where it would do you no good to know. The clearing in the middle of Cougar Island looked much bigger than when you stood in it. There

were the many places where the marsh split open into creeks, and then sealed up again. She could see all the way to where the Leigh and the Bella entered their own river, and to where their river entered Moss Island Sound, and then Indigo Sound, and beyond that to the bright blur of ocean. This was as close as you could get in these parts to a mountain, and one exactly where she would have wanted it, where it seemed at that moment that she was: on a mountain in the middle of an island.

*   *   *

Carver drew Adele while she slept, one rapid sketch after another. She wanted to get as many angles as she could. Adele's hands in her lap, her face, her head listing to one side, her feet, and the whole of her in the chair, from closer then farther away, from one side and then the other, and from straight in front. It was easy, for she slept without moving at all.

Carver chafed at the notion of asking the daughter permission to paint the mother, though she supposed she would need to. She'd pay Pauline a visit. She'd dress up, she'd put on lipstick. Women like Pauline always looked at you as if you were stark naked if you wore no lipstick. Granted, this was probably because they themselves felt that way without it. But wouldn't such obvious effort only make Pauline suspicious, or rather, more so? Carver had a good idea of what the ladies hereabouts thought of her, despite how much they tried to hide it beneath pleasantries. Pauline would worry that any portrait Carver did of Adele would be unbecoming. And, no doubt, to Pauline, it would be. Pauline would want Adele to be remembered as a lady, as a contributor to church and charity and society, not as someone who wandered and scowled and spoke only to curse or call names, as if somewhere in the recesses of her mind she had inverted the adage to: *If you can't say something ugly, better not to say anything.*

Carver sensed as well that there would be another, deeper place from which Pauline would resist. Not only was there something wrong with turning one's mother over to be made, so to speak, into art, but Pauline would also think most art was, at base, suspect, unseemly. A portrait done by someone's spinster aunt was one thing, but art was

quite another. No, Pauline could not be asked for permission. Indeed, she must never know. Carver could well imagine that were Pauline to be asked, and were Pauline to concede, she would find other ways to interfere, to prevent it from happening. So how then to go about it? The floorboards creaked overhead. There was her answer. She'd ask for Riddley's help.

Carver looked up from her drawing. Adele was awake, and staring at her. Carver gasped. Adele grinned then, in a way that seemed to Carver mischievous, and nearly triumphant, as if Adele were pleased by Carver's surprise. Carver burst out laughing. She rather liked this old woman. She found herself glad, too, for the company, such as it was. And she did very much want to paint her.

When Riddley returned downstairs, Adele was stacking cards on the tray table while Carver scribbled on a pad of paper. Neither looked up when Riddley entered.

"I was beginning to wonder if the ghosts up there might've done away with you." Carver glanced at Adele, then made a couple of long strokes on the paper. She was drawing, Riddley saw, not writing.

"I didn't see any," Riddley said, sitting on the wicker sofa. "Have you?"

"Not recently." She recalled her plans for keeping the local kids in line. But the way Riddley's voice had brightened at the mention of ghosts, Carver thought such a scheme might well lead to more curiosity rather than more caution.

"How'd you like my sleeping porch?"

"It's almost as good as sleeping outside."

"Yes, it is." She ripped the page out. "Those crabs of yours must be hurting in this heat."

"I covered them before I came up. But we should get going, now that Grandmother's up."

On the coffee table were the sketches of Adele. Riddley glanced at Carver.

"Help yourself," Carver said. "They're studies. Preparations for a portrait."

"Are you going to paint Grandmother's portrait?"

"I'd like to."

Riddley went through the drawings. Then she looked over at her grandmother, stacking cards in piles. It was odd how the sketches both did and didn't look like her. They made her seem more familiar, yet also more mysterious.

"She didn't seem to mind." Carver looked at Adele, then back at Riddley. "She wouldn't need to pose in a certain way. She could wear whatever she wants. If she didn't want to do it anymore, we'd stop at once. But I would try to make it pleasant for her. It would probably only take a few weeks, the part I'd need her for." Carver paused. "You look worried. Do you think she wouldn't want me to paint her?"

Riddley shook her head. "It's not that." She glanced in the direction of her house. "I don't think my mother would—" Riddley stopped herself. She was about to say, *let her,* but after that there would be no going around it. Then it would be outright disobedience. Because Riddley knew, just from looking at Carver, that it was going to happen, and that, unless she refused this very minute, she would have a part in it. What could possibly be the harm? But this was the kind of thing that, were Pauline to find out, she would look at Riddley and say, *You should have known better.* And the fact of the matter would be that Riddley had. She had known better. She knew better right now.

Riddley began again. "I'm not sure what my mother would think about it."

Carver gave her a long look. "It's not her decision, though, is it."

An idea of that sort, or that particular magnitude, had never occurred to Riddley.

"Adele won't stay put if she doesn't want to," Carver said. They both looked over at her. She did not appear to be listening. Carver looked back at Riddley. "Could you bring her over for me sometimes?"

Riddley nodded. A plan was beginning to form in her mind. She hesitated in the face of such treachery. "My mother wouldn't worry if I was the one on duty."

"On duty?"

"I look after Grandmother for a few hours a day. Usually we take walks or go on the dock."

Carver was stunned by how easily things were falling into place. Just a minute ago she had been thinking the whole thing was probably

too difficult to pull off. She leaned forward. "Adele, I hope you'll come back very soon," she said, in a voice, Riddley noticed, that did not alter from the voice she used with anyone else. Most people spoke extra loud and slow to Adele, as if Frazier had bequeathed her his deafness, or a loss of speech necessarily implied a loss of hearing, and of intelligence. "There's been no company in this house for quite a while. Decades in fact. You're welcome anytime, both of you."

Adele tilted her head to the right, and paused, the cards hovering in the air above the table. Who knew what she thought of the invitation? She resumed laying down the cards, covering the entire surface. But when she looked up she was smiling.

* * *

Pauline sat at the table while Riddley and Adele had supper. She cut up Adele's food and tried to keep her tidy. Pauline would wait to eat with Sam, following cocktails. Often they didn't eat until after Riddley had gone to bed.

"What did y'all do at Carver's?" Pauline generally preferred to ask at suppertime those questions which required an answer.

"Nothing much. Mostly we sat on the porch."

"You sat on the porch."

"Um hmm." Riddley scooped up okra, charred just the way she liked it. "After I took Grandmother to the bathroom, she played solitaire and napped. That's why we were gone so long. You know how grumpy she is if she gets waked up. Carver gave me some sweet tea and Grandmother some water. I remembered she shouldn't have tea."

"Good."

"She likes Carver."

"What makes you think that?" Pauline said, her mouth tight.

Riddley shrugged, recalling too late that that gesture was irksome to Pauline. "Carver said Grandmother and I are welcome to visit anytime." Riddley swallowed nervously. Her strategy was to have Pauline approve occasional visits. Then later, if the portrait were discovered, the offense would not be as grave. Such a strategy could, however, backfire. Pauline could forbid Riddley from taking Adele there at all, thus compounding Riddley's offense, for Riddley knew she would

take Adele there, regardless of permission. Carver was counting on her. And Riddley was counting now on the fact that Pauline would not wish to forbid it. Riddley continued, "I told Carver that I'd have to check with you."

This was just the kind of thing, Pauline thought, that Sam was so adept at: to present her with something that seemed to be a choice, but which, if she did anything but what he wanted, would make her appear a way she did not wish to, in this case, over-protective and suspicious. But what could possibly happen at Carver's? She may have been wild once, but she could hardly be considered so now. She seldom left the premises, and nor did anyone visit. She was eccentric, at best, and not even very much so, considering the local competition. So what was it about Carver that Pauline felt she should protect her daughter and mother from?

"I thought I'd take Grandmother over every once in a while. Just for a change." Riddley tried to sound casual, as if there were no conceivable reason Pauline might object, as if she had indeed already granted permission.

"All right," Pauline said, swiping a dishtowel over Adele's hand, which had, during Pauline's lapse in attention, again dropped the fork in preference for fingers. "I suppose y'all can go there every once in a while." She put the fork back in her mother's hand, then folded Adele's fingers around it. "Just don't make a nuisance of yourself. Or of Grandmother."

CHAPTER 15

Portrait

When Riddley and Adele arrived late the next morning, the carriage house was spotless. The porch's rattan chair had been brought in, and stood facing the easel. On the far wall, the squares of color had been replaced by Carver's sketches of Adele. Carver led Adele to the chair and said to Riddley, "Make yourself at home in the house. There's plenty in there to keep you occupied. Help yourself to anything to eat."

So Riddley went alone into Carver's house, that day and many days thereafter. The one day she and Adele never went to Carver's was Thursdays, Mattie's day. Were Mattie to find out, so too might Esther, and then perhaps Pauline. The fewer people who knew, the better.

Riddley favored the library for its books, and the living room for its high concentration of old and unusual objects. Such were found throughout the house. Many she was tempted to take. After four days of temptation and much consideration, she chose a small fish of nearly luminous green stone. It stayed cool in her pocket, despite the heat of her leg, her hand, her guilt, the day. She fingered it as she spoke to Carver outside the studio, which was what Carver called the carriage house. Riddley wasn't sure if she had stolen or merely borrowed the fish. She took to carrying it almost everywhere, especially when she went to Carver's, in case she should feel compelled to return it, or it was discovered missing, in which case Riddley could pretend she had just found it. At night, she often fell asleep with it in her fist, slipped inside the pillowcase. It was never in her hand when she woke. Once she found it on the windowsill, where she must have set it in her sleep.

Every day that she was in Carver's house, Riddley went up to the widow's walk. Once she watched a storm come in off the sound. Another time there was a wine glass on the railing, alongside a pack of cigarettes, matches slid under the cellophane. Something must have

happened to call Carver suddenly away. The next day, the glass and cigarettes were gone, and Riddley was sure then of what she'd suspected, that Carver also went up there often.

Riddley wandered through the house for about an hour or so, after which she fetched Adele. If Pauline asked where they had gone, Riddley answered vaguely—the woods, the road, the dock—and soon Pauline ceased to inquire. But Esther sometimes looked then with what seemed sternness at Riddley, as if she knew full well where Riddley had taken Adele, and why. Could Mattie have found out, and told Esther? But Carver said Mattie wouldn't go into the studio.

After turning Adele over to Pauline or Esther, Riddley ran down to the dock and checked her trap, after which, if it wasn't storming, she jumped in the water, swam awhile, floated. Then she went out in the bateau, crabbing if the tide was right. She took the stone fish with her, nestled in the deepest part of her shorts' pocket, where she rubbed and turned it, a cold green worry bead.

Despite Riddley's promise to visit Miss Byrd, the summer had more than halfway passed and she had not. Riddley had decided to show her the postcards, only to learn that she was too late, that Miss Byrd was gone. No one knew for sure what had happened. Just as when she had been among them, many things were said of her. Riddley heard, and overheard, a wide variety of explanations: Miss Byrd had been dismissed with apologies, because an older teacher had decided to return; Miss Byrd had been fired; Miss Byrd had quit without a word.

A good many of the parents had, naturally, taken issue with Miss Byrd's opinions, as had the parents of those few students who did not thrive under her tutelage. But despite her various peculiarities, most of the students and their parents thought her a good teacher. So what was it that had been discovered about her, or that she herself had discovered, that had brought about her departure? Riddley remembered then what Carver had long ago said about Miss Byrd: *her days are numbered.* How had Carver, never having met Miss Byrd, known she would not last?

Word of Miss Byrd would reach them, indirectly, over the weeks and months, as to why she had left and where she had gone. Which,

if any, of these stories were true was never ascertained. Rumor had it that Miss Byrd had opened her own school in Atlanta; she had run off with a man—an Oriental, or even a black?—to New York or California; she had moved to Washington to work for women's lib, or to protest the war; it had been found out that she was passing.

This last rumor perplexed Riddley. Could it mean that Miss Byrd was dying? But the comment had been made without any expression of pity, so Riddley doubted this was the case. She looked up the word in their dictionary, but nothing she found seemed applicable. Frazier's might have shed more light, but it was stashed in a box somewhere. It seemed too simple a word to benefit from Pauline's knowledge of Latin and Greek, but you never could tell. So one evening Riddley asked, "What does it mean to pass? I already tried the dictionary," she added, to intercept Pauline's usual injunction, *look it up.*

"Let's see. Pass a test, pass away." Pauline stood at the counter, beating a slab of veal with a mallet. "Pass a car, pass the butter, pass the word—but you know all those." She paused, resting the mallet on the pocked meat. She resumed pounding, and smiled. "A boy can make a pass at a girl. Is that what you heard?"

Riddley shook her head. "It's what some people are saying about Miss Byrd. That she was passing."

The mallet froze in the air. Pauline set it down, then placed the veal cutlets on a platter. "I never heard that." She scrubbed her hands under the faucet. "It means to pretend to be white."

It took Riddley a second. Worse than the shock of not knowing was the sting of not having been told. "Miss Byrd's black?"

"Of course not. People have been saying all sorts of things about her, just because they don't know what happened, and because—" Pauline broke off, drying her hands on a dishtowel. "She always meant well, but, well, she did tend to make a lot of people uncomfortable. So they talk about her. They don't mean any harm. It's just to try to make sense of someone who's a little out of the ordinary."

"But she never said she was white or black. She never lied about it either way."

"It's not something you do or don't say."

"She doesn't *look* black."

"I'm sure she isn't."

"So how come people believe it?"

"Well, with most *mulattoes,* as they're called, it's quite clear that they're mixed. But with a very, very few, you can't tell at all. Those are the ones who try to pass. I'm quite sure, though, that isn't the case with Miss Byrd. It was just somebody trying to be ugly. I don't believe it for a minute, and you shouldn't, either."

Riddley was not sure what to believe. All of the things that had been said about Miss Byrd seemed they could, in some way, be true. Yet at the same time, none of it seemed true in the least, for nothing got to the heart of what was different about—and, to some people, what was wrong with—Miss Byrd.

Riddley did not so easily dismiss the accusation of passing. It was another thing to ponder about Miss Byrd. If she were black, why would she hide it? The way she went on about slavery and civil rights and dignity in the face of suffering, you would almost think she'd be proud to be black. But if she were, she couldn't have been a teacher at their school. The only black people there were janitors, cooks, yardmen, and handymen.

If Miss Byrd were indeed black, what would she have done had Riddley shown her the postcards? Might she then have confessed it, and sworn Riddley to secrecy, or would she have distrusted or even loathed her, for having such things in her family?

Riddley thought about Miss Byrd's legs. Had they had anything to do with her dismissal, if indeed she was dismissed, and had not left of her own accord? The only other woman Riddley knew who had legs in any way resembling Miss Byrd's was Esther. On the hottest days when Esther did not wear support hose to work, Riddley had seen a few wispy hairs on her calf, nothing in comparison to Miss Byrd's leg. Nor did Esther make any attempt to conceal her legs. Did black women shave? Riddley tried without success to picture Opal's or Josephine's or Johnny Mae's legs. If they didn't, and Miss Byrd was, could that be what she was trying to tell Riddley by revealing her leg? If she had done so intentionally, that is, and not by accident.

Riddley replayed the moment when Miss Byrd, crouching, chanterelles in hand, had looked up at Riddley and smiled. Over time that

smile had come to seem different in kind from her usual one of teacherly benevolence. It was more like the smile Sam wore when he had gotten, or was in the midst of getting, away with something, and he knew that you knew, and was counting on you not to tell—that, by your very knowing, you would not want to tell. Riddley had previously thought that what Miss Byrd was getting away with was simply being herself, unaltered, unmodified. But could it be, on the contrary, that what Miss Byrd was getting away with was that she was black? Riddley pictured Miss Byrd's naked leg, the skin under the dark hair as pale as cotton in the boll. Surely she couldn't be black, with skin as white as that. But whether Riddley's glimpse of Miss Byrd's bare leg was due to purpose or mistake, and what such a glimpse was supposed to tell Riddley or to mean, Riddley would never know for certain, for, beyond rumors and hearsay and Riddley's occasional dream, Miss Willa Byrd, after she left them, was never seen or heard from again.

* * *

Most evenings Adele was content to stay in the house after supper, play cards, maybe watch a little TV. But sometimes she was hell-bent, as Sam put it, on being elsewhere, and would pace the driveway, or head to the dock or bluff. This evening she could not be persuaded to stay, and insisted on going back to her apartment. After Riddley had boiled the day's catch, she went to check on her. Adele was not there. Riddley guessed where she had gone. In the dusk, Riddley ran over to Carver's. Adele and Carver sat together on the lit porch. Riddley paused in the shadows a moment to look at them. Each held a glass and a cigarette and looked toward the river. When had Adele started smoking with Carver?

"I was hoping you'd figure it out," Carver said, turning her head in Riddley's direction, "so I wouldn't need to call your mother."

Pauline was sitting outside when Riddley brought Adele back. Luckily Sam was out of town on business.

Pauline stood as they approached. "Mother, you can't go wandering off like that, and at night," she scolded. "You went to Carver's, didn't you?" Riddley knew the question was really directed at her. Only later did she think to wonder how Pauline had figured it out.

Pauline turned to Riddley. "How did you know where she was?"

"She likes it there."

"As do you," Pauline said, in a voice that made Riddley wish she could deny it. "Y'all have gone there a number of times, haven't you."

"You said we could."

"I know." She sighed. "Well I'm thankful you knew where to find her. She's mighty lucky to have you for a granddaughter."

Riddley blushed, glad for the dark. Pauline would hardly say such a thing if she knew about the portrait. Riddley yawned loudly.

"All that dawn crabbing. You must be exhausted." Pauline kissed Riddley on the forehead. "You run on to bed. I'll come tuck you in once I've put Grandmother down."

As Pauline coaxed her mother up the apartment stairs, she wondered if you always ended up loving your children more than your parents. Maybe you had to. Maybe humans were simply built that way. She remembered her daughters' devotion, their hands like tentacles upon her, reaching and grabbing. They would have stuffed the whole of her into their mouths if she'd let them, if it were possible. Riddley much more so than the twins. The twins, having each other, were never as greedy for her as Riddley was.

She remembered finding Charlotte and Emmeline entwined in the crib, the fingers of one in the mouth of the other. Upon seeing them, Adele had frowned disapprovingly, as if two infants asleep together were improper. Pauline hadn't seen the logic of that at all. If they could comfort each other, why not allow them to? But she herself had grown uncomfortable with it after that. She had worried it was just her own laziness, her own exhaustion and willingness to let things be—or go, her mother might have said—if there was no pressing reason not to. She'd gotten a second crib, and placed the two side by side, but not near enough to touch. She thought contact might encourage them to climb out. Sometimes she'd go in there and each would have a hand stretched toward the other, or they'd have fallen asleep with their arms dangling outside the rungs.

But Riddley had turned her gaze, for her first five or six years, almost entirely on Pauline. Later, when Riddley began to shift her focus

elsewhere, Pauline was surprised how much she missed her daughter's attention, despite its often wearisome intensity. She missed it in that way you only miss things you know you will not get back. What power she had wielded, when her mere presence could make another downright blissful. It had been like that for a while with Sam, though in truth he was more the one who had such an effect on her.

Pauline sat Adele down on her hope chest at the foot of the bed. Crouching, she removed her shoes and then, taking care to keep her eyes averted, she undressed her, this person whom she had, presumably, once loved more than anyone else on earth, a notion quite inconceivable to her now. She did not quite believe it. It was her father she had most loved, certainly as much as she did her daughters. It seemed to have always been that way. No doubt some psychiatrist would have a heyday over that, but she had always loved her father as if he were her mother, or at least, what one traditionally thinks of as a mother.

But maybe it was all just a matter of memory. Maybe she had simply forgotten her early feelings for her mother. Heaven knew she had a terrible memory. Then again, segments of her daughters' early years seemed as vivid as last month. While to her daughters, whatever early memories they did retain were steadily receding, being buried under the present, the future. But how could they ever forget that time? It was, in a way, like forgetting her, forgetting what she was to them, all she had done for them. But they had and they would, just as Pauline herself had. Thus the bitterness so common to mothers: that their children did not recall all that had been done for them, the innumerable sacrifices the mothers had made. But the mothers never forgot. They told the children of these things over and over, and the children believed but disregarded them, or came to suspect that such sacrifices had either been grossly exaggerated or were to be expected, that indeed, that was what mothers were for.

Pauline bunched the nightgown into a tight roll and then pulled it quickly down over Adele's head, just as she had once done with her baby girls, so they wouldn't panic while the cloth covered their faces. It seemed wrong that Pauline remembered her children's childhoods better than they did. For the time being, anyway, until, that is, she forgot everything, even her own name. First her married, then her

maiden, her nicknames and pet names, and, she presumed, eventually even her given, at which point she would be free, like her mother, to answer to no one.

Adele hadn't reached the point of not knowing her own name—her given one, that is—though Pauline did not doubt that she would get there, in her own good time. Pauline could usually see some flicker of recognition in her mother's eyes, in the stiffening of her neck or the pause in her movement, when she said her name. Pauline said it now, and Adele glanced up from watching Pauline's fingers fastening the nightgown buttons. Pauline rarely said *Mother* anymore, except when speaking of her to someone else. Pauline was getting used to it, though it still made her feel a trifle impudent, as well as uneasy, that she might yet be scolded. But once Adele had started forgetting not just where and when but who she was, motherhood had been one of the first things to go. Naturally, it gave Pauline a measure of pain to realize that her mother no longer knew who they were to each other. Yet there was a strange comfort to it, too, for if Adele no longer realized that Pauline was her daughter, couldn't Pauline, in all fairness, occasionally suspend her knowledge that this strange and embarrassing and often frightening woman was her mother?

Pauline waited by the bed until, in moments, Adele was asleep. The amount Adele slept had increased almost as much as the amount she ate. She catnapped throughout the day, and slept as soon as she lay down at night. She could sleep through anything, and practically anywhere. Once she had fallen asleep on the toilet. She rarely stirred once asleep, and could be extremely unpleasant if woken. According to Frazier, last year Adele had been prone to nightmares, to thrashing about in bed and calling out. From what Pauline could gather, Adele no longer had bad dreams. Maybe, if her stillness were any indication, she had no dreams at all. Was it possible, she wondered, not to dream?

Pauline tucked the covers in and gathered the dirty clothes off the hope chest, which she still hadn't gotten around to sorting through. From the hallway, she glanced into Ray's cluttered room and sighed. She needed to get this whole place cleared out and organized, not

only her in-laws' things but her mother's as well. At the very least, she should decide which furniture to give to charity. In the driveway, she breathed deeply. It was always too close in there. Nothing she or Esther did managed to get the years of smoke and sickness out of the walls. Plus she guessed Sam smoked over there from time to time, now that she was trying to get him to stop doing so in their house.

If Sam found out that Adele had gone off tonight, he would insist on a lock. He had wanted to install one on the outside of the garage apartment, to make sure she stayed in at night. *What if she walks up to the main road?* he said. *She could get hit by a car, or worse.* Neither cared to specify what *worse* might be. At the time, though, Adele had done nothing wrong, so locking her in had seemed cruel and unjust. But Sam had insisted that justice was beside the point, that the greatest injustice, and certainly the greatest cruelty, would be to allow her to put herself in danger. Besides, locking her in could only be considered cruel if Adele herself thought it was, and Adele, he said, wouldn't care one way or the other. It was hard for Pauline to argue with him on that. If Adele were to find the door locked, she would probably just fall asleep on the sofa, or pace back and forth in the dark.

In the back room, Pauline gathered up the newspaper, her coffee cup, a book of Riddley's, an empty pack of cigarettes and numerous matchbooks. What if they locked Adele in and there was a fire? They'd been worried about fire with Isabel, who had, toward the end, taken to lighting her cigarettes off the electric range. More than once she'd left it on.

Fortunately Adele had shown no inclination to cook even so much as a piece of toast. But there were plenty of other ways the place could catch fire: an appliance or the elevator chair could short out, not to mention lightning, or sheer carelessness. Would Adele even know to flee? Pauline had to believe that she would, that she would know to avoid burning and suffocation, despite the fact that she seemed to have lost all caution when it came to such things as snakes, weather, choking, traffic. Crossing the street, she didn't just fail to look both ways. She did not look any way. She went. She was the proverbial child chasing the ball into the street, though what constituted the ball,

in Adele's case, was anyone's guess. That, Pauline realized, must have been why Frazier gripped Adele's hand whenever they were in town. Pauline had taken it, at the time, as a late blooming of affection.

She turned off the lights in the kitchen and made her way toward the stairs, picking up as she went. She would give her mother one more chance. But if she got out again at night, Pauline resolved to lock her in.

Much later that night, Pauline woke. She opened her eyes in the dark. She listened. It was quiet, inside the house and out. She didn't need to go to the bathroom. She'd had no bad dream. Nor had one of the girls. Riddley was silent overhead, and Charlotte and Emmeline were still at camp. Sam hadn't woken her, for he was away. So why was Pauline wide awake? In her throat and eyes she felt a familiar pressure. She had been woken, it seemed, by sorrow. She lay there a long while, searching that sorrow out, until it came to her. Who was there now, but herself, to remember her own childhood?

*   *   *

The door to Carver's room was unlocked, as it had not been for days. On the floor underneath the chalkboard were the silver candlesticks from the dining room table. These held the stubs of red candles. In the night they must have lit up the chalk board, which was entirely filled with figures and hands and faces. Was Adele among them? A pair of clenched hands and a head of hair reminded Riddley of her grandmother, but she couldn't be sure. She wondered when Carver would let her see the portrait.

Carver's paintings returned to her then, almost as if she were recalling dreams. Had Carver herself dreamed them? Riddley recollected those huge figures with their hands and faces weighed down, and the trees that resembled people, the stones that seemed suspended underwater, the somber man, the screaming girl.

Riddley knew all at once what she ought to do with the postcards: put them here, in this house. Now that Riddley was often at the garage apartment, the postcards nagged at her more insistently. In addition, their location was getting increasingly precarious. Pauline had again mentioned clearing out Ray and Isabel's belongings, and

putting Adele's in order. If Pauline did that, she would certainly find the postcards.

Carver alone, of everyone Riddley could think of, might appreciate them. For Carver seemed unafraid of ugliness. In fact she might seek it, though Riddley didn't understand why anyone would do that. She pressed the fish into her palm, turned it over, pressed again. Surely someone who could paint what Carver had, and who would want to paint Adele, would hardly flinch in the face of the postcards.

Not that Riddley intended to tell Carver about them, or at least not yet. She would stash them in the small cabinet at the end of the ground floor hallway. It was the perfect hiding place. The cabinet stood in an out-of-the-way spot, and resembled a safe, having a low boxy shape, and a lock and key.

That night, Riddley had a hard time getting to sleep. What if Carver or Mattie should find the postcards? But they would never guess their origins, for Riddley would take them out of the envelope. Besides, if the dusty clutter of the cabinet were any indication, no one had ventured there for a long time. And the postcards would be easy to reclaim, when the time came.

Late the following morning, after Pauline had gone to town and Esther, with Adele at her heels, had begun the long process of dusting, Riddley went next door. Upstairs, she held the envelope in her hand. She hadn't thought about what she would do with it, after removing the contents. She should keep it, and the note, in a safe place, in case proof was ever needed that the postcards had been a gift, if you could call them that. She put the envelope and the note in the drawer of a hutch, under an empty silverware container. Into the waistband of her shorts she slid the postcards. She pulled her t-shirt down to cover them. Then she went to fetch Adele.

Within the hour, Riddley had tucked the postcards into the drawer of Carver's cabinet, amid yellowed stationary, matchbooks, pencil stubs, and old photographs in black and white. The postcards blended right in, until you looked closer. As she shut the drawer and then the cabinet door she considered what she had veered away from considering before. What would Esther think, if she looked in Ray's bureau and found the postcards gone? Esther would know then for certain,

if she didn't already, that someone living had claimed them, that they no longer belonged only to the dead.

* * *

Much of the time Carver felt a sure contentment in her solitude, but occasionally it seemed that loneliness was gaining on her, and would soon overtake her, after which her solitude would be ruined. Those were the nights she couldn't read, nights she was too restless or weary to sleep, nights when if she let herself have another drink or watch TV she'd fall into a gloom that could last for days. That was when she drove. Sometimes the boat, more often the car, because not just movement but people were what she was after, not to talk to them but to see evidence of their existence, sitting on porches, the lights on in windows, a couple now and then out walking, an old person with a dog. But mostly the people she saw were, like her, driving, or getting in and out of cars.

Reed, too, had gone driving. He'd announce, *I believe I'll go for a drive.* He had hardly needed to tell them. Both Carver and her mother knew from the way he bounded up out of his chair what he was going to do, and that he would not be asking them along. Where exactly, Carver wondered now, had he gone?

She grabbed an extra pack of cigarettes, and filled an oversized plastic cup with ice water. She rolled down all the windows of Reed's old Buick and headed out the driveway. Why had she moved back here? It was a question she'd asked herself often, in alarm and bewilderment, the weeks after she first arrived. Only recently, on nights such as these, had she begun to ask it again. She felt cloistered, in the religious sense of the word, as in sequestered, and also in that there were many ancient, unspoken rules that one was expected to follow, and that one *did* follow, sometimes without even being aware of it. She used to think she had left the South too early to have its conventions imprinted upon her, but some part of her knew the rules quite well, or knew, at least, when she'd broken one.

She had made the decision to move here about a year ago, in the middle of a New York summer. She had at that time already been divorced and orphaned—as she did, in her more self-pitying moments,

think of it—for about a year. She was painting little, and what she did paint, she didn't like. She had a pretentious job in an art museum that made her feel farther from her own art, and art at all. It had seemed to her that she would never be a serious painter, nor perhaps a serious person, unless she did something drastic.

Above all, she had been tired of having change feel like something done to her, like surgery or an accident, something falling off a high building on top of her. She had wanted to change her life for herself, in some way not having to do with loss. So she had moved home, to the only home she could claim, where she had lived for no longer than a few weeks at a stretch during the last twenty-odd years. She could always leave, if it didn't work out. She still owned the brownstone in New York, though it was leased until January.

But why should she leave when she was getting so much work done? Painting Adele often seemed as easy as painting a wall, or that's how Carver would come to think of it. She didn't let herself think such a thing outright, not wanting to jinx her luck, or whatever it was that forged what felt at times like seamless connections between eye, brain, hand, brush, canvas. She put the paint on, and there Adele was. It was not really as easy as that, but the portrait was going easier than anything had gone in a long time.

Part of the reason painting Adele went so smoothly seemed to be due to the precariousness of the entire venture, that any day they might be discovered and, like illicit lovers, prevented from meeting again. For having made the decision not to ask Pauline, Carver felt certain that if Pauline found out, she would stop it at once. Thus each day Carver leveled a gaze on Adele that could last, if need be, well beyond Adele's presence, which it had. When Adele's time was up and Riddley had taken her home, Carver would often continue to work long into the afternoon, until the light grew too poor to do so.

She had an hour-and-a-half at most each day with Adele, and never knew when Adele might abruptly stand and walk out the door, as had happened a few times, before Carver figured out various means of getting her to stay put: music, a cigarette, food, cards, but most often and most reliably, speech. At first Carver had chattered about nothing in particular, bits from the news, weather, gossip she'd

heard from Mattie. But soon she had, without intending to, launched into what was now unfolding as the story of her life. What an odd audience Adele was, never responding in any way, so that Carver could not help but wonder after a while if she were listening at all, or following, rather, for it was obvious she listened. But following or not, she would settle down while Carver spoke. And Carver would settle down as well, under the strange comfort of her own voice, with none of her usual concern that she was revealing too much. In many ways, she might as well have been talking to herself, except that she said things to Adele that she never would have said to herself, and she heard things differently, too, in the way that, when trying to explain who you are to another, you become clearer, occasionally, to yourself.

Carver crested the top of the small rise at the intersection, her headlights illuminating one of the signs she'd illustrated for Riddley and Hayden. It was nailed to the trunk of the oak across the road. She flicked on her high beams. There then was her art. She pushed in the lighter and studied those crabs.

She lit her cigarette and turned left onto White Cliff Road. Some nights she headed right, into town, and went slowly around the darkened squares, but more often, like now, she drove south, toward more marsh, more rivers. Low brick houses sat at the far edge of wide watered lawns. Air conditioning units jutted humming from the windows. Chain link fences surrounded dog yards and kiddie pools. After a stretch of scrawny woods, and solitary live oaks in empty fields, came the clusters of old bungalows and shacks, the occasional trailer. This was Coffee Creek. She passed churches, swept dirt yards, small wooden houses set close to the road, screened porches. There were garden plots in back yards and side yards, corn wavering tall and human-like in the headlights, gesturing to her out of the corner of her eye.

She passed the road to Mattie's house, and then Mattie's church, and a small store, closed now. A hundred yards off the road was a bar. Pulses of music drifted into her car. She slowed. Black men and women stood out by the cars, laughing and talking and drinking.

They were hot from dancing, or just from being inside a place with few windows and no AC. They were looking to catch any bit of breeze off the river, a quarter mile distant. A man's head tilted back, drinking long and slow from a tall can. He looked familiar to her, and she wondered if it was Mattie's son Vernon, or someone else who worked on the bluff during the day.

What if she were to go in there, sit at the bar, order a beer? Curious looks, no doubt, but otherwise they would ignore her. Wouldn't they? Unless she was perceived as being there for other reasons. That did seem to be what she needed. Seeking a lover there, however, would be sheer insanity. If she had a lover in the South, he had best be white. Numerous lines were crossed in this town, but the line that never ever was—publicly, that is—was the one of color. No white person she had ever known or heard of or glimpsed here had a black girlfriend or boyfriend, much less a husband, a wife, a child. That such things still happened regularly she had no doubt. What amazed her was that it occurred invisibly, and in virtual silence. Invisible and silent to her, anyway. Maybe if she lived here long enough, or had never left, she would see and hear things.

She flicked her cigarette toward the side of the road and resumed her speed. She'd had attention from all variety of local men, some divorced, one widowed, the vast majority of them wed, a good many of them to girls she'd gone to elementary and middle school with, girls she'd come out with, girls who had been women for a long time now but nonetheless still called each other *girls*. Carver had felt not the slightest flicker of interest in these men in return. But she could start longing for some good old-fashioned romance, chivalry of the old school, with garter belts and martinis. The martini she wouldn't mind, nor the garter belt under the proper circumstances—but as for the chivalry, no thank you. Or maybe it wouldn't be chivalrous. Maybe chivalry had nothing to do with it at all. She had no idea. She'd had lovers from New England, New York, California, Italy, France, and Mexico, but for all her purported wildness, she'd had not a single lover from the South. How a Southern man would act in bed she really didn't know. Which assumed they would all act the same.

But were she to have an affair with someone in the social circle to which she supposed she did belong, she would soon be found out. Likewise if she brought anyone to her house, the neighbors would know in a matter of hours, or if by some miracle she managed to conceal it from them, Mattie would discern it at once. How Mattie knew what she knew remained mysterious to Carver. But that she almost always knew far more than she let on she was certain. Not that she would tell anyone, or anyone who might make such knowledge a problem for Carver. In fact she would most likely approve. Mattie had plenty of times stated outright that Carver needed someone to, as Mattie put it, *keep you company.* One time Carver had replied, *Why would I need anyone's company but yours?* and Mattie shook her head and said, *Young woman like you.*

Desire flitted about Carver's head like a horsefly, finding no one to light on, no one to bite. If she was ten years younger, or even five, or in a different place, she could have picked somebody up in a bar, slept with him, and that would have been that. Not that that was ever truly just that. And she had gone so long without sex she was not sure she could tolerate it without dire effects, like the starving's first contact with food, the thirsty's with water: you could overdose on what would have been a mere snack in the old and gluttonous days of plenty, or of youth.

But oh, the ease of it, and the temptation. Longing, she knew and saw and felt, was everywhere. Her own flared up at odd moments, like an old injury, something to be endured until it went away of its own accord, or she turned to sleep or drink to dull it. And should she choose not to endure or ignore it, she wouldn't even need to go to the usual bar or club. At the convenience store there were men filling up their tanks, buying six packs, bait, cigarettes, jugs of milk and soda. *No shirt no shoes no service,* the sign said, so some pulled on a shirt in the front seat or truck cab, elbows knocking against the window and ceiling, while the occasional one stood outside his open door and pulled the t-shirt over his head as sensually as if he were taking it off instead of putting it on. All it would've taken from her was a look

that lasted a half-second longer, or a glance returned. Most of them weren't used to looking at someone her age, she knew, but once they did look, they would have been willing. They would have been more than willing.

Once she had almost succumbed. In the grocery store a few months ago she had returned the gaze of a man. He was lean and angular with a mess of curly black hair. In the parking lot he had come up behind her as she loaded her car and asked, softly, if she had a light. She turned around. She was smoking, matches were visible in her breast pocket. She looked at him, and liked what she found, but after a long pause she looked him in the eye and said no, because a light, of course, was not what he was after.

Besides that once, she didn't look longer, return glances, pause, smile or half-smile, release her hair from beneath her baseball cap, ask for a light, drop her keys so she could bend down and pick them up, stretch herself or take a long swig of soda from the bottle before getting into her car. She kept her head down, her eyes averted, her cap on. She carried her own matches, thank you very much. Driving off, she put the cold coke bottle between her thighs, laughing to herself as she said, *take that!*

That was precisely where her ice water rested at the moment. She took a long sip. Again she turned left, and soon the road turned to dirt. Side roads dead-ended into stands of meager woods, or petered out into clearings, or led to big houses with swimming pools. The road she was on led out to an old causeway, blocked by a shut and rusty gate. A few times there had been a couple parked, or a group of kids drinking, or the mosquitoes were too many, and she had to go elsewhere, which by that point usually meant home. But tonight she had it to herself. She parked as close as she could get to the edge, and in such a way that the breeze could enter the car. She propped a leg up on the open door. The night sounds filled her, the hums and trills and cries.

She got out and lit a cigarette, squinting against the sudden brightness. Except while driving, she always used matches. She liked what

they entailed: the strike, the flare, the smell, shaking the flame out, the sudden dark. She stood beside the car, waiting for her eyes to adjust again.

She would have no lovers here. She understood that then. Or not for a long while, anyway. Had she known that when she made the choice to return? Indeed, that was part of the appeal of this place, how estranged she would be, how that would force her to focus. Isolation and loneliness did have their purposes. But she would have to be careful not to let her refuge transform into a trap. For you could, she suspected, keep turning inward until you caved right in.

CHAPTER 16

Fire

Long afterward, what would be remembered was how, in the dead of night, the birds began to sing. Other birds within range of hearing but beyond that of light did, after an initial hesitation, join in. The rueful and bewildered quality of many of the songs suggested that some thought they ought not to be singing at all, while the desperate shrillness of others indicated that some birds believed dawn was already long gone, and that they had slept right through sunrise.

Such birdsong might explain why the people who were woken by the birds felt at once that something was gravely amiss. Their bodies insisted the birds were wrong to sing. The sirens soon gave focus to their dread, though it did not entirely abate. Those who were woken not by birds but by fire engines found the sirens' ululations oddly comforting, signaling as they did that despite whatever injury, illness, death, fire, or theft had happened, the proper authorities were on their way. Not to mention the fact that misfortune was occurring elsewhere, to people other than themselves. Much of what else happened, and why, would later be disputed, but that the birds sang—everyone agreed about the birds.

Riddley was one of those awakened by sirens. Lights shone downstairs, and the phone was ringing. Below, in Sam and Pauline's room, someone picked it up. Had they come home early from the house party on Rice Island? Riddley pressed her ear to the carpet. It was Esther, who was staying the weekend in the guest room, to look after Riddley and Adele.

The sirens receded. Light reflected off the river. To the south, low in the sky, a thick cloud hovered, lit from beneath. It had to be coming from Carver's. Riddley pictured the candles burnt to stubs on the floor of Carver's room. She remembered that first day in Carver's house, when Carver held a match aloft in the cross breezes and spoke

of fire. It had been all Riddley could do then, not to knock wood. She hadn't wanted Carver to think her childish, even though it was not just children, of course, who knocked wood.

Riddley closed her eyes and saw flames swooping up the curved staircase as air rushed through the windows and doors and hallways, the house itself become a kind of bellows. *Every fire has a door,* she heard Hayden say, and there was Carver, running out into the yard, her clothes and hair on fire. And then it was Bernice in flames, her brother burning in her arms. For an instant Riddley glimpsed Bernice's terrible skin, charred, in places, clear to the bone. Riddley ran downstairs.

* * *

Riddley would've gone to Carver's at once in her nightgown, but Esther said she must put on proper clothes and comb her hair. Riddley did so faster than she ever had. Then Esther braided Riddley's hair. Riddley neither winced nor whined as Esther pulled each cord of hair tighter. Esther put the heel of her hand against the back of Riddley's head and gave the braid a final yank, to make it hang straight. Only when Esther braided her did it last all day.

They could hear cars passing, heading toward Carver's. Will Montgomery, who'd telephoned earlier, hosed their roof down in case of stray sparks. The sirens grew louder again. Where had the fire engines gone before? Birds called around the house. Esther put on a dress. Whenever she stayed overnight she took her uniform off once supper dishes were done. Then, in the mornings, she put it on again.

Esther examined herself in the mirror, and then gave Riddley a final scrutiny. "All right," Esther said, "but we ought to be ashamed. Like we're going to a circus."

Esther paused outside the garage apartment. There were no lights on, no movement behind curtains. She listened at the door to make sure Mrs. Wells was not up. She heard nothing. She didn't want to wake her by going in. Who knew what she might do if she saw the fire? Esther would check on her when they returned.

Most of the neighborhood had gathered on the back lawn to watch. The flames did indeed crackle and swoosh and roar, louder even than Riddley would have imagined. The night remained muggy, despite the dry heat of the fire.

Carver and men from the neighborhood carried out whatever was nearest to an exit, whatever wasn't too hot to the touch. People tried to stop Carver from going in, but she kept on. By the time the lost firefighters finally arrived, there was no hope of saving the house, but perhaps there never had been. The flames, urged along by the many open windows, bounded up the stairs and onto the roof and widow's walk, undiscouraged by the eventual salty drizzle of the fire hoses. As there were no hydrants for miles, water was pumped up from the river.

The women and children stood beyond where the walls could reach if they fell outward. The women held close those children who were afraid, or those who would consent to being held. The smell of the children's damp hair rose up, reminding the mothers of those same children as infants and toddlers, sweating during summer naps. How water had poured off them. The mothers had loved the smell of those moist fragrant scalps, the sweat of their children a pungent musk. What most did not recall was the near joy they'd felt that at last the child was asleep.

These same children, most grown far beyond napping, and not wanting to bring attention to how very far it was past bedtime, kept quiet. The older ones, when told they were forbidden to go any closer, even to help the fathers, grew surly, but that soon evaporated under the splendor of the blaze. The younger ones were glad to be held, or to lean against their mothers, to doze and wake again with a start, their eyes watering from the smoke and heat and brightness. Most of the children would remember this night long into adulthood.

Riddley did not doze. She watched it all. She stood before Esther, leaning back into her. Esther rested her hands on Riddley's bare shoulders. Riddley thought of Bernice's fire. How awful it must have been to watch, knowing people were inside, and knowing, too, that there was nothing you could do to save them.

* * *

Carver's legs and forearms had scratches and welts and dark streaks. The sleeves of her over-sized man's shirt kept coming unrolled, and at one point Carver paused in her jog, bent her head to meet her raised arm, took the cotton between her teeth, and with one jerk ripped the sleeve half off. With her hand she tore it the rest of the way. It was a shocking thing to do, in front of everyone like that, as if she had exposed far more than her elbow and bicep. Mid-stride, she tore off the other sleeve. She kept running in and out of the house while it was still possible to do so, before the firefighters told everyone to stand back, and then held her back when she refused, as one man holds back another, to prevent a fight. But before then, she grabbed anything she could, she didn't pause.

When Will Montgomery rescued a Victorian settee, she burst out laughing. *Christ Almighty, take that back in,* she said, *I've wanted to torch that since the day I was born.* Riddley felt Esther flinch, for Esther took it almost personally whenever someone took the name of the Lord in vain. Will didn't take it back in, of course. There was no time for that.

Riddley rubbed the green fish in her pocket, yearning for those objects she'd been tempted by, which, had she taken them, would have been saved. As the objects accumulated on the lawn, her misgivings grew piece by piece. Some of the furniture was upright, but much lay on its side or back or upended, feet in the air. It was scattered over a large area, with no relation to where each piece stood within the house.

Abruptly, she remembered the postcards. It had been less than a week since she had hidden them in the back hall. From this distance, she didn't see the cabinet. But it was small, easily lifted by one person. It stood to reason that someone would have hauled it out. With the clutter and chaos and shifting light, and the fact that so much had been removed from its context and turned wrong side up, Riddley was not sure she would know it if she saw it. Nor was she sure that she wanted it to have been rescued. Wouldn't this fire be a fitting way to carry out Frazier's request for destruction? But inadvertent destruction was hardly what he meant. He wanted whoever found the postcards to make a choice, the choice he himself had been unable to make.

Having them burn up by accident, while hidden in someone else's house, was not a real choice. Rather it was carelessness or cowardice, if not some kind of betrayal.

She pictured the postcards on Adele's broad lap. *Riddley,* Adele had said, as she held the postcard with the girl. Could Riddley have misunderstood her altogether? What if she had not been talking about her, Riddley, but about the postcard itself? That is, when Adele said *Riddley* was she referring not to her granddaughter but her sister? Could she have meant that the girl in the postcard was Aunt Riddley?

The glass blew out of a number of the windows on the upper floors, and there followed what Riddley at first took to be curtains, billowing out, from the wind the flames made as they ate their way through the house. But the curtains, as Riddley had thought them to be, did not catch on fire, as one would have expected of cloth. Instead whatever it was roiled outside the house and then dissipated. What she was seeing must simply be smoke, but why then was it such different shades? But the color of the smoke would depend on what was burning. She had once believed that in order for something to burn easily, it had to be dry, and preferably of wood or paper. But that night she saw that anything could burn, given enough fuel. And the smell, sometimes, was terrible.

* * *

Watching this fire, and watching these people watching this fire, Esther couldn't help but think of the postcards, especially of the one she'd brought home, the body burnt beyond recognition. And wouldn't these people have looked much the same, watching a black man hang, and burn? And for that, too, they had brought their children to see.

* * *

The mothers grew quieter, the children bolder, the longer it burned. The women had at first been talkative, but after a while, when it was clear there was nothing to be done but watch—after that they spoke only to call their own or someone else's children back from the fire. Gradually Riddley, like most of the other children, went back and forth

along the boundary of where they were allowed to go. *Stay close, now, Riddley,* Esther called out when Riddley passed within earshot.

Riddley looked back at her. Esther stood near the other women but apart from them. She stood very straight, her hands clasped below her breasts. Like those around her, Esther's face had been transformed by the fire. But it was more than just flame light. It was something about how she stood there, very erect and still, her face grave. She looked almost beautiful. The planes of her face, her cheekbones and forehead, were damp from the heat, and though Pauline said it was unattractive to have a shiny face, and to frown, on Esther it was not.

Esther's eyes closed and her lips moved. She was praying, but for whom, Riddley wondered, or what? Everyone was out safely. But Esther often prayed when others might not have. She prayed more than anyone Riddley had ever seen. Every single time she ate a meal, no matter what it consisted of, she said grace. She said it quietly, murmuring so low you couldn't hear anything but an occasional *Jesus* and *bless* and *Amen.* And her grace always went on much longer than the blessing Pauline had one of them say for Sunday dinners.

A few weeks earlier Pauline, reaching into the refrigerator, had spoken to Esther, not knowing that Esther was saying grace. Esther neither opened her eyes nor paused her prayer, but lifted a hand in front of her. Pauline had turned when Esther didn't answer, and seen her lifted hand, that hand which meant, *Wait.* Pauline had flushed, either from Esther's not answering, or from Esther telling her to wait, or because Pauline was embarrassed to have interrupted her in the midst of prayer. As soon as Esther was done she said, *Yes ma'am, I can stay 'til seven next Thursday,* and took a bite of ham salad.

Riddley picked her way through the salvaged furniture, searching for the cabinet. If the girl was Aunt Riddley, she wondered, what had she been doing there? Had she known the hung man? If the postcards had burnt up, Riddley would never know for sure who the girl was. And if they hadn't, didn't she have to try to find out?

Carver stood closer than anyone, as close as the firefighters would allow. When the walls fell in, the fire took on new life, the fuel stacked together like logs in a fireplace. Carver had to step back then from the heat. For the first time, she looked away from the fire. Her neighbors

avoided her glance. Her scattered belongings reminded her of an eviction she'd seen in New York.

When she saw Riddley moving among the furniture, she remembered Adele. That evening, Carver had paddled her surfboard until the last bit of dusk. When she came up to the house, Adele was on the porch in the rattan chair, which Carver had moved back to the house a few days earlier. They'd sat there in the dark, smoking, having a bourbon. Carver had assumed that Riddley would eventually come after Adele, as she had before.

Now Carver went up to Riddley and said, "Adele got back okay, didn't she?"

"Got back?" Riddley echoed. "Grandmother was here?"

Carver nodded. "We were sitting on the porch, and I drifted off probably sometime around nine-thirty, ten. When I woke up later, the house was on fire and she was gone." Carver squinted, looking off in the distance, remembering. "Right when I woke up, I heard a door slamming. That must have been Adele running out." Carver thought now how strange it was that Adele hadn't woken her. She could have burnt up in there. But Adele must have been very frightened.

Riddley recalled that day she had gone over to the garage apartment and found Adele smoking, the ashtray full of smoldering cigarettes. And Adele often smoked now with Carver. Riddley's face took on an expression common to mothers: worry not only that Adele might not be all right, but that she might not be all right because she had done something wrong. It was a notion that had not, until that moment, occurred to Carver.

Water splattered down then in big drops. Carver was taken completely by surprise. Usually she felt it coming long before it rained. People bolted, heads down and squealing a little, running for their cars. Riddley closed her eyes and tilted her face up.

The rain increased. A black woman appeared out of it, walking toward them, unstooped against the rain, her eyes on Riddley. She must be Esther. Carver remembered then that Riddley had told her Pauline and Sam were out of town.

Esther nodded at Carver, and said something to Riddley that Carver couldn't hear. The rain fell louder and harder. Riddley shook

her head, in answer or to say that she couldn't hear. Esther pulled Riddley into the curve of her body.

"Come in out the rain, Miss Varnell," Esther said.

When had anyone last said that sort of thing to her? Mattie had long since given up on that, after being so often unheeded. It was a kindness Carver would not forget, but one she could almost, at the moment, not bear. "Y'all go on ahead," she said. "I'll be right there."

Esther led Riddley away under the trees, and Carver heard first her mother, then Mattie, calling for her to come in, as one or the both of them always had at the slightest drizzle. *Carver Elliott Varnell, you come inside this very minute.* She had been ready with any excuse to go out, or stay out, in the rain. They never let her, though a few times she had done so against their wishes. She turned, back toward the house. Where was there now for her to go?

*   *   *

On the walk home the scrawny woods flickered and moved under the lights from the fire and the fire engines. Riddley led Esther along the bluff path. The rain stopped abruptly after they passed the studio, as if it had only intended to fall on the fire. About midway home the light from Carver's ceased to reach them, and after such brilliance the dark was thicker than before. It was a relief to enter it. Riddley stood still, letting her eyes get used to it.

"You lost?" Esther said, and in her voice Riddley heard that she did not like the dark.

"I'm not lost."

"You hear something?"

"I'm just giving my eyes a minute." Riddley turned her head from side to side, as if she could see, and then, quite abruptly, she could. From the corners of her eyes she saw them, and far off ahead through the darkness, those forms she had seen before only in daylight or in dreams. For a moment she was afraid. But whoever they were, she knew they were not there to harm her, but because they themselves had been harmed.

*   *   *

The last of the firefighters left after they had, as they stated over their radio, *brought the fire under control.* Meaning, there was nothing left to burn. Carver almost laughed at them, so much did they remind her of boys playing with walkie-talkies of cups and string.

Neighbors urged her to come home with them, have a bath, change clothes, eat, sleep. *It'll all still be here in the morning,* Audrey Mulrovey said, to which Carver had replied, *What will?* It would do her good, others said, to get away for a while. There was nothing, another said, left to save. One of the teenage boys was volunteered by his father to stay and watch over things, to make sure no thieves came by, or that the fire didn't restart. She did not need some boy around, thinking he was protecting her, his erection lurking in his bleached boxers. She almost had to be rude to convince them that she did indeed want to stay there, and alone.

* * *

Esther and Riddley checked the garage apartment, in hopes that Adele had returned on her own. Then with flashlights they searched the yard and Isabel's car and the dock. Adele was nowhere to be found. The flashlight beam shone on the rainwater in the bateau, left in by mistake. Riddley, forbidden to go out on the river while her parents were away, had forgotten to pull the bateau onto the dock.

Esther sat now on the side of Sam and Pauline's bed, where she had agreed that Riddley could, due to the circumstances, sleep. "She can't have gone far," she said, "in the dark." But her voice hardly sounded convincing, to herself or Riddley.

Esther said she'd wait up, and leave all the lights on outside, in case Adele returned. "If I'm not here when you get up, I'm out looking for her. You fix yourself a cold breakfast and stay put, so there'll be someone home if she comes back. Last thing I need is two of you to track down."

Nothing was said about contacting the neighbors, or the police, for both Esther and Riddley were worried, without saying so, that Adele had something to do with the fire. Why else would she have run away? Riddley's most recent worry was also too awful to say: that

Carver had heard an internal door slamming, not one leading out, so that all that time, as they watched, Adele had been inside, burning.

Riddley began to drift off, then lurched awake at the thought that not only had Adele started the fire and died in it, but that she, Riddley, would be blamed, and not just that she would be blamed, but that she was to blame, for taking Adele to Carver's to begin with, for keeping so much secret—Adele's smoking, Frazier's notes, the portrait.

And how would they ever tell Pauline what had happened? Riddley imagined saying, *Grandmother is dead*. But what Pauline would hear, what Pauline would feel was, *Your mother is dead*.

"Don't forget your prayers," Esther said, placing her hand on Riddley's arm.

"I said them already, before."

"No harm saying them again."

So Riddley clasped her hands together and prayed for Adele and Carver, and the poor and needy, and for the Lord to keep her soul, or, if necessary, to take it.

* * *

After everyone had gone, Carver looked around her at what was left. There was the studio, and the car and garage and stable. Rett Ogilvie, before the firefighters had arrived, had hosed down the roofs of those buildings for sparks, and left her a couple of packs of cigarettes and a lighter. Jasper Kane had left her a bottle of whiskey. And someone had left a cooler of ice and soft drinks and the kind of food one takes on a picnic. Tomorrow she would partake of the food, but at the moment she was most grateful for the men's offerings. Carver grabbed a pack of Marlboros, a bottle of water and another of Johnny Walker Red, and brought these with her to the edge of the bluff, to the wrought iron bench. She wiped rainwater off the seat. She was well beyond the smoldering ruins, but she was able still to feel the heat. Her skin felt hot to the touch, as after sunburn. She sat on the bench on the scalded lawn, that heat real or imagined behind her, and before her, the relative cool of the river. The tide was close to high, though she didn't know if it was about to turn or had already done so. What moon

there was had set or not yet risen. What had happened? Would she ever know? She couldn't think about it yet. She tipped her head back and gulped down water. Then she took a swallow of whiskey.

The sky seemed nowhere near dawn, though she thought it could not be too far off. What time was it? When she'd changed to go on the river, she'd left her watch on her bureau. Nothing had been retrieved from the top floor. When had the fire started? Ten-thirty, eleven, twelve? She had woken up coughing, the inside of her nose already blackened, as she had seen a few moments later, when she wiped it on her sleeve. How long did the fire take to burn itself out? For that was essentially what it had done, firefighters notwithstanding.

She lit a cigarette, not quite believing that she would wish to take still more smoke into her. It made her cough a while. She took another gulp of water, another wincing sip of whiskey.

She saw then, in the air and water and trees, flashes and glimmers of light. Heat lightning flared above the sound. Fireflies sparked in the hedges. Light flickered like flame over the marsh. Near the Crosses' dock, light pulsed white in specks and zigzags under the water. It moved upriver, flashing brightest around the pilings. Had her eyes been damaged by smoke and heat, by so much dazzling light? Then she knew what the light in the water came from. It was the noctiluca. There were millions of them out there this time of year. Their light, like that of the fireflies, was a light without heat. They gave off that cold glow whenever a porpoise or an otter or a school of fish passed through them, or when they came into contact with the bottom of a boat or floating dock, or got caught in the midst of a breaking wave. She inhaled deeply, the tip of her cigarette bright and hot, signaling back.

She sat a long while on the bluff, then stripped on the dock and dove into the dark river. She has always loved swimming naked, and at night, though swimming in the dark Carver felt less buoyant, as if it were the light, not the saltiness of the water, that kept her afloat. Plunging under, she swam hard upriver, against the current. Suddenly she began to sob, or that's what she would have been doing had she been in the air. Instead, she gulped in great mouthfuls of water. She

came up spewing and gasping. She made her way to the dock. She gripped the side, coughing. River water churned in her. She thought she might throw up, but the feeling passed.

She pulled herself onto the dock and lay on her back, panting. Her throat and tongue felt rough and thick. She swallowed and licked her lips. She was completely parched. Drinking saltwater, she knew, only makes you thirstier.

She got to her feet. She gathered up her clothes and walked across the ramp and the upper dock, then up the steep steps to the bluff, where she stood a long moment, naked, looking, seeing in the pre-dawn light what was there and what was no longer there.

*   *   *

In the huge expanse of her parents' bed, Riddley dreamed of shapes fluttering like cloth in the trees. But there was only smoke, and she was confused within her dream, because what she had seen had been falling, not rising. Had the fire spread to the trees? *Riddley,* Adele said, but she wasn't talking to her, she was talking to her sister. And Riddley saw only trees. Had she ever had a dream, Riddley thought within the dream, without people? Or no people, at least, that she could fully see. Could they see her? That thought tore her, crying out, from sleep.

Esther, who'd been mopping to keep herself awake, dozed with her head on the kitchen table. The mop handle which she had clutched throughout her own flitting dreams slid to the floor with a clatter when she woke from Riddley's cry.

"Hush, hush, it's just a dream," Esther said, even though she well knew that was rarely the case.

Riddley twisted in the sheet, caught in a half-sleep. She had to sit up, turn on a light. The nightmare was pulling her back into itself, calling to her in the voice of her grandmother, *Riddley, Riddley,* who was calling someone else, someone long dead. Her voice receded, grew thinner, wavery, a distance widening between her and Riddley.

"Where's she going?" Riddley said.

"Who?"

"Grandmother's getting farther away."

"She's not going anywhere, child, she's resting somewhere, we'll find her in the morning. You're dreaming still."

"No, I know it, she's going far off."

"Hush, hush. Go back to sleep, I'll sit here with you," Esther said, soothingly, but it gave her chills. Maybe old Ida Mae had been right about Riddley, about what she could see. Esther sat on the side of the bed and took Riddley's hand, and patted it, humming, praying silently, until Riddley slept again. Esther caught herself just before she too drifted off. She lay Riddley's hand down on the sheet, then rose slowly, her hips aching in the sockets, the bones of her neck feeling shifted out of place. She went back to the kitchen, to resume her cleaning, her vigil.

*　*　*

After Adele ran out of the burning house, she stood a long while in the bushes at the edge of Carver's property. When the sirens came close, she crouched down, pressing her hands over her ears, watching the fire through the trees, how its light trembled and flared and grew, reaching farther and farther outward, as if in pursuit of her. Some part of her was in another summer long ago, at the outskirts of another crowd, one she had eventually run and hidden from, when there had also, come nightfall, been fire, and that time too she had crouched in the bushes, afraid to watch but watching.

After a while she stood and entered the sparse woods between houses. She walked along the edge of the bluff, and then went down the stairs to their dock. The motorboat was in the hoist and she climbed in. Its rocking lulled her, and she slept. The rain pounding on the tin roof woke her, and then there were people calling. The worry in their raised voices, the cones of the flashlights darting over the planks and water, the lingering effects of the sirens and crowd and fire, and of memory lurking just out of the corner of her mind, along with that familiar sense she'd had as a child, of having always just done or been about to do something wrong—these things made her huddle in the space between the motorboat's seats, and keep still.

After they left, she went down to the floating dock. She climbed into the bateau. She sat there a long while, dozing. She woke from the splash of someone diving into the water, then kicking and coughing. When it was silent again, Adele untied the lines. At once the tide took her and spun her out, into the main current.

PART FOUR

CHAPTER 17

Aftermath

Early the next morning, Riddley went again to Isabel's car, thinking Adele might have gone there to sleep. It was empty. She slid into the front seat. She would just sit for a minute. She was very tired. Out of habit, she had woken up not long past dawn, and once she remembered all that had happened, she could hardly turn over and go back to sleep. On the kitchen table was a note from Cole, saying Riddley should wait there while he and Esther looked for Adele. Riddley couldn't stand to just wait inside, doing nothing, so she had taken *there* to mean their property, which included the yard as well as the house.

After returning last night from Carver's, Riddley had listened in on Esther's call to Cole. Esther had blamed herself for Adele's absence. She wanted to call the police, but Cole said wait. *It looks bad,* he said, *how she ran off.* And if the police got in on it, he added, it would look bad for Esther, too. Why would Adele run away, Riddley wondered, unless she had done something wrong? But if she had, wouldn't any evidence have burnt up?

Riddley looked in the glove compartment, as she had meant to do since she'd caught Adele smoking in the apartment. As she expected, the nearly full pack of Salems was missing, an absence which seemed, under the circumstances, a kind of evidence, for again she pictured the gravy boat with its smoldering cigarettes.

She adjusted the rear view mirror and placed her hands on the wheel. The air was heavy, despite the early hour and the shade. She rolled the window down and leaned her head back. She closed her eyes. The smells of smoke and cigarettes, talcum powder, wet fabric and hair grew stronger. Adele must be close by if she could smell her, Riddley thought from within her doze. She felt someone watching her. There in the rear view mirror was Adele, standing precisely where she would be reflected, to make sure she would be seen.

Riddley figured she should act nonchalant, so as not to frighten her. "Let's go for a ride, Grandmother," she called out, watching her in the mirror, "you can drive if you want." Riddley leaned out the window and looked back. Adele had disappeared.

Riddley searched the muddy ground to figure out which way she'd headed. She knew exactly what the print of Adele's shoe looked like, having seen it many times. She examined a wide area, and found many tracks, but the only human ones were her own. Could she have dreamed her? She straightened from her crouch. Didn't ghosts sometimes appear in mirrors? But last night's dread that Adele had died in the fire seemed foolish in the daylight. Adele was only missing, wandering or hiding or lost. And she would be found.

Riddley must have just been seeing what she was searching for, what she wanted to see. That was how Pauline always explained such things, including Riddley's various imaginings. Such an explanation hardly worked, however, on those occasions when what Riddley saw was something she would never wish to, something for which she would never have searched. She recalled her walk home the night before with Esther, how all around her had been those forms in the trees, and how they had returned in her sleep. She remembered then what she had dreamed. Adele was out there, too, in the darkness of that dream, though too far away to see, being already past the dock lights, and with no moon to reflect off the water. Dock lights. Water. Wouldn't Adele naturally, after fire, head toward water? Riddley took off running for the dock. At the edge of the bluff she saw what she already knew. The bateau was gone.

*　*　*

Carver, stretched out nude on the studio sofa, opened her eyes again, and looked sideways at Adele's portrait. She had painted her in the rattan chair, but that had come to seem wrong, so she had recently painted over it, intending to replace it with something less obtrusive, or possibly something that had more to do with Adele. The result, as she noticed now, was that Adele seemed to be almost floating, despite the solidity of her. And, though you could not see the chair, it seemed still present. If furniture could have a ghost, she thought, then this

chair surely would, it having witnessed much and then died a rapid, crackling death. From the lawn, she had seen it burst into flames. She would miss that chair. Having painted it, she'd lost her nervousness over it. She had sat in it yesterday evening, before she went out on the river.

She closed her eyes. She would drape the portrait with a sheet, until she could work on it again. Had Adele been found? Again she wondered why Adele hadn't woken her when the fire started. She must not have understood what was happening.

A throat was cleared outside the door, followed by a tentative knock. Carver sat up, looking around for something to cover herself with. The only thing within reach, and possibly the only thing anywhere, was last night's torn and filthy shirt, in a heap on the floor. She pulled it on. It smelled as if it had caught fire and been doused with stagnant water.

"Yeah?"

"It's Riddley."

"Oh, come on in." She swept her hair, stiff with salt and soot, back from her face.

Riddley slid open the door and screen and curtain and stepped into the room. One look told Carver something was wrong. "What is it?"

"Grandmother's missing. I think she's run away." Riddley looked down, but not before Carver saw anguish cross her face.

"You think she had something to do with the fire."

Riddley glanced up quickly. "Not on purpose. By accident." She looked away again. "She's careless sometimes."

"Everyone is. And it's certainly possible that she was. But even if she did run away, that doesn't prove anything. Guilt's only one of a thousand reasons to run away. Besides, Adele often runs away. She's probably just lost. The fire must've spooked her. She'll turn up soon."

Riddley shook her head. "I saw her just a few minutes ago, or what I thought was her. She was right there in the rear view mirror. But there were no tracks, even though tracks always show on mud," she said, her words coming out in a rush. "And last night in the dream I couldn't see her, it was too dark to see her, but I could hear her, I

could tell she was on the water, and I just went on the bluff and it's gone." This too, she realized, was her fault. If she hadn't left the bateau in, Adele wouldn't have been able to go out in it.

"Hold on, Riddley. What's gone?"

"The bateau."

"Sweet Jesus." Carver grabbed her cut-offs from the floor and thrust her feet into them. Then in one motion she stood and pulled them on. Riddley had never known anyone to not wear underwear. "What's the tide? Outgoing, isn't it?"

Riddley nodded.

"How long 'til low?"

"One-and-a-half, two hours."

"Does she know how to drive it?" Carver headed for the dock.

"I don't know. I've never seen her drive any boat."

"Which doesn't mean she can't. Let's hope she couldn't get it started, or it ran out of gas if she did, or she got caught on some nearby sand bar. We'll just have to assume she went with the tide." Carver looked at Riddley. "Unless there's somewhere particular that you know of where she might try to go."

Riddley, trotting to keep up, shook her head. "Not that I can think of."

"She can swim, can't she?"

"She used to could, as far as I know. I don't know if she still can." She halted. "I have to find Esther first and tell her. She told me not to go anywhere."

Carver turned and faced her. "Riddley, there's no time. We have to get to Adele before she reaches the sound. Once she's out there she—we might never find her." She looked, for the first time, at the sky. "Lord, there's another storm coming. A front must be moving through."

"Esther thinks it's her fault. She doesn't know Grandmother's snuck out before. She's worried she'll get in trouble. Her husband Cole came from town to help search."

"All right, you're right. Esther's got enough to worry about. Go leave her a note."

"She can't—" Riddley said, and then nodded. "I'll leave one for Cole."

"Run, then," Carver said, but Riddley already was. "I'll pick you up on your dock."

After Riddley climbed aboard, Carver put the boat at full throttle, despite the fact that it was near low. Riddley sat cross-legged in the bow. Water splashed her each time the bow crashed down between swells. The sky grew thicker and grayer. The wind picked up as they rounded the bend near Oakleigh. Soundless lightning flashed beyond the sound. They saw no other boats out, not even shrimp boats. A big storm must be headed in.

They were nearly to Moss Island Sound when Riddley spotted a boat. "There," Riddley called, pointing. Carver nodded, already veering toward it. They were too far to tell. Soon they could see that someone was in the bow. As they grew closer, they recognized Adele. She was slumped over, facing the stern, her arms resting on her knees. She appeared to be asleep.

"Another twenty minutes, half hour," Carver shouted above the wind, "and we might've been too late." Had the wind not been pushing Adele back, she would have been much farther out by then, perhaps as far as Indigo Sound, the last thing between themselves and the ocean. Out there the waves would be high enough to capsize a craft as small as the bateau.

More lightning flared. Riddley felt the thunder in her stomach and chest. Pauline would have been frantic, but against all reasoning Riddley felt anything but afraid. The lightning didn't want them, not this time anyway.

Carver pulled up alongside the bateau. On the seat beside Adele an oar balanced, its blade muddy. She must have run aground, or into the marsh, and pushed herself off. Carver and Riddley called her until she lifted her head. Her face and arms were streaked with dirt. She glared at them. She didn't realize they had come to save her.

"She's like this when she gets woken up," Riddley said.

The waves were such that Carver worried about Adele climbing into the motorboat, so Riddley got into the bateau with her. Underneath

the damp smoky odor of Adele's hair and clothes, Riddley could smell that Adele had wet herself. She hoped Carver wouldn't notice.

Carver had brought a rope for towing, but the bateau had plenty of gas. Adele must have been borne solely by the current. Riddley started the motor on the second pull. Carver led the way back. Riddley bailed as she drove. Water sloshed against their shins. The sky darkened to the west, thunder sounding behind them.

Once they passed the shrimp boat dock there was sudden light, in patches, on the water. The marsh across from their bluff turned luminous. The storm was passing to the west of them. Riddley leaned over and put her hand in. She hoped Esther would let her swim.

Carver raised her arm in a wave as she turned toward her dock. Riddley saw the blackened columns, and what looked like wisps of smoke. Beyond her view were Carver's belongings, still wet from last night's downpour. Had the postcards survived the fire, they might well have been damaged by the rain.

Esther and Cole waited in the spot on the bluff where Pauline always stood. The thought of Pauline, of telling her tomorrow all that had happened, broke the exhilaration of rescuing Adele, and of going with Carver into the sound, into a storm.

* * *

Grant us, O Lord, not to mind earthly things, but to love things heavenly; and even now, while we are placed among things that are passing away, to cleave to those that shall abide.

This prayer was said that morning in the church where Carver had long ago been christened and confirmed, where funeral services had been held for Evelyn and Reed, the same church where Riddley would have gone had Pauline been home. Other prayers like it were said elsewhere, and thus did news of the fire spread. Congregations were urged to pray for Carver in this time of devastation, and to give, along with material aid, comfort and sympathy and a shoulder for her to cry on, should she display any such inclination, which no one thought for a second that she would. As if Carver Varnell were some poor orphan!

When in fact she was beyond a doubt the richest single woman in town, as many a thwarted suitor was aware.

After church, or after dinner at home or the club, families drove out to offer condolences and food and to view, as with an open casket, the remains. But by then Carver had blocked off the driveway with some sawhorses from the barn. The better vantage, anyway, was from the river. The Ashburn saw more traffic over the next few days than it had seen since the Civil War, when Confederate maneuvers were launched from there against Union warships in Indigo Sound. People filled coolers with cocktails and ice and puttered by during the long evenings. Those who could visualize the house as it had once stood were particularly affected by the ruins, but even those who had never seen the house at all were not disappointed by the lonesome pillars, the charred trees, the heaped bricks and beams and rubble, which was said to still be emitting random gusts of smoke as much as a week later. *Remember Tara?* one mother said to her little girl, to give her an idea of the former grandeur, and the father added, *Remember Sherman?* The few who attempted to dock were quickly rebuffed by the padlock and chain at the top of the ramp, along with the signs proclaiming, *Trespassers will be shot on sight* and *This property guarded by one Doberman Pinscher, one trigger-happy Redneck, and one Sawed-off Shotgun.* Occasionally Carver herself could be seen, poking through the remains, but never did she return anyone's wave.

The fire, people said, was due to smoking in bed or drinking alone; to poor upkeep or the fact that the house was entirely in a woman's hands; to bad wiring, to old brittle wood made more brittle by the summer's searing heat and the unusually long periods between rains; to the beetles that had turned the nearby pines to kindling; to the fact that the fire engines got lost and arrived only after the fire was well established; to the family's long tradition of misfortune. These were some of the many explanations that were made, some of the blames that were cast. Was Carver smoking when she fell asleep, did she leave the oven on, or the stove, or a lamp whose shade brushed the bulb, melted through and caught, igniting a nearby curtain? One person suggested that Carver had, out of some convoluted sense of spite or malice, set the fire herself, but few held to that theory, for what

reason would she have to destroy all that? There was the insurance, but that was thought to be minor compared to the rest of her wealth, not to mention what she had lost. And so many of those things, being of historical, familial, or sentimental value, you really couldn't put a price on, though the insurance adjustors were doing the best they could.

Some people said they had seen it coming, that, really, they were not surprised. Underneath all the expressions of concern, the offerings of clothes and bedding, food and shelter, something else could be detected. It was not only that people had seen it coming. There was also the unspoken notion that Carver had it coming, that she had somehow brought it upon herself. Even after the fire was, weeks later, officially determined to have been electrical—that the fire, that is, had absolutely nothing to do with Carver's solitude, art, childlessness, reputation, attire, impropriety, wealth, curses, looks, lip or gumption, or with whatever kind of person she was or was not—still few would renounce their own theories as to the fire's cause. Rarely are people willing to change their opinion about someone due to mere facts.

Carver had her own theories, many of which likewise disregarded the official explanation. For one, she was by no means convinced that she, or Adele, hadn't left a cigarette burning. And the electrical explanation raised its own questions, such as, would the house have burnt down anyway, whether or not she'd been in it, whether or not she'd ever moved back? She had the distinct feeling it would not have.

After the fire there came a heat wave that even the violent rainstorms were unable to break. Instead the storms further thickened the air, and made the land seem constantly steaming. Among those who had no air conditioning, or could not afford to turn it on, nights brought no relief. Sleeplessness and electricity bills soared, as did the crime rate.

Along the bluff, the typical breezes for the most part ceased. Likewise did the temperature of the river seem markedly higher, like soup on a low simmer. Before that, the summer had been hot—summers always were—eliciting the usual complaints and grumbling, but the people along the bluff had always felt themselves to be better off than those in town, those without wind and water to soothe them-

selves with. Thus to suffer the heat the same as others seemed far worse, as if some punishment were being inflicted upon them.

* * *

Riddley had forgotten to consider how many questions Pauline would ask upon her return. The one that tripped Riddley up was this: *Did Grandmother go with you to Carver's?* If only Pauline had asked if Adele were there, or had seen the fire, then Riddley could have answered *yes* without hesitation.

"Not exactly," Riddley answered.

"Not exactly?"

In the back room, Esther was getting her things together. She came into the kitchen.

"Grandmother didn't go with us," Riddley said.

Pauline frowned. "But she went?"

Riddley nodded.

"She went by herself?"

"She was already there."

Pauline blanched. "She was there when the house caught fire?"

"It's my fault, ma'am," Esther said. "She snuck out after I put her down."

"If it's anybody's fault, Esther, it's mine. I should've listened to Mr. Cross about a lock."

"She'd already left by the time we got to Carver's," Riddley said. "Carver said she ran out right after it started."

"She didn't get lost on the way back, in the dark?"

Riddley shook her head, her breath held. Now Pauline would find out about Adele's bateau ride. But Esther kept quiet. Maybe she was waiting for Riddley to begin.

Pauline frowned. "Well thank heavens it worked out all right. But things are certainly going to change. Mother can't go traipsing around the neighborhood in the middle of the night." She looked in the direction of the garage apartment, and shook her head. "I'll run you on home now, Esther. I know your family's missing you."

"Yes, ma'am."

"Riddley, you stay in the garage apartment with Grandmother. Don't go out, and don't let her out of your sight for even a minute, you hear?"

"I won't."

"You take good care of your grandmother, now," Esther said, placing her hand on the back of Riddley's head.

"I will, I promise." Riddley wrapped her arms around Esther. They had another secret now, and one that they both knew they shared.

After Pauline returned from taking Esther home, she gave Riddley a long look. "There are other things you need to tell me, aren't there?" Pauline sighed in that way she had, when she knew she wasn't going to like what you had to tell her, but that you had to tell it, and she had to hear it, regardless.

Riddley nodded. This was just like Pauline: right when Riddley thought she had gotten away with something, Pauline revealed that she knew more than she'd been letting on. But how much more? That was what Riddley had to gauge in this instant, lest she give away more than was necessary. Had Esther revealed anything in the car on the way home? But Esther was better than any of them at resisting Pauline's probing. And the way Pauline brought the topic up made Riddley think she was mostly going off a hunch.

There were so many things she had not told Pauline, Riddley hardly knew where to start. And where had it all started, really? At so many points Riddley had failed to speak up when she should have. And it was more than just silence. It was concealing things, it was lying. One instance after another rushed into her mind: taking Frazier's postcards and his notes about Adele; the time she'd found Adele smoking next door, and at Carver's; how she'd left the bateau in the water the night of the fire, and Adele had gone to the sound; how she'd snuck Adele over to Carver's for the portrait. The portrait—that would satisfy Pauline, for the time being anyway, though it might be the least of Riddley's offenses.

After Riddley told her about the portrait, Pauline said, "Did it survive the fire?"

Riddley nodded. "Carver does all her painting in the studio. That's what she calls the carriage house."

"Have you seen it? This portrait?"

Riddley shook her head. "Carver said she'd show me when it was done."

That evening, before dark, Sam returned from the hardware store with the lock. Pauline had hoped that Riddley would not be around when he installed it, but as soon as he emerged with his tools, Riddley appeared. Just as the girls could be counted on to make themselves scarce whenever they were sought, likewise did one of them always turn up if there was something to be witnessed. Pauline herself couldn't stand to watch, and anyway, she was supposed to keep Adele away from the apartment. Sam later informed her that Riddley had helped him install the lock. He had given her a new responsibility, one she had seemed glad to accept: every day, first thing, she would unlock Adele's door. If she got there early enough, he said, Adele might never even know she'd been locked in.

The next morning, dawn still in the sky and Riddley still in her nightgown, she went to unlock Adele's door. As quietly as possible, she slid the chain out of its slot. As she let the chain dangle she felt a small thrill, as though she had just released the bolt on some wild animal's cage, one that did not yet know it was free. But of course it was Adele's captivity that they hoped would remain secret.

* * *

Pauline, after her long weekend away, had been quite shaken to see her mother. Could Adele's condition really have declined so dramatically over a mere three days? No doubt the fire had taken some toll, as, perhaps, had Pauline's own absence, despite how indifferent Adele seemed to her presence. Pauline realized as well that she had probably not been as aware of her mother's decline, watching it happen right in front of her. Everybody always said it was like that. Pauline pictured Adele at Frazier's funeral. She had not been anywhere near this bad. And that had been only four months ago. So what did that mean, Pauline wondered, for the next four months, the next, God help her, God help *me*, four years?

The thought of the portrait nagged at Pauline. Why would anyone want to paint her mother? She tried to picture it but her mind kept

shying away. She wanted to see it, but since Carver had kept it from her, it was awkward to ask her. But Pauline had to see it. She had a growing suspicion that the portrait might reveal something about her mother that she needed to know, that she hadn't been able to see for herself.

Riddley went to fetch Adele for supper. Adele pulled the apartment door shut, and then, quite matter-of-factly, slid the new lock into place, as if, like a regular lock, it was for keeping others out. Or as if there were someone else in the apartment, some prisoner or lunatic who might try to escape while she was gone.

*   *   *

Carver had refused all offers of shelter. In the garage she found an old canvas tent, which she erected on the bluff, beneath a live oak, to the northeast of where the house had stood. At the Salvation Army she bought pots, pans, cushions, bedding, and clothes, to supplement the donations she'd received. She covered the tent floor with the cushions, as if in a harem.

The neighborhood men brought her more whiskey, and advised her on which trash man to hire to haul away the debris. But mostly the men stayed away. They knew there was much to be done and that they, as gentlemen, should offer to do it, though they figured that Carver, no damsel in distress, would refuse. There was always the chance, however, that she wouldn't, so they sent their wives as emissaries. The women called on Carver more than they ever had. Some came by the bluff, but most parked on the road and walked up the driveway, calling out *Yoo hoo, anybody home?* as they approached, though their husbands said Carver was only bluffing about the shotgun. They came bearing food, and castoff clothes, linens, dishes. They didn't stay long. Carver made sure of that, by being herself and by acting a bit crazed, though which was which was not so clear to her.

Over the next days the women would bring food enough for a growing family. Carver received not the casseroles and cakes distributed to the just delivered or bereaved, but the cans and boxes normally destined for the needy, for where could Carver keep anything fresh? It would only have been a matter of hours in that heat, as the

studio's refrigerator had broken years before. In the evenings she built a campfire, over which she heated up the contents of a can, and beside which she sat, drinking her second bourbon, until she was drowsy enough to sleep. After all day in the sun, she didn't want to be in the hot studio, or to make it any hotter by cooking in there. And she had discovered the great pleasure to be had in making a fire. It focused her in a way little else could these days. It was a bit like getting back on the horse after being thrown. But she did not feel afraid of fire. If anything, she felt more entranced by it.

She went to bed and rose much earlier than she was used to. Most nights she slept salty from the river. Why rinse off when she would jump in first thing? That's what she did after coffee, and then at intervals throughout the day. Salvaging was hard, filthy work. She was exhausted by nightfall, from picking through and moving aside rubble, looking for whatever might have survived. And by what means *did* a thing survive? By chance or luck or fate, and what exactly, she wondered, was the difference between these? Thus far, very little had been worth recovering.

She took to making a fire in the morning, too, instead of making coffee in the studio, as she had the first couple of days. She generally avoided going into the studio. That was where she intended, eventually, to move, but she didn't like being in there when she wasn't painting. And when she'd be able to do that again, she couldn't yet say.

Riddley, crabbing from the dock or bateau in the early mornings, often glimpsed the smoke from Carver's campfire. It seemed a perfect existence to Riddley: swimming often, bathing seldom, cooking over a fire, sleeping outside. Perfect, that is, until she looked at Carver's face. The fire hadn't aged Carver, as tragedy was said sometimes to do. But it had, people said, made Carver more peculiar, and pushed her out to the edge of where she had, from all indications, been already headed.

For example, what she did with what she found. It began with the chandelier prisms. The first day searching, Carver found three prisms wholly intact, and a half dozen partially so. She hung them from fishing line in the branches of the live oak at the edge of the bluff. They spun and swung, carving slits of colored light into the rutted lawn.

She expanded from there. At any place on the property you might come across a mangled object—some identifiable, most not—hung from a branch, balanced atop a fencepost, or thrust into the crook of a tree. Some people thought such behavior tasteless, but someone had always thought and would no doubt always think such a thing about Carver. Others thought she had, as Pauline put it, *gone off the deep end,* to which Sam, who found Carver as pointedly sane as she'd always been, replied, *Well she better put some water in first.*

Why some things had survived while others hadn't became even more mysterious to Carver. For example, she pulled from the rubble an entire pane of diamond-shaped leaded glass, from one of the downstairs bathrooms. She made the pane a sling from fishing line and hung it in a water oak beside the tent. In the dark, the pane and the chandelier prisms picked up any available light—from passing boats, the sun or moon rising and setting, the campfire, a match, light from who knew where.

Riddley spent much less time crabbing. Instead, she often went by Carver's. Pauline couldn't object to Riddley helping someone in their adversity. Carver did not turn her away, though some days she might not speak more than a few words. Riddley looked for the cabinet among the rescued furniture, but Carver had covered all of it with tarps. In her pocket Riddley rubbed the stone fish, awaiting the perfect moment to discover and return it. *How lucky,* Carver might say then, perhaps even smiling.

Hayden returned from his mother's a few days after the fire, full of regret that he'd missed it. Most days he went with Riddley to Carver's. They gathered firewood and picked through the rubble, making piles of potentially valuable or curious objects. Carver looked through these, casting most aside, saving one or two for the trees or fence posts.

Sometimes Carver did not recognize an object. She would look at it for a long time, turning it round and round in her hand, putting it back down. Then she might pick it up again a while later and say, *Oh I know what it is.* If her mood had not been made too grim by her discovery, Riddley or Hayden would ask her what the object was. Sometimes she would tell them. *Sink trap, enamel basin, umbrella*

stand, door handle of the refrigerator, my Uncle Elliott's trombone.
More often she would toss the thing at their feet and say, *A reward
if you figure it out.* Not that that was much incentive. A reward from
Carver was likely to be something she might well give you anyway:
potato chips, a Coke, a drag off her cigarette for Hayden, the chance
to light it for Riddley, or, sometimes, and depending on what it was,
the object itself. Thus had Riddley acquired a deformed silver spoon
and a chunk of melted glass.

Carver hired Mattie's son Vernon to help her move the furniture off the lawn. Into the garage Riddley and Hayden hauled the
smaller objects, paintings and lamps and such, while Carver and
Vernon moved the larger furniture. A few things they moved into the
studio. The cabinet, Riddley saw, was one of those. The postcards
seemed then almost invincible, as though because they had not been
destroyed by accident, they'd proven that they should not, and perhaps could not, be destroyed by will. They had as well been made
more valuable by their rescue, and their near demise, and the time
had come, Riddley knew, to reclaim them.

* * *

The evening after moving the furniture inside, Carver found the postcards. She wondered which relative they had belonged to, her grandfather or uncle, possibly her father. She hoped not her father. The girl
in the postcard was eerily familiar, in a way Carver couldn't place.
Carver felt sure she had seen her before, and in the flesh. In terms of
timing, though, that seemed impossible. Carver must have known her
when she, Carver, was a child, and the girl was long grown. The girl
could well be a relative.

How fitting, Carver thought, that these postcards, of all things,
had survived the fire. It made an awful sense to her. She was sick-
ened, but hardly surprised. After the utter astonishment of the fire, she
wondered if she would ever find it in herself to be surprised again.
She had always rather expected to find something along these lines,
among the many papers she'd been through. It gave her a kind of
bitter satisfaction, though it made her wonder, too, at all she hadn't
found.

CHAPTER 18

Namesake

On a shelf in the garage apartment stood the picture of Aunt Riddley, perched alongside her sisters in a wagon driven by a black man. Riddley had always liked her own first name well enough, though rarely had she considered where it came from. But it was rather disconcerting to think that she was this girl's namesake, as if a similarity in temperament and destiny would also eventually be bestowed. Or maybe the similarity of the caul was enough, if Pauline was right about both Riddleys having been born that way.

According to Pauline, this was the only photo they had of all the sisters. With great care, Riddley extracted it from its frame. On the back, in faded block letters, was recorded: *Sophia, Eleanor, Riddley, Virginia, Adele, Roberta, 1903.* Below that, written in a darker ink and a different hand, it said *Elijah.* That must have been the name of the driver, or possibly the name of the horse, if they'd been particularly fond of him.

Riddley studied the picture a long time. Could this scowling girl, her hair tucked under a bonnet, be the same as the pretty one in the postcard? The two seemed utterly dissimilar, but they might still have been the same girl, years apart. Judging by Adele, a towheaded toddler in this picture, Adele's mother would have died just a year or two earlier. Perhaps that death, and Aunt Riddley's subsequent responsibilities, had caused her to lose her looks, an event which could, Riddley knew from Pauline, result from an unwillingness to look on the bright side. From everything Riddley had ever heard about her aunt, she had abandoned cheerfulness at an exceptionally early age.

But what Riddley needed to discover was if her Aunt Riddley had ever had any looks to lose. In this photo, there was nothing pretty about her. *Pretty is,* Pauline liked to tell her daughters, *as pretty does.* But in Riddley's experience it hardly mattered what you did, if you

were pretty enough, that pretty could pretty much do what pretty liked. And the girl in the postcard was plenty pretty, and knew it, as if prettiness were prettiness anywhere, regardless of circumstances. In fact, it was. The postcard proved it. The girl was still pretty, despite where she stood, despite the man hanging beside her.

Riddley replaced the photo in its frame and took from the bookshelf the few photo albums. Pauline had put most of them next door, for fear Adele might cut the pictures up, the way she had once with some photos of her and Frazier. One album was of a trip to Singapore; another was of Pauline's coming out; the last had many old black-and-whites, along with pages of faded newspaper articles, which Riddley didn't bother to read, as those she glanced at seemed mostly to be about weddings and deaths and the like. The first two albums had names, date, and place under each photo, but the last album's photos seldom had more than a date, if that. A few times she recognized Frazier and Adele, but with most of the photos, no one looked familiar. And no one bore any strong resemblance to the girl in the postcard, with her blonde hair and dark eyes.

Pauline was the best means of finding out if the girl was Aunt Riddley. But Pauline closed books and magazines and newspapers, and changed channels on the television when there was something she did not wish her daughters or herself to see. *What good could ever possibly come of looking at such dreadful things?* she might well ask upon seeing the postcards. And Riddley could think of no answer to that, though she felt certain there was one.

And even if Pauline did recognize Aunt Riddley, Riddley was not at all sure that she would admit it, perhaps even to herself. *People who would go to see such things,* Pauline might well say, *were common.* Nor was it only about Aunt Riddley having seen it. For an adult must have escorted her, a hanging not being the kind of thing a young girl would be allowed to see on her own. Nor could she have refused if told to attend. But even had she not wanted to go at the outset, she had seemed, by the look on her face, to be enjoying herself, or at least to not be sorry she was there. Riddley knew how it was to want to see what you shouldn't, at one and the same time to want, and not

want, to look. But she knew, too, that you could appear to be enjoying yourself and not feel that way at all.

*　*　*

"How's Adele?" Carver said. She and Riddley were sitting on the dock, eating watermelon, after scavenging all afternoon. Hayden, due home every day at five, had just left for his grandmother's.

Riddley shrugged. "Fine, I guess," she said, which was hardly true. Part of that was due to Pauline, who was spending more time with Adele, and keeping her inside as much as possible. But part of it was due to Adele herself. Something seemed to have happened to her the night of the fire. She had ceased, for a while anyway, to wander. When Riddley sat for her now, it was really sitting, and so it had come to seem more like a job, a task to be gotten over with, rather than something she might well be doing anyway and happened to get paid for.

"I had to tell my mother about the portrait. I'm sorry."

"Secrets tend to get found out, sooner or later. Most of them anyway."

Riddley's cheeks and neck reddened. What, Carver wondered, was she hiding?

"I hope I didn't get you in trouble," Carver said.

Riddley shook her head.

"I don't need Adele to pose anymore. I'd just like to see her again."

"My mother doesn't let her out much these days."

"Maybe that's for the best, considering where she went the last time she went out."

"I didn't tell her about that."

"That's probably wise." Carver spat seeds into the mud. "Well, bring her by sometime, if it won't get you in hot water. At least let her know I asked after her."

Riddley watched for an opportunity to sneak into the studio. There would not be many. Carver was always around when Riddley went by to help scavenge. These days Carver left the premises even

less than she had before. Riddley expected her chance to come when Carver went on one of her rare errands. One morning Riddley was crabbing on the dock when Carver put her surfboard in and began to paddle across the river, something she hadn't done since the fire. Riddley left her lines in the water and ran all the way to the studio.

She paused a moment at the threshold, then slid the door and curtain open. Right away she spotted the cabinet. It stood against the southern wall, next to the stacks of paintings. In the corner was the easel, covered by a sheet. After she recovered the postcards, maybe she'd take a peak at the portrait.

Packs of Camels, ballpoint pens and matches were stuffed into the drawer. Riddley pulled it all the way out. She had not even imagined that the postcards wouldn't be there. Could it be the wrong cabinet, a twin of the one she wanted? But Riddley would have noticed before if there were two of the same kind. She stepped back, examining it. It had to be the same one.

Carver must have found the postcards and put them somewhere else. She hadn't said a word, though, about finding them. But why would she? She wouldn't know they had anything to do with Riddley. And what if Carver had found them before the fire, and put them in a place which had been destroyed?

Riddley tore then through the studio. She looked in the bathroom cabinets, the closet, in the drawers of every piece of furniture. She climbed barefoot onto the kitchen counter to reach the high shelves. Behind her, a match flared. Riddley swayed, clutching at one of the open cabinet doors. She jumped down.

Carver, leaning against the back of the sofa, lit a cigarette and then shook the match out. Water dripped from the ends of her hair. Riddley had never seen Carver angry before but she could tell that she was.

"It's kind of hard to explain," Riddley said.

"I've got plenty of time." Carver refastened the towel at her waist.

"I hid something in your house," she said, "before the fire."

Carver exhaled a narrow stream of smoke. "Go on."

"I was worried they'd be discovered where they were, and I just wanted to put them somewhere safe for a while, until I figured out what to do with them. They were my grandfather's."

"Adele's husband?"

Riddley nodded. "He died right before Easter."

"And before that he gave you something you didn't know what to do with."

"Not exactly. I found them, and then my mother cleared out their house and sold it and I couldn't put them back, even if I'd wanted to." Riddley looked out the window. "They're not something either of them would ever want me to have."

"So why my house?"

Riddley glanced around the studio, her eyes resting on the easel. How strange her reasons seemed now. "When you were painting Grandmother, and I spent time around here, and in your house—" Riddley broke off. "I could just tell you were different."

"Ah," Carver said. "Different. Like your Miss Byrd."

Riddley blushed and looked down. "No, not like her. A different kind of different." She looked at the wall where the paintings were stacked. They were a large part of the explanation. It seemed the only hope she had of getting Carver to understand was to confess her trespassing, or some of it, anyway. She would rather avoid mentioning how they'd spied on her while she painted. "Hayden and I snuck in here a couple of times, last year after you moved in, and then earlier this summer." Riddley glanced at Carver, who appeared neither surprised nor outraged. Had she known all along? But why then had she never confronted them?

"Both times, I saw some of your paintings." Riddley gestured at the stack against the wall. "And then a few weeks ago I saw some pictures you'd drawn in your room on the chalkboard, and I thought that if you could draw and paint like that, and do a portrait of somebody like Grandmother, then, well, then the postcards wouldn't scare you. You were the only person I could think of," Riddley paused, thinking of Miss Byrd, and of Esther, "or one of the only ones, who wouldn't just want to get rid of them right away, or tell me I shouldn't have them."

"Postcards?" Carver cocked her head to one side. "Do you mean these?" She turned and pointed to the corner above the easel. The postcards were tacked to the wall, high up near the ceiling. How could Riddley have missed them there? But she'd been focused on

rooting out hiding places. It hadn't occurred to her they would be so obvious.

"Here I was assuming they belonged to my own fine family," Carver said, grimacing. "And I'm afraid you overestimate my bravery. They scared the hell out of me. They still do. But you were right in that it didn't put me off."

"Why'd you stick them up there?" Riddley walked over and squinted up at them, but she was still too far to tell if the girl was Aunt Riddley.

Carver came and stood beside her. "I thought that it would be good, every once in a while, to be shocked again by them. I didn't think I should just be able to put them away somewhere and forget about them. Though I doubt they'd be easy to forget."

"I didn't think I'd be able to, but I was. Only for a while, though, and even then I dreamed about them, and after a while I started seeing them everywhere."

Carver looked at her. "What do you mean?"

Riddley hesitated. But if she couldn't tell Carver, who could she tell? "Sometimes out of the corner of my eye, or from far away or in the dark, I see a shape in the trees that looks just like a person hanging. But when I turn to look, or come closer, it's gone. Usually there's something there that I've mistaken it for, like a broken limb or some Spanish moss." She took a breath and then continued. "But sometimes there's not. Sometimes there's nothing there at all that it could have been. I know it sounds strange. My mother says I'm given to seeing things, that I've got an over-active imagination, but I'm not making this up, I swear."

Carver studied Riddley. "I believe you," she said. "Has anyone else seen them? The postcards, I mean."

Riddley nodded. "That's why I wanted to move them. That one on the left was missing for I don't know how long. Then whoever took it put it back."

"Your sisters?"

"They'd already gone to camp by then. And neither of my parents would have left the postcards hidden if they knew about them. They wouldn't want anybody, especially one of us, to find them." She

paused. "I'm pretty sure it was Esther. She'd been putting stuff away in the same drawer."

"You haven't asked her?"

Riddley shook her head.

"I can see how that might be difficult."

"A few weeks ago I showed them to Grandmother. I thought maybe she might know something about them."

"What happened?"

"The only one she was interested in was the one with the girl. She stared at it for a long time, and then she looked at me and said *Riddley.*"

"I didn't know she still spoke."

"She hardly ever does anymore. I don't think she's said anything else since she moved out here."

"Why do you think she said your name?"

"At first I figured she was just scolding me, or letting me know she knew who I was, or it was because the girl in the picture is about my age. But then later I wondered if she was talking about a different Riddley, my Great Aunt Riddley, her big sister, the person I was named for. Maybe that's a picture of her."

Carver recalled her initial feeling of recognition when she'd seen the girl in the postcard. Perhaps that was due to a family resemblance between the girl and Adele. "Did you know your aunt?"

"She died before I was born. I've seen a photo, but in it she's older than this girl. They don't really look anything alike. But I wanted to compare the two pictures side by side."

"Would your mother know if it's her?"

"Maybe, but that doesn't mean she'd tell me. She'd probably just take the postcards away. She'd say I shouldn't see such things because I'm only a child."

"Well," Carver smiled, "you are."

"But I'm the one who found them."

"Ah yes. *Finders keepers, losers weepers,*" Carver said, though she wondered if, in this case, the converse might be true.

"My grandfather collected postcards. He had hundreds. My mother let me have them for a keepsake."

"Quite a keepsake."

"People were always mailing him postcards when they went away on vacation. Someone in Atlanta sent him these, with a note."

"What did it say?"

Riddley concentrated to recall. "'A little something for your collection. From your neck of the woods. So to speak.'" It occurred to her then that maybe these postcards had not merely been a part of Frazier's larger collection, but had in fact constituted their own. That is, that Frazier had specifically collected postcards like these, postcards of blacks killed by whites. But why would he ever wish to collect such things, and if he had, where were the others? Besides, if he'd bothered to collect them, why then would he contemplate destroying them? She cleared her throat. "It was signed W.S.D. I don't know who that is."

"Some wise guy."

"A wise guy?"

"It's a bad joke. All of them were hung by the neck, in the woods, or sort of. Hence, *neck of the woods*. Did you find out anything else?"

"On the envelope, my grandfather wrote: 'Destroy, or Donate to the Georgia Historical Society, or UGA.' He put question marks after *destroy* and *donate*, like he didn't know what he wanted to do."

"That he'd consider destroying them does make it seem more likely the girl could be your aunt. On the other hand, if she was, you wouldn't think he'd even consider preserving them."

"But he really liked history," Riddley said.

"Southern gentlemen tend to. Usually, though, they're interested only in certain kinds of history, battles and presidents, that sort of thing. Not history like this kind of history." Carver gestured at the postcards. "So, what are you going to do with them?"

"I don't know." Riddley's eagerness to reclaim the postcards had faded in their presence. Where could she keep them that they wouldn't be discovered? She looked back up at them. "When do you think they were taken?"

"I pondered that myself." Carver pointed to the one with the man tied to the palmetto. "I'd say this one's in the thirties or forties, judging

by the car. The clothes in this one," she pointed to the one with the girl, "made me think it's around the turn of the century, give or take a decade. It's harder to tell with these other two, as men's clothes don't change as radically as women's. They could have happened just a few years ago. Or Christ, last week."

"Last week?" Riddley echoed faintly. She remembered how she'd first thought the pictures must have been taken around the time of the Civil War, except for the one with the car.

"I'm exaggerating, but not by much."

"Where do you think they take place?"

"Here," Carver said, emphatically. "Or hereabouts, especially after what that note said. Lynchings were hardly uncommon in our neck of the woods."

"What would you do with them?"

"What would I do with them," Carver repeated. She tilted her head to one side, crossing her arms. "I guess, for starters, I'd find out as much as I could about them. Maybe ask older people, black and white, if they knew of any incidents around here, or had heard stories of such when they were young. Depending on how ambitious I was, maybe I'd see what I could find in local newspapers, history books, that sort of thing. Then again, maybe I'd just stick them up on the wall and study them from time to time."

"But you wouldn't destroy them."

"God, no."

Riddley gazed up at the postcard with the girl. Could that really be her Aunt Riddley, and if it was, what was she going to do about it? "I wish I'd never found them," she blurted out.

"Why?"

Carver's eyes were there, waiting for hers, when Riddley turned toward her. After a moment Riddley dropped her gaze, no longer sure that what she had said was true, that she would ever choose to know less, even when this might be what she knew.

"I'll get them down for you." Carver carried a chair over and climbed onto it. She detached the postcards and handed them down to Riddley. The one with the girl was last. Riddley stared at her for a long time. She was disappointed not to know at once who she was.

The girl looked familiar, but Riddley didn't trust that sensation. She could look that way simply because Riddley had seen the postcard before, or because she wanted her to look familiar. But why would she want that?

Carver jumped off the chair and looked over Riddley's shoulder at the postcard. It was one of the most disturbing photographs Carver had ever seen: the summer crowd moving with seeming obliviousness around the lynched man; the black men impassive in the background; the girl's unnerving smile. And part of what made it so disturbing, Carver realized, was how the photo appeared arranged, composed rather than candid. Who would take such a picture, she wondered, and for what purpose? The girl was practically a parody of whiteness: that huge white bow like a Luna moth landed on the back of her head, her white party dress with its wide sailor collar, her straight and glistening teeth, her luminous hair and creamy skin. All of this was accentuated by the shadows, and the blood crusted on the dead man's feet, and the girl's own dark brows, which were drawn together, Carver noticed now, in what seemed to be consternation, as if the rest of her face had not caught up with her smiling mouth.

"Is it your aunt?"

"I don't know. I thought I'd be able to tell once I saw it again up close. But I can't tell for sure. She does look sort of familiar."

"She looked familiar to me, too, right from the start, though that could be related to the fact that I thought the postcards belonged to my family, and so had some possible connection to us. They could just as well have." Carver looked around the studio. "Fitting, isn't it, that this is what survives of the great plantation."

Riddley glanced around her, uncertain what Carver meant.

"This used to be a slave cabin."

"Oh," Riddley said, "I forgot."

"That seems to have been the point of the renovation. I'm not sure why my grandparents didn't just tear the whole thing down and start from scratch. According to my father, it used to be dark and spooky and practically in ruins. He played here as a boy, before it was done over."

Riddley looked around again, trying to picture this house as it once was. It was hard to imagine, and harder, almost, to believe,

that this had ever been a slave cabin, that hundreds of slaves had once lived around here, that there had ever, in fact, been slaves at all. But plenty of times she'd had no trouble imagining that. It had been like any other game, a fantasy to act out. *Five Little Peppers and How They Grew, Little House on the Prairie, Little Women, Uncle Tom's Cabin, Gone with the Wind.* They had all seemed of a piece. *Prissy, go tell Mammy I'm ready to ride to Twelve Oaks,* Riddley or Charlotte or Emmeline would say, in their hula-hoop hoop skirts, glancing over their shoulder at that imaginary slave. There was never anybody there. Each of them always played a belle, except when they played Runaway. Just like in school, nobody ever wanted to play anyone black. Even at four, Riddley had understood that. Charlotte and Emmeline had tried to make her play a pickaninny and she would have none of it. *Fetch me my parasol,* Charlotte had said to her once, and Riddley had shot back with, *Fetch it yourself. I'm not your slave. I'm a belle dressing for the ball.*

Riddley looked down at the postcard. She tried to read the girl's face. Had she ever played games like that? Riddley lifted her t-shirt and tucked the postcards into the damp waistband of her shorts. When she got home, she would bury them within the rest of Frazier's postcard collection. Why hadn't she thought of that before? No one would look through those. She was supposed to allow her sisters a turn at them, but Riddley knew they'd have no interest.

At the door, Riddley faced Carver. "I'm sorry. I should have just asked you."

"No harm done. But no more sneaking around and spying, you hear?" she said, smiling ever so slightly. "At least on me."

* * *

The night seemed barely cooler than the day. The gibbous moon was covered and uncovered by fast-moving clouds, giving the effect of someone flicking a distant light on and off, on and off. The wind, strong way up high, never made it to earth, and it was more airless in the tent than usual. A mosquito had gotten inside, and Carver's many attempts to kill it had failed. She lay sweating and agitated in the middle of the tent. Every time a leaf or insect hit the roof she flinched.

She sat up and pulled on her clothes. She would go for a drive, something she hadn't done since the fire. She filled a cup with bagged ice from the cooler and grabbed a fresh pack of smokes. She drove out fast, noticing anew her junkyard in the trees. What had she been thinking? She was letting herself go a little too crazy. She would take those things down tomorrow, or most of them anyway. The chandelier prisms and pane of glass could stay. Possibly also a few others. But most of them would go.

At the intersection, she headed south. At some indefinable point, White Cliff Road became Coffee Creek Road. As a child she'd asked Reed why the same road had two different names, and he had said it was because the soil along Coffee Creek had more clay, which darkened the land and water. She felt now that astonishment she had so often felt since she had moved back here, when some belief or understanding from childhood was abruptly upended. The change in name did have to do with color, but not of marsh or river or bluff. This stretch of the road was called not White but Coffee because black people lived here, and judging from the buildings, had done so for a long time. Had Reed understood that but told her otherwise, or had he not known himself?

She thought of the lynched men in the postcards, and the many who had never made it to any postcards. How perfect these old oaks were for a hanging. No other tree so signified the South. But any tree would do in a pinch. Had a mob ever come to one of these houses, to drag a man from his bed? Or had he been tracked with dogs, into the woods and marsh, into wherever he had run and hid when he heard them coming? Or where he had been hiding perhaps for days, having feared they would come? And once they caught him, they hung him from one of the strong low branches of these moss-hung oaks. A live oak for the dead.

Carver put her hand out the window, cupping the wind. She was past the houses, almost to the turnoff. She looked out at the darkness, clotted with trees. She remembered the particular kind of fear that children have, that they do, perversely, like sometimes to feed. Sometimes she felt it when she walked down to the dock at night.

Branches around her like arms, and hands, and sounds like breathing and whispers and groans. Things she had imagined as a girl, which had mostly, but not entirely, dissipated. Carver recalled what Riddley had said about seeing figures in the trees. Carver had marveled then, and did so again now, at how completely Riddley believed in her own version of the world. And why shouldn't she? Childhood was by no means a time to which Carver longed to return, but she would not have minded some of its perspective.

The breeze was fine at the causeway. She parked and stretched her leg out the open door, but she could tell that it was not going to work. She would not calm down, she would not settle. Nor was this just about loneliness, or, to put it plainly, sex. She lit one cigarette off another and stood up, stretching. She walked onto the busted causeway and swung herself over the listing gate. A fish splashed loudly below her, and she jumped. Her throat clenched and she nearly cried out.

She sat at the causeway's edge, her feet dangling above the water. She flicked her barely smoked cigarette into the marsh, her throat too thick to smoke. How foolish she had been to think change might occur without loss. Didn't all change, by definition, require it? But why should the destruction of something she had lost, really, long ago— house, home, family—cause her such fresh grief? But it did; oh, it did. And how on earth to escape it? Grief like that, she knew, just follows you. You get to take it with you, like illness, like memory, wherever you go.

So it would still be hers elsewhere. She knew that, but she had to get out of here for a while, before she became unrecognizable even to herself, if such a thing were possible. She would go back to New York, see some old friends, maybe an old lover, walk on pavement until her shins ached, see a film every afternoon, spend the mornings in over-cooled museums. Besides, she needed more supplies. The art stores here were terrible. And she would arrange to sell the brownstone. If she didn't, then she would always have a place to run away to. She'd let herself run one more time, but just for a spell, before the city could get its teeth into her. New York, Carver knew, could make

you feel like there was no other place in the world to be. Overnight, without your even noticing, it could distract you from yourself, with the hoax and ploy of its glamour, its seediness, its self-importance.

So, yes, she'd go, and as soon as possible. She should get a few things straightened out before she left, things she wouldn't want to deal with when she came back. Finish her scavenger hunt, and arrange for someone to come in her absence and clear the whole mess out. Visit Mattie, whom Carver missed far more than she'd expected, now that, with no house to clean, there was no excuse for Mattie to come out regularly. Straighten up the studio, so that when she returned it would be easier to get at once to work. Ideally, she should finish Adele's portrait before she left. But she had not touched a brush since the fire. Her hands did not yet seem capable of it. It might help to see Adele again. But Carver could see her now with absolute clarity, sitting in the bow of the bateau, the sky behind her dark with rain clouds. She had only had to call her up.

Carver stayed on the causeway until the birds were beginning to sing, the breeze to still. As she made her way back, the sky began to lighten. In the near cool of dawn, light rising over the river, she killed the mosquito in the tent and then sprawled naked on the cushions, covering her face with a pillow so as not to be woken by the sun. The heat rose in the tent, and as she slickened with sweat she dreamt she was on the dock, jumping in the river, swimming and swimming, and when she woke, that was what she did.

CHAPTER 19

Spring Tide

ince Charlotte and Emmeline had returned from camp, they were even more like who they would be and less like who they were, or rather, had once been. They had become, over the course of the summer, *young ladies*. Riddley thought that was the opposite of what camp ought to do to you.

A few days after their return, Sam conducted a fire drill. "In a real fire you can break the glass," he said, and from the way he said it they could tell he would derive considerable pleasure from having, of necessity, to smash a window. Pauline gave him a look. "If it's a really big fire," he added.

When they'd done a drill a couple of years earlier, Riddley had found it exciting to pretend that their house was on fire and they had to escape, that someone would need to rescue them, escape and rescue not seeming, at the time, mutually exclusive. But now, with what had happened to Carver, not to mention Bernice, the drill seemed more like the enactment of a nightmare. She thought of the fire drill at Bernice's school, how little good it had done her, when it came down to it. *We laughed at the chief,* Bernice had said, *how he made his own kids crawl out blindfolded, so they could find their way out even with smoke. But smoke's nothing like a blindfold.*

Sam didn't go that far, but he was stricter than before. He stood below, where the end of the rope ladder dangled a few feet off the ground, yelling, *Move it out, move it out,* a command that only made them clumsier. Pauline stood to the side. She knew better than to interrupt him. He would make them do it until it was done to his satisfaction. And how could she argue with him? She could still hear those moans in the burn ward in Atlanta. But when Sam made the girls jump down to him from the second story porch, she thought he was going a bit far, though still she kept quiet. *It could happen,* Sam would snap back at her if she dared protest. And it was true. The

ladder could break, or be too tangled up to be of any use, or they could need to get out faster than that.

She thought of her mother, whose bed blocked the apartment's second story door. Were she to be trapped up there, and had she the strength to drag her bed aside, she'd be stranded out on the metal landing. Sam had never gotten around to installing the stairs, for a clump of camellias stood where the steps would have touched down. Would Adele try to jump? She had gotten out quickly enough from Carver's, though there was something in Riddley's account of that night that didn't sit right with Pauline. She figured Riddley would come out with it eventually, as she usually did.

Pauline looked up where her daughters stood, all of them gawky, bony-kneed, browned. How lovely they were. She was startled by how they had grown that summer, their limbs noticeably longer, their faces leaner. It was a low porch, barely nine feet high, but Pauline could barely watch, though she made herself do so, as each daughter climbed over the railing and either let herself fall or flung herself off, looking for all the world like she was trying to kill herself, and over and over, for Sam kept making them do it again. *To break them of the fear,* he'd said, as if to do repeatedly what scared you would eliminate that fear, instead of making it a habit, and justifiable, and ingrained in you even more deeply than when you'd started. His was the old school of thought, that fear was the best teacher. And maybe it was, though Pauline didn't like to think so. Or maybe it just taught you more about itself.

It was Riddley's turn. She hesitated. "Hey," Sam called. "Your nightgown's getting scorched."

Riddley looked out over the river. Then she leapt from the porch, one arm and one leg extended forward, aiming for the water. Sam had to back up to break her fall, and he stumbled as he caught her, but he did so just as her feet touched, and in one of those slow motion landings, *plunk,* they sat on the lawn. "For God's sake, Riddley, this isn't a track meet," he said, laughing. "Enough. I need a drink."

* * *

Pauline paused outside the door of the carriage house. The cracked cement, the dilapidated chairs and listing tables, the cigarette butts, the soot streaked across every surface, the years of leaves accumulated in and around the pool—the combined effect was of abandonment. How could Carver live in this? But Riddley had said Carver slept in the tent on the bluff. Pauline wasn't sure which was worse. She took a breath, raised her fist and knocked.

"Who is it?" Carver called at once from behind the curtain, as if she'd been waiting.

"Pauline." She cleared her throat. "Pauline Cross."

The curtain was moved aside at once, and the screen slid open. "Pauline," Carver said, stepping out onto the concrete, and the way Carver looked at her, Pauline wondered if Carver had been expecting her. Carver slid the screen shut behind her.

"Hello, Carver," Pauline said. Carver looked as if she were recovering from a long illness. She had lost weight, and cut her hair very short, in a haphazard way that reminded Pauline of how, when she had scarlet fever, her dolls' hair had been cut and their heads dipped in alcohol, to prevent the spread of infection.

"It's been a while," Carver said.

"Yes," Pauline said, trying to remember when they had last spoken. It had been months. She cleared her throat again and smiled. Why was she so nervous? "I'm so sorry about what happened. It's just awful."

"Thank you. Or I guess that's what I should say, though it sounds odd, doesn't it? Here, pull up a seat," Carver said, gesturing grandiosely at the many lawn chairs. "This is the closest I get these days to a parlor." She sat in an orange and yellow lounge chair in the shade, facing the river, or what little could be seen of it through the bushes. Pauline, in her pastel dress, was hardly eager to sit on a sooty chair. She picked a red and blue one across from Carver. The front legs scraped on the concrete as Pauline perched on its edge.

"Careful it doesn't collapse on you," Carver said.

Pauline sat farther back. "It's rather pleasant here in the shade."

"Pleasant is a bit of a stretch, don't you think? But it's better than in there." Carver nodded toward the studio. "It was bearable earlier in the summer, but now the heat's settled into the walls."

"I certainly hope it breaks soon. It's been dreadful."

"How's Adele? I haven't seen her since the fire."

Pauline was taken aback. She'd thought Carver would, out of awkwardness, avoid the topic of Adele. But she'd forgotten how seldom Carver found anything embarrassing or awkward. Pauline couldn't decide if that made things seem more or less so. "She's fine, I suppose."

Carver tilted her head to one side. Hadn't Riddley said much the same thing? "You suppose?"

"Well, you know how she is. Sometimes I think I don't know her at all, or who I knew no longer exists. But how can someone not know their own mother?" Pauline laughed uneasily.

Carver, taking out a cigarette, said, "Quite easily, I should think." She struck a match and drew hard on the cigarette, her cheeks hollowing.

Pauline, who had not smoked for over a decade, had a yearning so intense that her mouth went first dry, then wet. She swallowed, her eyes following the exhaled smoke.

"Cigarette?" Carver extended the pack.

"Oh, no thanks," she said, looking toward the river, perturbed that her desire should be so obvious. "We're keeping a much tighter rein on Mother these days. That's why you haven't seen her. I haven't let her out walking since the night—that night she last visited. I hate to restrict her, but I just can't have her running off. I couldn't live with myself if something happened to her." Pauline looked at her hands, and saw them sliding the lock into place. She folded them together. "I'd thought I could keep her here with me, but it's been so much harder than I ever imagined. I don't know how Daddy did it for so many years. But she behaved herself more with him, as far as I know. She wasn't as unpredictable, as likely to wander off." Pauline shook her head. "There're too many places she could go, and too much water. It's just not safe out here. It's the last thing I want to do, but I'm going to have to move her somewhere else," she said, astonished, not

having known what she was going to say until she said it. Not that she hadn't considered this option, but she hadn't known she'd made up her mind.

"I can understand that."

"I'm barely able to myself," Pauline said.

"She's hard to look after."

"But she's my mother," Pauline continued, as if Carver were the one trying to convince her to move her mother away.

Carver nodded. "Yes," she agreed, looking toward the deep end, where she could almost see her twelve-year-old self crouched, the day her mother died. She looked back at Pauline. "That is the problem, isn't it."

"I think I will have that cigarette after all, if you don't mind."

Carver handed her the pack and the matches. Something occurred to Pauline as she lit a cigarette. Twice she had come upon her mother smoking with Sam. *Sam, how could you?* she'd later scolded. *How couldn't I?* he'd answered. *She grabbed the pack out of my hand.* "Does Mother smoke with you?"

"Sometimes. She gets a look on her face much like yours a minute ago. That's why I asked if you'd like one."

"Oh my, how transparent." Pauline laughed and blushed. Her nervousness, in combination with the smoking, made her feel giddy. "Mother smoked for decades, starting in the twenties. She was a regular flapper there for a while, with a cigarette holder and a beaded dress and a bob. I have a wonderful picture of her from that time. She was a real beauty."

Pauline tapped the ash off and then took another drag. She'd forgotten smoking's many subsidiary pleasures—blowing smoke, tapping ash, holding, and gesturing with, a cigarette—not to mention the great comfort there was in simply having something to do with one's hands and mouth. "One of the most striking things about Mother was her hair. A deep black, against pale, flawless skin. The odd thing was that she was very blond as a child. She went dark when she reached puberty. Practically overnight, to hear her tell it. No gradual move from dirty blond to brown, but right into black. Her eyes and brows had always been dark, though, which often indicates the hair will

turn," Pauline said. "I remember hoping the same would happen to me, that I'd wake up one day as Bette Davis. I've always been dark-headed, and so of course always longed to be blond. But Mother assured me change never occurred in that direction, that the dark could not become fair, only vice versa. I thought it terribly unjust."

Carver smiled. "Rarely does one inherit the things one would like to have."

"How true. I didn't get her skin, either, or rather, I got the pale without the perfect. She was awfully vain about that as well. Years later I learned that she dyed her hair, though I've no idea when that jet black ceased to be natural, if, in fact, it ever was. She was quite secretive about it." Pauline paused, her ebullience suddenly gone. She took a long drag, her throat burning. "Strange, I never thought of her as beautiful, in person, I mean. Maybe it's always hard for a daughter to see that. I'm sure none of mine think much of my looks, though they have their reasons," she said with a laugh.

"I thought my mother was gorgeous, until she got sick. But I think she just died when I was too young, or when she was. No doubt I'd have unearthed countless flaws had she lived."

"That must have been terrible for you."

"Far worse for her. But yes, it was." After a long pause, Carver said, "You've heard about the portrait, I take it."

"Riddley told me, albeit reluctantly. She's quite loyal to you, you know. The few people she takes to she takes to quite fiercely. If you don't mind my asking, why did you want to paint Mother's portrait?"

"I rarely know why I want to paint anything." Carver glanced toward where the house had stood, recalling her first sight of Adele, there on the porch, in her mother's chair. "It was something about how still she is sometimes." She smiled. "When she's not covering miles." She leaned her head back into the net of her hands. "She just showed up on my porch one afternoon last month. That's when I started to sketch her. She seemed quite amenable to coming here." Carver hesitated. She might be getting into territory dangerous to Riddley. "Though I worked pretty hard, I admit, at keeping her enter-tained enough to stay put, while I painted her. I'd play my parent's old

records, give her a deck of cards, talk to her. She seemed especially to like to listen to me talk. It didn't matter about what. She never said anything back. Does she with you?" Carver recalled how Adele said *Riddley* when she was shown the postcards.

"Speak? Oh no, not for months." How relieved Pauline had been, when her mother had at last given that up. There had been nothing but terrible words, toward the end. But how seldom did Pauline speak to her mother these days, and when she did, her voice usually came out shrill or cajoling. It wasn't like that for Riddley or Esther, or even for Sam. They talked to Adele almost as if she were normal, or it didn't matter that she weren't.

"Has Mother seen the portrait?"

"Yes," Carver said, laughing. "I'm by no means convinced she realized it was supposed to be her."

"It's so strange, isn't it," Pauline said, shaking her head, "to have no idea what she does or doesn't understand."

"I guess I always assume she gets more than she appears to. But it could be quite the opposite."

"Yes," Pauline said, looking away. How it pained her, not to know how much her mother understood, of the lock, for example, or of what they said of her sometimes in her very presence. And soon, Pauline knew, there would be far greater degradations to bear: diapers, bibs, swabbed and bathed and wiped by strangers. Something deep inside her shuddered. Swiftly, as if just realizing she were supposed to be elsewhere, she stood. She smoothed the creases of her cotton dress. "I should get going. I didn't mean to keep you so long—"

"You're not keeping me."

"I hope I'm not being presumptuous, but I, well, would it be all right—"

"To see it?"

Pauline nodded, turning a deeper red.

How easily Pauline and her daughter blushed, Carver thought, wondering if Adele had once been like that. She was about as far away as she could get, these days, from blushing. "Of course," Carver said. "I'd assumed that's why you came."

Pauline felt such a fool. Here she'd been thinking she'd covered her true motives with some sort of condolence visit. But Carver had stated it matter-of-factly, as if of course Pauline would want to see a portrait of her mother.

"I usually don't show my work before it's finished, but I'll make an exception, under the circumstances." Carver led the way into the carriage house, hot despite the fans. Pauline was surprised at how clean it was in there, and how empty. Where had Carver put what had been saved? It must all be in the garage.

The easel, its legs visible beneath a pale yellow sheet, stood near the back wall. Carver peeled the sheet back. "Take your time," she said, without looking at the portrait. "I have something I need to take care of in the garage." At the door she opened the curtains wide, for the light, and then turned back toward Pauline. "You shouldn't expect to like it, you know."

, Pauline had no idea what to say to that, so, for once, she said nothing, a decision made easier by the fact that Carver was already out the door. Pauline stepped before the easel.

She was startled by how much the woman of the portrait looked like her, Pauline, like those glimpses of her mother's face she'd recently caught sight of in her own mirror. *It's only a picture,* she told herself, *not a prophecy.* Perspiration gathered between her breasts and shoulder blades, on her upper lip. She leaned back against the wall and glanced around the room. Where had her mother sat while being painted?

When she looked again at the portrait, it looked more like her mother. One of the strangest things was how Carver had managed to capture some of the qualities of Adele's face from when she was younger. Could Carver have seen some old photos? Yet at the same time Adele was undeniably old. It was not just the lines on her hands and face, the gray hair or sagging skin. Her expression allowed a glimpse back into her youth, but it also revealed how very old she was, far older than her age, and how alone, how she had already left them all behind. Could that explain the stillness, as well as the wandering? And there was something else that flickered back and

forth between who Adele had been long ago, and who she was now. Pauline drew her breath in, as struck as she had been when she'd said it herself a short while ago. Pauline needn't have told Carver that Adele had once been beautiful. Carver had seen that. There was something tragic about it—beauty gone, irreclaimable—but there was something triumphant as well, that Adele had once been beautiful, and that its imprint was still visible on her face.

*   *   *

After Pauline left, Carver returned to the portrait. She had not looked at it since she'd covered it the day after the fire. She still needed to decide what the backdrop would be. Once she had placed Adele, she thought she could more easily figure out the rest.

As she was about to drop the sheet over it again, she recalled what Pauline had said about Adele's blondeness, and her dark eyes and brows. Didn't the girl in the postcard, just beneath her pale slash of bangs, have dark brows? Yes, Carver was sure of it. She'd taken note of the girl's coloring because it was a type she'd always found particularly striking.

Could the girl be Adele herself, not Adele's sister? But if so, why would Adele say *Riddley,* rather than *Adele,* or *me,* or simply point to herself? Maybe Riddley had coloring or a dress like that, or Riddley had taken the picture, or taken Adele there. A far more chilling thought occurred to Carver. Had Adele's sister Riddley had some part in the lynching? That would certainly explain why Frazier had considered destroying the postcards. But there were plenty of other explanations for that, ones not nearly so dramatic or personal. What there was as yet no other explanation for was why Adele, who, apparently, remembered almost nothing, would remember that postcard, or what was shown in that postcard, and why the sight of it would cause her to speak, something she had otherwise forsaken. And why else would Carver have had such a strong sense of familiarity, of downright recognition, when she first saw that girl?

Surely though Riddley would have recognized the girl if she were Adele. Yet a person young and a person old were often, for children,

almost as good as two different people, while it was becoming ever clearer to Carver the many ways, at least internally, they were the same.

She wished she still had the postcard to look at. But images, particularly disturbing ones, tended to stay with her a very long time. She stared at the floor, concentrating on recalling the girl in the postcard. After a moment, she pictured her clearly. Then Carver looked again at the portrait. Beyond such generalities as the shape of the face, the placement of the eyes, the jut of the chin, there seemed no definite resemblance between the girl and Adele. But Carver had often found that to be the case between paintings and photos, and between the same person, say, during adolescence and during old age. The latter disparity was about far more than mere age. Often the expressions animating a face were particular to a period in a person's life. Similarly, the way expressions appeared on the face was altered by internal changes in the person, not to mention external changes in the face itself. This, she realized, had a great deal to do with what was so interesting about Adele's face. Adele did not censor or mute many of the expressions other people of her age and upbringing did. Thus when Adele was not in one of her states of blank repose, you might see raw greed or anguish, delight or longing cross her face, as they might the face of a child. But Adele, of course, no longer had the face of a child.

Carver well knew that the sheer boldness of a thought, however conjectural, could make it seem like truth, but nonetheless she couldn't rid herself of a growing assurance that she was right, that the girl was Adele. She would need to see Adele again in person, while also looking at the postcard. And to do that, Carver would need to tell Riddley of her conviction. Would that be a cruel thing to do? But she had never been of the opinion that children should be sheltered from difficult truths. As a girl, Carver had always despised adults' attempts to keep her, or make her, ignorant, innocent, naïve. Had they been willing to tell her more, to speak honestly to her, she might not have been compelled to find out so much for herself. But nor could she ever regret that.

* * *

Sam burst into the kitchen Saturday evening. "Let's go, troops." It was a term that now included his mother-in-law along with his wife and daughters. "The full moon's rising in less than ten minutes."

"They're just finishing supper," Pauline said. "We got a late start."

Sam made another round of cocktails and departed, drink in hand. "See you down there."

"Do we have to?" Charlotte said. Two months of camp had been more than enough of nature.

"It will be lovely," Pauline said.

"Lovely for the bugs," Emmeline grumbled.

"There's a breeze so they shouldn't be out. Besides, your father wants you to."

"Can I swim?" Riddley slid her plate into the dishwasher.

"Absolutely not. You just ate."

"But not much. I'm not even half full. Just a dip after the moon's up? By then it'll be nearly a half hour. A half hour for half-full in the full moon?"

Pauline smiled but shook her head. "It's too dangerous, especially in the dark."

"But it won't be with the moon out."

"You can swim tomorrow." Pauline wiped off Adele's hands and face with a damp dishcloth. "Y'all head on. I'll finish up in here and be right down. Somebody take Grandmother."

Somebody, Riddley knew, meant her, for Adele wanted nothing to do with Charlotte and Emmeline, as if she'd forgotten they were any relation to her, or else, as Riddley liked to think, Adele had never much cared for them and no longer made any attempt to hide her dislike. It didn't bother them. Their astonishment when they'd first seen her, and their steady embarrassment since, revealed how much Adele had changed in their absence. The few half-hearted attempts they'd made to interact with her, Adele had acted as if they aimed to steal her purse, which she had taken to carrying everywhere. At the outset it had nothing in it. Riddley had recently stocked it with a compact, lipstick, beaded change purse, and a key chain chock full of keys, none of which worked on anything around here. They were for her

old house, her old car, her old life, the one in which she'd had a car that ran, and a house with a door she could, with a key, unlock herself. To the purse Pauline had added an index card of contact names and phone numbers, in case, *Heaven forbid,* Adele got lost. *It's better than dog tags,* she'd added.

Once outside, Adele picked up speed. The dock remained a place she very much liked to go, though these days she generally seemed content to stay put. Pauline said her mother might be settling into her dotage at last, but Riddley had her doubts. She thought Adele was just biding her time, that she would soon start roving again. She'd begun to stare out windows, and watched doors open and shut with more interest than she'd paid much of anything besides food, since she'd drifted out to the sound.

At the edge of the bluff, Riddley paused. The marsh was rimmed with light. The tide would be very high tonight, as there was still a while before it turned, and the river was already well into the marsh grass. The edge of the moon appeared, so bright in that first moment that it almost could have been mistaken for the sun. Did the moon, like the sun, have a false and a true rising?

"Careful on the stairs, Grandmother," Riddley said, as Adele hurried down them.

"Hello Adele," boomed Sam, turning to watch them descend. He sat on one of the wooden benches edging the upper dock, an elbow propped on the railing, a cigarette in one hand and a drink in the other. He stood as she approached, as if she still cared about manners, that gentlemen should stand when a lady enters.

"You're just in time," he said, extending his arm for her to take it. Lately she'd shown more favor toward Sam, treating him, in fact, almost as if he were a beau. But without a glance Adele went straight past him, headed for the ramp. "I don't think your mother wants her down there, do you?" Sam said to Riddley, lowering his voice, though not enough Adele wouldn't hear. Adele fiddled with the rusty sliding bolt that kept the gate closed at the top of the ramp. "Grandmother," Riddley said, "Let's sit awhile and watch the moon come up."

"Have a seat, Adele," Sam said. "There's plenty of room here in the front row."

Adele pulled on the lock. The gate needed to be lifted for the bolt to slide.

"Grandmother, we'll go down in a bit. Won't you please come sit with me?" Riddley said, coming up behind her.

Adele twisted around and looked Riddley full in the face, then turned her gaze with clear purpose to the bateau, rocking below in the mild waves. Pauline and Charlotte and Emmeline descended the stairs from the bluff, Pauline exclaiming over the sky.

"We should pull the bateau up," Riddley said to Sam.

"Nah," he said, glancing overhead. "Not a cloud to be seen, and nothing in the forecast for tomorrow. There's that tropical storm forming to the south, but it's not expected to come in for a few days, and may well bypass us altogether."

"But it's hurricane season."

"Hurricanes don't just appear out of nowhere, Rid. Besides, won't you go crabbing first thing?" Sam said, having a sip of vodka.

"We should start chaining it up then when we leave it in," Riddley said. "Don't we have an extra padlock around? It'd be mighty easy to steal."

"Nobody in their right mind would want to steal that boat," Sam said.

"That's what we thought about your mother's car," Pauline said, and she and Sam laughed. Riddley remembered how mortified Isabel had looked at any mention of her stolen car, as if the theft had exposed some part of her that she'd hoped to keep hidden.

While they weren't watching, the moon had cleared the horizon. The bateau sat at the end of the path of moonlight. Adele strained toward it. Riddley wouldn't have been surprised if she climbed over the gate. "Why don't I go get Grandmother an ice cream sandwich," Riddley said.

"Would you like that, Mother?" Pauline asked, as though Adele had ever, in the last year or two, refused any sort of sweet. Adele kept struggling with the lock.

"Grandmother," Riddley said, tugging at her arm. "Sit down and wait for me right here, and I'll bring you some ice cream. Ice cream, Grandmother," she repeated. Adele glanced at Riddley, then resumed

her efforts to open the gate. Riddley sprinted up to the bluff, her sisters calling after her to bring some down for them as well. By the time Riddley returned, Adele was on the floating dock. Sam, in his chivalry, and in his worry that she'd do damage to the gate, had escorted her down. They stood together at the inner edge of the dock where the bateau was moored, her hand in the crook of his elbow.

"Heavens, Sam, watch out she doesn't fall in," Pauline said from the upper dock, where she leaned over the railing.

"Adele's not going anywhere," Sam said, patting her hand, "are you, Adele?"

"Mother," Pauline called brightly, "Riddley's brought your ice cream."

"Here we go," Sam said, attempting to turn her toward the ramp. Adele did not budge.

"Grandmother," Riddley said, "here's your ice cream."

"Can we go up now?" Charlotte took two ice cream sandwiches from Riddley, handing one to Emmeline.

"There's that show on TV you said we could watch." Emmeline peeled back a corner of the paper and took a bite.

"Is it already that late? All right then."

"Here, Grandmother, before it melts," Riddley said, but even sweets were no match for Adele's desire to be on the water.

"Let's go, Adele, before one of your granddaughters gobbles yours up," Sam said. Charlotte and Emmeline climbed the stairs to the bluff.

"You can have mine too," Riddley said.

"That's very generous of you, honey, but Grandmother doesn't need two."

Riddley stepped onto the ramp. "Adele," she called, her voice high, incantatory. Pauline's head swiveled toward Riddley just as Adele's did. "We can go out tomorrow, I promise, but we can't go out tonight. It's too late to go out now. It wouldn't be safe. It's dangerous to be on the water at night. Tomorrow I'll take you out, I swear."

"You'll do no such thing," Pauline said.

"I know," Riddley whispered fiercely, not taking her eyes from Adele's, as if to break her gaze meant she would lose her. "Come on

up now, Adele, it's time to come up," Riddley said, her voice containing more plea than demand. Adele stared back at Riddley. "Carver wants you to come visit. Carver's been asking for you. I told Carver I'd bring you right over. Carver's got your favorite deck of cards waiting, the ones with the butterflies. Carver wants us to go sit on her porch with her."

"But, Riddley—" Pauline said, then grew quiet as Adele smiled and moved away from the bateau. She extracted her arm from Sam's, took his offered hand and stepped up, onto the ramp.

CHAPTER 20

Departures

Plenty of terrible things happen with no foreboding, and seldom is foreboding later validated by events. Such knowledge did not, however, in any way appease Riddley's apprehension. Before going to bed she twice checked the lock on Adele's door. It took Riddley a long time to get to sleep, and when she did her dreams leapt about from one thing to another, jarring and hectic, as if they resented being dreamt, as if they meant to wake her. When they did, her room was so bright she thought in that first instant that it was morning, and that she was late for letting Adele out.

She went on the porch, into the full moonlight. It glinted off the magnolia leaves. The river shone, some parts rippling, others sleek. The tide had almost covered the marsh, the curves and edges that delineated it having nearly disappeared in places, making it seem a different river altogether. She had only seen it so high during the springtime, or hurricanes.

There was plenty enough light to see if the bateau was still there. But even leaning far out to the side, she couldn't see where it was moored. She climbed over the porch railing. She hesitated only an instant before jumping, arms outstretched and eyes on the moon. In the air she imagined that Sam was there to catch her, should she need to be caught. Her nightgown billowed up around her face, blinding her, but her feet remembered where the ground was.

She turned and looked up at where she'd come from. Only then did she wonder how she would get back in. If she went in through a door downstairs, the dogs would bark and wake Pauline before she could shush them. Riddley could pretend she was sleepwalking, but she had never lied about that and felt disinclined to do so, as if such might bring bad luck. The magnolia that grew outside her sisters' room had one branch that looked strong enough for her to climb out

on, then jump onto the porch, though she'd risk a loud noise when she landed.

From the edge of the bluff she saw the bateau. The floating dock floated so high that the bow looked wedged beneath the ramp. She was about to fetch her life jacket from the dockhouse when she heard something. From within came faint noises of one thing rubbing against another, what she took for fur against wood, water rats sliding through cracks. What need had she for a life jacket? The sky was clear, the water calm. It lapped gently under the upper dock. She turned away.

The ramp, unused to being at this level, creaked at the joints. The floating dock groaned against the pilings. The bow of the bateau knocked slightly on the underside of the ramp. It could have still been guided out, especially with someone weighing it down in the bow. If the tide came up any higher, though, the ramp might do it harm. To see if there was any danger of that, she turned toward the middle of the river and searched the surface for something floating. The water seemed still and rushing at the same time. A stick of marsh grass went by, heading seaward at a rapid clip. The tide must have just turned.

She went to the edge, her toes jutting over the side. She scanned for porpoises. Then she fixed her eyes on a spot mid-river. She watched the water a long while. After a time she began to sway. She looked across to the marsh. The eerie quality of the light made her wonder if she were dreaming, if she were still asleep. And what difference did it make if she were? In one movement she swept her nightgown off. Never had the river beckoned her so. Crouching, she looped one arm around the corner post. She put her weight on her right knee and dipped her left foot in, then lowered to ankle, shin, over the knee, halfway up her thigh. Within the constant press of the tide she felt a pulsing.

She stood then and went back up the ramp, leaving a line of single footprints across the upper dock, the salt tightening on her leg. She hurried past the dockhouse, remembering the sounds she'd heard. She tossed her nightgown up on the porch and climbed the tree, her white underpants glowing in the moonlight. She shimmied out onto the overhanging branch. It bent low, creaking, on the verge

of snapping. She jumped. She made a loud thump when she landed, and stood a long moment listening, but no one woke. Within moments of returning to her bed, she too was asleep, if, that is, she had ever been awake.

*   *   *

Carver woke long before dawn. She always found it hard to sleep before a trip. Or maybe it was because of the light. In the top branches of the oak behind the studio the moon rested, fat and gorgeous, its bluish light seeming to be what had, at long last, cooled the air. And how fine was the air, in it the ocean's rich salty breath. It spun the prisms and the pane of glass. They threw shards of moon across the ground.

The breeze kept off the mosquitoes while she made a fire. As the water boiled and the coffee brewed she broke the tent down. She draped it in the garage, so it wouldn't mildew. The bedding she stashed in the studio. She carried cigarettes and a cup of coffee down to the dock and let down the ladder.

She stripped and lowered herself into the river. It was almost the same temperature as the air. She did not expect to be back before the water cooled. She hung onto the bottom of the ladder, floating face down. The tide pulled hard at her. She hauled herself out. She sat at the end of the ramp, smoking, sipping the strong black coffee. The water drying on her skin could almost have been mistaken for touch.

Everything was ready. Her bag was in the trunk, the gas tank and cooler were full. The studio was clean, orderly, and the garage as well, or as much as was possible, with all the furniture crammed in there. But for the windowpane and the prisms, she'd taken all the objects out of the trees. A few she'd saved, but most she had piled with the other refuse. A dump truck would pick it all up next week, followed by another truck with load after load of topsoil to bury whatever was left. By the time she got back weeds might well have sprouted there.

The moon was behind the trees when she returned to the bluff, but it was still bright out. She poured herself the last of the coffee,

kept hot beside the coals. She kicked dirt on the fire, then squatted over it and peed. It made a muffled sizzling.

In the studio, she dressed in clean clothes. She rinsed the coffee pot and filled it with water. She took a final look around. Adele's covered portrait sat in the center of the room. Carver had, to her own surprise, worked on it intensely the last few days. First thing upon her return, she would complete the final touches. She took the sheet off the portrait, then turned the easel toward the door, to face whoever entered, and sunrise, and the river. So that Adele could keep a kind of watch.

The sky was just beginning to lighten as Carver poured water over the smothered fire, then hung the coffee pot from a low branch. She took a last look at the ruins. It would all be gone when she got back. She couldn't yet picture what she would put in its place. Wasn't it fitting, to have it burn down? How else to start a new life? But she hadn't wanted a new life. She'd wanted an old one, one not severed from the past. Had she thought the past something she could simply insert herself into, a plug into a socket? How presumptuous. But why not? Nor was it as if she had ever, regardless of where she was, not been here as well. Besides, the fire could hardly sever the past. Were it that easy, arson would be as common as shoplifting.

She was halfway over the bridge to South Carolina, her skin itchy with salt, before the sun was fully up. She was glad to be going, glad to be almost gone. Looking down, the muddy banks of the Savannah spread gleaming beneath her, she knew she'd want to come back, realizing at the same moment that she'd been worried she would not.

She would want that sooner than she expected. For a while she'd be rejuvenated by subways, by skyscrapers, by the nearness of millions of people who didn't know her or anything about her, and who likewise didn't care. But soon, more than the heavy air, the rich, rank smells of mud and marsh, the dense quiet, humming and buzzing with insects, more even than the luminous envelopment of greens, she would miss the constant nearness of water, how there was always the possibility of hurling your body into it, which she had done in all seasons, and which she would do as soon as she returned, no matter the month. It was the closest she would get to prayer. Swimming in

cold weather, in cold water, made her think of ascetics on mountains, in deserts, all things unnecessary and impure forced from them in the slow purge of fasting, and from her, in the ringing plunge into frigid, moving, salty water. That submersion was like baptism, as if she could baptize herself, not with a hand pressing on her head, but rather there seemed a hand beneath her, pushing her at a diagonal to the surface, the hand of the river, of buoyancy and of salt, and of the ocean, pulling the river into itself, or pushing it back into the land.

*   *   *

The first thing Riddley did upon waking was to lick her leg. It was salty, all the way up the shin, over the hard ridge of kneecap. So she hadn't just dreamed it. Or if she had, she'd also done what she had dreamed.

After dressing, she went next door. A reddish-pink was still in the sky. She'd woken with no sense of foreboding. Hadn't the bateau been there in the night? But by the time she woke there was no longer any need for foreboding. Adele was already gone.

After Riddley found the chain dangling, the pane of glass in the door broken, the drops of blood on the stoop, (Adele must have used her bare hand to break it, or cut herself reaching through) the gate at the top of the ramp open and the bateau missing—after that it all came out, things that could never be taken back. She confessed to Pauline anything she could think of, every secret she had: from stealing Carver's stone fish and spying on her, to Miss Byrd's legs; from finding and hiding and almost losing the postcards to Frazier's notes about Adele; from Adele smoking Isabel's cigarettes to Riddley's worry that Adele had started Carver's fire; from Riddley's life jacket-less visit to the dock last night to her and Carver's rescue of Adele in the sound. But all Pauline seemed to hear was that Adele had gone off in the night in the bateau, and that she had done so once before. *Hush Riddley hush,* Pauline said, grabbing her by the shoulders and shaking her once, and hard, *I can't hear all that now. Tell me where she's gone.*

Even with the heat, it was possible, for a while, to imagine Adele still out there on the water, scorched and parched and hungry, lying in the bottom of the bateau, going in and out of sleep, too thirsty, after a

while, to be hungry anymore. Wouldn't it be easier, Riddley thought, to sleep through thirst than through hunger?

The sun flared off the water, as relentless as a searchlight, but as if searching for something beneath the water, not on its surface. The visibility was such that you could see for miles, and see that Adele was nowhere out there, but still they kept looking. At low tide they saw what had washed up or sunk near shore. At high, they went into the marsh, up creeks and shallow waterways. They looked for anything that might be taken as evidence of her. There was nothing. Word had gone out, and they passed others searching, others who had also found nothing.

Sam and Riddley went first to the sounds, then along the coasts of Moss and Indigo Islands and Pelican Key, where they saw a Coast Guard boat doing the same. On the return, they investigated every nearby creek and river, up the Leigh and the O'Donnell and past the mouth of what Riddley thought had to be Runaway Negro Creek, at which point Sam turned the boat around all of a sudden, saying there was no way she had come this far. They came back, passing their dock, and went upriver as far as they could go. Then they turned and went back out to the sound. How could she have just disappeared?

After the night's reprieve, the heat had returned full force. Sam and Riddley drank bottle after bottle of water and soda. They seldom had to pee, most liquid leaving them in sweat. Riddley jumped in every time she could. Sam leaned over the side, splashing water onto himself from the river. He doused his hat, dropped ice from the cooler down his shirt. They got sunburned despite their shirts and hats and suntan lotion. And what would Adele look like, with no hat or scarf or lotion? Would she even think to turn her face away from the sun?

On the off chance that Adele had simply set the empty bateau adrift, neighbors, along with Esther, Charlotte and Emmeline, searched the woods, Carver's, any place Adele might have been besides the water, even though Adele's purse had been found on the floating dock, under the ramp, where it had not been, Riddley was positive, when she was on the dock that night. Adele must have set it down to undo the bow line.

Once Pauline went with Sam and Riddley in the motorboat, but Riddley had the feeling Pauline was scared of what condition they might find Adele in, if they found her. Sometimes Pauline stayed at the house, talking to the police and Coast Guard and neighbors or waiting for any word. Other times she had Esther stay at the house while she drove slowly up and down the roads with her hazards on, other drivers thinking she must be in search of a lost dog, unless they heard her when she leaned out her window and yelled, *Mother, Adele.* She tried to keep her voice cheerful, thinking her mother mightn't come if she feared a scolding.

As if Adele were indeed a missing pet, or a fugitive, they had posted signs. They got a few calls, but it was always about someone else, and once it was about somebody black, because Pauline had not thought to put *white* on the sign. If Pauline saw someone out in a yard, she stopped and asked if they'd seen an elderly lady go by, and in this way she learned of the many people, young and old, who had walked out the door and never been seen again, or else had turned up far away, with little ability or willingness to recount where they had gone. Why had those people run off, Pauline wondered, and why had her mother? Might she have learned she was to be sent away, and locked up elsewhere? But Adele could not have known that Pauline planned that. Pauline had told no one but Carver, and Adele hadn't seen Carver for weeks. Or maybe Adele had simply figured out what was to become of her. And if that were the case, what else might she have understood that Pauline had assumed, or hoped, she had not?

Riddley scanned Carver's bluff each time they passed. Why wasn't Carver, like the other neighbors, helping to search? Carver's boat swayed in its hoist, where it had not been for months. Charlotte and Emmeline said they'd seen no sign of her when they went by. Might Carver have had something to do with Adele's disappearance? Riddley hoped no one else was wondering the same.

* * *

Seafarers are reminded that if castaway they should NEVER UNDER ANY CIRCUMSTANCES DRINK SEA WATER. *A belief has arisen*

recently that it is possible to replace or supplement fresh water rations by drinking sea water in small amounts. This belief is wrong and DANGEROUS. Drinking untreated sea water does a thirsty man no good at all. It will lead to increased dehydration and thirst and may kill him.

Riddley blew the roach droppings from the spine of the sea survival manual and closed it. She leaned it back against the dockhouse wall. Adele might have glanced at it one of those times she had sat in here. But it had always been dark then, with the light off and the door shut. And besides, odds were she could no longer read. What were the odds she could still swim? *It's better to die by drowning than by thirst,* Sam had said, though he had been talking about horses, not people.

She scanned the shelf, then squatted, searching the ground for any remnant or clue. Nothing. She went out of the dockhouse, and stood in the shade before its door. It was noon of the second day. *The longer someone's missing,* the policeman had said, *the less likely they are to be found.* Riddley and Sam had been out in the boat since dawn, returning for lunch and supplies. Sam had gone to the filling station for gas and ice, so they could go out briefly again. Tropical storm Hortense was moving up the coast. The wind had picked up considerably, though the rain was not expected until that night.

Yesterday, Riddley had told Sam an abbreviated version of her midnight trip to the dock. But Riddley had not repeated all that she'd earlier confessed to Pauline, right after she'd found Adele gone. Those sins she would not reiterate. Nor had she mentioned what she'd come to suspect: that Adele had been in the dockhouse while Riddley was on the dock that night. For when she'd first discovered that Adele and the bateau were gone, she'd seen that the dockhouse door was open. Only later did it dawn on her that Adele might never have been lost had Riddley merely done what she should have, what she had always done before, and put a life jacket on.

That was only one of the many rules she'd broken that night, though most had never been stated as such. They'd never needed to be stated: *don't sneak out of the house after bedtime, don't jump off the porch by yourself, don't go on the dock in the middle of the night*

and strip and stick your leg in the water. But the one that had been stated, the one she knew even in her sleep, she had knowingly broken: *always wear a life jacket near the river.* She recalled the sounds she had heard that night, when she stood where she stood now, outside the dockhouse. Might Adele have been signaling her, or assuming Riddley would discover her at any moment, as in a game of Hide and Seek?

Riddley began to wonder, too, about the river that night, with its peculiar light, different in kind, it seemed in retrospect, from mere moonlight. And how very high the tide had been. Even at dead low, at midday, Riddley saw that moonlit tide overlaid, like a ghost tide, onto the marsh. Above all she wondered about how the river had beckoned her. Had Adele felt that as well, when the moon rose, and later, when she went out in the bateau? And what if Riddley had gone completely into the river that night? Would it have been satisfied with just her? For she believed it would not have kept her, not yet anyway. It would still have let her go.

That afternoon, across from the shrimp boat dock, Sam cut the motor. They drifted homeward backwards. Sam leaned against his seat and lit a cigarette. They watched the sky blacken over the ocean. A small craft advisory was already in effect. The promised storm was on its way.

Sam looked down into the water. "Full fathom five," he murmured. "Remember how much a fathom is?"

She nodded. "Six feet, so five fathoms would be thirty feet," she said, looking into the water as well, though she knew it only got that deep once you reached the sound.

After the storm came no one, not even a child, could believe Adele was still alive out there on the water. Lightning would have surely struck her, waves capsized her. Winds up to fifty knots, lightning, high seas, and ordinary fear and common sense forced everyone from the water for two days.

In bed that night, by flashlight, Riddley checked the charts, while outside it poured. The only way Adele could survive the storm was if she had made it beforehand to land. That would explain, as well, why there had been no sign of the bateau. Why hadn't they thought

of this before? The first time Adele had gone off in the bateau she'd reached Moss Island Sound in just a few hours. And wouldn't the unusually high tide two nights ago have swept her out even faster? Depending on when Adele started, on the tide alone she could have easily made it to the outer sound, though she'd need the motor to get to any shore. Riddley didn't doubt she could have started it. Adele was stronger than anyone seemed to think, and the tank, Riddley knew, had been near full.

According to the charts, there were a number of places Adele could have gone ashore. There was Shrimpboat Cut, an easy veer out of Moss Island Sound. From there she could head up Peach or Lyle Creek to Morrissey Island. She might have made it to the one spot where the water reached dry land, or else she could have crossed a small stretch of marsh. Was it possible to walk across the marsh without getting stuck? But alligators and water moccasins were purportedly crowded onto Morrissey, from the other places they'd had to flee.

Alternatively, she could have kept going up Lyle Creek until it widened into the Ogilvie River and took her to the ocean side of Pelican Key. Or she might've made her way through Devil's Door and onto Indigo Island. Conversely, she could have veered off into the Leigh, and disembarked on one of the river islands. Maybe she had pulled the bateau to shore and turned it over, and was sleeping underneath it right now.

Riddley looked up from the charts, toward the window. For an instant she mistook the flashlight's reflection for a lighthouse, which didn't exist on the rivers around here. Had they ever? A lighthouse could have helped Adele get home, if, that is, she wanted to get there. Riddley flicked the flashlight off. In the darkness, the rain grew louder.

Dawn of the next day, Riddley headed for Carver's in tattered sneakers and slicker. It was raining lightly now, but steadily. Sam had said they wouldn't be going out until the afternoon, if at all. They would have to see how the storm developed. When she came back from Carver's, she'd tell him of the places Adele might have put to shore. He had, she knew, already given up. The night before, she'd

overheard him say to Will Montgomery that if there were anything left of Adele to come to the surface, it might well do so today, for on lakes at least, the drowned floated up after three days down. *Jesus,* Will said. *Exactly,* Sam replied, *but minus the resurrection.*

When Riddley reached Carver's, even before she saw that Carver's car was gone and the tent had been broken down, she could tell that no one was there. She should have guessed it. That was why Carver hadn't helped look for Adele, why Charlotte and Emmeline hadn't seen Carver when they went by. Where had she gone, and why had she said nothing? Just as Miss Byrd had done.

The mud and standing water made the ruins look worse. The former lawn was pocked with puddles. Riddley wove her way between them. A pair of mallards rose, loudly flapping, from a puddle the size of a small pond. At the edge of the bluff she scanned the river. The sun had risen, though she couldn't see it. Again she wondered if Carver had anything to do with Adele's disappearance. But Carver would never take Adele somewhere without telling. That wouldn't prevent people from being suspicious, though, when they discovered that Carver had left around the same time.

The studio might reveal something. Riddley hesitated at the door, recalling the last time she'd entered uninvited. But Carver would have locked it if she didn't want anyone in there. And the door opened. Riddley slid the curtain wide, for the light.

She gasped at the sight of Adele on the easel. She remembered that other time when Adele had been lost, and she'd spotted her in the rear view mirror of Isabel's car and wondered if she were seeing Adele's ghost. But this time, she knew she was. Not really, of course. She knew this was only her portrait. But in that first instant she knew as well that Adele had not taken shelter on some island. The person she'd imagined steering the bateau up a creek, slogging past alligators and water moccasins, was not this person. No, this person, the person in the portrait, was dead.

Riddley stepped into the room. The air was stuffy. She slid the glass door and the curtain all the way open. She hung her slicker over a chair. Light seeped into the room. She stepped toward the easel.

Like all of Carver's paintings, this one had something unsettling about it. This was due in part to the fact that Adele was not in the center of the canvas. Nor was all of her there. Riddley had seen enough portraits to know they were rarely of the whole person, usually just of the head and part of the torso. But this one showed about two-thirds of Adele, down to her bent knees. It seemed an odd place to cut her off. In addition, one elbow was missing, from where it jutted past the edge of the canvas. Riddley wished Carver had scooted Adele over a tad, so all of her would fit in. And though Carver had not painted Adele's feet, she had gotten a sense of them in the knees, which were more relaxed, more forgetful of one another's whereabouts, than a lady's knees should be. Based on the knees alone—much less the face, the expression—Riddley knew Pauline would not like the portrait.

But the most disturbing part of all was where Adele sat. Riddley thought Carver had painted her in the big porch chair, but she was seated instead in the bateau. Why had Carver pictured her there? Had she known what would happen? Only part of the bow and the seat were visible. Carver had gotten the grayish-green color just right, with the paint weathered and chipping away in places. The backdrop was of the river, with a slash of emerald marsh, and a stormy sky. It was the sky that made Riddley understand. Carver hadn't depicted Adele's disappearance, though she could just as well have. Rather, she had painted her as she'd seen her that morning after the fire, when they'd rescued her in the sound. As they had not been able to rescue her again.

Riddley turned away from the portrait. Carver had cleaned the studio up. Against the southern wall, the cabinet remained. Now that Adele was gone, Riddley knew she had no choice but to keep the postcards, whether or not she wanted to, though she felt, for the first time, that she did want to. She would find out, if she could, what they might have had to do with Aunt Riddley. For starters, she would compare the girl in the postcard side by side with the photo of Aunt Riddley. She had to believe that Frazier would not have prevented her from knowing, though he might not have wanted her to. But the postcards were Riddley's now. What she did with them was up to her.

The counters were wiped clean, all painting equipment stashed away. The table was empty of everything but an envelope, the thick-papered, square kind used for invitations and thank you notes. On it was written *Riddley*. She blushed, as if she'd been caught at something. Inside were a note and a key.

> *Riddley–*
>
> *I've gone to New York. I aim to be back by Halloween, but don't worry if I'm not. I will be back. Help yourself to anything you find in the ruins—tell Hayden the same. But hurry. A truck will come next week, to haul it all away.*
>
> *Tell Adele I'm sorry I didn't see her before leaving, but that I'll go visit her when I get back.*
>
> *Your mother said something that gave me an idea about who the girl in the postcard might be. We can do a little sleuthing when I return.*
>
> *Please lock up the studio and stash this key in the coffee-pot, in the tree near the campfire. Keep an eye on the place for me, would you? Mattie will be coming out every once in a while to do the same.*
>
> *I give you free rein.*
>
> *—Carver*

Riddley folded the card shut. Clearly Carver had known nothing about Adele's departure. It was just coincidence, unless *before leaving* meant Adele's departure, not Carver's. But if it did, then Carver could not have expected to visit her later. And where had Carver planned to visit Adele? *Go visit*—that sounded as if Carver expected Adele to be elsewhere by the time Carver returned. Elsewhere, but still able to be visited.

And when had Carver talked to Pauline, and had she told her about the postcards? But Carver knew they were a secret, and she hardly seemed the type to slip up. Besides, if she had, Pauline would've said something by now, for she had never been any good, as Sam put it, at playing her cards close to her chest. So Pauline must have said something unrelated that got Carver thinking. Certainly Pauline would say to Carver things she would never say to Riddley. In the meantime,

Riddley would see what she could discover from Adele's belongings, which remained untouched in the garage apartment. And then when Carver returned, they would try to piece together who the girl in the postcard was, and, if possible, why she'd been at a lynching.

Riddley tipped the envelope, and the key fell into her palm. She dropped it into her pocket. It clinked against the stone fish. Outside, rain pinged on the blackened coffee pot. Water had entered through the spout. She emptied it, blackening her fingertips, and dropped the key in.

The rain came down harder. She thought of the rain the night of the fire, how it had come too late to do any good. But maybe nothing would have done any good. Could the same have been said of Adele? Maybe there would have been no stopping her, either that time or another. She had been so determined to be on the water. Where had she thought she was headed?

Riddley made her way over to where the house had been. She didn't try to avoid the puddles. There were too many amid the ruins. Her sneakers sounded as they did when she walked ashore onto one of the islands. Water spurted from the holes she'd cut in the canvas above her big toes. She went to where the outside steps had led up to the front door. She closed her eyes for a moment, and then, opening them, she entered her memory of the house. She passed through the hallway, by the curved stairs, through the kitchen and living room and out onto the porch. Where the wicker sofa had been, she squatted.

Something shone in the muck. She and Hayden and Carver had scoured this area and extracted anything salvageable. But the rain could have exposed it. She remembered what Sam had told her about fields up North, how stones surfaced each spring, from the ground freezing and thawing, freezing and thawing. But down here it would be due to drenching and drying and heat.

Riddley reached for the half-buried object, then pulled back. Carver had cut herself early on, and after that they'd always used some kind of tool to pull things out of the debris. Riddley grabbed a branch, knocked down by the storm. She broke off a stick. She pushed it beneath the object, and then, jiggling the stick to loosen the rubble, slowly lifted. The thing was heavier than she expected, and there was

more of it than she'd first seen. Much of it was encrusted with mud and debris, but she could tell from its heft, the way it shone in places where the rain rinsed it, and how it jangled dully as she lifted it, that it was made of metal, and part chain.

She bent her elbow, bringing the stick toward her face, the object hooked on the end. Mud fell off in clumps. After the rain had done what it could, she dropped it into her cupped hand. As soon as she touched it she knew what it was, and she wondered, as usual, why that knowledge had taken her so long. There were the pair of dice, the Tower of London, the cupid and the pierced heart, the Liberty Bell and the Washington monument, the Cherokee rose, the fish, the anchor, the cross—how glad she was to see Adele's charm bracelet again, having assumed it too was lost. Adele must have dropped it the night of the fire, when she'd been sitting out here with Carver. She liked to open and close the clasp repeatedly, and sometimes she would take it off and fixate on one of the charms. Riddley turned the bracelet over in her hand. From what she could tell, it was filthy but unharmed. Why hadn't they found it earlier, and for that matter, how could it not have melted, or been crushed by something falling? But Carver's salvaging had revealed how much managed to survive, though sometimes the damage rendered things almost unrecognizable.

Riddley recalled an afternoon some weeks earlier, when she and Carver and Adele had all sat together on the porch, after Adele had decided she was done with being painted for that day. Adele had been fiddling with her charm bracelet. Carver looked over at her and said, in that voice that suggested that Adele might answer, *Did you lead a charmed life, Adele?* Adele smiled, looking back at Carver. *What's a charmed life?* Riddley asked. *A charmed life,* Carver repeated, as she often repeated your question, and in such a way that it seemed different from the one you'd originally asked. Then for a long while she was silent, staring out at Cougar Island. Riddley thought she'd forgotten, or was thinking about something else, but then Carver said, *A charmed life is a lucky life, a blessed life, a life full, as Mattie would say, of grace.* Again she was silent. Then she added, *The kind of life that, as soon as you think you're leading it, you cease to.* And she'd stood abruptly and walked off, into the kitchen, leaving Riddley puzzled. It

was a jinx Carver had been talking about, Riddley realized now. That was something she understood.

Riddley untangled the chain and the charms. She gently shook the bracelet, to remove more dirt. The clasp still worked, though she didn't need it. It fit easily over her hand. She stood, straightening her arm. She cocked her wrist so the bracelet wouldn't fall off. She would have to hide it when she got home, lest she make her mother cry. But Riddley would give it to her later, as a keepsake, when she could bear to have it, when she would be glad to have it. Just as Riddley would one day show her Frazier's notes about Adele, and also the postcards, and tell her how when Adele had seen them she'd said *Riddley,* which might well have been, Riddley realized now, her last word.

*   *   *

By the time they resumed searching, no one had any hope of finding her. Her body had entered the body of water. Riddley did not want it to be found. What good would it do, at this point, to fish it out? Let the sharks have it, or the crabs.

Riddley and Sam often went out in the motorboat, those last days of the summer and on into the fall, as if the search had never been called off. They pulled out any boards or driftwood they came across. This was something they'd always done, to prevent boating accidents. But they were looking, too, for any remains of the bateau, though neither said as much. Not that Riddley knew how she'd distinguish a board of that vessel from any other piece of salvaged wood. *Flotsam and jetsam,* Pauline said, when she saw another nail-riddled board they'd picked up. But really it was only the flotsam, meaning whatever was lost at sea and remained floating. Jetsam, Riddley knew, were jettisoned objects that sank and didn't come up again, as opposed to lagan, goods sunk on purpose so they could eventually be hauled back up. And many things when fully submerged were preserved, like shipwrecks visited by divers. It pleased her to think their bateau might well be sitting intact on the bottom of the ocean somewhere, though with no buoy attached, of course, they'd never find it.

She was sometimes tempted, on certain blue-green dusks, to slide into the river just as the high tide turned. How pleasant to drift along

in the twilight, and how effortless, for a while, to stay afloat, salt water having far greater buoyancy than fresh, a fact about which many in that vicinity felt inordinate pride, as if they'd had anything to do with it. Borne downstream, house and lawn and dock lights turning on, lightning bugs flickering if mosquito control hadn't sprayed recently— everything would have appeared quite different, she thought, seen from within the water instead of atop it, and while traveling at the natural speed of the river, as had Adele, most likely, in her final ride in the bateau.

The Saturday after school resumed, Riddley was crabbing from the dock, wondering if she might inquire soon as to getting another bateau, when an oar floated by, about fifteen feet off the dock, heading downriver. She dropped her line and dove in. It took her until the Shippingtons' to bring it to land. It was heavy from all the water it had absorbed. She slid it onto the dock, a long sliver from the handle piercing the heel of her hand. She hauled herself up and the splinter broke off at the surface of her skin.

The oar could have been theirs. It was the same general size and shape and kind. She examined it closely, running her hands lightly along its surface, as if Adele might have scratched some final message into the wood. There were plenty of marks—nicks and cuts, and one long deep crevice, where it must have dragged along something sharp—but nothing Riddley could decipher.

* * *

How terrible it was, Pauline thought, to have no body to bury, to mourn. She understood then the particular grief of the mothers of soldiers, the son's body far away, in who knew what condition. And was Adele's body washed up on some shore, picked at by birds and crabs and raccoons, or long since eaten by every sea creature imaginable, down to those minnows that nibbled your shins when you stood in the shallows? Fish were nearly all carnivorous, she thought, or would become so in the face of abundant meat. *Meat,* she thought, and shuddered.

These thoughts she told herself not to think, but at night sometimes they came anyway. Nor could she help herself from further

pondering if her mother had known where she was headed if she stayed, that she had sensed she'd soon be leaving. And so she had gone ahead and gone. Or was that, Pauline wondered, just her own dread of those homes that seemed the opposite of home? For a part of her believed that it wouldn't have really mattered where her mother was, that she would have been just fine in such a place, as fine as she could have been anywhere.

Even years later they would refer to Adele's absence not as death but as departure, as disappearance. Weeks after all the searching was over, Pauline nonetheless kept expecting her mother to show up. Would she always feel like that? That was the practical problem, she figured, of having no one to put in the ground and put a stone over.

But Adele did not turn up, not even in Pauline's dreams. After Frazier died he'd appeared frequently in dreams, chatty and at ease, often with a cocktail in hand. After waking, she had missed him even more, but during the dream, his presence was a comfort to her. But not Adele. Even after death Adele seemed unwilling to comfort her.

Pauline recalled those nightmares she used to have of her daughters drifting out to sea. How wrong such dreams had been! She had been afraid of the wrong things. But how could she have known? Maybe fear could only teach by experience, by mistake, the worst fear being of what you had already suffered. Or maybe she hadn't been wrong, maybe that was yet to come. And should she ever lose a child to water, she would not remain on its shore.

The portrait was eventually what cured Pauline of the notion of Adele's imminent return. The portrait became, in Pauline's mind, a place for Adele to reside, or a place, anyway, where Pauline could imagine her. There on canvas, in that hot, dismal little house. Then Pauline could, metaphorically at least, bury her. They had a funeral without a casket or urn of ashes, a graveside service without a grave.

CHAPTER 21

Body of Water

Barefoot, clad only in her bathing suit, Riddley walked south along the shore of Indigo Island. The day was clear, the air warm and dry. It had been Pauline's idea to come out to the islands one last time, though it was later in the year than usual, just past the equinox. Because of Adele's disappearance, they had missed their usual Labor Day trip. Just as after Frazier died, Pauline was eager to do what they had always done. She thought that would bring things back to normal. But Pauline herself needed to return to normal before the rest of them could. And she'd been looking a bit too hollow-eyed for that, and been too oblivious to her daughters' many errors in manners, tidiness, dress, and grammar. Sometimes Riddley slipped up just to see if she'd be caught. More often than not, she wasn't.

As she walked, Riddley kept her eye out for bones, washed up on shore. Depending on where Adele had gone down, there was a decent chance she'd end up on one of the islands. Or would she be bones yet? It had only been about a month. But Riddley thought so. Things got eaten quickly in the sea.

She rounded the bend, and glanced back the way she had come. She couldn't see her family. She walked to the water's edge, the incoming tide lapping at her feet. A few hundred yards off shore, a porpoise surfaced, followed by another, and then two or three more, swimming parallel to shore, moving in the same direction as Riddley. She scanned the water, and after a few minutes they came up again, closer in and farther south. She jogged along the beach to keep up with them. After a while they stopped to feed, surfacing frequently and close together, forming a loose circle, tails thrashing. Two swam directly toward shore, and near enough to see eyes, spiracles, scars, mouths. Up close they looked a lighter gray, their skin irregular, rather than flawless and silky and dark, the way they looked at a distance.

Then they stayed down for a long time. Just as she had about given up, they surfaced, much closer to shore. They came up again, no more than a few feet from where the waves began to break. This was the best chance she had ever had to call them to her. Fishermen here or on nearby islands could well have summoned these very porpoises, or their kin. But what could she use for a drum? From the debris at the high tide line she found a thick piece of driftwood and an old plank.

She ran back down to the surf. She knocked the wood together hard, the driftwood drumstick for the plank. The sound was loud and solid. As if in response, the porpoises came up again. They were still close. She began to wade out. She spread her arms wide and then brought them together fast, knocking the wood as hard as she could, again and again. Waves slapped against her legs. The porpoises surfaced again, moving still to the south. She walked slantwise toward them. Soon the water reached her thighs.

They did not seem to be coming any closer, but nor did they seem to be going farther out. It was hard to tell. Everything looked so different from within the water. The porpoises stayed under for a long time. She struck the wood together harder. Had the noise caused them to sound or flee, or were they entranced down there? But maybe they couldn't hear it. Maybe the drumming was supposed to be performed beneath the surface. In that case, though, how could you pound with the necessary force against the weight of the water?

She kept walking out at a diagonal, hitting the sticks together. The water was past her waist. She was chilly, from the wind, and from being only partly submerged, so that she couldn't adjust to either water or air. She thought she felt the porpoises' echolocation signals rebounding off her body, in much the same way that a heartbeat concentrates in a wound. She would have gone under to listen, but to do so would have been a direct flaunting of Pauline's longstanding prohibition against swimming on the islands out of parental sight, not to mention without a life jacket, and alone. Wading was one thing, but to put one's head beneath the water could not but be deemed swimming.

She thought of the slaves walking in, somewhere not so far from here, into a body of water that probably looked much like this one. She wondered how far out they had to go before they could drown. Wading in, had they sang or prayed, or had they kept silent? In any case, she thought, porpoises must have been drawn to the commotion. And underwater, the chains might well have sounded like a kind of music.

A wave broke against her chest. Saltwater splashed into her mouth. She raised her arms higher. They began to burn. The waves seemed to have gotten much bigger, though part of that, she knew, was due to how deep she was. The wind had picked up, and the air felt cooler and heavier, making the water seem warmer.

Riddley pictured the porpoises turning around, approaching her. When they surfaced, they were still heading south. Maybe it was more than mere rhythm that drew them. She was not in need of fish or rescue, and maybe they could tell that. How, though, would they know? She wondered if the porpoises had tried to push the slaves toward the surface, to nose them back toward shore. Or maybe the porpoises could tell that the slaves did not want to be saved, and so had swum among the drowning and the drowned, as a kind of comfort, and to keep away the sharks.

Riddley stopped, her arms suspended in the air. How could she have forgotten what else might be summoned by her drumming? She remembered the baby hammerhead she had seen here months ago. It must be nearly grown by now. She could not have seen it were it down there. The sea around her was far too disturbed.

The porpoises came up again, riding a high swell. Their fins looked black against the dark sky. The silhouette of the one nearest the surface was for an instant backlit, visible inside the wave. There was no denying that they were moving offshore, that if she were to be attacked by a shark they would not come to her aid. The undertow, stronger now, wrapped around her ankles and tugged. She dropped the driftwood and the plank. They floated rapidly away.

A wave broke against her shoulders, cresting high up her neck, soaking her hair. If she survived the sharks, what trouble she would

be in, were Pauline to see her so far from family and shore, beyond where she could be rescued should she begin to drown. But as suddenly as it had come, fear left her. She took her feet off the bottom and began to swim. As Sam had said, there was no drowning mark upon her. Then she remembered what else he'd said, *Born to be hanged,* and she thought, as she had not for a long while, of the postcards. Having decided at last to keep them, they had ceased to haunt her. They had no need to haunt her, since becoming hers.

It didn't take long before she could no longer touch bottom. Treading water, looking out to sea, it seemed she was holding steady, but when she looked toward land, she saw by the trees that the current was sweeping her rapidly along. Again she faced the ocean. She took a very deep breath and blew it out slowly. She took another and did the same. Then she took one last breath and clamped her mouth and eyes shut. She dove down, her feet spiking into the air before her arms scooped out enough space in the water to pull her all the way under. She held her knees and feet close together and kicked.

The sound of her churning filled her head. She reached out her open hands, her eyes still shut. Sooner than she expected, her fingers touched bottom, that sand which seemed, out there, more silt than sand. It felt softer, muddier than sand, less abrasive, though she knew that, given time, it too could rub her skin raw and tender. She spread her hands and dug her fingers in.

She stopped kicking. She tightened her grip. She pulled her legs down, the muscles in her abdomen taut. She burrowed her feet into the sand and squatted, holding herself down with clenched hands and feet. The bubbles from her exhalation brushed her cheek. As more and more air left her body, it would be easier, she thought, to stay under.

With her eyes still sealed, she listened. She heard buzzes and whirs, whooshes and sighs, ringing, tapping, cracking, pinging, crashing. She imagined these as the noises of motorboats idling, accelerating, planing, of shrimp nets being dropped in and hauled out, a bow rising up on a swell and slamming down on the other side, a halyard slapping against a mast and the reverberations echoing into the hull, the bills of pelicans and cormorants and the talons of

ospreys plunging into the water for fish, fish leaping out of the water and splashing back in, porpoises signaling and searching, their tails stirring the water, their mouths and those of sharks opening, closing, teeth breaking cartilage, breaking bone. All those layers of sound, most of which she could not identify, and so many of which seemed, in the transforming medium of seawater, to be coming at the same time from up close and from far away.

Then she opened her eyes, as wide as she could. The brownish-green murk was full of specks. Bits of light filtered down, as if they were sinking. Above it was bright, sunny, the sky blue, but down here you would never know it. What a shock it must be, each time, for the porpoises to see the sky. The bubbles from the last of her breath pushed toward the air, which seemed more distant than she knew it was. Sand clouded at the bottom, from her burrowing. She saw no people familiar or strange, no porpoises or sharks, turtles or rays, no horses, no chains, no wrecks, no bones.

Her lungs were empty. They tugged hard at the inside of her chest. Had the slaves held their breath as long as they could, or had they inhaled the saltwater as gratefully as if it were air? Did they strive to keep themselves under, she wondered, or to bring themselves up? And what about Adele—when she went into the water, had she been trying to swim, or to drown?

Riddley clutched harder with her fingers and toes. Her limbs and belly, even her eyes joined her chest in the clamoring for air. Her heart struck at her throat and ribs like someone trapped and trying to get out. It pounded so loudly the porpoises must be able to hear it.

The water grew heavier, pressing on her, seeking a way into her body. It seemed to have found a route in through her ears, for the sounds had spread throughout her skull. Along with the relentless strike of her heart, there was a rushing, piercing sound deep in her brain, as if the ocean itself were breathing, and also, somewhere far away, as if it were keening.

She strained her eyes wider. Her eyeballs and lids and sockets felt parched as well as sodden. Just what was it she was looking for down there, what did she think she would find? She didn't know which she wanted more to see, the living or the drowned. They were

down there—Adele, the slaves, the horses, the turtles and sharks and porpoises—they would always be down there, whether or not she saw them, whether or not she looked or wanted to look, and that knowledge came into her like water, like something which, depending on its kind, its quantity, could save her life or take it. Her legs all at once straightened, her feet pointing, catapulting her off the bottom, her head tilting back of its own accord so that her open mouth, like a spiracle, would be first to break the surface, first to leave the water and enter the air.

AUTHOR'S NOTE

I'm indebted to numerous sources for background material. James Allen's *Without Sanctuary: Lynching Photography in America* provided crucial visual and historical material, as did exhibits in Detroit's Charles H. Wright Museum of African American History. Ida B. Wells-Barnett's *On Lynchings: Southern Horrors* and Ralph Ginzburg's *One Hundred Years of Lynchings* allowed me indispensable access to primary documents.

Other texts that I relied on include Leon F. Litwack's *Been in the Storm So Long: The Aftermath of Slavery;* Henry Hampton and Steve Fayer's *Voices of Freedom: An Oral History of the Civil Rights Movement from the 1950s through the 1980s;* Patricia Jones-Jackson's *When Roots Die: Endangered Traditions on the Sea Islands;* Julie Dash's *Daughters of the Dust: The Making of an African American Woman's Film;* and Mary A. Twining and Keith E. Baird's *Sea Island Roots: African Presence in the Carolinas and Georgia,* particularly William Bascom's chapter, "Gullah Folk Beliefs Concerning Childbirth." I am grateful to these authors for their scholarship.